The Great Caya

Fragments of the Gods
Book 2

JCR Paulino

For my wife, Ivy

Contents

"It's an old book named *Designing Gods*. You'll learn about *Homo ciberus* in there."

—The Invoker

Episode Seven

NOVUSLAND

Neojoppa

Gefyra Sea

Trivoli • *Casmare*

◉ TAORI

Bolenti •

Mohiri •

Sebes

Highlands

Lastrani •   ○ Ypsilos

SAPARI OCEAN

Isiagi •

Wetlands

VIPES OCEAN

Vepos •

N

Legend
‒
○ Village
• City
◉ Capital

Chapter Twenty-Four

7. Kendar

Kendar flies over the ocean, drowning in pain and rage. He'd fallen in love with a Sebesian spy, and her betrayal crushed him. In response, the Highlander lashed out, leveling Stargazer Hill and killing Tares of Coriplion. But it wasn't enough. Now Kendar can't breathe—a bitter image keeps choking his throat, the image of the woman who stabbed his heart, Lunai of Bolenti. She still lives.

*　*　*

Kendar's tears blurred the lights in the boat up ahead. His brain had stopped working, jammed by the storm inside his head. *Why?* was the only thought piercing through the chaos. *Why, why, why?*

He flew over the ocean, yet Kendar felt like he was sinking in it. He'd fallen in love at first sight; he had decided to trust and expose his heart. *I'm such an idiot!*

He'd imagined a life with her, a future without secrets. But even

Lunai's *name* had been a lie. The Madonalee, they called her—a professional sent to manipulate him into joining someone else's war. *Curse them all! I'll make them pay!*

She'd pretended to be a merchant and had feigned love for him. Kendar was the biggest fool in the world. He struck his chest as he flew and screamed her name with equal parts of anger and pain. *Why* couldn't he kill her when he found out the truth? He *never* should have fallen for her! *Why* hadn't he seen through her charade? And *why* couldn't he stop thinking about her?

"What am I to do with all this pain?" he asked the voices in his head with the last of his sanity.

Feed on it... the voices answered as Kendar neared the boat. *Feel it deeply. Grow stronger.* But that made no sense. Nothing made any sense.

He landed with a bang on the deck of the ship, cracking the wood and making the boat rock wildly. Panicked screams ensued. Kendar couldn't see any faces through his tears, but their noises hurt his brain. Why were they so loud? Why couldn't they simply *shut up?*

He covered his ears, begging for silence. He needed everything to stop moving. He wanted the entire universe to disappear and let him drift mindlessly until the end of time. Quietly. Alone.

Instead, the chaos around him intensified. Faceless figures shouted and hustled about him. Some screamed and ran away; some stayed, asking angry questions; others rushed toward him, yelling orders.

"Please, be quiet," Kendar murmured, his eyes glistening with still more unshed tears.

They didn't listen. Their incessant shrieks became unbearable, and Kendar's protective coat of feathers sprang up across his arms and neck. *Why?* Had someone threatened him? Probably, but Kendar didn't care. They could drive a hundred swords through him if they wanted.

But the yelling . . . the excruciating *yelling*. "Please, shut up," he begged. Couldn't they see what was happening to him? Their screams magnified inside his head, echoing over and over like waves ramming the shore, tolling like ever-ringing bells inside his brain.

"Shut *up!*" he yelled as he fell to his knees and covered his ears. "Shut *up!*" He lifted a fist as a final warning, veins protruding in his neck. "Shut *up!*" he screamed at the top of his lungs, trying to drown out all of their noise. But he couldn't.

Retribution came swiftly. Kendar lashed out, his invisible arms pummeling everything. The first wallop tilted the boat to the left, cracking the deck. More blows came; he unleashed a relentless assault, pounding and slapping blindly, hoping to squash sound itself. But the cacophony of misery only intensified. Wood splintered with every blow; passengers shrieked and wailed all the more.

Rage choked him, and Kendar struck even harder, bellowing, "Shut *up!*" over and over again. His invisible feet stamped the deck with all his strength, and the boat broke in half.

He stopped lashing out the second he plunged into the water—the ocean was so cold that it shook him out of his rage. His will to fight plummeted as the water engulfed his head, muffling the noises and promising relief.

Kendar sank as everyone else struggled to stay afloat. Even the broken boat put up a fight against the waters, yet it, too, did so in vain. He didn't resist drifting downward. Absent any conscious decision on his part, his invisible arms and legs turned into a bubble around him, shielding him from the depths. A transparent tube shot upward, stretching to the surface and providing him access to air. The tube kept stretching, elongating itself as Kendar sank ever deeper, still encased by his sphere. Cold and wet and barely aware inside his bubble, Kendar descended into darkness.

He stopped sinking a while later, reaching the seafloor. His limbs moved on their own accord—his knees drew into his chest, and his arms wrapped around his torso, curling his body into a fetal position and producing warmth. A familiar heaviness took over every limb and sealed his eyelids.

Wanting to forget that he even existed, Kendar of Ypsilos fell asleep at the bottom of the ocean. His mind slid into his mother's womb, feeling warm, safe, and quiet, not caring about anything.

* * *

Kendar had acquired his powers in a sickly darkness, and in pitch darkness he now healed, disconnected from the world. For three days and nights, he didn't move or even open his eyes, weightless inside his bubble as a thought in the mind.

Water surrounded him, yet it was thirst that eventually yanked him from hibernation—his mouth, lips, and tongue felt so dry that they hurt. Kendar opened his eyes and saw nothing. Still, he could feel that his eyes had shrunk backward in their sockets. He touched his cheeks and found that they, too, were sunken. He imagined how pale his skin must be . . . he must resemble a ghost.

Now that he was awake, the necessities of his body demanded that he return to the realm of the living. He *had* to survive; he *had* to prove her wrong. The pull of life beckoned strongly, and Kendar complied. Death was the new enemy, and her minions—hunger, thirst, and pain—had to be squashed.

He launched a set of invisible feet and pushed off the ocean floor. The bubble encasing him moved upward, crawling toward the surface. For a long while, he floated up, leaving his watery womb behind.

The darkness of night had enveloped the world by the time Kendar emerged. He hovered above the ocean but saw no sign of the wreckage he'd caused three days earlier.

Travel north, whispered the voices in his head. *Reach Belphi. Food and water first.*

Kendar nodded. He wouldn't spend another second thinking about Lunai. He'd left her behind in Casmare along with his gullibility and the rest of his humanity.

Get them all! the voices said in agreement.

"I *will* get them all," Kendar replied in a cracking voice. Half the world would pay and the other half would serve him, and none would know that was coming.

NEOJOPPA - WEST

Maraccia

Ivory Village

Macorie

Old Berkton

Lucierra

Naldora

Naldo Lake

Torinth

Friesven

Kasmana

NORTHERN MOUNTAINS

Palaumone

Soledad

Antilla

Rico

Cubile

Ionia

Carib

Gret Elp Lake

Vigani

Newisbel

Hellsmouth

Asmar

Mjikoni

Ababis

Belphi

Kartuch

VIPES OCEAN

N

Gefyra Sea

Casmare

Novusland

Chapter Twenty-Five

7. Anaya

Mean people had killed Anaya's family in Ivory Village for no reason, forcing the little girl to flee into the woods with her mom. But her mother died during their escape, and the six-year-old found herself alone in the cold mountains, accompanied only by the hands of the Naldorian goddess. Anaya would have been long dead if it weren't for Dian. The deity guided Anaya and lent her strength, empowering the little girl to do the impossible. Anaya had fended for herself, coming down from the mountains and learning to use Dian's powers as she traveled.

She met Jacob and Eva on her way to Palaumone, and the elderly couple took her in. It was nice not being by herself—the little girl felt safe for several weeks. But then mean gatalan riders pursued them. Although Anaya jumped to Jacob and Eva's defense, the couple died in the ensuing fight. Anaya's rage flared up, and she wiped out the evil people.

Now she's all alone again. Why do mean people keep killing the ones she loves? Anaya gives in to her despair, sobbing hopelessly and not knowing what to do. But then, exhausted and waiting for Dian's guidance, she encounters something weird. Curiosity pushes her sadness aside for a brief moment: a man carrying a purple glowing sphere is walking directly toward her! Did Dian send him to make her feel better?

The man reaches Anaya and introduces himself. His name is Marko Elsberra.

* * *

The tall man had a gray beard and white hair, just like her dad. Anaya liked the man's smile, too—it was kind. Still, Marko Elsberra was a bit funny. He wore a black cloak over his head and gloves on his hands, and a thick, broad band wrapped around his wrist. All of those were odd looking, but the gloves were the weirdest. Definitely the gloves.

Even during winter, few people wore gloves in Ivory Village—unless they were super-nice gloves, like the leathery ones. But those were hard to get. Mom once said gloves were too expensive and not worth it. Anaya liked them though; she would've bought them if she'd had money. But why in the cricket's name would anyone wear gloves in spring, far away from the snow? Weird.

But the purple orb the man carried wasn't weird at all. It was *awesome!* A light inside made it glow, and funny characters appeared, changed, and vanished from its surface. The letters behaved like they were little fishes trapped inside that kept swimming to the sides of their tank to peek outside. Marko told her that the orb was an eye—he'd used it to find Anaya. She opened her eyes wide. That sounded magical, like something Dian would do.

"Did Dian send you?" Anaya asked.

Marko smiled, then hunkered down and talked to Anaya face-to-face. "Well, someone did send me, yes, but their name isn't Dian. However—" he lifted a finger for emphasis "—I've discovered that sometimes people call the same thing by different names. It's very confusing, I know. But it's possible that Dian and the one who sent me are the same person."

Anaya frowned. "How can the same person have two names?" She trailed off and scratched her cheek. Wait—the goddess's real name was Dianasis, and she had changed it to Dian. Was it possible that other people had changed Dian's name too? She shrugged. "What's the name of the person who sent you?"

"Asage Bihram."

"Oh! Her name has two sounds, like yours."

The man smiled. "Where I come from, people's names always have two sounds. The first one belongs to the person, and the second one belongs to the entire family."

Anaya frowned, wondering if two-sound names could become confusing over time.

"Although," Marko continued, "I have to tell you this: Asage has the face of a pretty woman but the voice of a nice man. So I call Asage *he* instead of *she*."

Anaya wrinkled her forehead. That was so weird! She'd always imagined that Dian had a pretty face. Now she wondered why—after all, a goddess would remain a goddess whether she had a pretty face or not. But she'd never questioned whether Dian had a female voice.

"Then Asage and Dian are not the same person," Anaya said firmly. Then she hesitated. She'd never heard Dian's voice, at least not aloud. The only time Anaya had heard something close to an internal voice, it had sounded like her mother's. Anaya *felt* Dian's guidance; she gave Anaya certainty about what to do and the confidence to trust that it would be alright. But the goddess had never communicated with her using spoken words.

Marko half shrugged, half nodded. "Maybe you're right—they could be two different people."

A brief silence ensued. All of a sudden, Anaya felt exhausted. She'd fought mean men not very long ago and then had run for a long while, and she'd been crying her eyes out when she spotted Marko in the distance. All of that had been incredibly draining. She knew she should find a place to sleep soon, but she was too curious about the purple ball to say goodbye to Marko without learning more. "Did Asage give you the eye to find me?"

"He gave me the purple orb, yes. But he doesn't call it an eye—he calls it a synapse meter."

Anaya scowled. "That's an awful name! The ball is too pretty for that."

Marko laughed. "You can choose another name if you want to."

"I think I will."

He smiled and patted her head. "I'll ask Asage to give you the ball. He made it just to find you. The ball has no other use, I think. I'm sure it'll be okay if I give it to you, but I have to check with him first. And you have to promise not to let anyone else see the ball. Never ever ever."

The ball could be *hers*? Anaya giggled and gave a small jump. "I promise! I promise!" she said, her exhaustion momentarily forgotten. That ball was so pretty! She'd treasure it forever. But then she quieted, understanding why she'd have to keep it a secret. People had gotten scared every time they'd seen her use Dian's gifts. Perhaps the ball would cause the same reaction; it was magical too.

Anaya had been in stealth mode when Marko had found her. She wanted to ask how the ball did its magic, how it knew where to find her. But something else roamed at the back of her head. "*Why* did Asage want you to find me?"

Marko smiled. "He said you don't need protection—you can defend yourself against a hundred men." He paused and put a gentle hand on Anaya's shoulder. "But Asage said you need company."

Anaya froze at the sound of that. The sadness that had besieged her moments earlier pounced once again. She felt like someone had opened the front door during a blizzard and the punishing cold air had just slammed into her face. Tears pricked her silver eyes. Eva and Jacob had just died, and she was utterly alone again. Her mom, her dad, her brother . . . they were all dead, killed by mean people.

Her vision blurred, and pain wrinkled Anaya's face. She felt lightheaded, like her knees were about to buckle. And then out of nowhere, the kind stranger pulled her in closer and hugged her.

That felt so nice. Anaya leaned against him and wrapped her little arms around his neck, glad to let go, sure she wouldn't fall. Marko's beard was scratchy, much like her dad's. Oh, how much she had missed that. She nestled her head on his shoulder and lost herself in the warm embrace. She didn't want to be by herself anymore. Was that too much to ask?

Something broke free inside her, and Anaya started to sob. Images of home, of her mom, of her dad, all of what she'd lost flooded her mind. She missed her brother and felt terribly sorry about what had happened to Jacob and Eva.

Anaya had promised her mom she wouldn't cry, but she couldn't keep her promise tonight. She was sorry about that, too, but Anaya wailed as loudly as she could, letting her anguish out through her lungs, throat, mouth, and tears. She whimpered and shrieked and groaned, embracing a stranger, a man sent by Dian to keep her from falling. The goddess must've known that Anaya needed his company as much as she needed the air she breathed.

She held on to Marko tightly. *Thank you, Dian. Thank you, Mom.*

NEOJOPPA - EAST

Sandless

Norma

Nadie

Mesonia

Silver Lake

VETUS

Priene

NORTHERN MOUNTAINS

Narialy

Wet
Forest

Ghost Valley

Vasiliki Bay

Narian

Singing
Bridge

Kasmana

Caro Peninsula

Miramar

Cubile

Mercy River

North Katan

Platta

Small Mouth

Paraiso

Ionia

Carib

Triple Peaks

Asiana Harbor

Great Elp
Lake

South Katan

Newisbel

Hellsmouth

Belphi

Mongad

SAPARI OCEAN

Ababis

NARABI

Avianer

Prince Port

Fodora View

Gesyra Sea

Casmare

Chapter Twenty-Six

7. Rayla

The king-priest is dead, murdered with poison inside the holy palace. He died before announcing his successor, and the tragedy plunged the kingdom into chaos.

The conniving Kameiros framed Rayla for the murder, spinning a web of lies and plotting to take over the throne. Two of Rayla's master generals betrayed her to join Kameiros's side, including General Viembo, master of the army, who commands over one million soldiers.

Rayla is now isolated, pursued, and outnumbered. Kameiros's lies make it difficult for her to find allies or even a base of operations. Rayla's heart aches as she contemplates the inevitable events on the horizon. A shadow spreads through the kingdom: civil war is upon them, and thousands of Kasmanians will die.

* * *

The camp lay quiet in the predawn, tucked into the edge of the Wet Forest. Tents were submerged in a thick silence, punctuated only by the sound of crackling fires. All slept except for three dozen sentries on watch.

Rayla woke before sunrise and strolled through the site with Kaistan by her side. Her steps were slow, and her troubled expression mirrored what she felt in her soul. She'd been wrestling with three core questions for the past two weeks. How many fathers, daughters, husbands, and sisters would die in the upcoming battles? In this civil war, both sides would spill Kasmanian blood. How many of those lives could she save? If nothing changed, Rayla would lose this war. And if she did, how would she justify so much death?

She kept walking. Rayla's steps were as stealthy as Kaistan's—she didn't want to wake anyone. Over seven hundred Lathraias were recuperating their strength as they slumbered inside their three hundred black tents. Rayla smiled. At least the thought of her loyal troops gave her comfort—her Lathraias would cross oceans, deserts, and mountains by her side. They would even dare Hellsmouth.

"Three weeks," Rayla mumbled to herself as she moved through the maze of black canvas, poles, and ropes. She had three weeks before their food supplies would become a daunting problem. If things went her way, the number of mouths she'd have to feed would increase twentyfold in a few days. That was good news, of course, but it came with side effects. Now she had to secure a sustainable strong-hold as soon as possible to support all of her troops.

Rayla's aimless steps delivered her to a hundred-foot-tall atlas cedar. Its warm, sweet smell lightened her mood. She tickled Kaistan's chin and spoke in a teasing, deep voice. "Look, Kiwi. We stand at the edge of the forest *and* the edge of the camp. Don't let me fall, you hear me?"

In response, the massive midnight gatalan yawned lazily and licked his face.

"Oh, c'mon, Kiwi!" she chided him in her normal voice. "Don't be such a wet blanket. It wasn't my best, but Laramie would've laughed at my joke." Corina would have laughed too. Probably. She wished Laramie were here.

Rayla looked up at the sky. The first sunrays broke free on the horizon, painting the clouds with orange and red. She frowned. Before Altanarian's death, that view would've brought her joy. Today, the dawn's hues were an omen in the sky, a harbinger of Kasmanian blood spilling into rivers of devastation flowing throughout Neojoppa. A familiar sadness gripped her heart. How many would die? How many could she save?

Then a glimmer of hope sparkled somewhere inside her. The red clouds were going to give way to a bright sun in a few minutes . . . Her eyes opened wide. The ominous clouds would pass, just like the current suffering would eventually pass.

A fearsome expression overtook Rayla's face as a new thought became her shield: the way out of this mess was *through* pain and loss. The world was always changing; Kasmana was no exception. Only what came next mattered, what her nation would change into. She had to guide her people into changing for the *better*. She had no choice but to succeed and give positive meaning to the current suffering.

She decided it then and there: her path was to achieve a resounding victory quickly, shortening the war and minimizing casualties. She would act like a surgeon operating on a malignant tumor—she would ensure long-term health for the cost of a temporary wound. Doing the right thing would transform her into a divine instrument, into Kas's sword. She would do this for Altanarian, for Kas, and for her people.

Kaistan stirred beside her. "Good morning, my eken," came a soft male voice behind Rayla.

"Good morning, Cael," she said without turning. But the grassy smell of sweet rice tea made her head turn a moment later. Cael stood there looking rested and peppy, holding a steaming cup of tea. She grinned at him. "Have I ever told you that you're a lifesaver?"

"Only every three days or so, my eken. I'm striving to remedy that."

She laughed. "You know if Kaistan says it, it counts, too, right?"

Cael shifted his weight. "I'm glad to hear it, but I'll likely miss his compliments. I don't speak gatalan."

"Oh, it's not gatalan you need to speak, Cael. It's *Kais-ta-nian*."

The young man hesitated. "I . . . I don't—"

"I'll translate," Rayla said, bailing him out. "See how Kaistan is *not* growling at you or baring his teeth even though you're standing close to me?" Cael glanced at the five-foot-tall feline with sleek black fur. Kaistan seemed pretty relaxed. "That's the best compliment Kiwi could ever give you," Rayla added.

Cael gave her an uncertain smile. "I'm happy to hear it, my eken."

Rayla laughed, glad that Cael had lifted her spirits further. But that was enough teasing—she had important matters to attend to. "Have you seen General Gadai lately? How are his injuries?"

Cael nodded. "I brought him dinner last night. The general was in good spirits—he said he'll be ready to ride tomorrow."

Rayla's eyebrows went up. "That's great! Two days earlier than anticipated . . . Reach out to Aia and Rolan and tell them we're breaking camp tomorrow at first light." She'd leave the details to them. Her two trusted lieutenants would jump into action and make sure everyone would be ready to depart on time.

Cael's brows pulled closer together. "What about General Nereida and the rest of the Lathraias you summoned? They won't get here in time."

Rayla smiled. "That's why we need to get moving. Nereida will arrive with about twenty thousand riders, hopefully more. Add another fifteen hundred Lathraias to our forces. We need a garrison as a base of operations—we can't let food and logistics become the monsters that slay this army."

"I see," Cael said. His brows eased.

"We'll leave a small group of soldiers here to direct the new arrivals to our future destination." Rayla paused to sweep the campsite with her gaze. "I'm hoping Laramie will be among the first to join me. I need her input."

Cael nodded. "Yes, Laramie . . . Pardon me, my eken, but have you decided where to go? The garrison at North Katan or the one in Narian?"

Oh, Narian! That name brought back memories. During its heyday, Narian had been the capital of the now-defunct Normanian kingdom, and more recently, that city had served as the staging site for the biggest battle Rayla had ever fought. Under her leadership, Kasmanian armies had crushed over fifty thousand Maraccians holed away up north in the supposedly impregnable fortress of Narialy.

The Narialy stronghold had been the pride and joy of the Normanian army for centuries, but it was the Maraccians who had defended Narialy to the bitter end. The famed battle had taken place five years earlier, and Rayla's outstanding performance had cata-pulted her already meteoric rise. King-Priest Altanarian had honored Rayla with a special celebration at the holy palace and then promoted her to general at the tender age of twenty-seven.

"I'd love to go to Narian first," Rayla said, still feeling a slight flush from that day. "The Narian garrison is much bigger than the one in North Katan. Besides, if things go bad, we could ride north from Narian and take over the abandoned fortress of Narialy. With ten thousand soldiers, I could defend that fortress for months against the entire Kasmanian army . . ."

"But?" said Cael. His eyebrow twitched.

Rayla smiled. "*But* Rolan gave me great news last night. Brigade Leader Analia is in charge of the North Katan garrison. You remember her, right? We met Analia at the Yimin Tourney." Surely Cael would remember her, seeing as Rayla had decided to participate in that particular tourney and had then taken home the highest honors. The Yimin Tourney was a big deal—it was held during the most prestigious holiday in Kasmana, the one observed every six years to honor Kas and commemorate the arrival of the Canyo race to Neojoppa.

Cael gave her an enigmatic smile. "Brigade Leader Analia is hard to forget, my eken."

Rayla gave a soft nod. "According to Rolan, Analia refused to host General Fabris when he came knocking on her door three days ago. She asked lots of questions that Fabris struggled to answer, so Analia kept the gates closed and sent him on his way without giving him any provisions." Rayla laughed. "She wrecked Fabris's plans! And he returned to Asiana Harbor with his tail between his legs."

Cael's eyebrows went up. "Pretty bold for a brigade leader to stand up against a master general! Even for Analia."

"No kidding. So you see, Cael, there's a fantastic chance that Analia will join me, especially with Corina by my side." She grinned at him. "Analia might only have seventeen thousand soldiers under her command, but the North Katan garrison is looking like a pretty good candidate for our first base."

* * *

Rayla and seven hundred Lathraias arrived at the North Katan garrison's gates in late morning. It had taken them three days to travel here from the Wet Forest.

Rayla smiled at the sight of the garrison's unique shape—nothing else like it existed in Neojoppa. This garrison was one of fourteen strongholds the Kasmanian armies had wrestled from the Normanians during the Great War. They were easy to spot because these garrisons were much smaller than the ones erected by Kasmanian masons, plus the Normanians had used red limestones to build them. Even so, the North Katan garrison stood out due to the main building's bizarre pyramidal shape. It had earned the garrison the name "the Red Horn."

Upon their arrival, Rayla sent General Gadai and Lieutenant Corina to parley with Brigade Leader Analia while the rest of them waited outside the gates. In the Kasmanian armed forces, all officers swore allegiance to their respective generals, and Brigade Leader

Analia was no exception. The fact that she had rejected General Fabris, the master of ships, was a good sign. But Analia was still pledged to General Viembo; treason, vacating the position, death, or a royal decree were the only acts that dissolved a pledge. Rayla had to win her over. It was up to Corina and Gadai to make the treason case to Analia. But after four hours had gone by, Rayla began to worry.

"Are we gonna be forced to mount a rescue operation?" someone nearby asked. Rayla turned. The Herculean Aia sat atop her midnight gatalan, fully armed and ready to charge. Rayla flattened her lips. It was as if the lieutenant had read her thoughts.

"I would've been more concerned if the parley had only lasted for a few minutes," Rolan said, walking closer to them. "*That* would've made me suspect a trap. This is a consequential decision, not only for Analia but for her entire garrison. It makes sense that she's talking it over with her people."

Rayla nodded. Of course, Rolan was right. But still . . . those four hours already felt like twenty-four. She couldn't stop worrying about the safety of her friend Corina and comrade Gadai. Rayla contemplated the impossibility of storming a seventeen-thousand-soldier-strong garrison with just her seven hundred Lathraias to rescue them.

Right then, a battle horn blew inside the garrison, its bass bellow reverberating for miles. The gates opened slowly, hinges creaking as the heavy doors crawled inward. Six columns of soldiers marched out of the gates. Their feet thudded into the ground in unison, stirring dust into the air. Rayla watched them and nodded ever so slightly. She would've felt proud if she hadn't been so worried. The troops' sky-blue tunics underneath their neat armor said they were army soldiers, and their perfect synchronization proved that they'd been trained to Kasmanian standards.

The six columns of soldiers turned left and right to stand in formation along the outer walls of the garrison. Strangely, the soldiers didn't split themselves evenly—the group that turned right had about three thousand soldiers, while the group that turned left was about one thousand strong.

Rayla held her breath and waited. This display could mean anything, from an overwhelming attack to a military welcome. She felt sweat beading her forehead. These seconds were excruciating; just standing and waiting left her forces terribly exposed. Her seven hundred Lathraias would not survive a fight against an army of four thousand trained soldiers. If a battle broke out, Rayla's fledging rebellion would meet a tragic end.

She was risking everything by not telling her forces to turn tail immediately, but fleeing with their gatalans would destroy Rayla's standing with these potential allies. And she had reasons to feel hopeful—the garrison had blown its horn, announcing the movement of troops. That would've made no sense if Analia had ordered a surprise attack. The odds were on her side for once. But if Rayla was wrong . . .

The soldiers stopped marching; Rayla heard movement behind her. She turned. Cael rushed in, bringing Kaistan to her.

"Thanks," Rayla said, vaulting atop her midnight gatalan. She glanced at her troops. Every rider now sat on their gatalans, ready for anything. A shadow of a smile came to her lips. Her Lathraias were the best.

A second horn blew, and Analia, Corina, and Gadai came out of the gates astride their gatalans. Rayla heard sighs of relief from both Aia and Rolan and silently agreed with their reaction. Seeing Analia trotting between Corina and Gadai on her orange-furred mount was a good sign. Army soldiers didn't have gatalans, but all officers did regardless of their military branch, and Analia was no exception.

Analia's armor was more elaborate than that of her soldiers too. It was identical to the armor the Lathraias wore except that her tunic was sky-blue, signifying her allegiance to the army. In contrast, the Lathraias's tunics were black, matching their midnight gatalans.

Complete silence reigned as Analia neared Rayla. Thousands of soldiers inside the garrison watched quietly from the parapets even as the four thousand soldiers standing before Rayla and her troops gazed at them with flat expressions.

Analia's eyes locked on Rayla's face as soon as the brigade leader passed through the gates. She looked exactly as Rayla remembered her. She was twenty years older than Rayla, shorter than the average Canyo but robust and muscular. If she'd been taller, Analia could've passed for Aia's older sister. Strands of gray threaded Analia's shoulder-length hair; Rayla recalled that Analia had the habit of tying her hair into a ponytail and then undoing it every few minutes. "You get used to it," one of Analia's company leaders had whispered to Rayla on the first day of the tourney, back when they had first met in Vetus.

The sun had begun its afternoon descent when Analia, Corina, and Gadai reached Rayla. "My eken," Gadai started, "Brigade Leader Analia has questions for you before—"

Analia lifted a hand, cutting off Gadai. All eyes shifted to her. The brigade leader looked into Rayla's eyes for a few intense moments. Rayla remained relaxed and returned the stare. Analia's gaze was a groping hand frisking her soul, searching for her truth without permission, but Rayla welcomed the probing with a smile. She had nothing to hide and everything to feel proud of. Rayla understood—a worthy subject like Analia demanded a worthy leader. Analia could stare at her to her heart's content.

No one moved or said a word during the silent exchange. Then Analia's lips parted and her eyes widened. Rayla sensed warmth emanating from the other woman. Rayla smiled; she'd seen that before. The brigade leader had found her truth. But the truth wasn't about Rayla herself—she'd only served as a mirror, reflecting back some of Analia's values. Rayla wore her convictions like a second set of armor, making her certainty contagious.

Analia got off her gatalan and fell to one knee. A collective "Oh!" rippled out from the surrounding soldiers as Corina and Gadai looked on goggle-eyed. It was clear to Rayla. This wasn't what Corina, Gadai, and Analia had agreed upon while still inside the garrison.

Analia bent her neck and spoke in a husky voice. "Cacique Rayla, the light of Kas shines through you for all to see. You're a genuine leader, blessed by my god, endorsed by the mighty beyond the necessity for words. I embrace you. I hereby declare that General Viembo's treason has dissolved my pledge to him. Now, before my brothers and sisters, before Kas, I swear allegiance to you until the end of my days. I pledge to be your sword and your shield. I pledge my heart and mind to the fulfillment of your goals and the eradication of your enemies. I humbly request the honor of calling you my eken."

A murmur swept through the thousand soldiers aligned against the left wall, and they broke formation. Rayla glanced at them briefly and then returned her gaze to the brigade leader.

Before Rayla could answer Analia, Corina dismounted and rushed to kneel beside the brigade leader. "General Rayla, my eken, my friend, my sister. I should've done this days ago. Shame for my husband's actions will no longer rule my heart. Inspired by Brigade Leader Analia, I hereby declare all past allegiances void under Kasmanian law. I pledge my allegiance to you until the end of my days. I vow my sword and shield to you; I swear to give my heart and mind to fulfill your goals and eradicate your enemies."

Rayla spoke. "Brigade Leader Analia, master of the North Katan garrison, and Lieutenant Corina, it is my honor to accept your allegiance. Before Kas, I promise never to ask of you anything that would tarnish your honor. Now rise."

Rayla swung down from Kaistan to grab Analia's and Corina's forearms in greeting. A bubbly sensation filled her chest. She hadn't felt this rejuvenated in a long while. With Analia's pledge, Rayla's situation had changed drastically—she'd not only increased the number of soldiers at her disposal, but she had also secured a stronghold and addressed the food supply problem. More importantly, Analia joining her would likely make it easier to recruit other garrisons. Rayla's expectations of gaining support from central and western Kasmana garrisons now seemed justified.

The murmurs along the left wall became a commotion. Everyone turned to look. Of the thousand soldiers, half were arguing with each other while the other half were walking away from the garrison.

"What's going on?" Aia asked in a brusque tone.

Analia answered her. "I gathered all my soldiers inside the garrison and explained in detail what has happened since the death of King-Priest Altanarian. I gave them both sides of the story: General Kameiros's accusation and Rayla's position. I told them I'd make my own decision on whom to support after I had spoken with Cacique Rayla in person, and I gave them the choice of likewise following their hearts and deciding whom they wanted to support." She gestured at the ramparts. "The soldiers that stayed inside the garrison said they would follow me no matter what I decided." Then she tilted her head to the right. "Those three thousand said they would go with General Rayla even if I decided not to join her."

"I see," Aia said through gritted teeth. "So the bastards on the left decided to turn their backs on my eken no matter what."

Rayla reached out to put a hand on her shoulder. "It's okay, Aia. They believed Kameiros's lies. Be mad at him, not the soldiers. Look at the ones who are supporting us instead. If that isn't enough, look in front of you and praise Kas. Analia has joined our cause! This is a great day for us."

Gadai took a step closer to Rayla. "Where are they headed? The ones who are leaving, I mean."

"Some will go to South Katan, others to Asiana Harbor. The rest will journey to Mesonia," Analia replied.

Rayla frowned. "Asiana Harbor and Mesonia are too far away, especially on foot. The soldiers are ill-prepared for their journeys." She turned to Analia. "Could you please make sure they get enough provisions to make it to their homes?"

Analia barked a laugh. "I made the right choice! Very kind of you, my eken. It will be done."

"Thanks, Analia." Rayla turned and looked at the Lathraias gathered at her back, craning her neck until she spotted someone. "Cael! Cael, come here, please."

Cael hurried back to Rayla. "At your service," he said with a bow.

"Analia, perhaps you remember Officer Cael? He was there when you and I met at the Yimin Tourney."

Analia shook her head. "I'm sorry to say that I don't. I hope that doesn't offend you, Officer Cael."

"Not at all, Brigade Leader. My eken casts a large shadow."

"That she does, young one. That she does," Analia said with a smile. She turned to Rayla and looked at her expectantly.

"Cael is my assistant—he oversees logistics," Rayla explained. "Would you please put him in contact with your logistics officer? The two of them have a lot to coordinate, especially with General Nereida arriving any day now."

Analia's smile widened. "Sure thing; leave it to me . . . Ah, my eken! I'm feeling festive. Not only is this my first time hosting a cacique, but changing allegiances is a big deal. My soldiers are bound to feel anxious with a civil war brewing and the odds against us. Let's ease their minds a little. What do you think of an impromptu celebration marking our alliance? Meat, ale, and music until dawn."

Rayla's eyebrows went up. "Impromptu celebrations are my favorites."

Analia and Rayla took a step toward the gates, and the four thousand soldiers standing along the right wall began to cheer. Soon, the soldiers inside the garrison followed suit, joining the ovation.

Their thunderous welcome filled Rayla with joy. She grinned and waved as she walked through the Red Horn's gate, feeling ready for whatever came next.

Chapter Twenty-Seven

6. Danny

Danny crossed into Kasmana with his ranger party, searching for a child whose powers were similar to those of Newisbel's ruler, the Invoker. Danny had hoped to find the child as soon as possible and then look for his exiled father, Marko Elsberra, but a band of Normo rebels attacked Danny's party on the very first day. Although Danny survived the attack, Randal—Danny's grandfather and the captain of the ranger party—died during the fight. Farlie also passed away. Danny buried them both in Kasmanian soil.

Danny rushed to bring the injured Sandor and Eli back to the crossing terminal, where Newisbel physicians could save their lives. As soon as he got them there, though, Danny deserted the Newisbel Rangers Corps.

The fifteen-year-old then embarked upon a journey across the vast Kasmanian kingdom to find his exiled

father. Alongside the young Canyo walks his newly bonded friend, a gatalan youngling named Kara.

* * *

Danny woke when the first sunrays warmed his face. He raised a lazy hand to shield his eyes, realizing as he did so that his body felt stiff. He stood up and stretched his long legs and arms. Would he ever get used to sleeping on the hard ground?

He grunted. The instructors at Ranger Training School hadn't said anything about the rough realities of ranger life: sleeping on the ground, not bathing for weeks, pooping in open fields. They should've at least mentioned those things. The bastards. Did concealing painful details make the trainers a bunch of liars?

"Nah," Danny muttered. "Doesn't matter much . . ." He would've become a ranger anyway. At least he had the peace of mind to sleep soundly despite the lack of a soft pillow. Kara looked over him; she'd warn him if any sign of danger arose while he slept.

"Where is Kara, anyway?" he asked aloud, rubbing his eyes and looking for a spot to relieve himself. He chose a red cedar to receive his morning blessing. He walked to the tree, scratching his head and gazing at the surrounding woods.

Lack of comfort aside, the place wasn't so bad. This particular spot in Kasmana reminded him of the national parks throughout Newisbel, where it was illegal to build anything. The Neojoppa Preservation Park, for instance, had tall trees just like this red cedar—in fact, the flora here looked the same. The difference was the amenities, or better said, the lack thereof. Here, there were no tram stations, snack dispensers with remote phone-charging stations, or state-of-the-art bathrooms. And he could use a flasky right about now from one of the dispensers. Those refreshing energy drinks were the best—they tasted great and filled him up for twelve hours.

Still, something remarkable tilted the scale in favor of the Kasmanian woods: they wrapped themselves in calmness; a deep sense of peace emanated from the trees and leaves. That was impossible to artificially create in Newisbel. Danny smiled to himself. There was his positive angle! Right then and there, urinating on a red cedar, Kasmana was the place to be. If he ever attempted *that* in Newisbel, he'd be slapped with a hefty fine that would wipe out his credits for five months.

Mid-stream, though, Danny scowled. Where *was* Kara? They should be on their way soon. They had a long journey ahead of them —they couldn't afford to waste much time.

He finished his business and walked toward his knapsack to grab Randal's map. He was glad he'd taken it before he had buried his grandfather. *May his soul rest in peace*, Danny thought with a pang of sorrow.

He pressed his lips together. How was it possible to miss someone you'd just met? But he did miss Randal more than he could explain, especially the sense of safety he had felt around the old man. He'd felt that even before he'd known Randal was his grandfather. On top of that, he missed Randal for practical reasons, like dealing with maps. *I wish I were better at reading Kasmanian charts . . .*

Trying to decipher the various squiggles reminded Danny of what a rookie he was. He knew absolutely nothing about the places identified on the map. He knew nothing about Kasmana, period. That wouldn't have mattered if his ranger party was still with him— they would've taught him the ropes for a full year. *If* they had spent said year doing low-risk missions in Naldora, of course, and hadn't been sent into Kasmana. Danny had learned a lot about Naldora, its people, and its history at ranger school. That part of his training seemed wasted now. But he couldn't blame the instructors, seeing as rangers hadn't crossed into Kasmana for four hundred years. Novices simply weren't trained for Kasmanian missions anymore.

He tried his best, squinting over the map and eventually finding his destination on the map's western edge: Torinth, a large city next to Naldo Lake. It would take months to get there, but he was determined. Hopefully his father still lived in Torinth.

Danny's gaze followed a possible route. The first obstacle blocking his path was a large river that ran north to south across the continent—through Kasmana, Newisbel, and Belphi—and all the way to the Gefyra Sea. Kasmanians called it the Mercy River, and apparently the only way to cross it was via the Singing Bridge. Danny scoffed. *The Mercy River and the Singing Bridge? What kind of names are those?*

His stomach churned as he contemplated how much he didn't know about Kasmana's culture. If he talked to locals, he'd likely get confused by simple things, like the names of places, holidays, famous people, and historical events. The locals would smell the truth from a mile away—Danny looked like one of them, sure, but he didn't belong. He wondered how soon his ignorance would cost him. And how much. Perhaps he should avoid contact with people as much as possible.

At least not everything on the map made him stare blankly—one location close by was labeled the Reeky Forest. Danny stifled a laugh and made a mental note to avoid that place at all costs, no matter whether it was the official name of the forest or the mapmaker's opinion. He decided to travel along the outskirts of South Katan and make his way through the Plain of Carbel. Then he could continue northwest until he reached the Singing Bridge.

A movement caught the corner of his eye, and Danny looked up. Kara stood next to him. Gatalans could be so stealthy. "There you are!" He laughed and reached out to caress her stomach. "That's one full belly!" He *loved* the feel of her fur—it was so smooth and sleek.

The large feline licked her face in response.

"So you went out hunting this morning, ah? Guess you didn't find anything last night." He gave her a last pat and rolled up the map, then gathered the rest of his things. "Ready to go?" he asked Kara.

She yawned.

A few minutes later, they were on their way. Danny was planning on walking for three hours before stopping for a morning snack, and then they'd continue for another three hours until it was time for lunch. Dried meat was on the menu unless Danny spotted a quail along the way like he had the previous day. It was easy to recycle arrows he shot at small game. Preserving arrows was important, seeing as he didn't know how to get more.

He stopped and glanced at the feline loping along next to him. "Hey, Kara, mind if I try riding again?"

The gatalan twitched her ear. It would likely fail again, but being astride would make a massive difference in how far they could travel in a day. He had to give it an eleventh try.

He pressed down on her back near her tail. Kara stopped walking and sat on her hind legs. Danny climbed onto her and wrapped his arms around her neck. Kara stood up, lifting Danny up onto her back in one smooth motion.

He balanced himself as best he could. "Go easy," Danny said, hoping for better results today.

Kara consented and moved slowly, but Danny still slid off her slick fur ten steps later, falling sideways and hitting his shoulder on the ground. "Damn it!" he grumbled. He levered himself up, rubbing his now-sore shoulder. More walking it was, at least until he found a way to procure a gatalan saddle. If he could.

How much would a gatalan saddle cost? Not a fortune, he hoped. But a new problem stared him in the face. *How am I going to earn Kasmanian money?* That could become a major problem. If he couldn't figure that out, his trip to Torinth would take a year instead of a few months.

He dreaded it. He was going to have to deal with the locals despite his ignorance. *I have to find a way to make money!* The more he thought about it, the less optional it became. But just thinking about it almost gave him a headache. Except for in Newisbel, currency was quite antiquated in Palaios, with the kingdoms of Belphi, Sebes, and Kasmana using the same monetary system: metal coins. Stupid coins. They used silver coins of three different sizes, one gold coin, and palladium squares. It was so primitive! Coins were heavy, smelly, and full of germs, and they could be stolen or lost. And what about the sound coins made when you walked? They clinked and rattled, letting everyone know you were a prime candidate for smuggling.

He sighed. *Dammit*... There was nothing Danny could do about it. He had to earn stupid coins to buy a saddle for Kara.

As they resumed walking, he imagined how impressive Kara would look wearing a nice saddle like the ones Danny had seen in documentaries. Gatalans ran faster than horses by a long shot. A saddle would be a game changer.

His pulse quickened as he wondered how it would feel to ride a galloping gatalan. He imagined the wind on his face as Kara's powerful muscles vaulted him forward. The huge felines moved gracefully despite their size, and they didn't make sounds the way horses did. Riding gatalans likely felt smoother; Danny guessed that shooting arrows while astride a gatalan was probably easier despite their increased speed. He couldn't wait.

Danny went on walking alongside Kara. They traveled eleven hours each day, moving northeast toward the Plain of Carbel.

Danny reached the outskirts of South Katan three weeks later, hunting quail and small game along the way, shooting whatever came into view. One midmorning, a lucky arrow shot down two quail. Danny picked them up and carried them with him, thinking he'd save one for the next day. There was no point in giving it to Kara—one quail wasn't enough food for her.

Suddenly, the sounds of female laughter reached Danny's ears. He stopped in his tracks, crouched, and listened. He estimated that there were three or perhaps four women up ahead. Their merriment reminded Danny of the comradery he had enjoyed with his buddies in Newisbel. Danny wasn't alone—he had Kara—but he missed having human friends.

Danny approached stealthily. Just because the strangers were friendly with each other didn't mean they'd be friendly toward him. He glanced back at Kara. She sauntered along and showed no signs of concern. There could only be one reason for that. Danny reached over and caressed her neck. "These women are Canyos, right?"

She shoved her face into his hand in response. Still, Danny moved forward with caution. Perhaps Kara didn't sense any danger, but he still wanted to take a good look at the women before they spotted him.

A minute later, he found them sitting around a fire, teasing each other and cooking lunch. There were four of them, all Canyos. They carried bows and hunting knives and wore leather vests and wool pants, with belts strapped to their thighs and shins to carry extra blades. Were they huntresses from South Katan? Three of them appeared to be in their late twenties, and the fourth was closer to Danny's age, perhaps just a year or two older.

"Good afternoon," Danny said.

The four women jumped to their feet and reached for their weapons. "Declare yourself!" one of the women commanded.

"I mean no harm," Danny answered. He showed them his hands.

They gave him a stern look. Danny kept his hands up, aiming his eyes toward the ground to appear less threatening. He noticed the pot over the fire and the white smoke billowing up from it. They were cooking porridge; its nutty, sweet smell made Danny's mouth water. Then he glanced at the rest of their camp. They hadn't killed any game yet.

He studied their faces. Despite their initial distrust and hard expressions, none of them came across as ill-spirited. Their eyes softened the longer they looked at Danny. Slowly, their hands fell away from their knives.

"What do we have here?" one of them asked. "This one owns a gatalan youngling! Are you in the army, boy?"

"No way! He's too young. Pay attention, Suma—this one still sucks from his mama's tits."

Two of them laughed. "How old are you, boy?"

"I'm fifteen," Danny said. He lowered his hands.

"Too bad . . . That's a good-looking fellow. Right, Kame?" a third one said, slapping the back of the younger one.

Kame shrugged, dipping her chin and casting her eyes at Danny.

"Come back next year, boy, and Kame will let you suck from *her* tits."

Kame's nostrils flared as the other three laughed. "Shut up!" she yelled, reaching for one of her knives.

"Oh, little Kame is upset . . . Don't mind her manners too much, boy. Kame is a fine girl," the one named Suma said.

"Yeah. But it's hard being a virgin," the third woman said, and they all laughed again except for Kame. Danny scratched the back of his head. Not many people made off-color jokes in Newisbel.

The youngest huntress drew her knife and pointed the blade at the third one. "What about this knife up your—"

Danny stepped forward. "I'm sorry to have caused you any trouble, Kame. I have mean friends too. It's best not to mind them much."

Kame looked at Danny with narrowed eyes. "You talk funny. Where are you from?"

"Not from here," Danny said, wondering if he should try to sound less formal.

"Oooh. 'Not from here.' Handsome *and* mysterious . . ." Suma said with a grin. "What's your name?"

"I'm Danny."

Kame scowled. "What kind of name is *Danny*? Sounds like a Naldorian girl's name."

Danny tapped his chest and adopted a pained expression. "Mama's tits would be offended."

All four of them laughed that time.

"I'm Suma. This is Velle, that's Rue, and you already met Kame, your future wife."

Danny bowed his head slightly. "Pleasure to meet you."

"What kind of man carries two quivers on his back?" Rue asked.

Danny grinned at her. "One who likes shooting arrows."

"Are you any good?" Suma asked.

Danny shrugged. "Let's say that my grandma may brag about it."

"I like him," Rue said with a nod. "You better snatch him soon, Kame! This one won't be single for long."

Kame scoffed. "I don't sleep with bedwetters. I hate soggy sheets."

Rue snorted. "Oh yeah? And how many bedwetters do you know that have bonded with a gatalan, ah? That's good breeding material right there." She gave Danny an appraising look. "He can wet my sheets anytime he wants."

Kame shook her head and rolled her eyes. Danny smiled. Rue was only pulling Kame's leg. It was a religious taboo in Kasmana for adults to sleep with someone under sixteen.

"I see you already shot two quails," Suma said, jerking her chin at the birds he'd strapped to his back.

Danny nodded. "Would you like to trade some of your porridge for a quail?" He couldn't remember the last time he'd had a warm bowl of porridge.

The huntresses looked at one another. "Are you sure?" Suma asked. "You can get one or two kirins at Jamela's inn for that quail, depending on its weight."

A wave of relief swept through Danny. He knew what she meant —here, the smallest coin was a kirin. The medium-sized silver coin was called a double and was worth two kirins. One kirin was enough to buy a meal large enough to feed two people. Porridge, on the other hand, was usually offered for free to customers staying the night at an inn.

Danny thought about it and smiled. "How many quails do I have to sell to buy a saddle for my gatalan?"

Suma waved a hand dismissively. "Kas bless me if I know!"

"Common folk don't know such things," Kame said. "But you'll find soldiers everywhere these days—you can ask them."

Rue *tsked*. "Soldiers don't know either! Gatalan riders get saddles for free. But saddle makers do set up shop near garrisons. You could approach one of those. If you mean business, that is."

"I mean business," Danny said immediately. "Which garrison do you think is closest to here?"

Suma answered him. "There're two about the same distance away, I'd say. One is a red garrison in South Katan, and another is in North Katan. Which is closer depends on where you're headed."

Danny smiled. "I see! That's quite helpful. Thank you." North Katan was on his way to the Singing Bridge—he'd go there. He walked closer to the women and reached for a quail. "So, what do you say? Quail for porridge?"

"Fine by me!" Rue said with a grin.

"You're in luck, Danny. Valle makes the best porridge in Neojoppa," Suma said.

Danny looked at the fourth huntress in the group. Valle had laughed with the others, but she hadn't said a single word yet. He picked his way over to sit beside her. Kara followed him and chose a spot to lie down near Danny.

"You don't say much," he said to Valle.

The woman quirked an eyebrow at Danny as the other three huntresses spoke in unison. "The wise listen and the fools talk."

All four women burst out laughing. Danny joined their laughter and then reached for a bowl of porridge.

Episode Eight

Chapter Twenty-Eight

8. Rayla

Rayla took a moment to decompress late in the afternoon after a lengthy meeting with Brigade Leader Analia and General Gadai. They had discussed worst-case scenarios that might happen in the coming days and the best ways to deal with them. If dying was the benchmark, almost every scenario they considered that afternoon qualified as a worst-case scenario.

Rayla decided to reward herself by nibbling on freshly baked jelly rolls while stretching her legs. She strolled by the garden inside the Red Horn, seeing roses near and pine trees afar. A well-kept lawn stretched along the side of the road, but it was hard to enjoy the peaceful, lovely view—the first battle of the coming civil war would take place in a few days, and every clash would be crucial. The odds were stacked against her; she had to rout her enemies at every turn. She could afford neither to lose a single battle nor to win at the expense of too many casualties.

Her next steps were clear: Rayla would wait at the Red Horn for General Nereida to arrive with her gatalan riders, and then she and her troops would travel north along the east bank of the Mercy River to the city of Narian.

So much would depend on what happened at the Narian garrison, one of the largest in Kasmana. Rayla had decided she would try to secure Captain Quecia's allegiance, and by extension her sixty thousand army soldiers. That prospect excited Rayla—if she was successful, those sixty thousand soldiers would triple her troops. Even more importantly, her tactical options would be multiplied. However, if Quecia turned her down, the situation could turn dicey. Although the captain should allow Rayla to leave peacefully after denying an alliance request, if Quecia's mindset was anywhere near the attitude Rayla had encountered in Priene a few weeks back, she'd be in serious trouble—those seamen had tried to kill her without giving her the slightest chance to argue her innocence. Outclassed and outnumbered, the seamen had fought her with everything they had. But trained officers like Quecia were likely to be more objective and even-keeled, Rayla reminded herself.

The sun set beyond the Red Horn's horizon as Rayla continued to stroll. Her steps through the garden took her near the archery shooting range, where she caught sight of Rolan sauntering toward the stables.

"Hey, Rolan!" she called. The man slowed down and turned his head. "Can you please find out if there's any news about Laramie's arrival?"

"Of course, my eken," the lieutenant answered. He turned and started to rush away.

"Oh, no!" she hurried to say. "It's not urgent, Rolan—you don't have to do it right now. You can finish whatever you were doing."

"It's not a problem, my eken. My business can wait." He said something else, but the increasing distance between them blurred his last sentence.

Rayla sighed. Her question had been a personal one. A lieutenant like Rolan had lots of duties to fulfill; she hadn't meant to inconvenience him. Sometimes she couldn't believe how dedicated all of her Lathraias were. It was a blessing, truly. And a burden. She had to strive to deserve their devotion and reward them with a sense of accomplishment. They deserved no less for sticking with her, for succeeding at doing something bigger than themselves. It was up to Rayla *not* to give in, to keep fighting, to lead.

She resumed strolling. What a pity Laramie hadn't been at today's meeting. Rayla would've loved her feedback on the vital aspects of the plan. It would take four days for their gatalans to trot all the way to Narian, and General Viembo could attack Rayla's company at any point along the way. Would Laramie have challenged the four defensive tactics Rayla had conceived in case of an attack?

Depending on the number of Viembo's men, Rayla could fight him there and then. General Nereida would bring about twenty thousand gatalan riders with her, and Rayla would show Viembo no mercy. Coming after her with an equal or lesser force would be the end of him. She sighed. A miscalculation on Viembo's part was unlikely. General Helikex, her predecessor, had been right—Viembo was smart. Untrustworthy, but smart.

If Viembo attacked Rayla's company with an overwhelming force of army soldiers and seamen, she and her troops could gallop back to the Red Horn or use their swift gatalans to rush past their enemies toward the Narian garrison or the Narialy Fortress. Or they could cross the Mercy River and focus on recruiting entire garrisons in central and western Kasmana.

"My eken!" a melodious female voice called.

Rayla turned, recognizing Corina's voice. Her longtime friend ran toward her, prompting a smile from Rayla.

"I heard you were asking about Laramie's arrival," Corina said, somewhat out of breath. She fell into step with Rayla.

The cacique smiled at her. "You used to call me Ray."

"You used to call me Cori."

That was true. Rayla wanted to call her Cori again, and she did so in her mind. But Corina's recent formality seemed intentional—it maintained whatever distance had developed between them after Corina had married Viembo.

"You're right," Rayla said. "We let things change too much, didn't we? I'll make you a deal: I'll call you Cori again if you promise not to call me 'my eken' ever again."

Corina gave a short laugh. "Umm . . . I think I'll hold off on that deal. It wouldn't feel genuine just yet. I have to earn it first, work my way up to it. At least until I make up for the atrocities my husband is committing."

Rayla wrinkled her forehead. "You don't need to earn anything, Corina. Viembo's actions are not your fault."

Corina shook her head. "Not his actions," she said, "my own *in*action. I could've done many things to prevent all this."

Rayla nodded. "Same for me. But we have too many problems to deal with right now, right here in the present. We can't let the past distract us."

"I know. But we can learn from the past. That's what I'm trying to do."

Rayla forced another smile. "I'm proud of you. You know that, right?" Then she quieted, allowing the conversation to reach its end.

They walked on in silence for a few moments. "Do you have news about Laramie?" Rayla finally asked, remembering what Corina had said upon arrival.

Corina blew out a breath. "I'm not sure if it's news . . . Do you remember the soldiers who left the garrison when we arrived?"

"Of course! That's hard to forget. About a thousand of them." Rayla shook her head, half-smiling. "That encouraged me, you know? Only one out of every seventeen soldiers decided to leave." She liked that ratio, but something about it obviously troubled Corina. The cacique looked at her friend expectantly.

Corina sighed. "Well, listen to this, Rayla—some of them decided to stay after all, and a few who'd left that night returned the next day."

Rayla wondered what had made her friend suspicious. "Interesting. What changed their minds?"

Corina scratched her cheek. "They said your gesture of giving

46

them supplies for the road moved them. They thought about it overnight and decided to come back."

Rayla's eyebrows went up. "The supplies? Really? That's just common decency. They're Canyos, after all, with families to return to. How many of them came back?"

Corina knitted her eyebrows. "A bit over three hundred between the ones who stayed the first day and those who returned yesterday." Corina paused to glance at Rayla. "But Aia wasn't so impressed. She kept them separate from the rest of the garrison."

Rayla halted her steps. "That should've been Analia's decision."

"It was!" Corina rushed to say. "Aia asked Analia, and the brigade leader agreed wholeheartedly. Rolan agreed too."

"Is that so?"

Corina nodded vigorously, and they resumed walking. "I was concerned, too, you know?" Corina continued, her voice firm. "I had to make sure none of them were saboteurs, especially the ones who returned. If they meant you harm, they'd had time to plan something. Which is why I spent many hours talking to quite a few of them."

"Is that so?"

"Ugh! Can you please stop saying that? It's very annoying."

"Is that so?" Rayla said, and burst out laughing a few seconds later after Corina gave her a confused stare.

Corina chuckled. "You're the worst, you know that, right?"

"Oh, no! That's Kameiros, followed by Viembo."

Her friend snorted. "No arguments there."

"Did you learn anything of interest from the 'saboteurs'?"

Corina pressed her lips together. "I don't know, Rayla. Rolan said to disregard it, and I agreed with him. But Aia and Gadai said to let you know after I told them that the handwriting looked like Laramie's."

Rayla halted her steps, and Corina followed suit. "What handwriting?"

Corina reached into her pocket and withdrew a crumpled piece of paper. "*This* handwriting." Rayla extended her hand, but Corina shook her head. "Let me tell you the full story first."

Rayla almost protested but changed her mind. "Okay. Go on."

"One of the returning soldiers had an interesting history to tell. He said he was traveling with one hundred soldiers toward South Katan when they ran across a messenger rushing toward the Red Horn. The most aggressive members of the group detained the messenger. They questioned and killed her after realizing she carried a message for you from Laramie. That's what the returning soldier claimed, anyway."

Rayla frowned. "You doubt his story?"

"I didn't believe him," Corina admitted. "But then he showed me this, and I became doubtful. He said he felt ashamed that the men had killed the messenger—she was a young girl, around nineteen."

Rayla's eyes widened. "That's horrific!"

"It's horrific if it's true," Corina said, nodding. "Or he could be manipulating us to make us believe his story."

Rayla jerked her head back. "*That* kind of cruelty would be horrific too."

"I agree. The soldier said the men searched the messenger's belongings before they killed her, and they found this message. They crumpled it up and tossed it away. The soldier couldn't sleep—he kept thinking about what the men had done and what a contrast their actions were compared to the kindness you had shown them by giving them supplies for the road. So he got up before dawn, grabbed the crumpled paper, and returned to the Red Horn."

Rayla's eyes narrowed. "He's risking his life if he *is* lying."

"I think he's aware of that," Corina said. She finally handed the wrinkled paper to Rayla.

The cacique gently smoothed it out and examined it closely. "It does look like Laramie's handwriting . . ."

"That's the only thing that makes me hesitate," Corina said, watching Rayla read.

Dear friend,

I have important news. Kameiros's lies are crumbling. Meet me at our favorite spot in South Katan. I'll wait for you seven days after the end of the full moon. Be careful! Everything hinges on your well-being.

Kas's love,

Laramie

Rayla remained silent a long while, contemplating the paper.

"We all think it's a trap," Corina said. "Your enemies may not know your favorite spot in South Katan, but only one road leads to the city from here. They could set up an ambush anywhere along the way."

Rayla nodded and looked up. "There," she said, lifting her chin. Corina followed Rayla's gaze. Aia and Rolan walked hurriedly toward them. "I'm guessing they have more news about this."

"Probably," Corina agreed, watching the pair of lieutenants draw closer.

Aia stopped in front of them. "My eken."

"Greetings, Aia."

"My eken," Rolan said. "I received an unconfirmed report regarding Lieutenant Laramie."

Rayla nodded, ignoring the knot that was starting to form in her stomach. "Go on."

"Laramie left the Unburnt Hills while you were in Mesonia. She crossed the Mercy River into western Kasmana around the time we left the Wet Forest. There are no details about her destination or purpose."

"How do you know this?" Rayla asked.

"One of the riders we left stationed in the Wet Forest said Laramie sent a verbal message asking you not to wait for her but to depart from the Wet Forest as soon as General Nereida arrived. Laramie said she'd find you whenever you go—and that she'd hopefully bring you a trump card."

Rayla snorted. "Ha! Both messages are plausible, and both could be lies. We're dealing with spies, masters of deception."

"Yes, my eken. Both messages are plausible, but only one asks you to put your life in danger," Aia pointed out.

"True. We can ignore the message that asked for nothing since that's the same as obeying it. But you know the downside of ignoring this one?" Rayla asked, lifting the wrinkled piece of paper.

"What, Rayla?" Corina said after a few seconds of tense silence.

"If this message is true, Laramie is waiting for me in South Katan and her life is already in danger. Everybody knows how important Laramie is to me—Kameiros, Viembo, or Fabris could hunt her down and then kill her or use her as a bargaining chip. Can anyone tell me with *absolute* certainty that I should ignore this message?"

No one answered. Rayla sighed and began walking to her quarters. "C'mon. Let's find Gadai and have a longer conversation about this."

Chapter Twenty-Nine

9. Kendar

Night ruled the skies when Kendar spotted Belphi in the distance. He stopped his forward plunge and hung in midair, squinting at the southern coast of the biggest continent in the world—Neojoppa. If the sun were up, he would've seen nothing but land rolling away in all directions, just like the first time he'd seen the ocean, though the opposite of it.

After Lunai's betrayal, he was aching for revenge. Should he scorch the world, or enslave it? He frowned as he considered the question anew. Something had changed in the last hour. For some reason, neither path was very appealing anymore. Killing everyone and destroying everything would be a terrible waste. He didn't care about a world full of liars and untrustworthy people—they deserved to die. But Kendar did enjoy fine clothing, food, wine, and women. Getting his revenge by raining fire and causing earthquakes would ruin his own future. Very wasteful indeed. He needed more options.

Kendar took a moment to choose the best landing spot. Cold air tousled his blond hair as he hung motionless, his eyes roving over what he could see of Belphi. Then he grimaced at a sudden uncomfortable sensation. He glanced at his arms. The protective coat that had kept him warm was disappearing.

Kendar's grimace grew larger as the cold spread through his body and the smell of brine reached his nose. Would he ever learn to control that stupid protective layer? The coat, feathers, and scales came and went of their own accord, never listening to him. Dumb things! Too bad it was a waste of time yelling at them. He had better things to do right now; he needed to hurry. His extreme thirst masked any pangs of hunger, but it didn't lessen the biting cold.

He looked ahead again. Light from a thousand sun sticks was concentrated in a narrow patch to his right, while darkness engulfed miles of shoreline on both sides. He moved higher and closer to get a better look. The Mvivi Inlet stretched into an aggressive indentation in the new continent. It hosted Prince Port, Kendar remembered. He pursed his lips. Even though it was dark, he could tell that Belphi's seaport was nowhere near as impressive as Casmare's.

Kendar moved closer still. Prince Port featured two main sections: the harbors on the east side accommodated passenger boats, and the west side had nothing but fishing boats. Kendar veered right. At this late hour, he was more likely to find water and food on the east side.

He chose a dark spot to land. As he approached it, he realized he was angling through the Furaha ghetto, a business district featuring nothing but whorehouses, inns, and public houses the locals called drinkeries. Just what he needed! Kendar adjusted his path.

Dawn was only two hours away. The streets were almost empty, but a few establishments were open. He landed where no one would see him and hurried toward the closest whorehouse, impatient for water and food. After he'd tamed his hunger and thirst, he'd fuck someone just to get the taste of Lunai out of his mouth.

A drunken man laughed on the other side of the street. Kendar looked. The idiot staggered forward, glancing at Kendar and snickering, seemingly unable to keep his eyes away from him.

Kendar was used to strangers staring at him, but this was a bit mocking. He glanced down at his body and cursed, his eyebrows going up. He was wearing his sleeping shorts! He'd been in bed when Lunai's conversation with Tares had woken him. Everything after that had happened so fast, and he'd been so angry that clothing—or a lack thereof—had been the last thing on his mind.

He halted and dug his hands into his pockets. "Crap!" He carried not a single coin on him; he'd left everything he owned at Stargazer Hill. Heat made his face flush and his ears turn red. He was utterly broke. He couldn't pay for food or water or buy services at the whorehouse, not to mention clothing. The last time he'd found himself in such pitiful conditions, he'd been a child. Damn her! This was Lunai's fault. He should've killed that treacherous whore when he had the chance.

He felt dizzy with hunger. "Find me an unattended store with water and food," he told the voices in his head. They were likely to find a drinkery that had closed for the night. He'd break in, satiate his thirst and hunger, and steal money for clothing and whoring. There should be a bank or two near Prince Port, too. He'd be fine.

As you wish, the voices answered.

Kendar tilted his head, frowning. Most often, the voices gave him answers right away, but now he recalled other times when the voices had acknowledged his request, gone quiet for a few minutes, and then told him what he needed or wanted. Although he'd never given that delay a second thought before, he wondered about it now. Why did the voices sometimes not know the answers right away? In fact, how did they know the answers at all? Kendar hated to admit it, but he didn't have the faintest idea how his powers worked.

"Stop!" he said to himself. Was he going crazy because Lunai had betrayed him? It wasn't healthy to question one's innate abilities. Did normal people ever question their ability to walk? What a waste of time.

Walk back and turn left two streets down the road, the voices whispered. Kendar obeyed. When he turned left, the new street seemed empty—just one lone sun stick prevented total darkness.

Kendar spotted a one-story drinkery with large glass windows and walked up to it. He couldn't tell what the business to the right was, but a convenience store flanked the drinkery on the left. Kendar reached its front door, grabbed the handle, and pushed with his invisible arms. The doorpost broke with a loud crack.

He stepped inside and peered into the darkness, allowing his eyes to adjust. Wing chairs and chaise lounges sat in front of coffee tables seemingly at random. At the far end, a bar stretched for twelve yards, lined with a row of stools and topped with a showcase displaying cheeses, shelled peanuts, bread, and pastries. Behind the bar, barrels of ale stood against the wall, ornamented with colorful cloths and sashes. Bottles of wine and spirits sat on long shelves that ran above the barrels.

Kendar rushed to open a barrel of ale, ignoring the bottled spirits and wines. The barrel popped open, and the sweet, musty smell of hops and fermented malt swarmed Kendar's face. He grabbed a tankard from the counter and plunged it inside the barrel, scooping up a full pint, then gulped down the entire tankard in one go, dripping ale over his cheeks, neck, and chest.

He stopped to catch his breath, eyeing a loaf of bread inside the showcase. He smashed the glass with an elbow and reached inside, heedless of the jutting shard that sliced into his arm and drew a line of hot blood. He grabbed the bread, ignoring the scalding sensation in his skin and the blood dripping over the floor.

The loaf felt hard in his hand. Kendar submerged the tankard in the barrel again, drawing a new serving. He dipped the bread into the fresh ale, softening it slightly, and bit off a mouthful. He followed it with another swig of ale so that he could swallow the hunk of bread faster—he didn't have the patience to chew. He did that again and again until the bread disappeared. Finally, he felt warm and cozy. How many tankards had he gulped down?

He reached for cheese and a bottle of wine and dispatched them in no time. Then he noticed his injured hand. The bleeding had stopped and the pain was gone. He laughed at it without knowing why, then reached for peanuts and another helping of ale.

The ale and wine were making him feel like he was on top of the world. He couldn't sense any trace of his anger or emotional pain from three days ago. He laughed, praising the magic of alcohol. He'd never drunk so much before, but no one could accuse him of being wasteful—he was just making up for the last three days.

When he moved to grab a bottle of liquor, his head swayed along with the entire room. He tried to steady himself by grabbing the counter, but he knocked down the empty tankard instead. It exploded into a thousand pieces when it hit the hard floor. Kendar burst out laughing. The tinkling sounds of tiny pieces of wood scattering along the ground had become musical.

He grabbed another bottle of wine and drank it even as he reached for more bottles and tankards with his invisible hands. He threw them against the walls and ceiling, filling the drinkery with music—bottles exploded on contact, splashing glass and alcohol all over the place. Kendar laughed and giggled in between sips.

He ran out of wine and reached for more ale, but when he tried to take a step, he slipped on the pool of blood that had trickled down from his injured arm. The world tilted; pain flashed through his head when he hit the floor. His protective layer had apparently appeared a second too late.

"Stupid thing," he said as a loud ringing took over his ears. "Stupid thing," he mumbled again. Everything went dark.

"Hey, you. Hey! Wake up!" someone said, shaking him.

Kendar tried to open his eyes, but the punishing sunlight kept them shut.

"I told you he wasn't dead," someone said as a terrible headache exploded inside Kendar's skull. He grabbed his stomach, feeling an urge to vomit, still unable to open his eyes.

"Maybe all the dried blood isn't his, then. Do you think he killed someone?"

"Shut up!" Kendar hissed. Each word out of their mouths was landing like a punch inside his brain.

"Ha! Maybe you're right, Hami. This rude misfit isn't the bosi."

"I told you, the police will *never* bring the bosi here. Jail is for broke folks."

"He's too young to be the bosi. A bastard son or a nephew, maybe," a third man said.

Kendar finally managed to open his eyes. His vision was blurry, but he made out bars.

"Praise Lady Makena! Even his eyes are the same. This guy can easily pass for the bosi."

One of the men laughed. "He probably tried that—I bet it's what landed him here."

Kendar sat up, squinting. Even though the splitting headache and nausea were unbearable, he pushed himself unsteadily to his feet and looked around, forcing himself to think. Where *was* he?

The place was a square room with three walls made of cobblestones. It was big enough to accommodate twenty people. Floor-to-ceiling bars made up the front of the room, and a narrow, barred window ran along the top of the back wall. There was no doubt: Kendar was in a jail cell along with three other men.

He glanced down at himself and saw that he was covered in dried blood and puke. The combined smell made him even more nauseous. His left shoulder and hip hurt, probably from sleeping on the hard floor.

He checked the arm he'd injured the previous night. His eyebrows went up—not even a scratch remained. He'd never suffered an injury before and hadn't known he could heal so quickly. Hopefully that same healing ability would help him get through his horrendous hangover faster.

He glanced at the three men inside the jail cell. Their general features reminded him of Lucca, the pleasant man who had managed the property Kendar had rented in Casmare. More than likely, then, these men were Belphians, Normos who shared a common ancestry with the people of Normania and Maraccia. Like Lucca, these men had fair skin, broad noses, and light green eyes. And all three were at least eight inches shorter than Kendar.

He pointed at one of them. "You there. How long have I been here?"

The man threw up his hands. "Look, mister, I want no trouble."

"Then answer the question," Kendar said with hard eyes. Even the sound of his own voice hurt his head.

The man hesitated. "The afisa brought you in this morning. They said you wrecked Ormari's place in Furaha ghetto. Some balls you pack! The afisa put you down gently, so we figured you're fancy folk."

Kendar frowned at that. *Not* being thrown down onto the hard floor was considered preferential treatment? What puzzled him even more was that preferential treatment existed at all—how could anyone here know who he was to treat him differently? "Who's this bosi person you guys were talking about?" Perhaps that had something to do with this "preferential treatment."

One of the men snorted. "Ha! The rude misfit is fresh off the boat."

Kendar took a menacing step toward him, and the man shied away. Kendar towered at least ten inches over him. "Answer the question!"

"Relax, misfit," the third man interjected. "We're all paddling the same canoe here. No need to be aggressive."

"Dogs get free food; wolves have to hunt," the short man said. Kendar just frowned. What the hell was that supposed to mean?

"No one here is going to fight you, misfit," the third man continued. "Not after the afisa marked you."

"What is the *afisa*?" Kendar asked.

The man shook his head. "Fresh off the boat, indeed. Afisa are the people with the authority to beat you up and throw you in jail."

Kendar frowned. So they meant Belphian police. "And who is this bosi?"

"He's the ruler of this province."

Kendar ran his fingers through his hair. The headache was impeding his thoughts. These men had said Kendar looked like the bosi. That meant the bosi was a Highlander. But how could a Highlander be the ruler of a Belphian province?

Kendar tried to remember everything he'd read about Belphi during his time in Isiagi. Slowly, grudgingly, the information trickled in. Just like the other two kingdoms in Palaios, Belphi had a king. The Belphian monarch had absolute control over the military, the treasury, and interprovincial matters. But that was the extent of his powers. Belphi was divided into five provinces, each with its own ruler. Provinces weren't allowed to have a military, but they had a police force.

"How is it possible for a foreigner to become the bosi?" Kendar asked.

One man shrugged; another *tsked*. "What kind of stupid question is that?"

Kendar narrowed his eyes, and the same man rushed to answer. "If they pay the challenger's fee and win the election, anyone can become the ruler."

Kendar allowed himself to half sit, half collapse back onto the unforgiving floor. That was important information about Belphi. Why had the book he'd read been so incomplete? Odd . . . Well, that didn't matter now.

He leaned his head against the wall and closed his eyes, wishing his pounding headache would go away. The pain made it hard to figure out what to do.

The cold wall seeped its chill into his temples, lessening his headache ever so slightly. He chuckled. A Highlander ruled this province! If he remembered correctly—and if the book about Belphi hadn't been wrong about *this* aspect—Prince Port was part of the Mongad province, which occupied the Belphian eastern coast and part of the southern coast. It was the biggest province in the kingdom, second in importance only to the Narabi province, the province that hosted the nation's capital. How had a Highlander managed to rule over such a province? More to the point, could Kendar follow in his footsteps?

He put the thought aside for another day when he wasn't hungover. Right now, he could use a bath and a good bed, perhaps some chicken soup. None seemed remotely possible at the moment. Kendar had never been deprived of his freedom before. What was the best thing to do? He could bust out of this jail whenever he wanted, sure, but it was already apparent that he was as recognizable in Belphi as he'd been in Casmare. Destroying the jail cell now would waste a lot of time later, and wasting had landed Kendar here in the first place. Wasting was a spiral of death.

He clenched his fists and grunted. Thinking was leading nowhere in his current state; better to leave the planning for later, when he felt rested. Better not to rush into anything. Kendar could rest here awhile. Imagining a bed beneath him, Kendar's thoughts drifted into a drowsy haze . . .

"Hey! Hey, Highlander!" a potent male voice called.

Startled, Kendar opened his eyes. He realized that he'd fallen asleep. Twilight dimming the room through the narrow window told him the sun was setting outside.

He looked up. A man in a gray uniform—trousers, a shirt, and a brimless cap—stood outside the jail cell. He carried a sword and a truncheon at his hips, and he was staring at Kendar with the authority of a person in charge. Kendar connected the dots. This was a police officer, an afisa.

"Are you Kendar of Ypsilos?" the man asked.

Kendar remained silent, feeling the pain in his head coming back and mixing with confusion. How the hell did this man know Kendar's name? What was going on?

"Well, are you?" the afisa asked again, his voice hardening.

Kendar nodded, unable to come up with any ideas. The damn

headache was freezing his brain and making him only capable of a blank stare.

"Okay, then. Wait there." The afisa turned and walked away.

Once the officer was out of earshot, one of the men inside the cell jeered, "Where else is he going to wait, dumbass?" Kendar stayed silent.

Moments later, the afisa returned with a large set of keys. He unlocked the jail door and held it open. "You're free to go, Highlander. Someone paid your prison bill."

"Lucky bastard," one of the men inside the cell whispered.

Kendar frowned. "Prison bill?"

"Yeah," the afisa said. "The cost of the damages you caused plus an additional twenty percent for reparations to the owner and an additional eighty percent for the afisa fee."

His previous readings rushed back into his head. In Belphi, only three crimes were punishable with death by hanging: murder, rape, and treason. Everything else translated into a prison bill. The bill became months or even years of forced labor if the guilty person couldn't pay it. Prison charges included a punitive incarceration fee meant to finance the police and discourage offenders, and the amount tripled when a crime was repeated.

"Who paid my prison bill?" Kendar asked as he levered himself to his feet. He stepped through the open door.

"The lady is waiting outside with a bag of clothing for you. Go thank her yourself."

The afisa closed the cell door and walked toward the station's entrance. Kendar followed, still struggling with the headache and nausea. Just the idea of thinking about anything made him scowl.

He followed the afisa past empty jail cells and down a long corridor. His gaze swept over barren gray walls. Oil lamps were stuck into sconces, illuminating the hallway, and their light danced as an ocean breeze wafted in through the barred windows. "That's right," Kendar muttered to himself. A coastal city was waiting for him outside along with the mysterious woman. Whoever the stranger was, she saw an advantage in paying for his release, and *that* meant she knew too much.

Was she a threat? Even if she wasn't, what should Kendar do about people who knew too much about him? Crushing them like he'd crushed Tares of Coriplion seemed like an appropriate punishment.

The long corridor came to an end, and Kendar entered the waiting area. A young afisa sat behind a desk, clearly bored to tears, and a second equally bored one stood by the front door. Only one civilian waited inside: a woman, looking out the window and holding an overstuffed bag. Her silky black hair reached below her shoulder blades.

Kendar froze at the sight of her. She wore a blue dress that fit her body tightly, and she looked as breathtaking as ever.

She turned to Kendar, and her eyes filled with pity and relief. A sad smile grew on her rosy lips. Her voice came out soft and warm. "Hi, Kendar," said Lunai of Bolenti.

Chapter Thirty

9. Rayla

Rayla heard laughter coming from troops in the rear, and she took that as a sign of a lightened mood. The merry outburst came five minutes after the company emerged from the Reeky Forest on their way to South Katan. Then her shoulders slumped. *Who am I kidding?* She wanted to imagine that her soldiers now had a more positive outlook on the mission, but that wasn't quite true, and she couldn't ignore the reason why.

The company's heavy mood had not stemmed from the forest's foul smell or the toxic-looking green puddles that peppered the swampy terrain. The possibility was high that Rayla was risking her life by coming to South Katan, and her Lathraias knew it. Yet it was a risk that Rayla *had* to take. Laramie was a dear friend, yes, but heeding her call was more than Rayla just selfishly refusing to lose someone she loved. Laramie brought the best out of her, and Rayla needed her friend by her side to increase the chances of victory in the upcoming war. Rayla couldn't explain exactly why that was the case —not even to Laramie herself—but if Rayla didn't trust her instincts, what else did she have? Her conviction had taken her this far, and right now, that conviction was yelling, "Go to South Katan!" Listening to her guts could change everything. Hopefully.

"Let's never do that again," said Aia, wrinkling her nose, referring to the road they'd taken. Rayla nodded, wondering whether their clothes stunk like the forest. She couldn't tell. Maybe their noses had gone numb.

It had taken Rayla and her fifty companions seven hours to travel the winding, muddy road through the Reeky Forest. She'd chosen the route since it was unlikely that foot soldiers would use the arduous road—no one in their right mind would lie in wait anywhere along the foul-smelling path.

Half an hour after they'd left the forest behind, the company took a break to relieve themselves and nibble on snacks of dried meat and flatbread. "We won't be staying long," Rayla told Aia and Rolan. The pair of lieutenants agreed. From this point onward, they could be ambushed at any moment if Laramie's note had been a ploy.

They pressed on after twenty minutes of rest. Rayla calculated they had four hours of daylight left, and she intended to take advantage of every last minute of it. She wanted to be back in North Katan in three days, where she'd hopefully find General Nereida waiting at the Red Horn and ready to depart for Narian.

Then, an eerie, howling shriek thundered through the sky. The sharp screech seemed to echo in the clouds, and the entire company halted.

"For the love of Kas!" someone yelped at the back of the company.

Everyone looked up. Even though no one could see it, everyone knew what it was—the lord of the sky's call was unmistakable. Gavians were the largest birds of prey in the world, with a fear-inducing shriek that sounded like a combination of an eagle's screech and a wolf's howl. The gavian cried out again, and even the gatalans shifted uneasily underneath their riders, wary of the massive avian hunter and its skull-crunching talons.

"Is there anything more unnerving in the entire world?" a Lathraias behind Rolan asked. Rayla suppressed a smile. This fellow had probably never seen Hellsmouth up close.

"It means we've entered the Plain of Carbel," said Aia. The company resumed trotting along, their eyes still searching the sky.

Rayla agreed with Aia. Gavians were abundant near Belphian mountains, but they only nested on the cliffs of the Triple Peaks in Kasmana, and the Plain of Carbel was their hunting ground this side of Hellsmouth. Gavians wouldn't be spotted anywhere else in Kasmana.

"Can you believe I've never seen a gavian in person?" Rolan asked with a smile.

Aia gave him a surprised look. "Not even circling in the sky?"

"Not even. I've heard them, sure, but I've only seen pictures of them in books."

"What about you, my eken?" Aia asked.

Rayla's eyes twinkled. "I've seen them to my heart's content. Laramie is obsessed with gavians. She believes they are to Neojoppa what gatalans were to Quinquella. A few years back, she and I spent a week near the Triple Peaks and saw gavians in action."

"Is that when the two of you found your favorite spot in South Katan?" Aia asked.

"That's right! It's an inn on the outskirts of the city with a fantastic view of the Triple Peaks. Laramie and I liked the view more than the inn."

Rolan leaned forward on his gatalan with bright eyes. "Can you tell me about them, my eken? Gavians, I mean."

"Oh, gavians are impressive, Rolan," Rayla said. "Especially when they're diving to catch prey. It takes your breath away! They have slick gray feathers, and they glide in the air, not flapping their wings for long stretches. They hover amid clouds and then pounce down. I swear, they speed faster than an arrow."

"Is it true that their shriek paralyzes their prey?" Aia asked, clutching her gatalan's reins a little more tightly.

"Some prey, but not all," Rayla answered. "Quite a few try to run away. But I didn't see a single animal escape once the gavian swooped down on it."

Rolan's eyes shone with awe. "Wow! I'm hoping to see one today."

"Is it true they can lift a toddler?" Aia asked.

Rayla hesitated. "I don't know about that. Although they *are* enormous compared to other birds."

"How big?" Rolan blurted out.

Rayla grinned at him. "The big ones have a wingspan of up to fifteen feet; Laramie said they weigh up to forty pounds. But she also said adult gavians can only lift between ten and fifteen pounds." Rayla lifted a finger and aimed it at Rolan's disappointed face. "How*ever* . . . gavians can kill animals of any size with their long talons. They go for the spine or the neck, and if they grab you, you're done for. When their prey is too big for them to carry away, gavians simply carve out a chunk of meat to fly off with and then leave the rest behind."

Rolan's expression shifted back to awe. "Wow!"

Rayla nodded. "That's why small animals stay within the areas where gavians hunt—gavians share the bounty."

"You said they're the same as gatalans, my eken, but there is one big difference," Aia interjected.

"I didn't say that; Laramie did. But, yes, gavian meat is delicious."

Aia had a hungry look in her eyes. "Yes! That's what I heard."

"It sounds like you've had gavian meat, my eken?" Rolan asked.

"I did, yes. But only once. Do you remember the big celebration in Kassapea after we defeated the Maraccians? Altanarian promoted me to general, and they served gavian that day. It was the best meat I'd ever had. They told me it came from Belphi and cost a fortune."

The gavian shrieked again, and this time, the source of the sound was much closer.

Rayla tipped her head back and surveyed the sky. "You're in luck, Rolan. Three screeches in a row usually means the gavian locked in its prey."

Rolan suddenly looked worried. "It isn't one of us, right?"

Rayla suppressed a laugh. "I doubt it—they don't mess with humans or gatalans. Unless they're really hungry," she added with mischief in her eyes.

"There!" Aia said. The entire company halted again and looked. A hundred yards away, the massive bird plunged down from the sky, its gray wings tucked against its body. It shot along at a breathtaking speed, just as Rayla remembered. Awe still widened her eyes. Nothing moved swifter in the world than a pouncing gavian! Not even a gatalan possessed that speed. All of the Lathraias watched with bated breath as the aerial raptor slid down from the clouds faster and faster. Then the gavian spread its wings and took on an angle, turning horizontally.

Then, out of nowhere, an arrow shot toward the gavian from the opposite direction. The sharp-tipped projectile barreled toward the bird and hit it squarely in the chest. The gavian lost control in midair and crashed, tumbling to the ground in a chaos of legs and feathers.

Rayla's mouth fell open, and Rolan gave a small yelp. A trail of dust rose where the gavian had crash-landed.

"That's an impossible shot!" Aia said as a murmur spread through the company. "You all saw that, right?" she asked no one in particular. Many nodded in disbelief.

Rayla had to agree. If one hundred Lathraias had shot at the gavian at the same time, perhaps one of them would have hit it, but even that would have taken a tremendous amount of luck.

Seconds later, a boy came running after the gavian, clutching a bow tightly in one hand. A gatalan youngling ran along next to him. It was a tall gatalan with orange fur, but it hadn't developed any black stripes yet.

Rayla focused on the boy. Although he couldn't have been older than fifteen, he was fit and well-armed, with a sword strapped to his side and two full quivers on his back. He reached the gavian and jumped up and down excitedly, then played with his gatalan in a childish celebration. Rayla smiled. The boy and his gatalan reminded her of herself and Kaistan.

"That was one lucky shot!" Rolan exclaimed.

"Maybe," said Rayla with wonder in her eyes. Sometimes "luck" was just a way to label forces people didn't understand.

"I don't think he's noticed us, my eken," Aia said.

"No, he hasn't . . . C'mon, Kaistan. Let's go meet them," Rayla said. She gently pressed Kaistan's side with her right leg, and the gatalan started walking slowly toward the boy. She didn't want to startle him by approaching too quickly.

Rayla glanced behind her. Fifty Lathraias followed her with raised eyebrows. She smiled. They were obviously curious about the boy's skill *and* the gavian. She couldn't blame them; both were quite rare.

"Only you two for now," Rayla said to Aia and Rolan. Then she spoke to the rest of the troops. "I know you don't see something like this every day, but we don't want to overwhelm the boy. I'll call for you once I've spoken to him."

She moved ahead while Aia and Rolan gave instructions to the rest of the company and then followed Rayla. Up ahead, the boy finally noticed them. He immediately became still, blinking rapidly at them as if not understanding what he was seeing. Then his gaze became an open stare.

"Look, Kara! Those are midnight gatalans!" he gasped. "Can you believe it!" A wide smile overtook his features, and he hurried to meet them with Kara at his side, squealing with joy as he ran.

Rayla tilted her head, frowning. She sensed sincerity in the boy's childlike enthusiasm about their midnight gatalans, but only Canyos living in rural communities deep in the north would have never seen one before.

"He's more awestruck by our gatalans than by you, my eken," Aia commented.

"It's not a crime not knowing my face, Aia."

"No, my eken. It's just odd."

They neared the boy, who had stopped running. He bubbled with enthusiasm, bouncing from foot to foot.

"Hi! Is it okay if I touch them?" the boy said. He didn't wait for an answer before sticking out a hand to caress Kaistan's head.

"Be care—" Rayla started to say, but the boy was already tickling Kaistan behind the ear. Rayla gawked as Kaistan moaned and licked the boy's face in response. The teenager's giggles robbed Rayla of words, and she glanced at Aia, wide-eyed. Except for Laramie, Kaistan was reluctant to let anyone other than her touch him, including veterinarians and people who fed or washed him.

"Hi there," Rolan said to the boy. "What's your name?"

He stepped back, looking down with embarrassment. "My apologies. My name is Danny, sir. And this is Kara," he pointed at his gatalan. "Pleasure to meet you," he added, lowering his head.

Rayla, Aia, and Rolan looked at each other. His tongue held a slight and pleasant accent. They'd never heard anything like it.

"Where are you from, boy?" Rolan asked.

Danny paled. "I'm . . . from . . . from a faraway village, sir. I'm on my way to Torinth."

Rolan narrowed his eyes. "What's waiting for you in Torinth?"

"I'm trying to find my father, sir. His name is Marko. I haven't seen him since I was four."

"That last part is probably true," Rolan muttered to Aia and Rayla. "But he's hiding something."

"He's probably a runaway," Aia said baldly. Danny stiffened.

"Let him be," Rayla told them, turning back to the boy with a smile. "My name is Rayla, Danny. Pleasure to meet you. This is Lieutenant Aia, and this is Lieutenant Rolan. And this is Kaistan. It seems my gatalan already approves of you."

Danny bowed his head without any hint that he knew whom he was addressing. Rayla glanced at Aia and Rolan to read their reactions. It was justifiable for the boy not to recognize her face, but he should've recognized her name. She was the cacique of armed forces, after all, and second only to the king-priest.

"It seems he grew up alone on a mountain," Aia said in a neutral tone.

"And yet he has good manners," Rayla said. She smiled at him again. "Where did you learn to shoot?"

Danny smiled, seemingly oblivious to any suspicion. "I practiced many hours a day every day, ma'am. Archery is my best skill."

Rolan wrinkled his brow. "So you're saying that shooting down the gavian wasn't a lucky shot?"

Danny shifted his weight. "It wasn't, sir. Happy to prove it."

Rayla laughed. "I hope you aren't jealous, Rolan. This young man may be a prodigy." She looked at Danny with approving eyes. The boy fidgeted with embarrassment, and she liked that, too. He had a sense of pride *and* a sense of humility. "What do you plan to do with the gavian?" she asked.

"I was just hunting for dinner, ma'am. I didn't know it was this big."

Aia laughed. "Shooting down a gavian for dinner is probably the biggest accomplishment of your life, boy!"

A shade of sadness briefly veiled his eyes. "Thanks, ma'am."

"You seem to disagree," Rolan said. "What else have you done with your bow?"

"I've defended people I care about, sir."

"When—" Rolan started to ask, but Rayla lifted a hand, halting him. Rolan lowered his eyes. "Sorry, my eken. You've already said to let him be."

Rayla nodded at Rolan and then looked at the boy. "Danny, would you consider selling the gavian to me? You could dine with us if you wish, and we'll feed your gatalan too."

The boy caressed his chin, and his eyes turned bright as he considered her proposal. She smiled again. The boy's expressions were easy to read, and his innocence was genuine. No wonder Kaistan liked him.

"Do you know how many gavians I'd have to sell to buy a saddle for Kara, just like the one you have? That saddle is so nice!"

Rayla, Rolan, and Aia burst out laughing. That gavian was enough to buy at least two saddles, probably three.

"If you come with us, I'll give you a brand-new saddle for Kara plus enough money for a round trip to Torinth," Rayla said.

Rolan edged closer to her. "Are you sure, my eken?" he said in a low voice. "The boy is hiding something."

"I know," she answered just as discreetly. "But whatever it is, it's not malicious. I trust Kaistan's instincts. Besides, I was a teenager once myself, Rolan. And I had *lots* of secrets."

Aia couldn't resist butting in. "Oh, secrets belong to mere humans, my eken! Rolan never had any." She could barely contain her laughter.

"Fine! But if he comes with us, I'll keep an eye on him," Rolan said in a stubborn tone.

Rayla nodded. "That's part of your job," she said loudly and clearly. "But you're to treat him with kindness. You may be looking at the best bowman in Kasmana since the Cayacoa."

The boy made a puzzled face at the sound of the legendary name. Rayla nearly shook her head. His ignorance was as remarkable as his shooting. Perhaps his father was to blame for abandoning the child at an early age and not taking care of his education. She wondered if Danny even knew how to read.

"What about it, Danny? Would you sell your gavian to me?"

The boy gave Rayla a bright smile and then turned to his gatalan. "What do you say, Kara? A new saddle, food, *and* money?" Kara looked away and twitched one of her ears. Then the boy turned back to Rayla, pushing his chest out and lifting his chin. "I accept your proposal, ma'am."

"Excellent! You'll be quite popular once my companions taste gavian meat tonight." She grinned at him. "You're headed for Torinth, so I'm guessing you'll cross the Mercy River at the Singing Bridge?"

"That's my plan, ma'am."

"Please, call me Rayla."

71

"Will do, ma'am."

Rayla laughed. "We have to ride south for a few more hours. Then we'll return north tomorrow afternoon and reach the Red Horn the next day. I'll give you a new saddle for Kara and your payment then. You can be on your way to Torinth the same day. Does that work for you?"

He bobbed his head eagerly. "Yes, it does. Thank you! I appreciate your kindness, Rayla."

"My thanks to you! Gavian meat is a rare treat . . . Do you see all those soldiers over there?" Rayla tilted her head at the Lathraias.

"They're hard to miss," Danny answered.

"Well, they're dying to meet you," Rayla said, waving at them. To the boy's delight, fifty midnight gatalans came trotting toward him.

* * *

Danny had been riding Kaistan for the last fifteen minutes, sitting behind Rayla. The boy had tried to follow the Lathraias astride Kara, but he kept sliding off her sleek fur every other minute. Rayla realized she herself had never ridden a gatalan without a saddle. Judging by how it was going—or wasn't—for Danny, riding without a saddle seemed impossible. Someone had told her years ago that Belphians could ride horses without a saddle if they had to. Rayla hadn't doubted that at the time, but now she'd have to see it to believe it.

After giving up on riding Kara, Danny had tried to follow the Lathraias on foot, but he had quickly fallen behind, delaying the company. Although veins had started to protrude from Rolan's neck when Rayla had offered to let Danny ride with her, her lieutenant was wise enough to keep his thoughts to himself. Rayla understood that Rolan was trying to protect her from a complete stranger, but Rayla wouldn't have it. The boy was more than her guest; Danny was her responsibility now. She would not leave a teenager behind in potentially hostile territory.

They went on for another half hour. The riderless Kara walked at the back of the pack of gatalans, far away from Danny. He seemed to have understood Kara's hierarchical spot amid the midnight gatalans and didn't make a fuss.

Rayla studied the sun's position as the white star made its way west. She had over two hours of daylight left, and so far, so good. No ambush; instead, they would have gavian meat for dinner. She planned to camp near South Katan at sundown. If all continued to go well, on the following day, she would reach the inn where Laramie was supposedly waiting for her.

The company was passing a foothill near the Triple Peaks. A fading brook trickled along in front of them; on their left, the ground sloped up the hill; on their right stood a grove. Rayla remembered this particular section of the road—she'd crossed it with Laramie a few years back after a rainstorm, when the brook had turned into a creek. The two women had climbed up into the grove to get through. Rayla would've chosen to pass through the grove again today if the climbing wouldn't have put unnecessary strain on the gatalans. The view was much better up there.

Suddenly, a burst of dry laughter echoed down the hill. The entire party halted. "I told you she always rides at the front," someone out of view said.

"Ambush!" a Lathraias shouted from the middle of the company. The side of the hill shook, and Rayla looked up to her left. Dozens of boulders were tumbling toward her company, bringing with them a rain of smaller rocks.

"*Take cover!*" someone yelled. But where?

Rayla's mind raced, searching for the best move. Her hands clenched on her reins. The enemy had the higher ground, while she and her Lathraias were sitting ducks. Then Danny shouted at her back, "Look to the right!"

Rayla turned. A large boulder rolled toward her from the grove. "Hold on tight!" she yelled, spurring Kaistan ahead. "Move up into the grove!" she yelled at her Lathraias as Kaistan jumped forward.

The agile gatalan leaped onto the side of the hill, barely avoiding the giant boulder.

Rayla looked down the hill. The boulder lay squarely in the middle of the road, cutting her off from the rest of her company, while dozens of rocks rained down upon her Lathraias.

"Move up into the grove!" she yelled again despite not being able to see her troops. "Attacking speed!" she commanded Kaistan, and the gatalan pounced to the right, burying his claws into the slope and leaping toward the grove. He breasted the terrain in four jumps, with Danny still holding on to Rayla tightly, his arms wrapped around her waist like a belt.

They stopped and glanced back. Rayla had expected a better view of the battlefield below, but a makeshift wall blocked her view of the ambush. She could hear Aia and Rolan shouting orders.

Danny yelled, his voice overloud in her ear. "Straight ahead! Incoming arrows!"

Rayla ducked left and spurred Kaistan on. A volley of arrows raced past her head as the gatalan leaped out of the way and rushed to the left. Her mind searched for clues, trying to grasp the situation. Then Rayla spotted a clearing ahead just as more arrows whistled by. Her chest tightened. Danny was in tremendous peril—he wore no armor and had turned into a human shield against the archers shooting at Rayla's back.

Kaistan increased his speed, and they flung themselves ahead, finally outdistancing the arrows. When Rayla pulled on the reins, Kaistan stopped abruptly.

Rayla jumped off the gatalan. "You stay there!" she told Danny as the boy likewise began to dismount. "They're after me, not you." She hurriedly drew her two spears from the holder strapped to Kaistan's side. Her sword already hung at her hip. "You'll be safe as long as you're away from me. Ride straight ahead." Her intense gaze shifted to Kaistan. "Take care of him, okay? Do this for me, Kiwi. I'll come find you soon."

When she glanced back at Danny, she saw a fearsome look radiating from the teenager's eyes, transforming his innocent face. Rayla knitted her eyebrows together. Danny had aged ten years in an instant! He looked like a seasoned warrior had taken over his body.

The boy shifted forward to sit in the saddle as if he would comply with Rayla's order. But she knew the facial expressions of soldiers who obeyed her commands, and that wasn't one of them.

Danny said nothing—he simply spurred Kaistan on ahead. The two disappeared from view. What was all that about?

Rayla heard noises at her back and turned, assuming a fighting stance. Three men came into view atop orange-furred gatalans. They got off their mounts and approached her in a crescent moon formation, with the man at the center lagging the ones walking at the far ends. All three were strongly built, holding their shoulders back, their chests out, and their chins high. They wore full suits of armor; confidence oozed out of them as if they were sure they could take on Rayla.

She raised an eyebrow when she recognized the man at the center. She couldn't remember his name, but he had taken fourth place at the last Yimin Tourney. He was a master swordsman—not as good as Aia, but still an elite. Rayla chuckled. Perhaps the other two were as good as him. That would explain their cockiness. She smiled, welcoming the challenge.

The men stopped moving once they were within striking range. "Time to pay for your crimes, cacique," the one in the center said.

She chuckled again. "Who named you judge and executioner?"

"We'll let Kas pass judgment through our swords," another one said.

"Fine by me," Rayla said with a smirk. But it would be her spears passing judgment, not their blades. She held the long, red-painted spear with her right arm, its tip pointing toward the ground; with her left hand, she rested the smaller, yellow-painted spear across her shoulders in a near-vertical position.

"What's with the spears?" one of the men asked with a hint of surprise.

She shifted the small one off her shoulders and pointed it at him, twirling it several times. "They're my weapon of choice." The men glanced at each other, and Rayla chortled. "If you prepared for this thinking I'd use my sword, you're out of luck. You came here to die."

"We've seen you fight dozens of times, but never with spears," the one to the right said.

She snorted. "Spears are not great in a melee, you fool! Four of you would force me to draw my sword. I'm glad you're one shy. I haven't used these girls in a while."

If they insisted, perhaps she *would* draw her sword out of sheer curiosity. Rayla had never seen master swordfighters attack a single opponent as a group. More than two of them meant they'd get in each other's way. But these three confident warriors had likely choreographed a specific attack based on a supposed flaw they'd noticed in her swordsmanship. That made her curious. Maybe she'd let them test their theory if they asked nicely.

"It doesn't matter what tricks she uses! We'll kill the witch here and now," the cocky one sneered.

That sealed the deal. "Enough chat," Rayla snapped. She lifted the red spear like a lance and charged the man at the center. He prepared to parry the strike, but she spun left and went after the man in the corner position.

She spun a second time, swinging the red spear at the man's head and thrusting the yellow one at his chest. The man parried the red spear, and it slipped slightly around his sword, nearly striking his head. At the same time, the yellow spear pierced his armor and drove deep into his chest. The man yelped as he fell, grabbing at the shaft sticking out of his body.

"No!" the man at the right yelled. He and the center man came at Rayla simultaneously.

She eyed the incoming enemies and tried to retrieve her short weapon, but it was stuck in the fallen man's armor. She looked down. The dying soldier was holding on to her yellow spear as blood oozed from his mouth. Rayla was forced to jump back and abandon the short spear.

The two men abruptly halted before her. The man from the right glanced at their fallen comrade, and his lips quivered.

"Lari's death wasn't in vain," the other man said to him. "She'll fight with her sword now. We'll avenge Lari *and* the king-priest."

The other man nodded, and they stood there waiting for Rayla to make her move. But she didn't reach for her sword—instead, she walked in a circle around them, holding the red spear with both hands, assessing their stances. Suddenly, she lurched forward, thrusting her spear in quick, short strikes. She spun, slashing left and right, then reset her feet and thrust forward again. She twirled to one side and then the other, keeping the two men in front of her and darting the tip of her spear at their faces and chests. Her precision and speed were breathtaking. The unrelenting attack overwhelmed the two men; they could do nothing but fend off Rayla's strikes as she continued to drive them back.

A fourth man burst into the clearing, panting and drenched in sweat. Rayla ignored him. "Run, now!" the man yelled to his comrades. "He's coming this way!"

"What the hell are you babbling about?" one of them hissed as he kept fending off Rayla's spear. "We're not leaving until we've killed this hag!"

"Give us a hand!" the cocky one yelled at the newcomer.

The man hesitated, glancing back the way he'd come. Then he reached for his sword and attacked Rayla's open flank.

She jumped out of the way. The first two went on the offensive, quickly joined by the newcomer. Rayla dodged, spun, and struck even faster than before. Her long spear forced them to keep their distance, but they collectively began driving Rayla back. She couldn't switch to attacking without her short spear—she had no choice but to wait for an opening to draw her sword and put an end to this.

Then a fifth enemy soldier suddenly joined the struggle, a

woman with wide, panicked eyes. She was drenched in sweat, as if she'd been running for her life until just a moment ago.

Rayla stifled a curse—the woman charging toward her was carrying a throw net, and she was clearly ready to cast it over Rayla. She tried to move out of the way, but her movements were curtailed by her need to block the rain of sword strikes coming at her from three angles. Out of the corner of her eye, Rayla saw the woman cast the throw net at her; she could only watch helplessly as it fell, ensnaring her from head to toe. Rayla tripped and fell backward.

As the three men rushed forward to deliver a mortal blow, the woman yelled at them with dread in her voice. "It's him! It's too late!"

Even before the men could turn, an arrow pierced the skull of the one closest to Rayla. His corpse fell onto her, knocking the wind out of her. Rayla caught a glimpse of Kaistan's midnight fur partially hidden in the surrounding trees, but the heavy body obscured her view of what happened next. She struggled to free herself from the net and the dead man's weight. More hissing sounds followed, and three bodies thudded into the ground in rapid succession.

Then silence. Rayla waited, lying on the ground, unable to move. She heard Kaistan moan somewhere nearby. "Kiwi!" she cried out, nearly giddy. Her muscles relaxed. She was saved! But someone had killed her attackers. "Who's there?" Rayla asked in a firm voice.

Someone pulled the dead body off of Rayla. She saw Danny's face. "Are you hurt?" he asked her, the piercing look still in his eyes.

"No, I'm okay," she said. Danny drew a knife and cut apart the throw net, freeing her. Incredulity flooded her face as she scrambled to her feet. "*You* did this? You killed the four of them?"

Danny glanced at the gatalan, and a shadow of a smile came to his lips. "Kaistan and I did," he said.

She looked around; there was no one else in sight. No doubt Danny had saved her—he'd shot the arrows now stuck in her attackers' skulls. "Dear Almighty," she murmured. Danny wasn't bluffing about being a good bowman! And it seemed he didn't believe in striking opponents in the chest. She took a closer look at him and Kaistan and smiled to see both of them unharmed.

"The fight is over," Danny said. "All of the rebels are dead. But your people don't know we're here. I'm sure they're worried about you. We have to go around a long barricade the rebels built." Danny stood up. "C'mon! I know the way," he said, offering his hand.

She took his hand, and Danny helped Rayla to her feet. She stood still, looking at the young man, studying him. Her eyes turned soft. "You saved my life, Danny," she said, laying a hand on his shoulder. "I have no idea how I can ever repay you. We just met. We're strangers, yet you risked your life for me."

Danny looked down and shook his head. "No, that's not how I see it. Earlier, you could've fled on Kaistan and left this danger behind." He gestured vaguely at the scattered bodies. "But you decided to protect me instead even though that meant putting yourself at risk. You're a good person, Rayla. I'd never leave someone like you behind."

A tingling warmth spread through Rayla's limbs, and her eyes became moist. She reached for Danny's shirt and pulled him closer, giving him a hug. "Thank you, Danny." She could never repay him. He'd saved more than Rayla's life—he'd saved what she was fighting for and the hopes of the people who supported her. "You're very young, but you're already a remarkable man."

Kaistan joined in the hug, licking Danny's face. The boy giggled like he'd done a few hours ago. Rayla smiled. The innocent side of him had returned.

When she released him, Rayla noticed Danny's quivers: one was empty, and the other only had a few arrows left in it. She chuckled. The teenager had been busy . . . "Wait a minute!" she said, stepping back and looking at Danny with disbelief. "Did you shoot at these people while galloping on Kaistan?"

Danny gave her a half shrug. "Yes." He caressed Kaistan's ear. "He's amazing! He runs incredibly fast, but he's smooth and steady. It's easy to shoot while riding him."

Rayla's eyebrows ran to the middle of her forehead. No one she knew could do that! Such an unrivaled skill had made Cayacoa a living legend during Queen-Priestess Vetania's reign. Rayla's breath stalled. And this unassuming teenager had already mastered it.

She glanced at the last two soldiers who had joined the fight against her. They'd been sweaty and scared when they'd appeared. She pointed at them. "Were those two running from you?"

Danny's face was split by a sudden grin. "Nah! They ran from Kaistan—he corralled them for me. He's amazing! I can't believe how intelligent he is. Can we please go? I want to make sure Kara is fine."

Rayla shook herself a little. What this boy could do . . . "Right!" she said. She climbed onto Kaistan and then helped Danny up. "But Kara isn't worried about you—she would've come to find you if she were. Your gatalan knows when you're in danger, hurt, or have been killed."

"Really! That's so cool!"

Rayla blinked at the unusual expression. But Danny had saved her life, and he could say whatever he wanted. "Yeah. *Cool*."

They trotted back along the path Danny had taken when he'd come to Rayla's aid. Soon, the barricade he had mentioned rose before them. That same barrier had blocked Rayla's view of the ambush at the edge of the grove and cut her off from her Lathraias. She had to admire how much work must have gone into building that wall. These enemies were committed! Misguided, but committed.

Kaistan loped around the barricade. Rayla hoped everyone was okay. She had reason to believe they would be—her enemies had likely sent their best fighters after her while the rest of them had focused on keeping the Lathraias from coming to support her. It was a good plan. And it would've worked if it hadn't been for Danny.

They moved on. Two more bodies lay on the ground with arrows through their skulls. Rayla almost glanced back at the teenager. That was clearly his handiwork. A smile came to her lips, and the sliver of pride in her chest surprised her. Who could have predicted the boy she had decided to welcome would turn out to be a prodigy? Who would have said he'd risk his life to save hers? But all credit should go to Kaistan—his approval of Danny had won her over.

As they moved along, another corpse showed up on the road, and another, and another—all with arrow shafts planted in their skulls like flags. Then a new clearing came into view, and Rayla gasped at the gruesome sight: over twenty corpses littered the ground, all with arrows driven into their heads. She pulled on the reins, and Kaistan came to a complete stop. She stared at the scene with incredulous eyes. These troops would've come after her but had never been given the chance. Danny had saved her from certain doom in more ways than she'd thought.

Rayla looked a while longer, visualizing what had unfolded here. She saw the panicking faces of two dozen men and women. They cowered, terrified by a madman running in circles around them atop a massive midnight gatalan. The man shot arrows from everywhere, piercing head after head with deadly accuracy. The beast ran and growled, and the man shot and shot so quickly that the defenders couldn't even see the arrows coming at them. Their horror had mounted as dead comrades kept toppling to the ground all around them.

Rayla spurred Kaistan ahead, and they moved through the field of bodies in silence. It was hard to believe, but the cheerful and innocent teenager she'd just met had another side—he was hell on four legs.

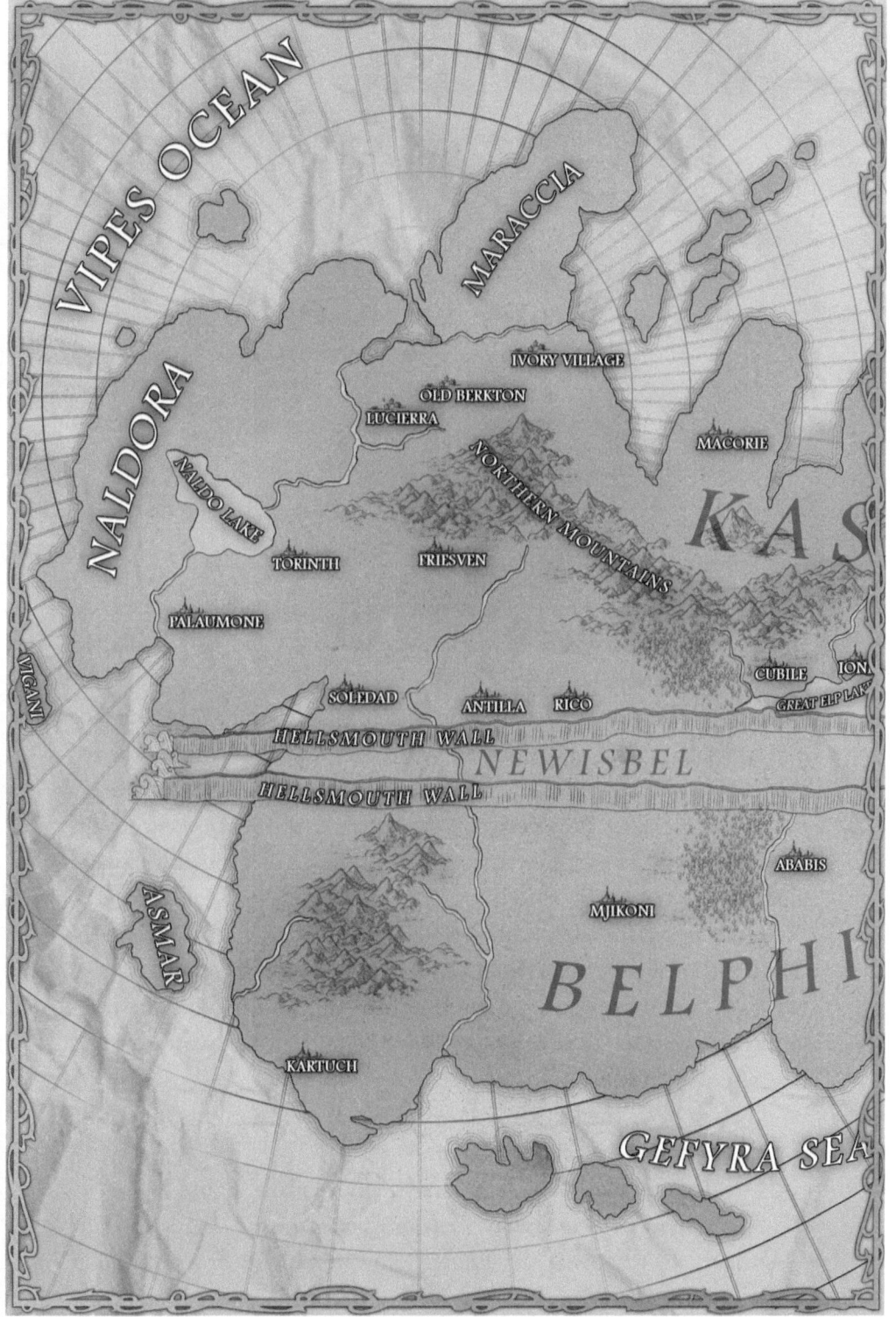

Chapter Thirty-One

8. Anaya

Marko's home had a backyard filled with rows of raised beds where he grew batatas. Funny enough, he called them potatoes.

Anaya had never seen anyone farming in Ivory Village, but her dad had said people in the nearby village of Old Berkton grew carrots that they sold at the market, and folks in Lucierra Village grew beets for the king-priest. Very few of those made it to the market. Anaya would always remember the beets—those red vegetables were amazing!

Once her dad had brought home two boiled beets for Yael's birthday, and her mom gave Anaya the last bite. The red taproot melted like sugar in Anaya's mouth, sending her eyebrows flying. The little girl asked for more, but there was none left. Beets were a rare treat, her parents told her.

"I want to be the king-priest!" Anaya had said, pouting. Then she could eat all the beets she ever wanted.

Her dad laughed. "You'll have to become a cacique first."

Anaya had no clue what "cacique" meant and thought she'd never eat sweet beets again. Except now she might. She pointed at the raised beds rippling through Marko's garden. "Can you grow beets?" she asked him.

"I don't have the seeds," he said. "But growing beets is as easy as growing potatoes, just a little different."

Easy, the man said. Anaya smiled mischievously. Beets were a royal delicacy, but a person who cooked scrambled eggs for breakfast could do anything in Anaya's mind. "Can you teach me?" she asked. If she learned to grow batatas now, she could grow beets later.

Marko smiled and patted Anaya's head. He did that a lot. Anaya said nothing because she liked it. Casar and Jamal used to caress her hair with approving smiles. "It'd be my pleasure," Marko said.

He built a raised bed for Anaya to grow potatoes that same day. She spent the following morning learning about planting seasons, sunlight, soil consistency, and watering.

Anaya's suit and protective coat had gone dormant since she had arrived at Marko's home. She felt safe here. With no other homes nearby, the place felt like a combination of vacation spot and hideout. No mean men would find her here—Anaya could take her time rebuilding her resiliency and deciding what to do next. There was no rush; she liked the place and the company.

Spring weather was awesome in Torinth. There were always clear skies and a lukewarm sun. Anaya wore a red tunic and gray leggings that Marko had procured for her. Those were all she needed to feel warm. Marko, though, wore a brown coat anytime he went outside, which was puzzling. Anaya scratched her head the first time she saw it, but it was best not to make fun of him. Having delicate skin wasn't his fault. Two winters in Ivory Village, and Marko would lose that brown coat when spring came.

"I heard you talking to someone last night," Anaya said as she worked on her raised bed.

Marko stood behind her, watching her work and occasionally giving her instructions. "Really! Oh, my . . . That means you've already developed remote surveillance."

Anaya stopped digging in the dirt and turned to Marko. "What?"

He half winced. "Sorry! I shouldn't use fancy words, but I got a bit excited. Remote surveillance is a useful ability. I'm glad you already have it—it will help you." Marko paused and cocked his head. "Although I bet you're only using half of it." Anaya wrinkled her forehead. "No worries!" Marko rushed to add. "I'll explain everything."

"Okay, but who were you talking to last night? I thought you lived alone."

He laughed. "Oh, Anaya, the answer will blow your mind. The friend you heard last night wants to meet you, too, but we were waiting until . . . well, we didn't want to freak you out."

Anaya smiled. She'd taught Marko that phrase. "Why? Is he very ugly?"

Marko burst out laughing. "Not at all! His appearance is quite cute. I nicknamed my friend Asa, but . . . Anaya, what's the weirdest thing you've ever seen?"

"Umm," she said, bringing a soiled hand to her chin. "You mean weird creepy or weird like, 'Oh my god, that's so weird!'"

Marko scratched his head. "The second one. Weird but nice."

Anaya grinned. "Easy, then! When Albi peed on me."

"Albi? The albino gatalan?"

"Yes."

He chuckled. "Well, that wasn't peeing. But, yes! Weird like that. You see, Asa is weird like . . . wait . . . I'm not sure anymore. Maybe what Albi did takes the cake. I'll tell you what, Anaya, why don't *you* decide?"

"Okay."

"Good. You see, Asa is a talking doll."

Anaya's head jerked back.

"You've seen dolls before, right?" Marko asked. "Rag dolls?"

Anaya gave him a slight nod. "Can I see him?"

"Yes, I'll introduce you. But let me tell you a few things first. One, Asa is a real person."

"Okay."

Marko raised an admonishing finger. "He's not a toy!"

Anaya nodded, curiosity bubbling up inside her. "I heard you talking to him last night—he sounded like a real person."

"Yes, he is."

"What does he look like?"

"Like a small bear, this tall," Marko said, holding his hand about two feet off the ground. "He's fluffy and nice to hug."

Anaya opened her eyes wide. "Can I hug him?"

"You'll have to ask him, but you need to wash your hands first in case he says yes."

Anaya leaned forward. "Do *you* hug him?"

Marko's face tightened. "Not really, no."

"But you said he's cute *and* your friend."

"Yes, but I'm a grownup; that'd be weird. Like, weird weird. And Asa is heavy! I couldn't lift him even if I wanted to." He smiled at her. "But *you* could lift him using your powers. We'll teach you how to—I mean, *Asa* will teach you how to lift anything and make it look like your arms are doing it. He has powers, like you."

Anaya blinked. "Powers? A *doll* has powers? Asa can do everything that I can?"

Marko chuckled. "He can do more, actually."

Anaya frowned. "More like what?"

"Well, for instance, I mentioned remote surveillance. It means you can hear and see from a distance. That's pretty nice, right? Asa will teach you how to do it."

Anaya frowned. "See at a distance . . . see what?"

"Anything you like. Albi, for instance. He's still a cub, but he's your gatalan. You could find him remotely and see how he's doing if you want."

Anaya grinned and gave a small jump. "I want!"

"Also, flying. You can already move through the air, but Asa will teach you how to fly really fast. And go underwater in your suit. And Asa will teach you how to fight."

She pouted. "But I can fight already!"

"Yes, you can. But you'll learn to protect yourself against very strong enemies. And you'll learn to keep people you care about safe."

Anaya fell silent. Marko had promised to take her to Palaumone in search of her grandparents, and she'd said she would ask him to take her there when she felt ready. Mean people had killed everyone Anaya cared about, and she was afraid to find her grandparents because mean people might hurt them too. Could Asa really teach her how to protect everybody?

Anaya stood up. "So, Asa has Dian too?"

Marko laughed. "Yes. But he doesn't call it Dian, he calls it bionanobots."

Anaya frowned. "That's a weird name."

"I know. But remember what we talked about—sometimes people use different words for the same thing. And that's okay."

Anaya nodded. It was like *batata* and *potato*. Different words, but the tuber still looked and tasted the same. It didn't confuse her as long as she knew what they meant, and it was nice to let people use the words they knew.

"One more thing, Anaya: even though Asa is a real person, he doesn't have muscles in his face like you and me, so his mouth doesn't move when he talks. It sounds like the voice comes from inside his head."

"That's weird."

"I know. That's why I didn't want to introduce you before we had this conversation."

Anaya's expression was resolute. "I want to see him. I want to meet a talking doll."

Marko arched an eyebrow at her. "And one last thing. Asa doesn't walk . . . he sort of glides."

Anaya laughed. "I want to see that!"

It was Marko's turn to laugh. "I'm sure you'll be gliding everywhere as soon as you see him do it."

* * *

Asa was cute for only five seconds.

He waited for them, standing in the living room like he knew Anaya and Marko were about to come inside. A grin blossomed on her face when Anaya saw him. Asa was the tallest doll she'd ever seen, reaching her belly button. He looked like a toy bear, with a round face, short ears, a fat belly, and short limbs. A fluffy layer of wool covered his body, brown like a peanut. His appearance made Anaya think that this doll was made for hugging. And she wanted to comply.

Then Asa spoke, wiping away Anaya's smile. "Hi, Anaya! Nice to meet you," he said in a soothing male voice.

The little girl stepped back, startled. Marko had warned her, but still. The talking doll was the weirdest thing ever, and it wasn't weird nice but weird weird. The voice sounded human and all, but nothing moved in the doll's face when Asa spoke. Anaya narrowed her eyes; a real person *must* be trapped inside the doll, like a ghost in disguise or something.

"Asa gave me the recipe for your porridge," Marko told her.

Anaya turned to him. Marko was rubbing the back of his head like he was embarrassed. "You haven't cooked any porridge," she said with stern eyes. Marko had probably tried to smooth the awkward introduction, but he'd chosen the wrong thing to say.

He held out his hands with his palms up. "But you know we're out of oats! We're going into town tomorrow to buy them, remember?"

Anaya crossed her arms. "And chocolate."

"Yes! We'll pick up ingredients for your hot cocoa too."

Something that resembled a laugh came out of Asa. "Less than two weeks, and you're already ruling this house."

Anaya stared at Asa for a moment. He was weird, but Marko trusted the doll and had said Asa could help her. Should Anaya be nice to him, then? She unfolded her arms. "You've been here all this time."

"Yes. I've been hiding," Asa replied.

"Why?"

"I didn't want to scare you. I know I'm . . . unusual. Sometimes people react with fear to things they've never seen before."

Anaya nodded. Not long ago, a group of Normo men had seen her eating apples while in stealth mode, and they had freaked out. Anaya had turned visible for their sake, but that had terrified them even more. They'd called her a she-devil and tried to kill her. Fear made everything seem dangerous, even a fluffy doll.

"I'm glad I don't have to hide anymore," Asa went on. "I was a bit lonely. All I've had for company is Marko. I'd love to make a new friend."

Anaya's heart twitched, recognizing that type of pain. It lasted much longer than a tummy ache. She remembered the boy with crooked ears who had worked at the convenience store across from the church in Ivory Village. He was three years older than Anaya, and the other boys had made fun of him. He had no friends, but he was always attentive and eager to help whenever Anaya visited the store with her mom. Anaya would've been his friend if they had been the same age. She'd felt sorry that she couldn't help him. Perhaps she could help Asa instead.

Anaya stepped forward and touched Asa's head. It felt puffy and soft. It tickled, too. Anaya brought up her other hand to rub his head, giggling.

"You get used to the voice," Marko said.

Anaya looked at him. He was smiling at them both. She nodded again. Weird things became normal over time. She gently pulled on one of Asa's ears. "I'll be your friend," she said. "But no sneaking up behind me!"

"Thank you," he replied in a warm voice. Anaya blinked—she'd almost expected a smile from him. Without facial expressions, his answers felt incomplete.

She glanced at Marko. "You sure I'll get used to this?"

"I am," Marko said with a slight nod.

"Hmm." Her eyes returned to Asa and her hands to his head.

Touching him made her feel fuzzy inside. Maybe that could make up for the rest. "Can you really help me protect my grandparents?"

"I can teach you how to see enemies coming."

"With the remote thingy?"

"Yes. You'll have time to prepare for or even intercept them before they get close to your grandparents."

Anaya smiled. That should work.

Asa floated up, his face rising to the same level as Anaya's. "Before we do anything else, though, Anaya, I need to confirm one thing."

Anaya couldn't resist—she pulled Asa in close and hugged him. It was delightful! The doll's body was pleasantly warm, and his woolly outer layer made her feel like she was hugging Albi.

"Go on," she said, tightening her arms around his neck and looking over his shoulder. From there, she could imagine his facial expression and improve the conversation.

Asa took a moment to respond. "You call the source of your powers Dian," he eventually said.

"Yes," Anaya answered, still hugging him. "Dian has looked after me since Mom died. Dian is a goddess—she can do anything. She helps you, too, right?"

"It's complicated. *Your* Dian is very, very special. A different Dian helps me; I call her by another name."

Anaya stopped hugging Asa and looked at his face. *Another Dian?* How could that be? She stared a bit longer, but Asa's face remained expressionless. Anaya returned to hugging Asa, thinking. She'd met a handful of Naldorians in her life, and most of them had paintings or statues of Dianasis. But almost every painting or statue looked different. Could Asa mean something like that? Probably not. Those paintings and statues all referred to the same goddess.

"What's the name of your goddess?" Anaya asked.

Asa hesitated. "I call it bionanobots. But we'll talk about that later, okay? To unlock more of your powers, I have to explain a few

91

things that will be new to you. But I need to confirm something first that will tell me about your full potential."

Anaya didn't understand the word "potential," but she shrugged it off. "Okay."

"When Dian communicates with you, do you hear a voice in your head?"

That was an easy question! Dian never spoke to her using words. "No," she answered immediately.

"That's excellent!" Asa said. "We've finally found you."

"Ah, I'm sorry," Marko interjected. "Pardon the intrusion, but why is that important?"

"Anaya doesn't hear voices in her head. That means she's a perfect match for Isbel's bionanobots."

Marko frowned. "I thought we'd already established that she's a perfect match."

"No, we didn't. You probably assumed it. Anaya has over forty percent of Isbel's bionanobots, so there was a good probability, true. But we still had to confirm the level of integration."

The little girl let go of Asa, grimacing. "Are you okay, Anaya?" Marko asked.

"Who is Isbel's bio-something-something?"

Marko came closer and kneeled before her, talking to Anaya face-to-face. "Bionanobots are what Asa and I call the source of your powers, and his powers, too. Keep calling yours Dian—that's totally fine. Isbel was a very special girl, just like you! When she was alive, Isbel was the most powerful person to ever exist. No one else came close. Isbel had the same relationship you have with your Dian."

"Oh," Anaya said, tilting her head. "You mean the same Dian as me?"

Marko nodded. "Yes. Exactly the same one."

Asa came closer. "You and Isbel are the only people in history to have . . . this relationship with your Dian. Because of it, Isbel did things no one else could. When I'm done teaching you, Anaya, you'll be a new Isbel."

Episode Nine

Chapter Thirty-Two

7. Danny

The Plain of Carbel was a cold place at night, and Danny was grateful to Officer Cael for setting up a black tent especially for him. Danny loved the tent's sleek, crescent-shaped design reminiscent of an upright horseshoe. Someone in Newisbel had once told him that Kasmanians liked parabolic and oval shapes. That person had been right. This particular tent was big enough to accommodate five Lathraias, and its roll-up canvas panels made it warm during the winter and ventilated during the summer.

Cael was the most vocal of the Lathraias about thanking Danny for saving Rayla's life. The young officer promised Danny he would give him a mini fold-out tent for his journey to Torinth once they returned to the Red Horn. Danny appreciated the gesture. He'd learned to enjoy sleeping outdoors, but he also liked the idea of having a small tent for rainy days. Carrying it wouldn't be a problem once Rayla had given him the promised saddle for Kara.

Danny's eyes sparkled whenever he thought about having his own saddle and trotting to Torinth atop his gatalan. Something like that would've never happened back home. He wished his friends from Newisbel could see him riding Kara and snap a few photos.

Danny grinned, picturing how they'd react if they saw him astride the gatalan. Tenis Lockfield would pull him closer and give him a surprisingly strong hug, proud of him, and perhaps Castellana would give him a smile with her pretty lips.

His grin faded, replaced by a worry. What if the Invoker got mad at him for abandoning the mission and deserting the rangers corp? Would the Invoker exile Danny like he'd exiled his dad? Danny wanted to believe the chances of that were pretty low—surely someone as powerful as the Invoker was too busy dealing with real problems to concern himself with a small fly like Danny. In all likelihood, the Invoker didn't even know Danny existed. After all, *he* hadn't smuggled forbidden technology into Kasmana. Danny decided to stop worrying. Besides, right now, things were looking up for him.

The Lathraias spoiled him, and Danny didn't mind that at all. Cael had granted his request to keep Kara by his side inside the camp, a special request he'd had to have approved by Lieutenant Rolan—normally, whenever a company with riders spent the night outdoors, all gatalans slept around the outer edges of the camp. According to Cael, they served as a deterrent and early warning system. Even though a few sentries would keep watch after everybody else went to sleep, if there were ever any intruders, gatalans would wake up first and cause a fuss.

Danny felt lucky to have found Rayla's party. These Kasmanians had treated him like a celebrity ever since Rayla told them what unfolded beyond the grove. And something else surprised him—he'd expected to feel like a stranger in a strange land while searching for his father, and instead, every cell in his body felt at home with these locals. The blood in his veins sang to him, overjoyed by a sense of kinship with the Canyos and their gatalans. They were Danny's people; something primal inside him told him so.

Still, many Kasmanian customs were new to Danny. He endeavored to assimilate their traditions, eager to blend in as seamlessly as possible. His introduction to their ways started with a military ritual: Danny ate his first serving of gavian stew with pleasure, although he had to do so alone in his tent. This small portion, known as *kasalla*, served as a first course meant to be eaten in silence inside one's tent. Kasalla provided a moment for reflection, offering gratitude to Kas for life, country, and victory. Cael himself delivered the kasalla to Danny, taking the time to explain the tradition. Beyond its religious significance and emotional comfort, kasalla also fulfilled a logistical role after battle, ensuring that everyone was accounted for and nourished.

The small portion of stew was the first delicious meal Danny had had in weeks. Alone in his tent, he moaned at the fatty, juicy taste of gavian meat. Potatoes, peas, and carrots melted in his mouth, making the stew an experience he'd never forget. He gobbled it down like he was a prisoner who'd been penned away for decades. As soon as he finished eating the kasalla, Cael told him he could join the rest of the company and eat as much food as he liked while mingling with the others. He devoured the last morsel of stew and rushed out of his tent, eager for more.

As soon as he stepped outside, Lieutenant Aia ambushed him. "Come here!" she nearly shouted, pulling him closer and giving him a back-crushing hug. It was the third bear hug Aia had given him since he'd returned with Rayla. "Oh, I know that look!" she added with a grin. "Food tastes much better after a life-or-death battle. Come! We prepared a fire for you near my eken. You can eat as much stew as you like. I'll make sure of it."

She grabbed Danny's hand and pulled him through the camp, hauling him along like one of the tow trucks in Newisbel. Danny couldn't resist or even voice a single word in protest. His neck and ears burned with embarrassment as he became on the receiving end of more hugging and touching than ever before in his life. Proper manners and gender boundaries from Newisbel were out the window, that was for sure. More than half of the Lathraias accompanying Rayla were female warriors—most quite attractive—and none had the slightest problem with showing him gratitude with tight embraces for having saved their cacique. The teenager bit his tongue, feeling mortified as he was crushed against so many soft breasts. The male Lathraias behaved in a more normal fashion—they showed their comradery with cough-inducing slaps on the back. Even Rolan expressed heartfelt gratitude and apologized for his previous rude attitude.

"My eken!" someone called out. Aia and Danny stopped and turned. A soldier ran toward them and fell to his knees. He was in his mid-thirties, had long flowing hair, and carried a dagger on his right thigh. "My eken, is the Cayali still in need of a saddle for his gatalan?"

"Yes, he is," Aia said. Danny watched the exchange, wondering what the heck the word "eken" meant. He'd wanted to ask Cael earlier but also hadn't wanted to look like a complete idiot. Should he call Aia "my eken" as well? All of the other titles the soldiers used were familiar, like lieutenant and general. Danny furrowed his brow. He decided he'd call everyone by what he assumed their name or rank was until someone scolded him for having bad manners and explained the "eken" rules.

"In that case," the soldier kneeling before them continued, "would you please allow me the honor of offering the Cayali my fallen gatalan's saddle? It is in perfect condition, my eken. I swear it before Kas."

Aia brought a hand to her chin, and the soldier held his breath. Danny felt sorry for the man. He'd been with Kara for only a short while, but just the thought of losing her already saddened him greatly.

During the ambush a few hours earlier, nine Lathraias had been injured, mainly from falling rocks. None had suffered life-threatening injuries. But gatalans had not fared as well—five had died during the attack, and six others had been so badly injured that they had to be put down afterward. Now this soldier was offering his gatalan's saddle to someone named Cayali. He called it an honor; Danny hoped the gesture would lessen the soldier's sense of loss.

"I'm sorry about your gatalan, Ruque—she was a fine one," Aia finally said. "I'll allow your request in her honor, but it's only temporary until we reach the Red Horn. Cacique Rayla promised the Cayali a brand-new saddle, and I'm sure my eken wants to keep her promise to him."

Danny's eyes widened, and Ruque hastily stood, a sad smile on his face. "Thank you, my eken. It means a lot to me. I'll fetch the saddle right away." The soldier ran back the way he'd come and disappeared behind a row of black tents.

Aia's hand landed on Danny's shoulder. "Why the fish face? I thought you'd be delighted to get your first saddle for Kara."

Danny blinked rapidly, his eyes darting toward where Ruque had disappeared. "Sorry, Aia. I'm . . . I'm just a bit confused. Why would that soldier call me Cayali? He was talking about me, right?"

Aia gave him a blank stare, shook her head, and resumed walking. Danny let out a slow breath. *Was that a dumb question?* It seemed like it, but he couldn't tell why. He hastened to keep up with Aia's long strides.

"I should issue an arrest warrant for this Marko character," Aia said a moment later. "What an awful father! You know nothing about anything, Danny. It's a disgrace. A young man with your talent . . ."

"Sorry, Aia. It's probably my fault."

"No, it's not." She sighed and slowed down. Then she stopped and looked Danny in the eyes. "Whatever happened was for the best. The will of Kas shapes the world in obscure ways, Danny. If such an irresponsible man hadn't raised you, you wouldn't be who you are today and my eken would've died during that ambush. Thank Kas for you, and thank Kas for everything that influenced your upbringing. Thank Kas for that awful father of yours too."

Danny tilted his head. Aia's words were full of passion—there was gratitude in her voice, but also fear. She'd almost lost her eken. Given that Aia was the strongest human being Danny had ever seen, he hadn't been expecting her to share her feelings with such readiness. But perhaps he should've suspected it. Aia had been the first to hug him when Rayla told them that Danny saved her life. He started to get the idea that he could do no wrong in Aia's eyes for the rest of his life.

"Thank you, Aia. I take that as a compliment," he said, briefly dipping his head. "But could you please explain why the soldier called me Cayali?"

Aia gave him a smile. "Cayali means 'little Caya.'"

"Okaaay . . . ?"

Aia laughed, slapping Danny's back so hard that he took an involuntary step forward. Danny smoothed out his expression even as he felt a burning sensation in his right shoulder. Suddenly, those bear hugs seemed less embarrassing.

"Caya means 'divine bow' in our aboriginal language," Aia said. "You see, Cayacoa was the Great Caya. The title became the name. You are the Cayali, or the little Caya." Aia paused, her brows pulling closer together. "In all honesty, Danny, your current name is a bit lacking. Another blemish on your father's record. We saw you shoot down a gavian with our own eyes, and the cacique of armed forces acknowledged your skill in shooting from atop a galloping gatalan. People will call you Cayali partly because the title is very exciting to us and partly because your name is so . . . well . . . hmm. Get used to it, Danny."

Aia paused to study Danny's face and smiled at his impassive expression. She placed her hand on the boy's shoulder. "Being the Cayali is a good thing. A Caya is a symbol of victory, a sign of Kas's approval. We're overjoyed that Rayla found you—it means that Kas favors her. We haven't had a Caya in centuries! If you ever decided to join the army, people would go overboard for the chance to fight under you." She winked at him. "You'd make general within twenty years."

Danny lifted a single eyebrow, and they resumed walking. There was absolutely nothing wrong with his name in Newisbel! Castellana loved it, and Danny loved how she said it. On the other hand, the Kasmanian army desperately needed kinetic target shooting instructors. There was nothing divine about shooting while riding horses or gatalans—it just required proper technique and *intensive* training. In any case, the skill he had worked so hard to acquire back in Newisbel would translate into more gavian stew in a few moments. No complaints there!

"That's your spot," Aia said, pointing at a fire. To the right of it, Rayla and Rolan waved at him from where they were sitting. Danny waved back as Aia left him to join the duo. To the left was a station serving food. Danny went straight to it, got a bowl of stew, and walked to the fire Aia had pointed out. He gobbled down his stew, barely noticing when Kara came and sat behind him, until she nudged him ever so slightly.

"That's a big belly, Kara!" he said, rubbing her fur. "Did you say thank you?"

The gatalan licked her nose in response. Cael had said his team would feed Kara along with the other gatalans, and Danny could obviously trust his word.

Danny looked at his bowl and jerked back his head, startled to find it empty. He beelined over to the food station to get more stew. By the time he was on his third bowl, he heard laughter coming from behind him.

Rayla was watching him with amusement. "I had forgotten that teenagers eat more than gatalans!"

Rolan chuckled. "He's only fifteen. He's already tall, but he'll grow a few more inches, and that big frame will fill up with muscles. He'll be quite strong."

"And incredibly handsome," Aia added.

"My eken, I think we should give him a guacanari," Rolan said. "A Cayali can handle it, especially this one as he grows stronger."

Rayla raised her eyebrows. "I thought they stopped making them. When I was at the academy, nobody could use a guacanari. I was awful with them; I couldn't shoot a darn thing."

"You and everybody else, my eken," Rolan said, nodding. "But I'm confident that Cael could find one of those bows for the Cayali somewhere."

"I'll think about it," Rayla answered after a moment. "Danny is on a quest to find his father, and I won't ask him to delay his journey waiting for a bow he doesn't need."

Kara growled softly behind Danny just as something thudded onto the ground beside her. Danny put down his bowl and looked up. The soldier who had intercepted Aia and Danny earlier stood there with puffy eyes.

Danny looked back down to see a leather saddle lying at his feet. It had a padded seat that swooped up at the front and rear; a bridle and the rest of the riding gear lay next to it. The leather had a brand-new luster, like it had been cleaned and waxed within the last few hours.

"I apologize for interrupting your dinner, Cayali," the soldier said earnestly. "I'm hoping you'll accept this gift. This saddle belonged to my dearest Tempest. As you can see, it's in perfect condition—she only used it for two months. It would honor her memory if you would use it, even if for just a day."

Danny gave him a sad smile and stood up. "What is your name, sir?"

"Oh! My name is Ruque. Please don't call me sir, Cayali. It's embarrassing."

Danny put his hands in his pockets and leaned forward awkwardly. "My apologies, Ruque. It's an old habit."

"I understand. I was like you at your age . . . except for the saving caciques and shooting down gavians part."

Danny scratched the back of his head. "Now I'm the one who's embarrassed . . ."

"I understand that, too," Ruque said.

Danny shifted his weight and then extended his hand. "It's a pleasure to meet you."

"Believe me, Cayali, the pleasure is mine." Ruque shook Danny's hand.

"Tempest is a beautiful name," Danny said. "You obviously loved her very much, and that tells me she was special."

"Quite so," he said with sad eyes.

"It'll be my honor to use Tempest's saddle," Danny said. Then he pointed at the two bags at the back of the saddle. "What are those for? And the harness?"

"I just installed them. The bags are to carry extra quivers or anything else you want, and the harness is meant to carry a rolled-up tent. The accessories are easy to detach if you don't want them."

"Are you kidding me?" Danny said, his eyes widening. "They're perfect!"

"Would you like me to help you install the gear on Kara? I'm guessing this will be your first time doing so."

Danny's body perked up. "Yes! I'd love that!" He couldn't wait to feel the wind in his face as he rode Kara for the first time. They began to work on it right away. Getting the saddle on Kara only took a few minutes.

"Hey, Cayali!" a potent female voice called when Danny and Ruque were nearly done. Danny looked up and saw Rayla approaching him with a smile on her lips and a bow in her hand. Over forty Lathraias had gathered behind her, including a handful who had bandages wrapped around various parts of their bodies.

Danny's gaze was drawn from Rayla to the furious activity in the open field in front of them. Six soldiers were rushing to install a dozen sun sticks at random; after them came Cael, who lit each stick and then placed a net holding a melon midway up the shaft of each one.

Rayla stopped in front of Danny and offered him the bow. Her smile widened as she jerked her head at Kara. "Care to give us a shooting demonstration?"

Behind them, the Lathraias started cheering and whistling in eager anticipation.

Danny smiled and grabbed the bow. "Anytime."

Chapter Thirty-Three

9. Kendar

One glance, and Kendar recognized Lunai's back. That petrified him. The ensuing shock dispelled his headache, yet thinking clearly was still difficult.

A few seconds went by before a coherent thought formed inside his skull. *What the hell is she doing here?* Lunai was the last person he'd expected to see, but there she stood, glowing.

She turned as if sensing Kendar's presence. He caught his breath at the sight of her face—the soft angles, the smooth skin, the rosy lips, the gray eyes. Damn it! It wasn't right. Why were her eyes still mesmerizing? Would she ever look like the hideous monster who'd betrayed him? But hideous monsters didn't come to people's aid. *What the hell is she doing here?*

Lunai gave him a sad smile. Kendar's lips parted. He shook his head, refusing to believe his eyes, then closed them. He forced himself to feel the anger she deserved. Instead, Kendar noticed that his headache and nausea were gone. He opened his eyes and stared in silence at Lunai's face for a little while. Everything else in the room disappeared. Despite his best efforts, a warm sensation grew inside him.

Kendar looked down. *What the hell is wrong with me?* He should've been furious; he should've lashed out and trashed the place. He should've killed everybody! But clenching his teeth was the best he could manage. He forced his mind to imagine his invisible hands stretching across the room and snapping her neck like a twig. Except not a single muscle moved; the thought of harming her hurt him instead.

His eyes stayed down, and he noticed his clothing again. Kendar's pajamas were filthy, covered in dried blood and vomit. He looked and smelled absolutely horrible. What would Gemina have said if she'd ever seen him like this? Kendar sighed. Had his self-esteem ever sunk this low before?

His face inched back up, but he didn't look Lunai in the eyes. "Did you pay my prison bill?"

"Yes," she said, almost whispering. He had to look away. Lunai's smitten tone triggered memories of intimacy, when her lips had whispered sweet words into his ear and her warm breath had set his groins on fire.

Kendar squeezed his eyes shut. His headache returned suddenly, taxing his thoughts. Lunai had come to help him, and in doing so, she'd put herself at risk. She had to know that Kendar could kill her on the spot, crumpling her like a piece of paper just like he'd crumpled Tares of Coriplion. He could break every bone in her body and make her suffer horribly. And she would have deserved it!

Lunai should've stayed the hell away from him, but she hadn't. She had come to help him. Her help meant that Kendar would save an incredible amount of time. He would avoid the complications that would've arisen had he used force to break free from the Belphian jail —that would have ruined everything for him.

Kendar clenched his fists, struggling to maintain self-control. Although he was in her debt now, Lunai was still guilty of betraying him and breaking his heart. No one had ever hurt him this much.

His nostrils flared, and he took several resolute steps toward the door. "I'll repay you," he said as he walked by her. He hoped she would mistake that as a threat.

"Kendar, wait," she said, reaching for his arm.

Kendar flinched at her touch, but he stopped.

"Take this," she said, offering him the bag she carried. "And there's someone in this city you should meet—a Highlander just like you. His name is Darios."

Kendar scoffed. He didn't know how, but there she was again, still manipulating him. His gaze turned hard. "Do you ever regret who you are?"

She looked down and brought her hands together, the bag of clothing hanging limply from her fingers. "Who I am led me to Casmare." Then she looked into his eyes. "I'll never regret meeting you there." The quiet smile in her eyes disarmed him. She placed the bag at his feet. "There's a bit of money inside for lodging. Clean yourself up; eat and rest. Then go see Darios. It's important."

Lunai looked at him with hesitant eyes. She opened her lips to say something more, but then she just turned around and walked away. She stopped a few steps later and half turned back. "Goodbye, Kendar."

The finality in her voice stung. Kendar said nothing as he watched her walk away. His hands twitched, almost reaching for her, and his voice caught in his throat, almost calling her back.

Kendar walked the streets, getting the lay of the land and scowling at the prevalent smell of spilled sewage.

Afisa patrolled Prince Port's streets atop horses whose fresh manure peppered the stinky dirt roads. The midmorning sun exposed worn-out buildings and sweaty people in a city abuzz with activity that resembled a proper commercial hub. The energetic bustle stood in sharp contrast to what he'd initially witnessed the night he'd arrived. Prince Port's nonexistent nightlife had made the place seem more like the Highlands than a mega city, yet during the day, the city told a different story. Perhaps it was just that no other place in the world came close to Taori in terms of its nightlife.

Kendar looked at the people bustling around, allowing the scene to lighten his mood. Belphians wore colorful ankle-length dresses, including most of the men. A scarce few wore trousers—those were mostly laborers and officers riding horses. Some men wore long-sleeved shirts held closed with strings at the sides instead of buttons on the front, but they were the minority. Most preferred flamboyant colors and long-hemmed attire that was tied with a sash at the waist and sported square necklines and puffed sleeves.

Kendar saw many faces that morning, most smiling; here, people moved with vigor. Prince Port was nowhere near as affluent as Taori, but the Belphians Kendar saw seemed to be much happier and more carefree than the Sebesians had been. He wondered if that was a coincidence or if there was a deeper meaning at play. Perhaps that was irrelevant; maybe thinking about it was a waste of time.

He continued to stroll along. Amid the colorful Belphians, Kendar stood out like a green cloud drifting through the sky. In addition to his height and general appearance, he was wearing the leather pants and silk shirt Lunai had procured for him—Kendar's typical attire in Novusland. He smiled, enjoying the attention. Belphian children pointed at Kendar as he walked by, calling for their parents to come see, and even the grown-ups joined in the overreaction. Nothing remotely close to that had ever happened in Sebes.

Most Belphians waved at Kendar when they made eye contact, including the afisa astride their horses. Kendar thought about the buzz he was creating, hearing people whispering about him as he kept moving through the crowds. The mystery of how a Highlander had become the ruler of a Belphian province dissipated a bit. If Kendar decided to be friendly and establish relationships via generosity as he'd done in Casmare, he would likely be in a position to win an election in less than a decade. *I could become the bosi if I wanted*, he reflected. *That could be interesting.*

Then he sobered as his mind returned to the matter at hand: he was broke. He soon spotted three banks within walking distance of the inn where he'd stayed the previous night using Lunai's money. One bank had the same design as the financial institutions in Sebes. He nodded, satisfied. He'd visit the bank once everyone had gone home and make a withdrawal.

He kept walking and located a clothing store and a barbershop. He nodded again. Tomorrow, when he had money, he would visit them too.

When he walked by a whorehouse, he turned his head away in disgust. The building was revoltingly dirty, with flies and rats feeding on rotting food and puddles of stale beer near the entrance. Kendar could not imagine anyone becoming intimate in such conditions. If the other whorehouses in Prince Port were remotely similar to this one, he wouldn't be staying in this city for long.

Someone is following you, the voices in his head whispered.

Kendar kept an expressionless face. He stopped in front of a fruit stand on the side of the road and grabbed a mango from the stand. He examined it as he exchanged pleasantries with the merchant, a plump woman in her late fifties. Glancing back surreptitiously mid-conversation, he spotted a Belphian man spying on him. The spy hid behind three afisa horses tied to a hitching post in front of an inn. The man wasn't dressed like an afisa officer, but he was wearing one of their gray brimless hats.

Kendar smirked. The spy was at least a hundred feet away. There'd be no evidence of Kendar's involvement, but whoever had sent the spy would get a clear message. Then Kendar hesitated. Would it be better to capture the spy alive and question him? "Nah," Kendar said aloud. Fear would serve him much better than information.

"Excuse me?" the fruit merchant said.

Kendar looked at her, realizing he'd said *Nah* out loud. "The mangoes smell great, but I'm thinking of buying some tomorrow instead," he told her, trying to save face. "I'll be walking for a few more hours, don't want to carry things around."

The woman smiled, her mouth missing two front teeth. "Here's a free one for you," she said, handing him a perfectly ripe specimen. "I get fresh fruits every day. Come see me tomorrow—I'll give you a good price."

"Thank you," Kendar said with a slight bow. He liked the gesture; this woman had won his business. He would come to see her the following day, when he'd have enough money to buy as many mangoes as he wanted. Hopefully this woman didn't have a hidden agenda like the last fruit merchant he'd met in Trivoli. If she did, Kendar wouldn't hesitate to kill her.

He grabbed the mango and then jerked his head at the tethered horses. He wanted an audience for what was about to happen. "All of the afisa horses I've seen are so well-groomed! It's impressive." He unleashed two invisible hands as he spoke.

The woman looked at the mounts tied up in front of the inn. "Oh, yes! Afisa hire the best stable hands. They pay well. My nephew works for them."

One of Kendar's hands wrapped itself around the spy, encircling his chest, neck, and mouth, immobilizing and gagging him. Out of sight behind the horses, the man struggled to free himself, only able to make muffled sounds.

The struggle spooked the horses; they nickered and snorted. A second invisible hand slid underneath one of the horses and tapped its underbelly. The animal whinnied and kicked in protest, prompting everyone to look at the three horses.

"Something is bothering them," the merchant said, puzzled.

Kendar yanked the spy, causing him to tumble toward the horses' rear ends. Kendar kept him upright and then tapped the same horse's underbelly a second time. The animal bucked and unleashed a savage kick, bashing the spy in the chest and sending him hurtling backward.

The crowd gasped as the man flew through the air and then

crashed onto the ground. Kendar snapped the spy's neck while he was rolling in the dirt in agony. A murmur grew, but when it became clear the man was dead, the crowd fell silent.

"Lady Makena," the merchant whispered, tapping her forehead in a silent prayer. Kendar looked around. Over half of the gathering crowd were making the same gesture.

Kendar glanced at the dead man. "That wasn't too smart," he said, referring to the audacity of spying on him.

"No, it wasn't," the merchant said, shaking her head. "Even the children know it. You never walk behind a spooked horse."

Kendar returned to the inn late in the afternoon. He needed a bath to remove the layer of dust he'd accumulated while walking all day on dirt streets. After that, he planned to enjoy a hefty dinner, rest, and visit the Sebesian bank after hours. Being broke didn't suit Kendar of Ypsilos.

On his way in, Kendar approached the innkeeper, who was bent over a ledger behind the counter. "Hi there. Do you know where I can find a map?" he asked. He'd seen enough of Prince Port—no nice eateries, entertainment, or clean whorehouses. He'd be out of the city first thing in the morning after buying mangoes from the merchant woman.

Get them all, the voices in his head told him. Kendar agreed. The time had finally come to visit Kasmana. No doubt, the military super-power of the world would have better cities.

"Oh!" the innkeeper said, looking up at Kendar. "You're finally back. I have something for—"

The front door opened with a bang, and two men dressed in identical clothing walked in. Everyone looked at them. The men were in their mid-fifties and wore light brown trousers and sky-blue shirts with side laces. Both reminded Kendar of Lucca.

The first man flushed. "My apologies!" he said with a bow. "I didn't expect the door to work properly."

Kendar laughed as the innkeeper shook his head. He grabbed a rolling pin from the counter and waggled it. "I'd throw this at you if you weren't the bosi's servant. The blow might fix your damn head!"

"My sincere apologies," the man said, still red-faced.

The second one walked closer and placed a hand over his heart, tilting his head down. "Master Kendar, greetings. We'll provide your ride."

Kendar blinked and opened his mouth, but the innkeeper cut him off. "He doesn't know yet," he told the bosi's servants. "The Highlander has been out all day—just got back now. Don't blame me for your late invitation." He reached below the counter and withdrew a small wooden box. He opened it, took out a golden envelope, and gave it to Kendar. The envelope bore a seal depicting a bird in flight.

"Here," the innkeeper said. "That's the official seal of Bosi Darios, ruler of Mongad. Another servant came at noon and left this for you. The bosi is expecting you for dinner tonight."

Chapter Thirty-Four

1. Rayla

R ayla and her Lathraias traveled north in the company of the Cayali, heading for the Red Horn. Midafternoon rolled in as they rode on and left behind the Plain of Carbel. A gentle spring breeze caressed their faces, and Rayla welcomed its freshness.

As she rode, Rayla shook her head every so often. For the first time in seven years, she rode far behind the vanguard, surrounded by a watchful escort. The last time she hadn't steered her Lathraias, she had been twenty-five years old. Since then, she had always ridden at the front, knowing firsthand what was happening. Now, it felt like walking blindfolded through a forest of hawthorns, letting someone else lead her by the hand. She stomached the maddening change, trying to quiet her restless fingers and twitchy neck.

Assuming such a passive role mortified Rayla, but the days of riding in front of her company and leading the charge into battle were over—she hadn't argued with Rolan and Aia when the lieutenants had demanded changes be made. Rayla had survived the ambush near the Triple Peaks, yes, but the reason it had even happened in the first place was that her enemies had exploited a vulnerability: she always rode at the front, wide open and exposed. Her behavior seemed foolish now. Emerging alive from that ordeal had been a wonder, a miracle that had come in the form of a fifteen-year-old boy with an odd name.

The company had set off at dawn, galloping through the morning and trotting during the afternoon. They had crossed into North Katan territory and now expected to arrive at the Red Horn in two hours. Rolan and Aia rode next to Rayla while Danny trotted at the back of the company next to Cael. The thought of those two brought a smile to Rayla's face. They'd hit it off the previous night—Cael had been happy to answer a deluge of questions from Danny.

"My eken, have you thought about my request?" Rolan asked, breaking a stubborn silence that had lasted for over an hour.

"No, I haven't," Rayla said. She took a few seconds before continuing in a neutral tone. "I won't ask Danny to stay. I understand your point, Rolan, I do. But as impressive as he is, Danny is just a child trying to find his dad. It wouldn't be fair of us to insist that he stay. Praise Kas, we were lucky to meet him. I'll be indebted to him for the rest of my life, and I won't ask any more of him. Being a prodigy doesn't mean the boy must lose his freedom. Danny should follow his own path. Let's wish him well on his journey."

"But . . . My eken . . ." Rolan swallowed the rest of his words.

Rayla glanced at Aia. The lieutenant was looking straight ahead as if she were avoiding eye contact. "You're quiet," Rayla said, probing her.

Aia shook her head, her eyes still on the troops in front of her. "Forgive me, my eken, but I'm too old to believe in coincidences. Meeting Danny was no accident. He's the first Cayali in four hundred years. His presence here is the will of Kas."

Rayla looked down, absentmindedly caressing Kaistan's neck. She wouldn't admit it to her lieutenants, but she'd had the same thought the previous night. Initially, she had set out for South Katan to find Laramie, and that had turned out to be a plot that had nearly claimed her life. Instead of finding her friend, she'd met a Cayali, the first divine bow since the Great War.

Back then, Cayacoa—the greatest bowman in history—had galvanized the Kasmanian armies, single-handedly decimating a horde of Normanian Nephilim on the western shore of the Mercy River. The giant Nephilim were the enemies' trump card, but Kas spoke through Cayacoa's bow, asserting with divine certainty who his chosen people were.

The battle at Mercy River had sealed the fate of the war. The Great Caya's fame spread throughout the Kasmanian army and beyond, and the divine bow's legend reassured all Canyos that they enjoyed Kas's blessing. Queen-Priestess Vetania galloped to victory, riding on the back of Cayacoa's stature, crushing the allied forces of Normania, Maraccia, and Naldora. In a single decade, Vetania and Cayacoa delivered half of Neojoppa to Kasmana for the glory of the Almighty.

Rayla bowed her head in silent prayer, praising Kas the Almighty yet again. A new Caya had risen in this time of war, and that innocent-looking child had found his way to her—a miracle of its own accord—to deliver yet a second miracle. After saving her life against all odds, he'd electrified the Lathraias with a flawless display of his skills. The gatalan underneath him had run like the wind, and to the delight of all onlookers, that lovely boy had shot cleanly through target after target with a smile on his face. "Cayali!" her Lathraias had chanted. "Not a coincidence," Aia had said. "Keep him by your side!" Rolan had begged.

Rayla would not deny it: Danny's presence alone would sway entire garrisons into joining her. Most Canyos would agree at once—after all, through a Caya, Kas had pointed at his chosen side. Still, Danny had no clue about his importance, and Rayla would not burden him with it. He was fifteen, for crying out loud. She knew in her heart that this wasn't Danny's war; this wasn't what he was after.

"Please forgive my insistence, my eken," Rolan said. "But the Cayali is a gift from Kas. We must accept his providence!"

Rayla didn't answer. It wasn't her doing that had found Danny, and it wouldn't be her doing that would keep him by her side. If providence was afoot, divine grace would guide Danny into fulfilling Kas's will. Rayla squinted at the horizon. It was final: she would *not* manipulate the boy into doing her bidding.

"Speak of the devil," Aia said.

Rayla looked back. Danny trotted toward them atop Kara, flashing his endearing smile.

"Good afternoon," Danny said. He angled his gatalan to take the spot next to Aia, on the opposite side of Rayla.

"Kas's peace," Rolan and Aia said at the same time. Rayla smiled and nodded at Danny in greeting, but Kaistan swung his head up and down in protest.

"Oh! Hi, Kaistan," Danny said with a sparkle in his eyes. Kaistan stretched his neck forward and moaned. "Oh . . . I'm so sorry, buddy. Coming right away!" Danny spurred Kara and went around Aia to reach Rayla's midnight gatalan. The boy tickled Kaistan behind the ear, making silly sounds as if talking to a baby. "Who's a good ga-ga-gatalan, ah? Ga-ga-gatalan."

Rayla shook her head, barely containing her laughter—Kaistan clearly loved every second of Danny's nonsensical babbling. "Laramie will hate you," she said to Danny.

"Laramie?" the boy asked with a frown.

Aia was the one to answer. "She's my eken's best friend."

"Don't let Corina hear you saying that!" Rayla admonished her.

Aia laughed. "Laramie is close to Kaistan, but I don't recall ever seeing him this excited to see her."

Rayla nodded in agreement. "No, he's never been this way with anyone before." She slanted her gaze at the boy. "Laramie is a jealous type, Danny. Don't let her see you playing with Kaistan like this. If you do, your life expectancy will drop drastically."

Rolan laughed. "She's the wrong person to cross, Cayali. Laramie is the master of knowledge. If she decides to end you, she'll get away with it . . . and no one will ever find your corpse."

Danny scratched his head. "Understood. Whenever Laramie is around, I don't know you, Kaistan. But for now . . . tickle, tickle, gatalan. Ga-ga-gatalan, tickle, tickle. Who's the best boy in this party, ah?" Kaistan purred in response.

"Hey, what's that around Kara's neck?" Aia asked. She pointed at the five cobalt-blue, slightly curved stones dangling at equal intervals across Kara's chest. The pendants were thin and long, with their tips cut off.

Danny grinned. "Cael made this necklace for Kara. Isn't it beautiful? They look like jewels, but they're talons from the gavian I shot down yesterday. It turns out that the talons have an external layer—this is how they look when you peel it off. Mind-blowing, right? Cael trimmed them to make them the same size and then cut off the tips." He reached over and ruffled Kara's fur. "Otherwise they would have been incredibly sharp and dangerous for her neck."

Rayla lifted her chin, feeling proud of Cael. "That's a thoughtful gift. Quite rare. It will mark the moment we all met."

Danny's eyes widened. "That's exactly what Cael said!"

Of course Cael would say that, Rayla thought. That was her assistant: always aware of other people's needs.

"Hey, wait a minute," said Aia. "Aren't there supposed to be six talons?"

Danny jerked his head back in surprise. "Busted!" He guided Kara back around Rayla to ride alongside Aia once more, then looked at her with a smile and reached into his pocket. "I was planning on giving you this when we parted ways tomorrow, but what the heck . . ." He pulled out a small item wrapped in a piece of cloth and gave it to Aia.

She pointed at herself. "For me?"

"Uh-huh."

Aia reached for the item and unrolled the cloth. The sixth talon came into view, a bit longer than the ones in Kara's necklace but otherwise identical. Aia's eyes bulged. "I . . . I don't know what to say . . . It's beautiful!"

Rayla didn't know what to say either. She hadn't noticed that Danny had become close with Aia; she would've imagined that Cael would be the one to receive such a gift.

"Now I'm the one who's jealous!" Rolan exclaimed with a laugh. "How come Aia is the only one to get a gift from the Cayali?"

Danny shrugged. "It's hard for you to compete with Aia's charm, Rolan."

"No arguments there," Rolan said a tad too loudly.

"So, this is your way of proposing to Aia?" Rayla joked.

Danny laughed. "No, no such luck for me! Aia reminds me of someone who helped me a lot growing up. I lost my mom when I was two, and that person was always there for me."

"Interesting. Was she the one who taught you how to shoot? Is she a moving wall of muscles like Aia?" Rolan asked.

Danny shook his head, amused at the thought. "She looks nothing like Aia; she's a Normo. Her name is Tenis, and she's a very gentle soul—the furthest thing from a warrior you'll ever find."

"Tenis?" Aia repeated. "What kind of name is Tenis? Does everyone have funny names in your village?"

"I don't know about that," the boy answered. "Tenis isn't an odd name to me at all. Same goes for my name. 'Danny' is absolutely fine; the name slides off the tongue." He grinned at Aia. "Go ahead and try it . . . 'Danny.'"

Rolan laughed. "Don't fret, young man. Cayacoa had an odd name too."

"Really? What was it?"

"Satsani, believe it or not," Rolan said.

Danny rubbed his chin. "Hmm . . . I could see myself calling him Satsa after a while . . ."

Rayla jumped back into the conversation. "I'm curious, Danny. How does Aia—one of the most fearsome warriors in Kasmana—remind you of a gentle Normo woman?"

Danny shifted his weight atop Kara. "Well . . . it's not about Aia's looks, and it's not her swagger either. It's something deeper, something at her core. It's Aia's genuine caring, if you know what I mean—sincere dedication to someone else's well-being without expecting anything in return. Aia is like that with you. Tenis is like that with her family and with me. Even if Aia had been born in a different body, that part of her would still shine through."

"Wow," Rayla said, glancing at Aia. Her lieutenant never got many compliments; she was just too intimidating for most people. But now that Herculean woman was clearly trying not to tear up.

"Thank you, Cayali," Aia said, bowing her head. "I'll treasure this gift forever."

Danny grinned, his eyes shining. An uncomfortable silence swallowed the four of them.

Rayla's chest tightened as she realized one of her flaws. Even though her loyal subjects didn't *need* compliments, Danny had just shown Rayla that her people would appreciate them now and then. True, they served Kas and not Rayla, but she wouldn't be here without them. Her stomach churned; she'd been taking them for granted. Kas taught his children in many ways, and now it was her turn. Who would've thought a fifteen-year-old boy would teach an experienced leader how to be a better boss?

"Hey, Aia—the gift was supposed to be for later, actually. I came to ask you something," Danny said, ending the awkward silence.

Aia gazed at him with almost-moist eyes. "After that gift, you can ask me anything."

"Except to marry her, of course," Rolan said.

Aia gave a soft laugh. "He can ask for that too—he just won't like the answer. I'm sure this good-looking young man isn't used to rejections."

Danny didn't say anything, prompting Rayla to glance at him. The teenager had shrunk into himself slightly, dipping his chin and caving in his chest.

Rolan laughed. "What do we have here? It seems we've stumbled into something, haven't we? Our mighty Cayali is a virgin!"

"I'm not a virgin," Danny said softly, straightening his spine.

"Of course not," Aia said to Rolan, then turned back to Danny. "You're experienced with girls your own age, right? That's natural."

"I wouldn't say 'experienced,' no. I'm not going to lie."

"But you've tumbled with a couple of young girls, right?" Rolan asked.

Danny shrugged. "'A couple' is a stretch."

"Okay. I think we get the picture," Aia said to Rolan in a stern tone. "He had an unusual upbringing, that's all. Blame that irresponsible father of his. Danny may be strong and handsome, but he's still underage. Parents educate; adults don't meddle. Let's stick to the rules and let the boy be, Rolan."

Rolan threw his hands up in the air. "I wasn't going to say anything else! I'm not his dad. But if the Cayali were one year older, a few female comrades would offer to remedy his lack of experience."

"That's enough!" Aia snapped, staring down Rolan. He threw his hands in the air again. "I apologize for him," she said to Danny. "Rolan has the sensitivity of a crocodile."

Danny forced a laugh.

"What did you want to ask?" Aia prompted him.

The boy caressed Kara's neck. "Well, I overheard you last night talking about a guacanari bow for me, and it made me curious. Is the bow going to make me a better archer?"

Aia grinned. "I'm glad you're curious about that. A guacanari is a special recurve bow that Cayacoa used. It's quite heavy compared to other bows, and it's bigger than a longbow. According to historical records, guacanari bows are incredibly powerful . . . *if* you can use them. Cayacoa was the first to master one. A single shot from a guacanari can kill a Normanian Nephilim, piercing through their armor plates."

Rayla moved a bit closer. "Cayacoa was the first and only person to ever use the bow in battle."

After the Great War ended, the Kasmanian army made hundreds of guacanari bows, hoping to perpetuate Cayacoa's success. It should've been a game changer just like gatalans had been. The problem was that no one else could use the bow on the battlefield. Rayla had experienced that truth firsthand. The guacanaris were insanely taut, requiring a great deal of strength to bend, and even the few trainees who managed to draw the bow—Rayla included—missed their practice targets nearly seventy percent of the time. Worse yet, the trainees were exhausted after just a few rounds.

"You need a longer and heavier arrow than what's standard," Rayla went on, "but when you *do* manage to shoot an arrow with a guacanari, it travels over three hundred yards."

Danny gasped. "Three hundred yards! Can you imagine what a trained army could do with that? If arrows from a guacanari can pierce armor, they can blow apart doors too."

The three Lathraias smiled at the boy's enthusiasm. Average Kasmanian bows had a range of one hundred yards, double that of other nations' bows, but even the best Kasmanian bowmen and women were accurate only within sixty yards. The Lathraias had already seen Danny hit a moving target over one hundred yards out. If the boy could wield a guacanari, that would turn him into a Great Caya.

"They say Cayacoa reached four hundred yards sometimes," Rolan said. The comment almost made Danny faint.

"Yeah, but that's when he shot while galloping," Aia pointed out.

"That makes sense," Rolan mused. "The speed of the gatalan added impetus to the shot."

"The truly amazing aspect of Cayacoa was his accuracy," Rayla added, her eyes still on Danny. "That's why the Lathraias keep calling you little Caya. You have the same accuracy as the Great Caya, but no one has seen you hit a target three hundred yards out."

"I see," Danny said. He became pensive, dropping his gaze to watch the ground going by underneath Kara's paws. "Who made Cayacoa's bow?" he asked eventually.

Rolan blew out a breath. "Nobody knows where his bow came from. But our best crafters had access to the guacanari after Cayacoa's passing, and they made perfect replicas."

Danny frowned. "Is it possible that's where the problem lies? Did the crafters perhaps fail to copy a vital part of the original design?" He looked at Aia, Rayla, and Rolan one by one. Each gave him a blank stare.

Danny's next words came out fast as he clenched the reins more tightly. "With the right tool, the right technique, and the right training, dedicated people can match Cayacoa's results, I'm sure of it. Maybe even surpass him over time."

Rolan chuckled. "There've been thousands of deeply dedicated Canyo warriors throughout history, Danny. Probably hundreds of thousands. But there's only been one Cayacoa."

"It's true, Danny," Rayla said, nodding. "The divine tool is *the person*. Kas's grace flows through them. It's not about their equipment."

Danny shook his head, pinching his lips together. "Is the original bow still around?"

"I'm not sure . . . Perhaps—" Rolan started to reply.

"It is," Rayla interrupted him. "It's at the Ministry of Knowledge's headquarters in Vetus. I saw it myself—it's in perfect condition. Laramie keeps it inside a glass box next to Cayacoa's armor. They're both magnificent pieces decorated with sleek gold stripes. Laramie considers them to be national treasures."

"Oh," Danny said, lowering his head again. "Then I guess there's no way for me to get my hands on it."

Rayla's heart skipped a beat. *This* was the role Kas wanted her to play! It was the one thing she could do for Danny: procure the original guacanari for him. Rayla glanced at Rolan and Aia in turn. The two lieutenants nodded at her.

"Are you really interested in testing Cayacoa's bow? You're a Cayali, Danny. I can make that happen," Rayla told him.

His face brightened. "That'd be awesome! I'd love to compare the original bow against a duplicate. If Cayacoa's results haven't been exaggerated, I believe dedicated people could replicate them with hard work. I think we're just missing some aspect of the original bow."

"A Caya makes the bow, Danny, not the other way around," Rolan said.

Rayla agreed, but she thought it best not to keep arguing with the boy. Danny did things the Lathraias could only dream about; it made sense he would think differently than the rest of them. But Danny's interest in the original guacanari was significant because it revealed Kas's will. Rayla would do anything to put that bow into Danny's hands.

She gave a decisive nod. "Rolan, take two of your fastest riders and retrieve Cayacoa's bow from the Unburnt Hills. Bring Cayacoa's armor too. Laramie won't be there, so talk to Alcalion and tell him the order came from me."

"As you wish, my eken," Rolan said. He turned his mount and raced off.

Rayla glanced at Danny's beaming face. She smiled. "I'll see if Cael can find a guacanari duplicate for you at the Red Horn—you can give that a try first. It will take a couple of weeks for Rolan to return with the original bow. You'll be gone by then, but I'll keep Cayacoa's bow and armor with me. I hope you'll stop to see me on your way back from Torinth."

Right then, a commotion ensued at the front, and the company came to a halt. Rayla gripped her reins tighter. She *hated* not knowing what was happening at the vanguard. She spoke through her teeth, craning her neck to try to see what was happening. "I'll never get used to this, will I?"

"Messenger!" someone yelled up ahead.

"It's a fast runner from General Nereida," Aia said, her height allowing her to see ahead better than the others. "Make way!" she yelled at the soldiers in front of them. "Let her through!"

The Lathraias in front of Rayla moved to the side, and seconds later, a messenger riding an orange-furred gatalan approached Rayla. The young, slender woman dismounted and fell to one knee. "Kas's peace, Cacique Rayla. I bring an urgent message from General Nereida."

"Go on," Rayla said.

The messenger spoke louder, using a deeper voice. "My eken, General Fabris leads an army from the west. General Viembo brings an army from Mesonia while three brigades from Ionia come through central Kasmana to block access to the Singing Bridge. All windows are closing. Please, my eken, make haste. I wait for you at the Red Horn."

Chapter Thirty-Five

9. Anaya

Asa sat at the table with Anaya and Marko while they finished dinner. "What do you call this again?" Anaya asked, taking another bite of dessert.

"Cheesecake," Marko said.

"Cheesecake," she repeated, sticking another spoonful into her mouth. She let the creamy piece of heaven melt on her tongue, savoring every bit of the tangy sweetness.

Anaya would've never imagined there could be something better than beets in this world, but now she'd found the first upside of leaving Ivory Village. "Does the king-priest eat cheesecake at the holy palace?" she asked.

"No, I don't think so," Marko said, reaching for a spoonful of his own.

"Ha!" Anaya replied. She didn't have to become a cacique after all.

"Would you like to know where that cheesecake comes from?" Asa asked Anaya.

"Do you think it's time to show her the kitchen?" Marko said before the girl could answer.

"No doubt. It's time for her next lesson," Asa replied.

Marko turned to Anaya. "Well, little one, you could learn to bake cheesecake yourself if you wish."

Her face beamed. "Awesome!" The possibilities were endless. She could bake all the cheesecakes she ever wanted. She'd even bake one for the king-priest. She'd become the most famous baker in all of Kasmana! Everybody would want to be her friend and share their toys with her. Perhaps the king-priest would share his boiled beets in return.

Anaya glanced around Marko's home. It was bigger than her house in Ivory Village, but not by much. A living room with a couch that served as Anaya's bed, with a clean floor but barren walls—they almost announced that a single man lived here—and a small kitchen with a dining table. Marko had his own bedroom, but it was always locked.

Asa floated up from his chair and glided through the kitchen, stopping before Marko's bedroom. "It's time," he said.

"Well, Anaya," Marko said, putting down his spoon and standing up. "What you're about to see will blow your mind all over again."

Anaya stuffed a final chunk of cheesecake into her mouth. "Is it better than a talking doll?" she asked with her mouth full.

Marko laughed. "Probably not. But it's darn close."

They walked to the bedroom, and Marko unlocked the door. A sun stick in the shape of a bulb lit up by itself when Marko opened the door. "Nice magic," Anaya said. Sun sticks were awesome, especially outdoors, but they still required someone to light them up. Perhaps Dian was in this room too.

The little girl scanned the bedroom with eager eyes. It had one bed and a desk with a chair, but something was wrong. She looked at Marko, narrowing her eyes.

"Something bothers you, Anaya?" he asked, moving to the back of the room. Asa followed him.

"You don't sleep here, do you?" Anaya said. Nothing in the room showed natural wear and tear—it wasn't anything like the living room.

Marko just smiled.

"Very perceptive, Anaya," Asa commented.

"Don't worry—you'll understand everything in just a second," Marko said with bright eyes. He lifted his right hand and touched the wall with an open palm. "Don't be afraid, Anaya. You're about to see my real home."

Anaya squinted at the wall. *Real home?*

The spot Marko touched on the wall glowed pale blue, and a section next to it split in two. Each side rolled away in opposite directions, revealing a metal box big enough to accommodate three people. A white light illuminated the box and made the metal shine like a brand-new sword. Anaya's eyes opened wider and wider.

Marko tipped his head at it. "This is an elevator. It will take us down to where my real kitchen and real bedroom are." He and Asa walked into the box, but Anaya remained frozen where she was.

"It's safe, Anaya, I promise. Please, come inside," Marko said, extending a hand toward her.

Anaya said nothing. She wanted to believe it was safe—after all, Marko and Asa were already inside, looking calm and carefree. But what if the doors closed after she walked into it? She didn't want to be swallowed by a metal monster. What to do?

She reached for her pendant and closed her eyes. *Guide me, please*, she asked Dian. She opened her mind to the goddess's answer. Anaya trusted Marko, and she wanted to be Asa's friend. But was it smart to go inside that thing?

In answer to her plea, an adrenaline rush accelerated Anaya's heartbeat, quickened her breath, and made her sweat. An excited smile came to her lips—she remembered those sensations! Dian was promising a thrilling experience.

She nearly jumped into the elevator. The doors closed, rolling toward each other, and Anaya imagined how it must look from the outside: the wall *had* closed its mouth and eaten them. But it wasn't true! They were alive inside, hiding from the rest of the world. Anaya giggled, and Marko patted her head.

The elevator moved downward, making Anaya yelp. It felt like the floor was disappearing beneath her feet, and the falling sensation turned the pit of her stomach cold. Then everything stopped and the doors opened. A living room with a hard floor and egg-shaped chairs came into view, but Anaya didn't care. She burst out laughing, leaning against the elevator's wall and grabbing her stomach.

"Can we do it again?" she asked amid her laughter. That ride was like the time she used a red shield to glide down the snowy Kasmanian mountains, going faster and faster. She loved it!

Marko smiled at her. "Yes, we'll do it again later. You can ride the elevator as many times as you'd like, but for now, there's a lot of stuff for you to see."

He walked out of the elevator with Asa, giving Anaya a moment to compose herself. Dian had been right! She could always trust the goddess, and it seemed like she could fully trust Marko and Asa too.

Anaya stepped out of the elevator, and the doors closed behind her. *That's so awesome!* The elevator closed its own mouth, remaining a secret. She gave it an approving smile. Anaya liked the elevator a lot . . . although the best thing about tonight was the still the cheesecake. But her brother would've chosen the elevator over the cheesecake, she had no doubt.

She turned, gazing at the living room. A soft light illuminated the place even though she couldn't spot any sun sticks or candles or a fireplace. The magic here was next level! *Dian must really like Marko and Asa.*

A humongous white egg sat on a small pedestal near the elevator. Its front had been sliced off at an angle, and it had a padded red interior. Anaya looked at it with wide eyes.

"That's a chair!" Marko called out. She couldn't see him, but he seemed to be reading her mind. "And, yes! You can try it."

Anaya gave a small jump and hurried to climb into the egg chair. The pads lining the interior were soft, and the backrest was deep, so deep that the chair encased her completely. "Wow," she said out loud as she sank into the soft cushions. This chair was the most comfortable thing ever! "Can I sleep here?" she bellowed with excitement.

"If you want!" Marko called back. "But come over here! You can play with the chair later."

As she tried to worm out of the chair, Anaya discovered that it swiveled. She giggled. The chair was the best thing ever! Not counting the cheesecake, of course. Or Albi.

Finally, her feet were on the floor again. She resumed her examination of the living room. Other lounge chairs and couches punctuated the space, and the walls displayed paintings and wiggly decorations Anaya had never seen before. A long kitchen island rose on the other side of the living room; stainless steel appliances lined the wall behind it. Anaya didn't recognize any of those devices, but their black-and-silver colors pleased her. Marko's real home was nice.

The largest bed Anaya had ever seen lay to the left of the living room in an open area that seemed like the bedroom. She gasped. Her entire family could've slept comfortably there! It was so big that she doubted her initial assumption. "Is that a bed?" she asked in awe.

Marko nodded at her from behind the kitchen island. "Yes. Come over here."

Anaya walked closer, taking short steps, gazing at every detail. Then she saw it: the furthermost wall in the kitchen showed nine different images of Marko's home aboveground, as well as the surrounding areas.

"That's called a screen," Marko said, pointing at it. "This one is divided into nine monitors. Each one is showing what's happening at different spots above us."

Anaya squished her eyebrows together. "They aren't paintings?"

Marko grinned. "No. What you see here is what's happening up there right now."

"But nothing is moving," Anaya said in a disbelieving voice.

"That's because nobody is up there," Asa said, joining the conversation. "I'll show you. Look at the monitor in the lower left corner."

"The one showing the kitchen upstairs?"

"Yes," Asa answered. "Now, pay attention."

The chair Anaya had been sitting on when she was eating her cheesecake slid back from its spot at the table and rose into the air. She inhaled sharply, her eyes huge and fixed on the screen. "Are *you* doing that, Asa?"

"Yes, my darling friend."

That made her look away from the floating chair and at him instead. No one had ever called her that before. "And guess what, Anaya?" Asa continued. "You can do it too."

She gasped again, even more loudly this time. "No way!" Sure, she could lift and pull things toward her or cast them away using her steel threads, but she would've never thought about moving them in any other direction. Especially if she couldn't see the thing with her own eyes.

Asa laughed. "You can! I'll teach you how it's done, and then we'll practice until you've mastered it."

"Look at the monitors again, Anaya," Marko urged her. "They let you see what's happening someplace else. Your remote surveillance works like that—with it, you can hear and see things at a distance."

Anaya scratched her head. "So this room has Dian too?"

"Not exactly. This room uses a different type of Dian. We call it technology. Remember that word, Anaya. Technology."

"What is technology?" she asked.

Marko walked closer and lifted Anaya, putting her on the kitchen island's counter. "Do you remember when you told me your father made nabilon swords?"

Her eyes glittered. "Yes! My dad was the best."

Marko patted her head. "Would you believe that people could *not* make nabilon swords five hundred years ago?"

"Why not?"

"They didn't know how. But then someone figured out how to

mine Arawan ore and make it into steel. And then someone else figured out how to make swords out of that steel. The process of learning more about how the world works is called *science*, and using that knowledge to make new things is called *technology*."

"Oh," Anaya said. She was proud of her dad's nabilons. "Technology is pretty awesome."

Marko smiled at her. "That's right! Now, tell me: who has better technology, people five hundred years ago or people now?"

That was an easy question. "My dad and the people from now," Anaya answered.

"Exactly right. Think about people living five hundred years in the *future*. Who would have better technology, the people from now or the people from the future?"

Anaya thought about it. "Will people in the future learn more?"

"That's a good question," Marko said. "I believe they will. Humans, as a group, tend to learn more, make better tools, design deadlier weapons, build taller buildings, and construct faster ships."

Anaya nodded firmly. "Then people in the future will have better technology."

"Right again." Marko pointed at the monitors. "This is an advanced technology built by people who have learned much more than Kasmanians have learned."

"Are they from the future?" Anaya asked.

"No—they've learned more because they began to learn before Kasmanians did."

Anaya nodded. That made sense. Casar knew a few things she didn't, but only because he was older. "So Kasmanians will build monitors one day?"

"They will, but that will take them many, many years. Meanwhile, we cannot show this to them because . . ." Marko looked at her expectantly.

Anaya knew the answer because it had already happened to her: Kasmanians would be confused and afraid, and many would react by trying to protect themselves. They would call Marko and Asa she-devils and shoot arrows at them.

"Because of fear," Anaya said, and Marko smiled, patting her head approvingly. Anaya tilted her head. "The purple ball you gave me, is that technology too?"

"Yes—that ball was designed to find the type of Dian you have. I'll teach you how to read it." His expression shifted, becoming more somber. "At least one more person out there has Isbel's bionanobots, and we believe he'll come after you one day."

She stiffened. "What do you mean, come after me? He won't be my friend?"

Asa answered this time. "We're afraid not. He wants to take your Dian for himself."

Anaya paled. Her mom's essence lived within Dian! She could never allow anyone to take Dian away.

Marko's hand went to her shoulder. "No worries, Anaya—with the ball and your remote surveillance, you'll see him coming from a mile away."

"Yes. And I'll teach you how to fight better," Asa said. "You're Isbel's perfect match! The odds are in your favor."

Anaya breathed a sigh of relief. Things weren't hopeless; she'd be able to defend herself. But then her eyes hardened. She'd *had* it with mean people coming to take loved ones from her! She'd make that man regret trying to steal Dian from her. Anaya would train as hard as she could and make him pay. "Can you teach me remote surveillance now?"

"Sure thing, my darling friend," Asa said.

Pride shone in Marko's eyes as he let his hand drop from her shoulder. "You must be thirsty from that cheesecake," he said as he reached for a glass of water. "This is an oven, by the way," he added, pointing at an appliance beside him. "It's where I baked the cheese-cake. I'll teach you how to make it another day."

Anaya smiled. She was about to learn a bunch of good stuff! "Thank you," she said to both of them. Asa bowed his head slightly, and Marko smiled. Anaya smiled too. No doubt Dian had sent Marko and Asa to look after her. She appreciated that.

Marko handed her the water. Drinking it made Anaya feel much better.

"Now, Anaya," Asa said, "let's begin."

Episode Ten

Chapter Thirty-Six

8. Danny

Danny's eyes beamed with pride. Kara's speed and stamina were incredible. She galloped along all morning with him on her back, then trotted for three hours in the afternoon following a short break, and then raced at full speed toward the Red Horn after that urgent message from General Nereida. Kara ran as fast as Kaistan—she was head-to-head with a pack of the best midnight gatalans in Kasmana. And when they finally reached Nereida's camp in front of the Red Horn, Kara held her head high while most of the gatalans in Rayla's party looked exhausted.

"She's impressive," Rayla said, "and she's still young! Kara will grow stronger and faster, just like her master."

Danny grinned at Rayla and muffled a giggle. But Rayla was partially wrong. He wasn't Kara's master, he was her friend.

A sea of white tents rose to meet the Lathraias as they approached the Red Horn. Danny gawked at the sheer size of the camp—at least four thousand of them had turned the area into a snowfield. For some reason, the white tents were bigger than the black ones in the Lathraias's camp.

Rayla galloped at the front of the company with Aia and Danny racing by her side. The entire party slowed to a trot when they neared the first row of white tents. Thousands of soldiers came into view, mingling and chatting, clearly waiting for their next orders. Their clothing was similar to what the soldiers in Rayla's company wore, except that the tunic underneath their armor was orange, while the Lathraias wore black.

"Nereida's soldiers," Aia said to Danny. His eyes glowed at the sight of thousands of orange-furred gatalans roaming around the camp's edges. Then Aia looked at Rayla and chuckled. "She did it again."

Rayla smiled and shook her head. "Nereida is amazing! This is about thirty thousand riders. I wasn't expecting this many with so little notice, I must admit."

Danny tilted his head, his attention drawn away from the gatalans. "Can you tell me a little bit about General Nereida? How should I carry myself around her?"

"Oh, Nereida is the reason General Helikex never got married," Aia said with a twinkle in her eyes.

"Can't blame the man," Rayla agreed. "Even in her mid-sixties, Nereida is still a beauty and a force of nature. She can be severe, funny, or distant, but no matter her mood, she has a weakness for talent—she can smell it like most of us smell flowers. She'll like you, Danny."

Danny frowned. He didn't know what to make of all that, plus none of it told him how to behave around her. He shrugged and decided to go with short sentences and immaculate social manners. "Helikex was your predecessor, right?" he asked Rayla.

"Predecessor *and* mentor," Aia chimed in.

Rayla nodded. "Right. Even with all the skills I worked so hard to hone, I wouldn't be here if it weren't for General Helikex."

That's exactly right! Danny almost shouted. During all that talk about divine bows and God-given skills, he had bitten his tongue. But they were wrong—whatever remarkable skills Rayla had, she'd worked hard to hone them. Plain and simple. The same was true for

him. After the end of each school year, his classmates always vaca-
tioned, visited theme parks, or chased after romance. Danny, on the
other hand, had worked his butt off perfecting his kinetic target shooting. And he would bet every credit he owned that the same had been
true for Cayacoa. If he was indeed a real person rather than just a
legend, Cayacoa had mastered archery through proper form and
relentless training. It had nothing to do with divine intervention.
That was an insult to all his hard work.

That said, superior equipment *did* make a difference in performance, of course. Shooting an arrow with a Belphian bow wasn't the
same as shooting with a Kasmanian bow. If Cayacoa really *had*
existed, Danny would've loved to wrap his fingers around Cayacoa's
original guacanari. It was probably a fantastic weapon the locals
couldn't copy. Hopefully, the original bow still worked. Just the
thought of it made his hands twitch eagerly.

It pained him, but arguing about divinity versus hard work was a
losing proposition outside of Newisbel. Best just to steer clear of
Kas's domain. "You really appreciate General Helikex, Rayla!" was
all he said. The rest of his thoughts could stay just where they were:
in his own head.

Rayla's eyes turned soft, filled with a faint glow. "He opened
doors for me that I would have never unlocked on my own, at least
not for a long time. I owe him my career and my success. I still
consider Helikex to be my eken."

Danny moved closer to Rayla. "So, the next gavian I shoot
down . . ."

Rayla laughed. "Yes! I'll take those talons, please. They'd make a
nice gift for the general."

A horn blew inside the garrison, announcing Rayla's return. "The
gates will open soon," Aia said to Danny.

He nodded, eager to see the interior of a garrison, then looked
more closely at Nereida's soldiers as he and the others trotted through
their midst. "How come the vast majority of these soldiers are
women?" he asked Aia. At least sixty percent were women, probably

closer to sixty-five percent. And most riders in Nereida's army were in their mid-twenties, much younger than the average soldier in Rayla's party.

Aia cast an approving glance at the soldiers. "Gatalans choose who they bond with—if they bond with a human at all—and since the beginning of history in Quinquella, gatalans have bonded more often with women. We don't know why."

The lieutenant paused for a second, and her eyes took on a melancholic air. She resumed talking in a softer voice. "Many gatalans live in the wild, but the army has large fields where gatalans roam free. Thousands of them live there. Students about to graduate from battle school are allowed to spend time in those fields if they wish. Even though it isn't mandatory, every student visits the fields at least three times during their final year. If a gatalan bonds with a student, the student becomes a gatalan rider."

Danny nodded. "I see. Lucky for me, Kara didn't care I hadn't attended battle school."

"Lucky for you both," Aia said, smiling. "Just look at the size of her already! Kara will grow into a prime gatalan. She's unlikely to have bonded with anyone else. And gatalans that bond with humans tend to live longer. Again, we don't know why."

She waved an arm at the crowds of soldiers. "In all four branches of the Kasmanian army, after a third promotion, officers must be gatalan riders to advance to the next rank. So you're looking at the future brass mingling before your eyes."

Danny's eyebrows shot up. "Really! Why is that?"

"We've learned to trust gatalans' selections. Other kingdoms have nobles, but *this* is our version of nobility, at least in the army. People chosen by a gatalan are remarkable in one way or another." She grinned suddenly. "Civilians go overboard trying to woo gatalan riders."

"That's so cool!" Danny exclaimed. Natural selection had clearly taken on a new meaning in Kasmana.

Aia shook her head. "'Cool . . .' You use the weirdest words. Why not 'warm'? Sounds nicer to me."

He stifled a chuckle. "Good point!" He'd been striving to avoid Newisbel slang, but sometimes he slipped. At least he was no longer too worried about it—being the Cayali had brought him goodwill and much patience with his shortcomings.

Danny looked again at the orange-furred gatalan riders and remembered something Cael had said the previous night: Lathraias were composed exclusively of midnight gatalan riders. "What about midnight gatalans?" he asked Aia. "Where do they come from? There are none in General Nereida's army."

She nodded. "True. We have roaming fields for midnight gatalans too. They're much scarcer than orange-furred, partially because not all of their offspring are midnight gatalans like their parents. Another difference is that midnight gatalans rarely connect with humans. However, they do bond much more easily with Canyos who have previously bonded with another gatalan, so soldiers who've ridden orange-furred gatalans and who have stellar records—and students with the highest marks—are allowed to visit the midnight gatalan fields. If a midnight gatalan chooses them, they become a Lathraias."

Danny nodded slowly. "Ah . . ." That explained the age difference he'd noticed—most Lathraias had spent years excelling as orange-furred gatalan riders before joining the ranks. But Cael was much younger than the average Lathraias, so he'd probably been chosen by his gatalan right out of battle school.

Danny caressed Kara's neck. "No worries, Kara! I will never replace you, not even with a midnight gatalan."

Aia laughed. "She's not worried about that, Danny—no other gatalan will bond with you while Kara is alive, at least not until she becomes too old to ride. You are hers, my dear boy, and hers alone. Gatalans don't share and they don't cheat."

Danny looked at her with awestruck eyes. "That's just amazing! So gatalans know who is a rider even when their gatalans are nowhere near them?"

Aia gave a firm nod. "They do. And they'll know it when the bond is broken, either because of death or old age. Only then will other gatalans be attracted to you. And they won't ask for permission! As far as they're concerned, it's first-come, first-served."

* * *

Soon after they arrived at the Red Horn, Rayla rushed into a meeting with General Nereida. But before leaving, she gave Cael specific instructions about the Cayali.

Danny waited for Cael, looking around and wondering why the Kasmanian army called this installation a garrison. He would have described it as a fort. In his mind, garrisons were small military posts, and there was nothing small about the Red Horn! Its grounds could easily house twenty thousand people. Sixty buildings made up the complex, most of them two stories high. The buildings had been erected in the pattern of a perfect circle and were guarded by a twenty-foot-high wall. Right at its center rose a red pyramid twice as high as the walls. Danny scratched his head. The buildings made complete sense, but the pyramid struck him as bizarre.

"Cayali!" someone called, and Danny turned with a chuckle. That name was apparently here to stay. He spotted Cael walking toward him. "You're to stay by my side at all times," Cael said once he was standing in front of him.

Danny lifted his eyebrows at Cael's impassive face. What the heck had Rayla instructed him to do? From that moment on, Cael stuck with Danny like a shadow, blatantly keeping Danny isolated from the others and showing no remorse about it.

"What's going on?" Danny asked after Cael maneuvered him into having dinner at a remote table. The young officer weaseled his way out of answering with a remark about what Kara would be fed. "What's going on?" Danny asked again when Cael waved away people coming to meet the Cayali.

Cael sighed. "My eken wants to make sure you're on your way to Torinth tomorrow."

Danny frowned. "C'mon! Give me a little bit more than that."

The young Lathraias smiled. "We like you a lot, Cayali, but you're not a soldier. Brigade Leader Analia allowed you inside her garrison as a guest of the cacique. But now it's best if you keep to yourself."

Danny pressed his lips together, smelling bullshit in the lieutenant's words. Cael obviously wasn't at liberty to say what was happening, so Danny didn't insist. In any case, the night didn't go on for long after dinner. An order came from Rayla instructing all Lathraias and gatalan riders to get plenty of rest in preparation for a long day. The sun sticks went out around 9:00 p.m., and everybody went to bed whether they were tired or not.

Having a soft bed under him meant that Danny slept soundly for the first time in weeks. He would've loved to lie on that feather mattress all morning long! But a thunderous horn blew before dawn, waking everybody inside the garrison. Danny whimpered, covering his ears and refusing to open his eyes. Eventually, though, he gave in and struggled to his feet with a sigh. Rayla had said they would leave North Katan at first light, but he just hadn't been expecting such a brutal wake-up call.

Still, Danny was thankful—he'd been given a private room for the night. Only a handful of people had enjoyed such a privilege. The gray-walled chamber was small and barren, but it came with a metal bathtub big enough for one person, half-filled with warm water. The bath had been relaxing, no doubt contributing to his good night's sleep. Most of the soldiers inside the Red Horn had slept in massive co-ed dormitories with access to gendered bathrooms at opposite ends of the huge rooms.

"Cayali!" a muffled voice called outside Danny's door. "You need to hurry if you want to have breakfast. We're leaving in twenty minutes."

Danny recognized Cael's voice. "I'll be out in a jiffy," he said, rushing to get dressed. It didn't take him long to gather his few belongings, although he did pause to give the bed one last wistful glance.

When he opened the door, it was still dark outside. "Good morning, Cael! I'm ready to go."

Cael bowed his head slightly. "Kas's peace."

Danny hesitated. He should greet people the same way; almost everybody said that. "Kas's peace," he responded, barely able to stop himself from wrinkling his forehead. Using the name of a god he didn't believe in felt a bit disingenuous.

Cael smiled. "Follow me, please," he said, leading the way. A moment later, he asked, "What's a 'jiffy'?"

Crap! Danny couldn't believe he'd done it again, but he often lowered his guard around Cael. "Sorry, Cael. My bad. 'Jiffy' means a very short time."

The young officer smiled. "You're so weird, Cayali."

They walked past a garden and entered a building across from a dormitory. Inside, a large lunchroom came into view, filled with cafeteria tables. The room accommodated over 150 tables neatly aligned into four columns. The place was abuzz with nearly nine hundred people eating and chatting.

"Is this the only lunchroom in the garrison?" Danny asked as they walked inside.

Cael chuckled. "Oh, no! There are twenty lunchrooms in the garrison, one across each dormitory. Each lunchroom can host up to one thousand people." He pointed at the far end of the lunchroom, indicating they were heading that way. Danny looked. Aia sat there alone at a round table covered with a white cloth and decorated with a vase filled with pink tulips.

Only one other table was decorated as nicely as Aia's. It was next to hers, and two people were already sitting there. Danny didn't recognize either of them, but both wore a golden ear cuff in the shape of a gatalan's claws on their left ear. The cuffs looked just like Rayla's. Cael had said that only Kasmanian generals wore ear cuffs. Perhaps that table was reserved for generals and Rayla would join them shortly.

He looked closer at the two generals. The man had a shaven face and braided long white hair. He was in his sixties; the black tunic underneath his armor meant he was a Lathraias. The woman wore an orange tunic underneath her armor. *That's General Nereida*, Danny told himself, *the master of gatalans*. So then the gentleman next to her was General Gadai, master of Lathraias.

Danny did a double-take. Had Rayla been mistaken when she'd said Nereida was in her mid-sixties? The woman sitting next to Gadai looked barely into her fifties! Frankly, she could have gotten away with saying she was in her late forties. Nereida's long hair shone as black as a midnight gatalan, and her short, round face had a well-defined jawline. There was a smile in her eyes as she spoke with Gadai, who listened to her with a serious look on his face, constantly nodding at whatever she was saying.

Danny reminded himself that using his best social manners with Nereida began by not staring at her. He looked at Aia instead and flashed a smile. She wiggled her fingers in greeting, then waved at a server. The man immediately stepped to her table and took notes as Aia made her request.

It happened then: the room became quiet, all eyes turning to Danny. He raised both eyebrows and kept walking, glancing at the four columns of cafeteria tables. Even Gadai and Nereida were staring at him now.

Danny couldn't remember a time when so many eyes had been on him. He smiled suddenly, a bubbly sensation fluttering in his chest. He didn't mind the attention at all. In fact, he enjoyed it! So much for Oscar's theory that Danny Elsberra was an introvert in disguise. By the time Danny reached Aia's table, only the clinking of plates and silverware tickled the thick silence.

"Kas's peace," Danny said to Aia with a slight bow. To his surprise, the greeting felt alright this time. He didn't believe in Kas, but the local custom conveyed to Aia the happiness he felt at seeing her. He liked the feeling. Would he turn into a real Kasmanian in no time?

"Kas's peace," Aia said with a smile. "Please, sit down. We need to eat as soon as our breakfast arrives—we're leaving as soon as we can." Danny nodded and sat down. Then Aia addressed Cael. "Please ready our gatalans, Kaistan included. We'll wait for you in front of this building."

"As you wish," Cael said. He quickly turned and left.

"Ah . . . Cael is bringing Kaistan too," Danny said. "That means Rayla is going to join us for breakfast."

"She is." Aia's gaze danced around the room, never settling on a person or thing. Then she rubbed an eyebrow.

It was the first time Danny had seen Aia with a worried expression. It was not a good partner for her herculean build. "Are you okay?" he asked.

Aia looked at him and frowned, tilting her head. "You're enjoying this, aren't you?"

"What? Me?" he said, flinching slightly. Perhaps he *was* smiling . . . "Well, maybe a little. I don't mind being a temporary celebrity."

"*Celebrity* . . ." Aia scoffed. "Another funny word." She straightened her spine. "Listen, Danny. Perhaps you don't understand the situation. Three enemy armies are closing in on us—one from the east, one from the north, and most importantly, another from the west rushing to cut off our access to the Singing Bridge."

"I think I understand that part," Danny said, nodding. "I want to cross the Singing Bridge to be on my way to Torinth. You want the option to cross it because you'll have more room to maneuver in Central Kasmana, plus Rayla can recruit entire garrisons there." Aia's frown didn't go away. "Am I missing something?" Danny added. That look on her face worried him.

"Well, yes. It's not your fault, and my eken doesn't want anyone pressuring you. But lots of people here have strong opinions about your future."

Now he was also frowning. "Like what?"

Aia almost answered, but instead her eyes darted to the right, behind Danny.

"Good morning, young man," a melodious female voice said at his back. Danny turned. General Nereida stood there, her piercing eyes absorbing every detail of his face. "Kas's peace," she added with a sincere smile. Something electric touched Danny's bones. He recognized the sensation—he was in the presence of a true leader.

He rose to his feet and bowed his head. Nereida's height matched his. "Kas's peace, General. It's a pleasure to meet you."

"The pleasure is mine, Cayali," she said, extending her hand in greeting. Danny reached out and shook her hand. His eyes opened wide. That slender, sweet-looking woman gripped his hand with surprising strength.

Danny did his best to match the squeeze, being careful not to overpower her. She leaned into him with a smile, and Danny gently swayed back, maintaining their original distance. Then her hand slid up to grasp Danny's forearm. He followed suit. She pushed ever so slightly to the left, and Danny moved with her without thinking; she leaned back and pulled him in, and Danny moved in tandem.

Nereida smiled and let go of Danny's arm. She looked into Aia's eyes. "Care to guess how many riders I've trained in my lifetime, Lieutenant?"

"Dozens of thousands," Aia said.

Nereida lifted a finger as if awarding a point. "I knew it the moment I saw the way this young man walks, and I confirmed it just now: he's a superb gatalan rider."

Aia nodded sharply. "Indeed! I've seen it firsthand. He can shoot while galloping, guiding his gatalan without using the reins."

"So I've been told, Lieutenant. I'd pay a pretty gold coin to see it."

Then her gaze returned to Danny. "Tell me, Cayali, isn't Kara your first gatalan?"

Something about her tone made Danny's temperature rise. He stopped himself from rubbing his hands down his pant legs. "That is correct, General."

"And isn't it true that Kara's first saddle came into your possession not two days ago?"

"That's true, yes."

"Then how is it that you're already an outstanding rider?"

Danny's mouth turned dry; a cold sensation spread through his chest. He couldn't reveal the years he'd spent riding horses at ranger school, or the six months he'd spent training like a madman astride his horse in Newisbel. He didn't know what to say, so he just stood there rigid and wide-eyed, his face turning pale.

"He was born that way," Aia said a few seconds later. "He's the Cayali—Kas has touched him."

Nereida chuckled and showed her hands to Aia. "Kas touches my students through these hands. Sometimes he caresses, other times he slaps, but always he guides."

Danny tilted his head. She was talking about instruction and training, exactly what *he* believed in. Could it be that not all Canyos were superstitious? "Forgive me, General," he said. "You still believe in divinity, don't you?"

"I certainly do, young man. But I substitute the word 'divinity' for 'perfection.' I believe in perfection. Canyos have to achieve it through labor." She looked behind her. Everyone in the lunchroom was listening to her every word. She spoke a little louder. "Everything in this world is born with the potential to shine with Kas's divinity, all of you included. It happens in nature every day. But Canyos have to apply themselves to manifest their innate divinity in this world."

She pointed at the flower on Aia's table. "See that tulip? It's radiating with Kas's divinity. It is perfect." She looked at Danny with penetrating eyes, and he felt naked under her gaze. "Have you seen my eken Rayla fight? *That* is divinity, my boy," she said, not waiting for an answer. "*That* is perfection."

Danny's mind was blank; he was in awe of the confidence that flowed out of Nereida with each word, and he had to make an effort not to gape at her. Silence grew around Danny, prompting him to think of something to say before he looked like an idiot, but no words came to his aid.

He was saved by the sound of resolute steps echoing inside the lunchroom. Everyone turned to see Rayla walking toward Danny's table with fire in her eyes, her gaze drilling into Nereida's face. "What's the meaning of this?" Rayla asked loudly. "I made my intentions clear, Nereida. No one is to interfere with the Cayali."

Everyone lowered their heads, Nereida included. "Forgive me, my eken," Nereida said. "I wanted to evaluate this young man for myself."

Rayla raised an eyebrow. She had reached Aia's table. "And what's your verdict?"

"The boy is brimming with talent," Nereida said. "I doubt he's reached his full potential. We can expect much more from him."

Rayla sighed.

"The will of Kas brought him to us!" someone yelled. Danny's eyes widened, remembering what Aia had said a moment earlier—lots of people had strong opinions about his future. He understood them wanting him to fight alongside them in the bloody battles to come. Was this what Rayla and Cael had been trying to shield him from?

Danny sighed. Just thinking about bloody battles was unnerving: death everywhere, swords clashing, arrows whizzing by, the smell of blood, and the screams of dying men. War was disturbing. He didn't want to be a part of anything so barbaric, not after being raised in a peaceful society like Newisbel. Yet, he had already been in two brutal fights, and he wouldn't run from a third if it came his way. After all, he had to defend himself. More importantly, he was determined to protect his friends and comrades; he would save the people he loved. Killing was detestable, even when the foes were enemies. But Danny would not feel guilty or afraid while doing what was right.

Someone had told him that his mother had died while protecting strangers. That made him proud. His mom had shown him the way to live and die—*she* had done the right thing. It was a sacred duty that Danny had committed to honor. Maybe that was why as soon as the fighting had started, he had entered a fear-free zone, one where his training took over and his body moved on its own accord with lethal precision. But pain had arrived in full force after the first fight, when he'd found fallen family and friends on the battlefield. That pain was unbearable. Could he have saved them if he'd been stronger and killed their enemies faster?

Inside the lunchroom, Rayla turned to face the soldiers as the attitude in the room became more and more agitated. All eyes were on her, begging her to say the words and order Danny to fight at her side.

When she spoke, her voice filled the room. "If Kas wills Danny to fight for us, can any mortal stop that from happening?"

Nobody answered. Rayla let their silence settle the matter. "The Cayali shall follow his own path. There will be no more meddling with him."

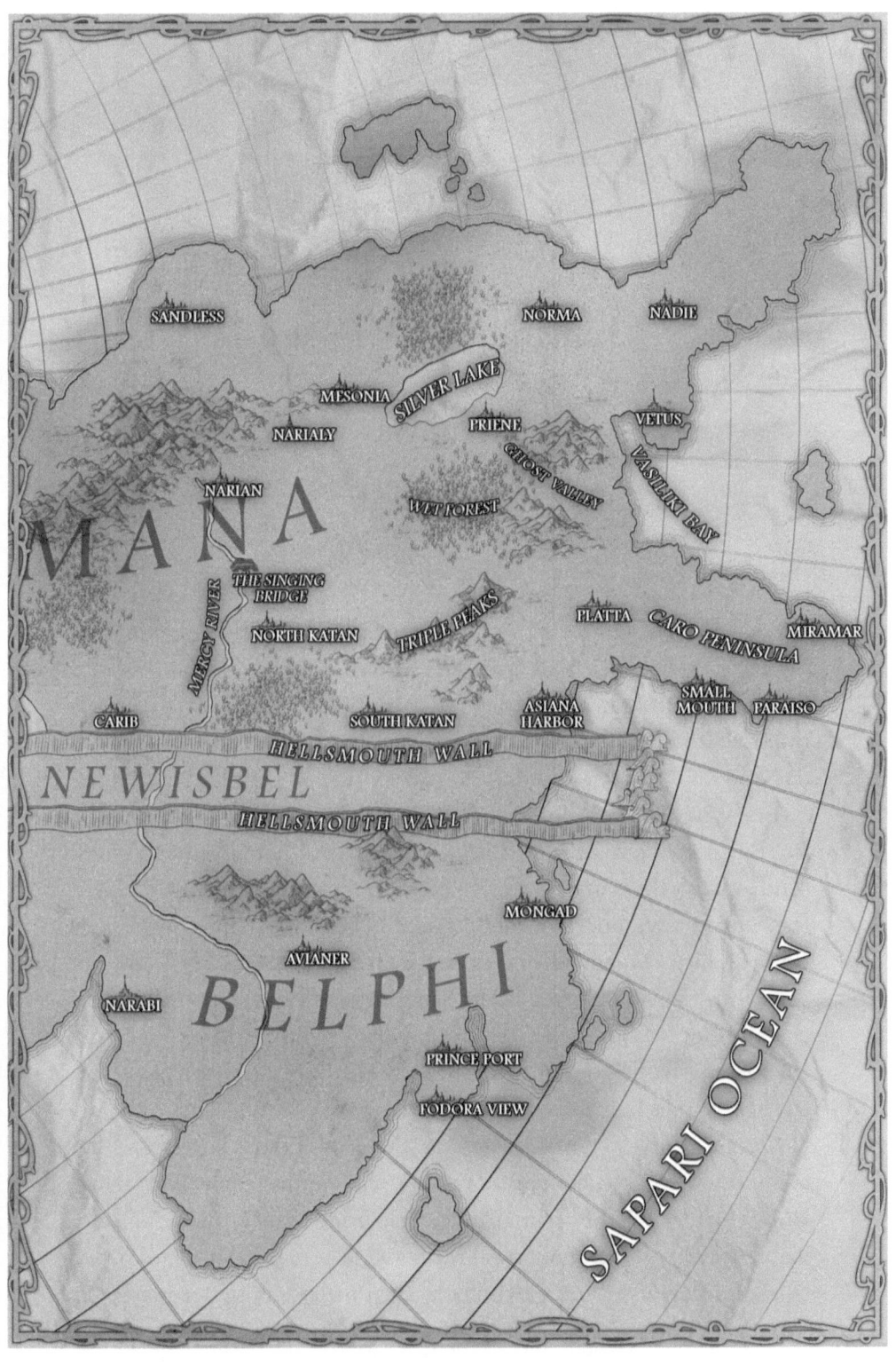

Chapter Thirty-Seven

11. Rayla

At first light, Rayla set out for the Singing Bridge alongside Generals Nereida and Gadai. Her party had grown considerably in the last twenty-four hours, with fifteen hundred additional Lathraias arriving at the Red Horn the previous day and boosting her elite unit to twenty-two hundred riders. Nereida's mounted soldiers numbered thirty-one thousand.

Rayla ordered Brigade Leader Analia and her seventeen thousand army soldiers to stay at the Red Horn. Speed would be crucial in the coming days, and foot soldiers simply couldn't keep up with trotting gatalans. Meanwhile, General Fabris and his eighty thousand seamen marching toward them from Asiana Harbor posed a clear threat—they could attack the Red Horn en route to the Singing Bridge, and Rayla couldn't afford to lose the garrison. It was her only stronghold and fallback. She had to secure it.

Rayla didn't plan to return to the Red Horn in defeat. She wanted to keep the momentum going; she *had* to reach the Singing Bridge before Viembo's men did. That bridge constituted the only viable way to cross into Central Kasmana, where she'd have plenty of space to maneuver and garrisons to turn to her cause. Crossing the bridge would level the playing field; it might even give her the advantage. General Viembo appeared to be well aware of that fact, considering that he was sending three of his armies to converge at the bridge.

Rayla and her party traveled north for a day and a half along the eastern shores of the Mercy River, stopping for a much-needed break when the morning of the second day came to an end. Once they resumed their journey, the entrance to the Singing Bridge would come into view in less than an hour.

As the short break was ending, Rayla approached General Gadai and Aia. "Any news from the missing scouts?"

Gadai cast his eyes down and shook his head softly.

Rayla's jaw tightened. That extinguished the last of her hopes. They should've been back by yesterday morning. She had no choice but to finally admit it: the missing scouts were dead or captured. The worst possible scenario was unfolding before her eyes.

"It could just be an advance party," Aia rushed to say. "We could take them out and still cross the bridge."

Rayla sighed. She wished that was a realistic scenario. Three sets of scouts had been dispatched on their way when she and her company had left the Red Horn. The group of scouts with the longest route had returned the previous night, bringing information about Fabris's army. The eighty thousand seamen had marched from the east to South Katan and then turned north, the scouts said. It would take Fabris's men seven days of brutal marching to reach the Singing Bridge, at which point they would be exhausted. On the plus side, apart from cutting off a potential southern retreat, the seamen posed no immediate threat.

The scouts Rayla had sent to the northeast had returned the previous morning with information about General Viembo. He marched from Mesonia straight to the Singing Bridge with sixty-five thousand army soldiers. The bulk of his army would arrive a day after Rayla's troops, but an advance party of five thousand soldiers would likely reach the bridge a few hours before Rayla did. By now, Viembo's scouts had probably informed him that Nereida had joined Rayla. He couldn't have known that when he'd sent out his advance party—he'd expected to meet twenty-two hundred Lathraias in battle. That advance group of five thousand soldiers was unlikely to engage Rayla now. But she *was* likely to engage them if they showed their faces, even if only to thin out the enemy.

The true concern came from the scouts Rayla had sent to gather information on the troops coming from Ionia. Fifty thousand Ionians marched from Central Kasmana, aiming to block the western side of the Singing Bridge and take up favorable positions. If they had already arrived on the other side, the bridge would be a bottleneck, with any rider daring to enter the bridge being slaughtered before they could possibly reach the other end. Even a small advance party would be able to inflict catastrophic losses from such a favorable position.

And now Gadai was telling Rayla that the scouts she'd sent to check on the Ionians hadn't returned. That meant the scouts had either been killed or captured. It also meant that an advance party— or worse, the entire Ionian army—could have already taken up unassailable positions on the other side of the bridge.

"What about you, my eken? Do you have better news?" Gadai asked, referring to the reason Rayla had visited the rear.

She bit back a sigh. "Unfortunately, no. Most of the gatalans look exhausted after the intense travel of the last few weeks. A few don't, but we certainly can't break into a gallop as a cohort—we have to maintain our current pace or risk losing the majority of the gatalans."

Aia frowned. "If Central Kasmana is out of play, should we go straight to Narian? Even trotting, we'd avoid a skirmish with the bulk of Viembo's army."

Rayla let out a hissing breath. "I'll visit the vanguard and talk to Nereida, but you're right—we can't cross the bridge now. Mobilizing the Ionians was a good move by Viembo. We'll take a peek as we ride by the bridge just to be sure though. The Ionians couldn't possibly hide fifty thousand soldiers. If we spot them, we'll move to plan B and ride north toward Narian. Our hopes would then rest with Captain Quecia joining our cause."

* * *

Rayla didn't know what she was going to do about Danny. The Ionians cutting off access to Central Kasmana had changed everything. Only a miracle could fix his situation now, frankly. Unless the missing scouts suddenly appeared and said the Singing Bridge was clear to cross, Danny would be forced to delay leaving for Torinth. How would he react to such news? With anger? Danny was a teenager, after all, and he just wanted to find his dad. The whole situation was unfair to him—far too many people were expecting incredible feats from the boy.

Rayla's brain scrambled to find a logical explanation for her troops' behavior. Word of the Cayali had spread like wildfire among her soldiers. Most hadn't seen him in action, but they still felt awe toward a fifteen-year-old boy they didn't know. Rayla shook her head. Her soldiers were fearsome warriors, willing to risk their lives for her, yet they seemed desperate for a symbol—they were grasping at reasons to hope that somehow everything would be all right.

Part of her understood that desire. The odds were stacked high against them; dying was more likely than succeeding. Another part of her felt guilty. Was it her fault Danny found himself in this predicament? By now, Viembo's men knew about him, surely. Some of them would shoot Danny on sight; others would kneel before the first Cayali in four centuries.

Danny would've been better off if Rayla hadn't asked him to accompany her. She had inadvertently put the boy in danger—within hours of him joining her, her enemies were throwing rocks and shooting arrows at him. Was she being selfish when she approached a child prodigy who'd shot down a gavian right in front of her? Rayla sighed. She had sincerely liked Danny from the first moment she met him and had wanted to help him by giving him a saddle. She also wanted him to make it to Torinth and find his long-lost father. But now all of her good intentions may have doomed the boy.

Reality butted into her thoughts. "Hey, Danny," Aia said with a smile. Rayla turned to see the Cayali trotting their way.

"Kas's peace," Danny said once he was in front of them. Rayla nodded. His manners had become more conventional as of late—he'd even stopped calling people ma'am. Thankfully.

"Kara looks quite lively," Aia said to Danny.

"She's one of the few not-exhausted exceptions I mentioned earlier," Rayla agreed.

Danny beamed. "Thanks to Cael! He's been feeding her well at night—she's getting extra rest because she doesn't have to hunt." He chuckled. "I'm worried she's getting spoiled. At this rate, she'll expect me to hunt for her once Cael is no longer around."

Rayla frowned. That comment probably meant Danny expected to be on his way as soon as they reached the Singing Bridge. "Listen, Danny, I need to apologize—" she started to say, but then she heard, "Up, up, up, up," coming from the vanguard.

Each rider repeated "up" once in a hushed voice. As the word rippled to them, Rayla and everyone around her whispered "up" once. All of the riders mounted their gatalans after repeating the word, Rayla and Aia included, and soon the whole company was on the move.

Rayla angled Kaistan toward Danny; Aia moved to ride at his other side. "I need to apologize to you, Danny. You won't be able to cross into Central Kasmana today. I truly am sorry, but trying to cross would be quite dangerous."

"Oh, I know," Danny said nonchalantly. "Cael explained the situation last night when those scouts didn't return. My plan went up in smoke."

Rayla frowned again. She'd expected him to be upset.

"You're taking this quite well, Cayali," Aia said with raised eyebrows.

"Do you understand that your life is at risk?" Rayla asked, gripping her reins more tightly. "You'll be in the middle of a bloody battle if you stay with us." She paused, forcing her tone to remain even. "Then again, if you cross the bridge alone, Viembo's men will either kill you or force you to join them."

Danny's eyes turned hard. "I'll put an arrow into the skull of anyone asking me to fight against you or Aia. Don't get me wrong— bloody battles are scary. It's awful having to kill another person, even when they mean to kill you. But those rebels leave us no choice! We *have* to do what's right. We *have* to defend ourselves and the people we care about."

Aia smiled. "You'd put yourself at risk defending us?"

A tinge of sadness crept onto Danny's face. "My mother died protecting strangers. What would she have done for her friends?"

Rayla sucked in a breath, understanding him a bit better. "Sorry about your mom." Danny nodded at her.

"Just to be clear, are you saying you'll stay with us?" Aia asked.

"For the time being, yes. I can't cross the bridge anyway, right?"

Rayla looked down. This was her fault, and she didn't like that sense of hopelessness one bit. Danny would be in danger no matter what she did.

Raising his chin, Danny said, "Rayla, I'm sorry, but we've had this conversation already." She looked at him with surprise; it felt as if he'd read her mind. "You're a good person. I would never abandon people like you and Aia while your lives are in danger. I'll help you take care of these rebels." Danny nodded, seemingly satisfied. "It's the right thing to do."

"Praise Kas!" Aia shouted.

Rayla suppressed a desire to hug him. "That means a lot," she said softly. She was glad he wasn't upset, but still . . . Danny was risking his life again, without hesitation. To think that he was only fifteen years old! Then Rayla squinted. This was the second time Danny had called her enemies rebels. Why that word?

He didn't seem to be reading her mind any longer. "Hey, Aia, I actually came to ask you something," Danny said, turning to her.

Aia sat taller atop her gatalan. "Right now, Danny, I'll help you with *anything* you dare ask."

Rayla smiled. Aia's eagerness to help Danny reminded her of the mission she had entrusted to Rolan. She hoped his task of retrieving Cayacoa's bow and armor was going well. If the Cayali stayed with her, she could give him the armaments as soon as Rolan returned with them. She had no doubt that Danny would be able to do marvelous things with the original guacanari.

"I wish I had something cool to ask," Danny went on, "but I'm just curious about something."

"Go ahead—ask away about the *cool* stuff," Aia said with bright eyes.

"Why do they call it the Singing Bridge?"

Rayla almost shook her head. Danny was probably the only person in Kasmana who didn't know the reason.

Aia grinned at him; she was probably used to his peculiarities. "Oh, you'll see for yourself when we get there. Actually, you'll *hear* the reason in half an hour or so."

Danny leaned forward as if he were already straining his ears. "Hear what? Can you tell me? Knowing won't ruin it, I promise!"

Rayla smiled. Danny's burning curiosity made his ignorance endearing. "It's not easy to explain," she said.

Aia nodded. "Yeah, it's a bit weird . . ."

"Something happens with the sound of the rushing waters and an echo that somehow involves the bridge," Rayla half explained.

Danny opened his eyes wide. "A water echo?"

"I . . . don't know. But something about it produces an eerie sound."

"It's not eerie!" Aia said firmly.

Rayla chuckled. "Sorry, you're right. Some people find it relaxing, even spiritual."

Aia smiled. "It makes me sleepy after a while."

"Can you describe the sound?" Danny asked in a hushed voice.

Rayla tried. "It's like . . . like a group of women vocalizing, soulfully and continuously. Honestly, it would drive me mad after a few hours."

Danny gave a slight gasp. "Wow! I can't wait to hear it. I've never heard of any place that produces a sound like that."

"At least not in Neojoppa," Rayla said, nodding.

"What about the Mercy River? Why is it called that?"

"Oh, that's an entirely different story!" Aia replied, still grinning. "And a much more interesting one."

"It involved Cayacoa, actually," Rayla said. "And the reason he became the Great Caya."

Danny's eyes glowed. "Can you tell me? Please?"

Rayla smiled and went on to recount the legend of the Great Caya.

Kas's wrath had left them no choice—the Canyo people had been forced to abandon their ancestral homeland and cross the vast Sapari Ocean five hundred years ago when an unrelenting series of earthquakes and volcanic eruptions leveled their home, a magnificent island continent called Quinquella. Canyos paid dearly for their sins. There was no end to their suffering once the calamities started; their only remaining hope was to appease their god and do his bidding.

At first, Canyos didn't know why the event known as The End of the World had hit Quinquella harder than any other place in Palaios, triggering natural disasters that killed hundreds of thousands of Kasmanians. Children of all ages fell alongside elite soldiers, farmers, caciques, and gatalans. Centuries of cultural heritage were wiped out overnight, along with friends, families, neighbors, and livelihoods. Death and despair were all the Kasmanians knew.

With loss and anguish seared into the Canyos' minds, King-Priest Lazarus gathered the survivors and promised them that they would emerge from their ordeal even stronger. He asked for their forgiveness, acknowledging that he, as their king-priest, had failed them.

The almighty god Kas had punished their entire race for failing to spread his rule to other nations. All Canyos knew that they should have expanded his influence, but they'd erred and instead relished the abundance Kas had provided in Quinquella. They'd grown complacent, satisfied, and secluded, an existence that ultimately cost them more than they could afford.

The survivors didn't blame the king-priest—rather, they thanked him for lighting a candle in the darkness. They didn't resent their god, either. Any loving father disciplined his children, and Kasmanians had learned their lesson: from now on, they would spread Kas's rule throughout the world.

Their voyage across the ocean took eighteen months. Kasmanians brought along their religion, masonry knowledge, weapons, and gatalans. But by the time they arrived in Neojoppa, Kasmana was no longer recognized as a nation. Still, guided by their king-priest, the homeless race bonded into a single family. They shared a love for their god and a deep pride in their ancestral heritage. After arriving on the new continent, the warlike and highly organized Kasmanians enjoyed a renewed sense of purpose. For a century, spearheaded by their gatalan riders, they spread unchallenged from Neojoppa's east coast, taking over the Caro Peninsula and the Vasiliki Bay in a few short decades and then invading South and North Katan. During the next sixty years, Nadie, Norma, Priene, and Mesonia fell to the Kasmanian armies, who triumphed without suffering a single meaningful defeat. But when the Canyos built the Singing Bridge and threatened to cross into central Neojoppa, they encountered serious opposition for the first time.

Building that bridge triggered an alliance between Normania, Maraccia, and Naldora, the three kingdoms that occupied Neojoppa north of Hellsmouth. A forty-year-long war ensued, reshaping the continent and birthing the kingdom of Kasmana.

Normania was by far the largest of the three kingdoms when the alliance was founded four hundred years ago. Their army alone had numbers equal to Kasmana's—it was about seventy thousand strong.

Although Normanians had no gatalans, their territory included a clan of giants from the Carib village near the Great Elp Lake. Normanians called these giants Nephilim; the males were between nine and eleven feet tall.

Nephilim fought like beasts, wearing armor plates and swinging spiked maces in the heat of battle. Their long reach and tremendous strength negated the Kasmanians' gatalan advantage—anytime a dozen Nephilim fought alongside a Normanian army, they leveled the playing field. Fortunately for the Kasmanians, there was just one Nephilim village in the entire realm, meaning that even at their peak, only sixty giants could take up arms against Kas's children.

Thirty years into the war, a decisive battle took place along the west bank of the biggest river in Neojoppa, the one the Normanians called the Caribe River. The Nephilim' village was named after that same river. The Carib village went on existing after the war—albeit without the giants—but the river took on a new name.

Queen-Priestess Vetania crossed the Singing Bridge, followed by the bulk of the Kasmanian armies. She led them south for the pivotal showdown against the allied forces. Vetania allowed the opposing general to believe that he had outmaneuvered her by approaching her forces from the rear and pinning the Kasmanian armies between the Caribe River and Hellsmouth. Twenty-three Nephilim fought on the Normanian side; not surprisingly, the fierce battle went on for eight days in an apparent stalemate.

When the Nephilim appeared to be exhausted, the queen-priestess played her trump card: she called for her Lathraias to join the battle, and fourteen hundred midnight gatalan riders crossed the Singing Bridge, planning to attack and decimate the enemy's rear. But the Normanians were waiting for that maneuver and played their own trump card. They had reserved twenty-eight Nephilim and two thousand Naldorian soldiers to wait for the Lathraias and ambush them as they exited the Singing Bridge.

It should have been a massacre. The largest cluster of Nephilim ever assembled, supported by a small army, should have crushed the elite Lathraias. Afterward, the victorious forces should have joined the Normanians in finishing off Queen-Priestess Vetania downriver.

But amid the Lathraias crossing the Singing Bridge rode an eccentric new recruit from Mesonia. His name was Satsani. The clean-shaven twenty-one-year-old wore unusual armor decorated with gold stripes on every joint and edge—a family heirloom, he had said. Satsani wielded a matching recurve bow, heavier and larger than anything ever seen before in the Kasmanian arsenal. He called his bow guacanari, and no one else could shoot straight with it. Satsani shot larger and heavier arrows that were capable of piercing through plate armor.

When the Nephilim ambushed the Lathraias, Satsani ambushed the Nephilim, shooting arrow after arrow at the oversized targets. From three hundred yards out, he missed not once. Satsani killed the whole lot before the giants' long maces could strike a single midnight gatalan rider.

The massive bodies tumbled one after another into the Caribe River, the giants' blood flowing into the wide stream and tainting the water. The Canyos chanted, "Divine Bow!" over and over in their aboriginal language. Their celebrated hero was no longer Satsani—he was Cayacoa, the Great Caya.

During the ensuing battle against the Naldorian foot soldiers, one of the few Lathraias casualties fell into the river. Her body traveled downstream, floating on a river of Nephilim blood. Hours later, the Normanian armies fighting downriver saw the Lathraias corpse first. They cheered at the auspicious sign, praising their prophets and waiting for the victorious Nephilim to join them and finish the job. They mocked the deflated, trapped Kasmanians for two days, telling them to look at the river and ask for mercy.

But when the ground shook two days later, it was midnight gatalans that rammed the Normanian rear, led by a golden Lathraias. He galloped alongside the river in front of the pack, wielding the glittering guacanari and slaying the remaining Nephilim. And he showed them no mercy.

* * *

Rayla finished telling her story as the three of them reached the vanguard. The sun had reached its highest point in the sky; soon, the Singing Bridge would come into view.

"Shooting from three hundred yards out!" Danny said, shaking his head. "That's unbelievable accuracy!"

"You can do it, too, with a guacanari," Aia told him.

Danny gave her a doubtful look. "I don't know, Aia. Maybe I can shoot an arrow that far with the right equipment, but I'm not sure about hitting the target . . . If it's stationary, maybe?"

Rayla reached over and slapped his back. "I have confidence in you, Danny. You're a Caya!"

The boy opened his mouth to protest, but before he could speak, General Nereida trotted closer and joined them. She rode her orange-furred gatalan, a smaller-than-average cutie named Celina. Rayla smiled at the sight of her. She'd always liked the undersized Celina very much. Somehow, that gatalan exuded the same mystical elegance as her master did.

Nereida smiled at the three of them and pointed at the curving road ahead. "The ears appear first."

They looked ahead and fell silent. Two massive gatalan statues that guarded the Singing Bridge's eastern entrance rose into view above the trees, the sun shining furiously on the gilded ninety-foot-tall statues. In the background, the wind brought the murmur of rushing waters into their ears.

"Wow!" was all the boy could say. He was staring at the statues with wide eyes, his lips frozen in an O-shape. He would have to step onto the bridge to hear the water sing, but right now, he seemed captivated by the statues.

Rayla smiled, filled with pride as she thought of the Kasmanian builders who had created the gatalan statues. She wanted to tell Danny about the carved gatalans that welcomed Canyo ships in Vasiliki Bay—those dwarfed the ones now before his eyes. And she wanted to add that sculptures of Cayacoa greeted travelers on the other side of the Singing Bridge. But she never got the chance to say any of it.

"Queen-Priestess Kalaria ordered the gatalan statues to be coated with a thin layer of gold," Nereida said to Danny with a chuckle. "History said she did it to honor Cayacoa's golden armor, but everyone knows the real reason: Kalaria loved orange-furred gatalans."

Danny glanced at Aia's pursed lips and burst out laughing. Then he stopped suddenly and wrinkled his brow. "What's that?" he asked, pointing ahead past the bridge.

Rayla looked while Nereida lifted her hand. The entire company stopped. Beyond the cobblestones that paved the entrance to the bridge, large wooden posts had been driven into the ground at equal intervals. They were about nine feet tall and two feet in diameter and only interfered with the road to the north. Rayla gauged the spaces between the posts. They were wide enough to allow a gatalan passage, but still, the situation felt ominous. What in Kas's name was going on?

Rayla looked beyond the posts. Nothing else seemed suspicious. To the right, the road east was clear. To the northeast, the sloping ground turned into hills that rolled away out of view. And to her immediate left lay the wide and fast-flowing Mercy River.

Rayla frowned. An ambush from the right flank was possible, but unlikely. Viembo's advance party was only five thousand strong—it would be suicide for them to attack over thirty-three thousand gatalan riders. Even with equal numbers, gatalan riders were much better fighters than army soldiers, gatalans or not.

Then, without any warning, Danny reached for his bow, and Kara broke into a full gallop straight ahead.

"Danny!" Aia yelled. The boy didn't look back.

Rayla clutched Kaistan's reins but subdued the urge to chase after Danny. Everyone would follow her if she did, and whatever Danny was going after could be a trap. What in Kas's name was he thinking? He was breaking so many rules by rushing ahead like that! Rayla's eyebrows drew together. Danny had made himself a target by being so far ahead. Should she send Aia after him?

"Up the hill!" Aia shouted, pointing northeast.

Everybody looked. In the distance, a cluster of men were advancing, carrying two dozen logs toward the posts. Each piece of wood was so heavy that a group of five men could only carry one; the group struggled to keep moving forward on the sloping terrain. They were organized into six columns of four rows each.

"It's not an ambush!" Rayla exclaimed. "They're trying to block the road north!"

No doubt this was Viembo's advance party at work. The Ionian army had already negated access to Central Kasmana. If the emerging barrier in front of them were completed, its presence would force Rayla's company to either move east or spend time dismantling the roadblock. Both scenarios would be detrimental, but heading east and winding up in open ground was out of the question. The advance party likely hoped to delay Rayla long enough for Viembo's main army to arrive and pin her down while Fabris's men made their way from the south.

Up ahead, Danny looked at the bridge as he ran past it. Something inside held his attention for a few seconds.

"What the hell is the boy doing?" Nereida asked with impatience. She cast a glance back at the troops behind them. "Don't break formation!" she called out. "Wait for my eken's orders!"

Rayla could only imagine the expression on Danny's face—it was probably the same one he'd had during the fight near the Triple Peaks, when he'd looked as if an ancient warrior had taken over his body. Danny had saved her life that day. Should she trust him now?

Rayla glanced behind her. Thirty-three thousand riders watched Danny in complete silence, charging the air with their electric anticipation. Rayla felt the same excitement. Danny had broken all military rules by charging ahead on his own like that, but he was the

Cayali, touched by Kas. Rayla had no idea what she was about to witness.

She turned back to watch him. Kara ran like the wind, still heading straight ahead. Then, suddenly, she veered right, and she and Danny ran in parallel to the men carrying the logs up the hill.

Danny reached back into his quiver and then fired arrow after arrow in rapid succession, ten of them in all. The arrows soared into the air in two separate groups—they looked like two sets of five fingers slowly curving as they flew higher and higher up, the two sets finally spreading apart. He turned Kara around and rushed toward the bridge's entrance while the arrows were still aloft.

The first set of five arrows swooped down onto the men carrying the first log, hitting the group highest up on the hill. The arrows struck in rapid succession, piercing all five men in the ribs. They immediately fell, and the heavy log they'd been carrying thudded into the ground. It rolled down the hill, tumbling into the next group and taking out those five men. Their log rolled down too. The two logs smashed into the third row, then crashed into the fourth. In seconds, an entire column was wiped out.

Nereida gave a small yelp. "Praise Almighty Kas!" she said as murmurs grew amid the troops. "I can't believe my eyes!"

"That's a Caya," Aia said softly.

"Divine Bow!" someone shouted.

Danny kept rushing back toward the bridge as the second set of arrows neared its targets. The arrows bypassed the men carrying the log in the second column at the top of the hill, hitting the third one instead. The five men collapsed, and their log tumbled down the hill, taking down three other rows below them.

"Cayali!" soldiers began shouting at random.

Ahead of them, Danny stopped at the entrance to the Singing Bridge, sitting tall astride Kara. He looked straight ahead, his eyes piercing something on the bridge. Everyone fell silent.

The boy was so still that Rayla wondered if he was even breathing. Then he reached for more arrows and fired a dozen shots in rapid succession at targets no one else could see. He reached for a thirteenth arrow . . . but then waited. His shoulders relaxed, and he put his arrow back into his quiver. He stared a while longer before turning to look up the hill.

Four columns of men with their logs remained. They had all stopped, doubtless aghast at what had befallen their comrades, but a man atop an orange-furred gatalan gestured angrily, apparently ordering them to carry on with their mission.

"Aia!" Rayla shouted, about to order her mightiest lieutenant to lead the charge uphill. She could *not* allow Viembo's men to obstruct the road north now that Central Kasmana was out of play. That blockage would likely cost her troops thousands of lives.

But before Rayla could finish her command, Kara broke into a full gallop again. Rayla held her breath as the gatalan raced toward the men and Danny reached for an arrow. He fired a single shot. The arrow flew straight this time, hissing through the air, hungrily seeking its target. It struck the apparent commander in the back of the head; he slid off of his gatalan with the shaft sticking out from his skull and then rolled down the hill just as the logs had.

The men standing around him gawked at each other, then looked at Danny and the thousands of riders on the brink of charging them. They dropped the remaining logs and ran away, leaving the logs to tumble harmlessly down the back side of the hill.

Danny stopped galloping and turned back. The threat was over.

Thousands of gatalan riders erupted into victorious cheers. "Cayali! Cayali!" they chanted, lifting their swords into the air. Danny looked at Rayla. She lifted her sword and stabbed the sky, joining the chant.

Danny raised his bow in response. The soldiers' frenzy reached a fever pitch, their collective roar reverberating through the storied stones of the Singing Bridge. "Cayali!"

Chapter Thirty-Eight

9. Danny

Danny turned to face the gatalan statues as the chanting died down. The moment felt surreal. "Cayali! Cayali!" thousands of battle-hardened soldiers kept calling him. He couldn't stop smiling, surprised at how it felt to receive so much attention. He wished he had his phone with him—he would've snapped tons of selfies with the chanting Kasmanians in the background. He would have cherished the epic photos forever, immortalizing his on-top-of-the-world moment. Too bad electronics were a no-no during missions. He laughed, shaking his head. Something like this would never happen to him again, especially after he'd returned home.

He was so very, *very* glad he'd chosen to become a ranger. Coming to Kasmana was like traveling back in time; outlandish experiences were part of the deal. This superstitious frenzy over hitting bull's-eyes would've never happened in Newisbel.

Would his friends back home even believe him if he told them what had happened here? Castellana Loen would. Oscar Lockfield would find a way to spin this nice moment and make fun of Danny. Well, screw Oscar! Even though shooting arrows while astride a galloping animal wasn't as much of a big deal as the Kasmanians believed it was—that skill was useless in Newisbel—Danny had saved lives with his kinetic shooting ability in Kasmana. Here, it counted for something.

In any case, stopping those rebels from blocking the road north had been the right thing to do. "Well done, rookie," Eli would have said. Captain Randal Highthorn would've been proud of him for staying alert and spotting those rebels in time to stop them.

Danny smiled, remembering the sparkle in his grandpa's eyes when he'd told Danny that he was one of the best bowmen on the continent. It was nice to be the best at something. That made people around him proud. He wished his friends would likewise strive to become the best they could be at something. That would set the stage for their own special moments.

His musings were interrupted by Rayla spurring Kaistan toward him, Aia and Nereida following suit. All of them were grinning.

The chanting finally stopped, allowing the river's murmur to reach Danny's ears for the first time. He muffled a giggle. Now that his adrenaline had subsided, he remembered what awaited him when he stepped onto the bridge. He couldn't wait to hear it sing—that would be yet another unique experience.

Danny once again gazed up at the massive gatalan statues guarding the bridge's entrance. The sculptures were magnificent, and the bridge itself was equally impressive—it stretched for over nine hundred feet, sprawling across five stone arches, and it was wide enough to allow ten gatalans to cross it walking side by side.

Danny shook his head softly. At ranger school, the instructors had said the Sebes kingdom in Novusland had the best masons in Palaios, often telling students about fantastic Sebesian designs and tall spires. But those instructors hadn't ever been to Kasmana or seen the Singing Bridge. Whoever had erected this bridge could build anything.

Danny knew it firsthand. His second chosen career in Newisbel had been structural engineering. During his last year of prep school, he had amazed the instructors when he programmed millions of nanobots to coalesce into an arrow. That arrow had been smaller than usual, but now, he'd bet all of his credits that his nano-engineered arrow would've pierced through Nephilian armor. Cayacoa had nothing on him! If he'd kept working on it, Danny could've made an arrow powerful enough to punch a hole through a concrete wall. But that would've been useless, too, in Newisbel. There, it made more sense to program virgin nanobots to coalesce into buildings, bridges, and sophisticated tools and devices.

The trio reached him. "What's with the smile?" Nereida asked Danny. She wore one of her own. "Feeling proud of ourselves, aren't we, young man?"

Danny just grinned at her.

"Well done, Cayali!" Rayla said warmly. "That was much more impressive than shooting at melons dangling from sun sticks."

Danny gave her a coy smile. It was the same skill, but who cared? "Thanks, Rayla. I just did my job. Those rebels had to be stopped."

Aia snorted. "Your 'job'! Stop with the annoying modesty. Look around you—this moment isn't only yours, Cayali. Don't you dare diminish it! I'd crush your ribs with a bear hug if everybody wasn't looking."

Danny raised his eyebrows. There was a smile in Aia's eyes, but coming from her, a bear hug felt like a threat.

"Ladies!" Nereida called out, jerking her chin toward the middle of the bridge. "What's going on there?"

They looked. The bridge was empty except for a bizarre scene fifty feet away: six yoked oxen lay dead, with just a single arrow wedged between their eyes. Behind the oxen, large metal panels and supporting paraphernalia jutted straight up. The panels were high enough to shield standing men; their aggregated width blocked most of the bridge. Before the panel, six army soldiers lay crumpled next to the animals. They'd been killed by precisely shot arrows too.

Three pairs of eyes landed on Danny. He cleared his throat and straightened his spine. "An army of foot soldiers was crawling forward behind those shields," he explained. "I couldn't estimate their numbers properly, but I guessed that two thousand had entered the bridge already." He shrugged. "I took out the oxen pulling the panels—that stopped their advance. Then a dozen soldiers jumped out from behind the shields and ran toward me, but someone called them back. Six made it; six didn't. The whole group withdrew to their side of the bridge."

The three women looked at each other with hard faces. Danny remained silent. He felt like he had become momentarily invisible, as if the grownups around him had entered into a private discussion. The trio moved closer to the bridge's entrance, trailed by Danny. They craned their necks, looking at the western riverbank.

"Yeah . . . at least fifteen thousand," said Nereida after a moment. Danny opened his eyes wide. She meant the soldiers from Ionia, obviously, but he couldn't see a single one of them.

Rayla made a *hmm*ing sound. "The entire army is here. Over thirty thousand are farther back."

Aia nodded in agreement. "Those metal panels may have seemed like a good idea, but frankly, they're lucky that Danny stopped them. Many of them would've died as soon as we saw them nearing our end of the bridge."

Nereida tapped her fingers on her thighs. "Perhaps they were planning to rush at us with those panels on our south flank while the rest of them exited the bridge."

Aia shook her head doubtfully. "Even so, we're thirty-three thousand, and it's easy to loop arrows over those panels. The sheer number of corpses piling up would've made it hard for them to advance."

"If the panels were in play, the soldiers could've lifted their shields overhead to form a tortoise formation," Rayla pointed out. "But the bridge still would have become a bottleneck for the rest of them." She glared at it. "The same will happen to us if we try to cross. It's not a fight that can be won . . . Perhaps they wanted to delay us long enough for Viembo's men to finish their blocking maneuver."

Aia grunted in agreement as Nereida came closer and slapped Danny on the back. "In that case, this young man stole their thunder twice!"

"It's something he likes to do," Rayla said with a smile.

Aia shifted her weight atop her gatalan. "We should head for Narian right away. Thanks to Danny, we avoided the worst scenario, but we're still at a disadvantage here."

Rayla nodded. "Viembo didn't achieve *all* of his goals, but he scored a clear victory by blocking our way into Central Kasmana. He negated our best option."

"Now everything hinges on Captain Quecia," Nereida said. "And Laramie succeeding at whatever she's planning. Maybe. Only Kas knows what the heck she's doing in Central Kasmana."

"She said she'd bring Rayla a trump card," Aia said. "Laramie is not one to bluff about stuff like that."

Rayla raised an eyebrow at her lieutenant. "That's assuming the report about her crossing into Central Kasmana is true. The other seemingly plausible report about Laramie turned out to be a lie."

"True," Aia acknowledged. "But she has to be somewhere. When Rolan returns, he'll confirm whether or not she left the Unburnt Hills."

"If Laramie has indeed crossed the bridge, what in Kas's name is she doing in Central Kasmana?" Nereida asked. "It's not like she can recruit garrisons to join our side. That's not her forte."

Rayla lowered her head and sighed. "No, it's not. Corina could do it on her own, but I doubt that's what Laramie is doing."

With that, the three leaders appeared to be done talking. They turned their gatalans around and began to trot away, going back to their troops.

"Just give me forty seconds," Danny said to them. They stopped, and Danny guided Kara toward the bridge. He couldn't take a selfie or record a video, but he was *not* going to miss this opportunity.

Kara moved forward and entered the Singing Bridge. The

susurration of flowing waters beneath Danny gradually turned into a soulful song, filling his ears and his heart.

* * *

Their path to Narian took one and a half days as they traveled north and veered slightly away from the riverbank. The waters kept giving Danny goosebumps as he remembered his experience inside the Singing Bridge. The bridge had made him feel like he was surrounded by a chorus of tiny invisible women, thousands of them floating around him and singing directly into his ears. Perhaps they'd meant to say something, but he had no idea what they were telling him—they sang in an alien language. Yet, something had traveled within the sound, something peaceful. When he closed his eyes, their singing had permeated his skin, bathing him in warmth.

As they rode toward Narian, Danny kept thinking about it with a tingling sensation spreading in his belly. He couldn't fathom designing the impressive series of precise angles and arrangements that caused human ears to hear the river echoing as a song. The configuration of the hills surrounding the bridge, its size and height and every inch of its contours . . . all of it influenced the sounds and vibrations produced by the fast-flowing water underneath. There was no way Kasmanian masons could have set out to achieve such an effect—far too many variables were involved. It was equally astronomically improbable to have achieved such a bridge by accident. And yet the Singing Bridge stood. It was perfect—a genuine wonder in Neojoppa.

He remembered the brief conversation he'd had with Nereida when they first met inside the lunchroom at the Red Horn. She'd said that she substituted the word "divinity" with "perfection." Cast in those terms, the Singing Bridge was divine. At least subjectively. A dense mind like Oscar Lockfield's would call what Danny had so deeply enjoyed "noise."

The thought slapped Danny in the face: was he being dense like

Oscar? Rayla's troops kept calling him Cayali, the little Caya. Now he knew that meant "Divine Bow" in their aboriginal language. He had labeled the idea as being superstitious and primitive, but was it really so wrong? Wasn't his archery in fact nearly perfect? He pursed his lips. He was overthinking things. "Divine" was just a word that described an action he could do perfectly.

Then Danny shook his head. Divine *wasn't* just another word—it elicited a different set of emotions. Such words were hard to stomach for someone raised in the technologically advanced society of Newisbel. He'd worked hard at kinetic target shooting, but it wasn't as unique as the Singing Bridge. It wasn't divine. Any Kasmanian could shoot the way Danny did . . . *if* they could stop feeling awe about it and start to practice instead. That sense of awe was a barrier in disguise, and the Kasmanians' minds would not let their bodies achieve such mastery as long as they felt that way. The skill had to become mundane first—otherwise, they wouldn't even try.

Then Danny's eyes widened as another thought struck him. Perhaps divinity and perfection were nothing more than how people felt about stuff. His Kara was perfect, even if she had a flaw or two. Same for Castellana Loen. Danny nodded softly. *That* was what Nereida had meant when she'd said the tulips on Aia's table were perfect and radiating Kas's divinity. If Nereida had hated tulips, she would've never felt that way.

His shoulders drooped. He'd been obtuse in thinking that the Kasmanians were superstitious for believing in divine bows. He was an idiot. Rayla, Aia, Cael . . . they were great people, and the fact that they believed superb skills were a sign of Kas's blessing didn't change that. Danny could list worse views . . . like thinking oneself superior by judging the beliefs of others.

"You okay?" Aia asked. "You've been awfully quiet."

Danny twitched, startled. He hadn't noticed Aia joining him—he'd been so lost in his head that he'd forgotten his surroundings. Captain Randal would've slapped the back of his neck in disappointment.

The boy looked around. It was late afternoon already; thirty-three thousand gatalan riders were trotting toward Narian in one wide, long column. The terrain was sloping a bit. That reminded him of Oscar, who—weirdly—enjoyed biking uphill. Danny and Kara were a few hundred feet behind the vanguard, while Rayla, Nereida, and Gadai had moved to the front after the morning break. That new rule for Rayla never to ride at the front didn't last long.

"Sorry, Aia . . . Just been thinking."

Aia had accompanied the top brass all day; Danny had no idea how long she'd been riding next to him. She sat atop her midnight gatalan with a concerned look on her face. "You were so deep in your thoughts that I got curious."

"Sorry," he repeated. "Don't mind me much—I was trying to figure something out." He looked into Aia's eyes and smiled. It was clear that she cared for him just as Rayla did. Both of them were good people.

Musing about that made the thought nibble at him again: it didn't matter if Aia and Rayla believed in divine bows. That belief wouldn't matter much to Danny once he'd returned home, anyway. He should just be happy that these Canyos had found a Cayali. It was their experience, their reality. Who was he to take that away from them?

He nodded to himself. That was all that mattered to each person —how the experience felt to them in the moment. Experienced reality became one's truth. And nobody needed someone else's permission to feel the way they felt. Danny could imagine saying exactly that to someone like Oscar Lockfield.

"Let me know if I can help," Aia said to Danny. "I was a teenager once. It was long ago, but don't you dare repeat that last part."

Danny laughed. "I won't. Promise." He fell silent for a moment. "Hey, did you train under Nereida before becoming a Lathraias?"

Aia opened her mouth to reply, but just then, the riders ahead of them murmured, "Halt." Aia and Danny reined in their gatalans and repeated, "Halt," as the word echoed down the length of the column. Soon enough, everyone had stopped.

"Any idea what's happening?" asked Danny.

Aia wore a carefully controlled expression. "We'll find out soon enough. Sometimes it's nothing. We're close to the Narian garrison—maybe it's something to do with that."

That made sense, but it didn't comfort Danny. "Can we go to the vanguard and see?"

"No," Aia said sternly. "The command was to halt, and we're going to do exactly that." She sighed. "In general, Danny, you need a very good reason to disobey a valid order. You have to be absolutely certain that you possess critical information that the people in charge *don't* have and that it's something that would change their minds. Would you say that's the case now?"

Danny hunched his shoulders. "No. Sorry."

Aia reached out and patted his shoulder. "No need to be sorry. You didn't attend battle school; you're not a soldier. Nobody expects you to know these things."

"Thank you for making me feel better, Aia," he said, but his forehead remained wrinkled.

She half laughed, half sighed. "Oh, dear Kas! I'll answer your question about Nereida—maybe that'll distract you. The answer is no, she didn't train me. I joined the Lathraias straight out of battle school. Rayla did too. Why do you ask?"

He forced himself to relax in his saddle. "Well, I was thinking about something Nereida said when we first met. You were there. It was about divinity versus perfection."

"Ah! That's simple for us Canyos," Aia said with a smile. "It doesn't matter what you are—farmer, soldier, mason, cacique—if you achieve perfection in what you do, you're Kas's instrument. Divinity flows through you and into whatever you do for the benefit of others. When that happens, you're a blessing from the Almighty no matter your trade."

Danny's eyebrows went up. That was quite the thought—simple but effective. If they truly lived by that philosophy, their belief empowered Kasmanians to outperform the peoples of other nations.

Maybe it wasn't a coincidence that Canyos had conquered northern Neojoppa. According to what Aia just said, most of them strived to reach high standards in whatever they did to reach communion with their god.

"Kas's instruments," Danny murmured to himself. It surprised him to realize that religious dogma could be useful. He made a mental note to discuss the matter with Castellana and Rael. Even with Oscar over drinks. Danny could see Rael and Castellana bringing up interesting angles. Perhaps dogma *had* helped the Canyos, but Normos and Naldorians had religious views, too, and those hadn't helped them stop the Kasmanians. During prep school in Newisbel, the teachers had said that dogmas were like clothing for toddlers: they stopped fitting as society evolved and no longer provided good guidance for prosperous behavior.

"'Kas's instrument' sounds quite fancy, but I like it," Danny said.

Aia came closer and tousled his hair. She looked into his eyes and spoke in a neutral tone. "When someone reaches *your* level of proficiency, Danny, they're beyond being Kas's instrument. They become a fragment of the god."

Danny's eyebrows inched up even higher, but before he could reply, a rider came rushing toward them from the vanguard. "Lieutenant Aia, my eken!" she gasped when she halted in front of them. "The cacique requests your presence at the front at once. Please bring the Cayali with you."

Danny and Aia approached the front. Ahead, Rayla, Nereida, and Gadai sat atop their gatalans, talking to someone Danny had never seen before. The visitor wore a sky-blue uniform that reminded Danny of Brigade Leader Analia from the Red Horn, but this woman's uniform featured a brooch in the shape of gatalan claws. She rode an orange-furred gatalan, which meant she was an officer and likely held a higher rank than Analia. The visitor was in her mid-forties, with caramel skin, green eyes, and long, flowing black hair.

Another woman—a pure-blooded Canyo riding an orange-furred gatalan—intercepted Danny and Aia before they could reach Rayla. Frowning, she signaled for them to follow her. Danny hadn't met her before either, but Aia complied instantly with her request. He shrugged and trotted after them. The woman guided them to a position where they would be out of the newcomer's line of sight.

"Hi, Corina. Is that who I think it is?" Aia asked as soon as they stopped.

Danny recognized her name—Cael had said Corina was one of Rayla's best friends. Weirdly enough, she was also General Viembo's wife. One of the many horrible things about civil wars was that they pitted family members against other family members.

"Yes, she is," Corina said to Aia. "We were more surprised than you are."

Aia ran her fingers through her hair. "Praise the Almighty . . . This is either very good or very bad."

Corina tilted her head. "I'd say it's right in the middle."

Danny had to jump in. "I'm sorry to interrupt, but could you please explain to me what's going on?"

Corina turned to him. "Yes, of course, Cayali. My apologies. My name is Corina. We haven't met yet," she said, extending a hand.

Danny shook it. "Pleased to meet you."

"The honor is mine," Corina said with a smile. Right then, she looked just like Rayla except for the length of her hair and the color of her eyes. "The woman with Rayla is Captain Quecia," Corina went on. "She's the master of the Narian garrison—and right now, a vital potential ally."

"The Narian garrison has over sixty thousand army soldiers," Aia added. "It's one of the largest in Kasmana, behind the two garrisons in Mesonia and the one in Ionia." Danny nodded as Aia returned her attention to Corina. "Why is the captain here? Couldn't she have waited until we arrived at her garrison?"

Corina's expression turned serious. "She hasn't shared many details yet, but Captain Quecia did tell us that she had planned to meet us in battle when the sun rose this morning. She almost came here with her entire army."

Aia's face turned ashen. "That's pretty bad! If she were to fight us, we could manage a victory, but we'd suffer catastrophic losses."

Danny's throat bobbed. If such a scenario came to pass, Rayla's troops wouldn't be able to fend off the incoming wave of Viembo's men from Mesonia—not to mention General Fabris's forces or the Ionian army. Each of the three armies opposing Rayla already outnumbered her troops, and if Captain Quecia decided to support Viembo's men . . .

Corina nodded. "The situation is certainly dire. But something gave Captain Quecia pause." Her gaze settled on Danny. "She came alone and asked to meet the Cayali."

Danny jerked back. "Me! But why?"

Aia answered him. "More than likely, her scouts told her what happened at the bridge yesterday. I know you're only fifteen, Danny —and this isn't fair to you—but your presence and support for Rayla are quite significant."

Danny frowned. The situation was a bit too much. The cacique of the armed forces and the legendary General Nereida were here, yet a captain who commanded sixty thousand soldiers had come here to meet *him*? Sixty *thousand* soldiers!

"Why . . ." he began. Then he remembered what Rayla had said a few days back: half of Viembo's men would shoot at him on sight, and the other half would ask him to join them. "She came alone, so she isn't here to kill me. Is she going to ask me to join her?" The question sounded silly to Danny as soon as he asked it. Was there a third possibility?

Corina gave him a grim smile. "We'll find out soon enough." She tilted her head in the captain's direction. "Rayla asked me to give you a heads-up about what's happening. Nereida trained Captain Quecia years ago, and she's likely to still have some affection for her mentor. Rayla wants all of us to follow Nereida's lead."

"Understood," Danny said with a nod, doing his best to smooth out his expression. "I just have one more question. Captain Quecia's appearance is quite different from everyone else's. Is she a Canyo?"

"Of course she is," Aia said with hard eyes. "Don't you see the gatalan between her legs?"

"Yes, sorry. I . . . I just—"

"One of her grandparents was a Normo," Corina said.

Danny raised his eyebrows. "That doesn't matter, right?" He'd been taught that Normos and Canyos were mortal enemies, and according to the rebels who had killed Captain Randal and Farlie, that hadn't changed.

Corina wrinkled her brow. "Why *would* it matter?"

Danny hesitated and then smiled. He found her answer fascinating. Race didn't matter at all in Newisbel—back home, Danny had been a pure-blooded Canyo in love with Castellana Loen, a Normo, and nobody would have thought twice about it. But Canyos had fought bloody battles against Normos for centuries in northern Neojoppa. Still, though, some had intermarried once they'd stopped fighting, and other Canyo-Normo relationships had sprung up, driven mainly by commerce. Corina's answer seemed like a window into Neojoppa's future: what divided the two nations was artificial.

Corina nodded, accepting his silence as understanding. "Follow me," she said. The three of them trotted toward Rayla and her group.

As Danny and the others approached, Rayla gestured for her companions to form a semi-circle. The new arrivals completed it.

"Praise Kas, he's just a child!" Captain Quecia said in a husky voice, her eyes latched onto Danny. She turned to Nereida. "And you swear before Kas he is a Cayali?"

Nereida smiled, suddenly looking younger than Captain Quecia. "Witnessing what this young man can do is more impressive than hearing a thousand legends. I'm blessed to have seen his skills. The light of Kas shines through him, my dear. It warms the heart."

They all fell silent as Captain Quecia came closer to Danny, still looking at him intensely. She touched his cheek. Danny didn't flinch. He'd begun getting used to Kasmanian's touchy-feely society, and besides, the color of Quecia's eyes made him think of Castellana. Danny couldn't help smiling at her.

"Very well," Captain Quecia said in a commanding voice. She turned to Nereida and Rayla. "I won't fight against you, Cacique Rayla, but I can't join your cause. I won't apologize for that. I swore allegiance to General Viembo—he's my eken. A vow taken before Kas cannot be broken lightly."

Corina chuckled. "My husband swore fealty to Cacique Rayla, yet he rises against her out of greed."

The captain dipped her chin. "I understand, Lieutenant Corina. But my eken claims to have valid reasons for his actions. Cacique Rayla is accused of murdering King-Priest Altanarian, and that is a serious crime. My eken thinks his actions are justified—he says that Rayla is trying to evade judgment. I must give him a chance to prove his claim."

"I'm innocent, Captain, I swear it to Kas," Rayla said in a firm voice. "Corina is right—nothing but greed motivates Viembo. Same goes for Cacique Kameiros. It's only a matter of time before the truth comes out."

"I agree," Quecia said. "Time is key, and time is what I choose to give you. I won't raise my sword against a Cayali. But I must give my eken the opportunity to defend himself against your version of events. I cannot break my vow to him before he has done so. I know that's not what you wanted to hear, but I'm sure you can understand it."

Rayla sighed. "Unfortunately, I do."

"My child!" Nereida broke in. "Can you imagine the Almighty Kas raising the first Caya in four centuries to come to Rayla's aid if she were *not* telling the truth?"

Quecia shifted her weight atop her gatalan. "As I said, I won't raise my sword against him."

General Gadai finally spoke. "Captain Quecia, if I may. You are faced with a momentous decision. I'll be blunt. Denying us your aid could have catastrophic consequences. You're choosing to step aside, and, yes, that's better than trying to kill a Cayali. But will you sleep soundly tonight believing that you're following Kas's will by *not* helping us now?"

The captain lifted her chin and sat taller atop her gatalan. "Catastrophic consequences, you say? What tomorrow will bring is anyone's guess. All I can do right now is follow my conscience."

"What about following your heart?" Nereida asked.

Quecia held her proud posture for a few more seconds, but then she looked down.

Rayla sighed. "Let Captain Quecia be. As disappointing as her words are, I can't fault her for showing integrity. We wouldn't be in this position if Viembo had acted like her."

Quecia cleared her throat. "What do you plan to do now?" she asked Rayla. "It'd be hard for you to return to the Red Horn with General Fabris and the Ionians advancing from the south, and I don't see a good reason to go east."

Rayla gave a grim nod. "You're right. My last option is to continue north and take over the abandoned fortress of Narialy. I can defend it for months with a third of my current numbers."

Nereida smiled. "The Narialy Fortress . . . I was there. The last major battle in Neojoppa was fought within her walls. If I remember correctly, you were there, too, Captain Quecia."

"Yes, I was," she said quietly. "I was a lieutenant in your army."

"Then we both witnessed greatness that day, didn't we?" Nereida asked rhetorically. "Kas's light shone through Rayla when she defeated the Maraccians holed up inside that fortress. No one had ever taken Narialy before my eken did it five years ago. Rayla ended the war."

Quecia's eyes softened. She nodded at Nereida and then turned to Rayla. "Cacique Rayla, General Viembo may not breach the fortress as you did, but don't you fear a long siege?"

Rayla met her gaze evenly. "At the moment, all I can do is buy time."

"You believe that time is on your side, don't you?"

Rayla nodded. "When you woke up this morning, you planned to meet me in battle today, didn't you? Look at us now; see how much things have changed in just a few hours."

Quecia bowed her head. "You have my respect. I pray for the time when Kas's truth is revealed." She bowed a second time to Nereida and then turned her gatalan, ready to leave.

"Excuse me, Captain Quecia," Danny said suddenly. Everybody froze. Rayla's face turned impassive, but Nereida's eyes seemed bigger than usual. Danny gave them a slight smile. "I apologize if I'm speaking out of turn," he said to Quecia.

The captain turned to him. "Not at all, Cayali. I'm eager to hear anything you have to say."

The captain's eyes were so strikingly similar to Castellana's! Danny forced himself to focus on the matter at hand. "I understand that you won't break your vows. Like Rayla, I wish more people were like you. But I want to ask something of you, if that's okay."

She nodded. "As long as it doesn't involve swearing fealty to Cacique Rayla, I will consider what you ask. You have my word."

He bobbed his head briefly. "I appreciate that. I wish to ask for provisions, Captain, as much as you can give me. I need lots and lots of arrows, food, blankets, and general supplies. I understand that the fortress has been abandoned for a while, so I'll need construction materials to patch holes here and there. I have thirty-three thousand friends coming with me, and I'd like to keep them fed and warm for as long as possible. Would you please help me, Captain Quecia?"

A long silence ensued; a few people held their breath. Captain Quecia took a while to consider Danny's request. Then she let out a long sigh. "It's a fair compromise. If Cacique Rayla is guilty, a few weeks' worth of supplies won't matter. But if she's innocent, they may make all the difference. I will help you, Cayali."

"Thank you so much!" Danny said, almost squealing with happiness. He noticed a half smile on Aia's lips.

The captain looked at him with fondness. "No, I must thank you, Cayali. Fulfilling your request eases the storm in my heart."

"In that case, Captain, I have a request of my own," Rayla said. Quecia turned and looked at her. "The Narian garrison has a large archery field, correct?" Quecia nodded. "I wonder if you have a guacanari bow somewhere." Rayla tilted her head in Danny's direction. "I have someone with me who's eager to try one."

Chapter Thirty-Nine

10. Anaya

Marko's real home was amazing! First of all, it was hidden underground, and Anaya was in on the secret. She loved that so much that she giggled whenever no one was looking.

Then there was the elevator. At night, Anaya pretended it was a toothless monster that tried to swallow her aboveground . . . but she was so cute that the monster changed its mind after a few seconds, opening its mouth and letting her into Marko's real home as an apology for its initial rudeness. During the day, the elevator was a magical closet. The doors closed above ground and transported Anaya to a new world.

And that was just the beginning; the elevator wasn't even half of it.

Stuff Anaya had never seen before filled the underground home. Marko had called it "technology." He had lots of devices with awesome colors and names, like *toaster*. His real home was like a rainfall of candy. To top it off, Marko baked something that he called cookies and kept them in a glass jar on the counter just for her. Cookies were the best thing ever!

But training with Asa was a different story. The first two weeks were a bit rough.

Her lessons began the same night she rode the elevator for the first time. She wanted to learn right away, because someone strong was coming to steal Dian from her. Anaya would *not* let that happen! She'd teach that mean man a lesson.

"I'll use words you know as much as I can," Asa said when the training began. "Sometimes I'll use new words though; that's important too. Let me know if you need me to explain something I said in a different way."

Asa started by explaining the two types of Dian in Anaya's life. Much of it was confusing. First, there were bionanobots, the kind of Dian that lived *inside* Anaya. They were so small that the human eye couldn't see them, and Anaya had millions and millions of them, Asa told her.

Anaya had always thought Dian was invisible, but Asa made things sound so weird. He said bionanobots replaced brain cells and nervous system cells, giving rise to a new species of humans he called *Homo ciberus*. Anaya cringed at the sound of those weird words and was glad when Asa moved on from the subject. All Anaya cared about was that Dian lived inside her—that was how she felt the goddess, and that was her truth.

"You're one in a hundred million," Marko said. From his smile, Anaya assumed being one in a hundred million was a good thing, but she wasn't entirely sure.

Asa told her that the second type of Dian was nanobots. They were invisible, too, at least until they gathered to form a material he called *fasma*. Anaya had billions of nanobots. They were self-replicating—that way, they could replace any damaged ones. Nanobots lived *outside* Anaya's body, and they could gather into anything, like her suit.

Anaya frowned at that. Marko chimed in and asked her to imagine sand on a beach. Anaya could never count all of the grains of sand, but she could play with the sand and make sandcastles. The wet sand could take on as many shapes as Anaya could think of. The same thing happened with her nanobots: although she had a finite number of them, she had enough to make a battle suit, plus they could take on other shapes too.

Anaya smiled for the first time since the conversation had begun. She liked Marko's explanations much better.

Asa took over the lesson again. When nanobots coalesced, they formed fasma. Anaya controlled the fasma thanks to the first Dian, the one that lived inside her. Anaya's nanobots were an extension of her body—they responded to her subconscious just like her arms and legs did. But her subconscious prioritized survival and safety, so her suit would appear on its own if she was in danger. When it did form, the suit took up most of Anaya's nanobots, limiting what else she could do.

Anaya glanced at Marko. She wished he'd offer his own explanation, but Asa continued. "With remote surveillance, you send out nanobots, and they gather into tiny surveillance cameras. You see what they see because they're part of you."

That made Anaya frown harder. "I don't like the word nanobots! It's just weird."

"What would you like to call them?" Asa asked.

There was clearly only *one* answer to that. Why would Asa ask something so obvious? "Dian's power," Anaya said, reaching for the cookie jar.

"I see. And what about your bionanobots?"

"That's easy too! If they live inside me, they're Dian."

"Understood. Dian and Dian's power. We have a deal, my darling friend."

Anaya smiled and bit into her cookie. She had won this round.

"Dian is always inside," Asa resumed. "But Dian's power is outside, and it can travel up to fifty miles away from you. Do you understand how far that is?"

Anaya shook her head.

"Well, why don't you test it out tomorrow?" Asa suggested. "Once you learn how to do remote viewing, you can use it to see how far Dian's powers can travel."

Anaya nodded. That sounded like fun! She could sit in the egg chair tomorrow morning and search for Albi while drinking cocoa. She missed her albino gatalan so much.

Asa went on to teach Anaya how to see remotely. She soon discovered that practicing was much easier than listening. Marko compared remote viewing to the kitchen monitors, and that helped a lot.

At first, Anaya had to close her eyes to see her own personal live feed, but she mastered it eventually and could see remotely while still keeping her eyes open. It was the same as hearing two sounds at the same time, except with images instead of audio. She deployed her remote surveillance consciously, but her subconscious chose which image or sound took precedence in her awareness. After a few weeks, seeing remotely became second nature.

"Remote surveillance occupies a lot of Dian's powers," Marko told her during one of her learning sessions. "Be mindful not to send them too far out. If you fall into a trap, you'll have less defensive power until those nanobots return."

Anaya frowned. That was a surprise. Dian could do whatever she wanted—the goddess didn't have any limitations. But Anaya trusted Marko. He did say that she had a finite amount of nanobots. Perhaps Anaya was the one who had to do something, like pray the way her mom had taught her. "Can I increase Dian's powers?"

"Yes, you can. And you will," Asa said. "When you grow Dian's presence *inside* of you, you'll increase Dian's powers *outside* of you too. Right now, you have about forty percent of Isbel's original bionanobots. That limits the amount of external nanobots you can control. Even if they were swirling around you right now, you wouldn't have the means to assimilate and use them."

Part of that made sense to Anaya—more of Dian inside meant more of Dian's power outside. "How can I grow Dian's presence inside?"

"You don't need to do anything—it'll happen on its own," Asa answered. "Isbel's bionanobots were dispersed throughout Palaios when she died. Over time, they gathered in small pools around the planet. When a pool becomes large enough, they rove, looking for a host. That's what caused the terrible plague called the Demuse." He paused and exchanged glances with a somber Marko. "Bionanobots have no awareness that they're deadly to little children, that they've caused terrible tragedies. And when they fail to find a host, they disperse again, starting the cycle all over."

Anaya didn't know what the crickets Asa was talking about, but the doll continued. "Anyway, Isbel's bionanobots are attracted to you now. They'll find you on their own and become part of you. You won't notice a thing unless a big chunk of them finds you all at once."

"What will happen then?" Anaya asked, frowning.

"It'll be uncomfortable if there are too many. You'll feel like you're coming down with the flu—you'll be dizzy and nauseous, and maybe you'll develop a fever. But don't worry! All you'll need to do is rest for a few days, and then you'll be stronger than ever."

Anaya flinched. "That happened to me already. It was awful," she said, remembering when she almost died in Ivory Village. She didn't want to go through *that* again.

"Oh, it won't be like the first time, Anaya. You'll be fine, I promise."

Marko walked closer to them, his eyebrows knitted together. "Asa, I think you need to make this information a bit more digestible for Anaya. I know she's special, but let's remember that she's only seven years old."

Asa's eyes moved to Marko. "You're underestimating her, Marko. Anaya is *Homo ciberus*. She's remarkably more intelligent than any child you've ever met before."

Marko shook his head. "Forgive me, Asa, but she seems to struggle with the deluge of information coming from you."

"That's because we need to increase Anaya's vocabulary. Her mind hasn't enjoyed proper stimulation, that's all. New concepts will unleash her reasoning capabilities. She'll be alright. Trust me—her mind is like fertile soil. If we don't plan good seeds, it'll grow nothing but weeds."

Anaya scratched her head, wondering what "vocabulary" meant. Was it like the amount of clothing she owned? She wouldn't mind increasing that, but the reference to fertile soil confused her. Although it probably had to do with growing potatoes. Or beets.

Marko sighed. "Anaya, once you've increased Dian's powers, you can ask her about anything. She'll have access to a lot of information, and she'll find answers for you. You'll be surprised. All you have to do is ask about anything; she'll do the rest."

"Oooh," Anaya said, bringing a finger to her chin. What Marko said made sense. When Anaya came down the Northern Mountains alone, she had wanted to know the way to Palaumone, and Dian had given her the answer. Anaya had known where to go and had walked in the right direction. The same thing had happened when she'd needed places to spend the night—Dian had guided her to those places too. And now Marko was telling her that she could ask Dian about other things. Anything!

An idea came to her: to surprise Marko, she'd ask Dian how to make a cheesecake, and then she'd bake it herself. That would be fun. She couldn't wait to see the look on his face!

"I want to increase Dian's power now," Anaya said, reaching for another cookie.

"No worries, my darling friend. It will happen on its own," Asa said. "And I'll tell you something else: once you have seventy-eight percent of Isbel's original bionanobots, you'll unlock a skill that will make you unstoppable. I hope to still be here to see it happen."

"What skill?" Anaya asked, crumbs from her cookie drifting down between her fingers.

Asa came closer and hovered before her within hugging distance, but Anaya wasn't in the mood. "It wouldn't make much sense now. I'll explain it once you've mastered the skills you already have," he told her.

Anaya pouted but said nothing. Asa came even closer. "Tomorrow morning, Anaya, I'll teach you how to fly."

Episode Eleven

Chapter Forty

10. Danny

Danny rode in the middle of the column for the second day in a row. After leaving the Narian garrison, Rayla, Aia, and Nereida had ridden close to the vanguard with Corina and Gadai nearby. Danny had wanted to ride with them, but Rayla gave Cael the responsibility of looking after the boy's safety, and Cael had responded by confining him to the safest possible spot in the caravan. Cael surrounded him with a convoy of fearsome-looking Lathraias, all of whom took the job of protecting Danny too seriously.

Danny didn't mind it the first day, but by the second day, his face had turned into a perpetual frown. Rayla had probably thought Danny would have fun with Cael, but instead his friend had morphed into a warden. "This is a bit much, don't you think?" Danny complained when his guards wouldn't let him move a bit up the line to chat with Corina. They kept him boxed in, giving him nothing but headshakes. No one aside from them was allowed near the Cayali, not even during breaks. Danny couldn't even relieve himself in private. He wanted to keep up his manners, but he couldn't stop himself from glowering at Cael and the Lathraias. His freedom had been taken away, dammit. Danny hated it.

The only saving grace was that the road toward Narialy had turned into an impressive scenic route, with green hills dwarfed by snow-capped mountains creating a kind of magical background that Danny had never seen in Newisbel. Patches of cherry blossom trees were interspersed with tulip fields and orange-tinged wild roses. Green meadows rolled away in the distance, hosting Maraccian hurrs and flocks of wheeling birds. Danny could've blissfully stared at the scenery for hours . . . but his jailers didn't allow him to slow down his pace at all, and it was impossible to get a decent peek at his breath-taking surroundings when he was surrounded by tall, robust riders wearing black armor.

Toward the end of the second afternoon, Danny's frustration reached its peak. What was the point of risking his life as a ranger if he couldn't enjoy good experiences along the way? It was his rightful payoff for enduring primitive conditions, and they had taken it away. Curse words slipped loudly from his tongue, but no one understood the meaning of terms like "dickheads" or "ass-kissers." Yet when Kara began growling and hissing at everybody, the jailers finally under-stood the Cayali's ill mood. They expanded the circle, giving him a little breathing room. Then Rayla came to ride next to him an hour later, just as the Narialy Fortress became visible on the horizon.

"Sorry about the asphyxiating security, Danny," she said. "It went overboard. I can imagine how it must have felt."

Danny looked down and didn't answer, feeling childish. Despite having three armies on her heels, Rayla was still taking the time to comfort him. Was he being an idiot? He didn't need the computing power of the now-infamous infinity intelligence processor to under-stand Rayla's intentions. After witnessing what had happened with Captain Quecia, Danny realized "the Cayali" was more dangerous to General Viembo than Rayla herself was. Killing Danny would prove he wasn't divine, and that would probably break the troops' morale, alienate Rayla's allies, and end the war. Danny had become a highly valuable target in a high-stakes conflict. Worst of all, he was easy to kill—any old arrow would do the trick. It made sense that Rayla was taking extra measures to protect him. Still, she didn't have to go out of her way to comfort him. Danny felt ashamed and grateful at the same time.

They rode in silence for a while as the Narialy Fortress came more into focus. It was nothing like the two garrisons Danny had seen so far. This fortress rose fifteen stories high and had been carved into a cascading-stairs design that descended from two mountains and formed a vertex. Most of the high walls had been chiseled from the original mountains. Flat land rolled out from the front of the fortress, making enemy troops' movements visible from three miles away. It was a masterpiece of engineering.

Danny leaned forward, curiously contemplating the front gate. Two massive horizontal iron cones jutted out of its sides, forming a three-hundred-foot-long bottleneck. The cones resembled gigantic lances. Danny imagined how easy it would be to block the entrance to the narrow corridor framed by the cones, trapping storming armies inside and then slaughtering them. From every angle, the Narialy Fortress was daunting.

Danny glanced at Rayla. He didn't want to be ungrateful, considering that she'd come to see him despite everything else that was happening. He fumbled for something to say. "That looks formidable," he finally commented. "Why did the Kasmanian army abandon it?"

"The location," Rayla answered. "It's not efficient. It worked for the Normanians when Narian was the capital, but now it's too far from anything of importance. The garrisons in Mesonia and Narian enjoy better strategic locations, so they ended up replacing Narialy."

Danny nodded. "Oh, that's right . . . Cael mentioned that the Narialy Fortress is much closer to Mesonia than the Singing Bridge is. Viembo made a mistake in leading the Mesonian army to the bridge."

"I disagree with you," Rayla said, still looking straight ahead. "All a general can do is make the best decision in the moment based on what they know and what resources they have. Viembo had no way of predicting that a Cayali would be on my side. Coming after me at the bridge almost worked—Viembo could've landed a decisive blow if he'd managed to delay me long enough. And then he got unlucky a second time when Captain Quecia stepped aside. He could've won this war then too." She finally looked at him. "But Viembo knows about you now. There are no more surprises."

Danny fought the urge to drop his gaze. "I guess you're right."

Rayla faced forward again and shrugged. "He doesn't need to rush here."

Danny frowned. "How come?"

"First, we're not going anywhere—Viembo can take his sweet time coming up with a plan to breach the fortress." Even from the side, Danny saw her eyes narrow. "The main features of Narialy are well-known. Viembo needs to figure out a gadget or a strategy that would give him an advantage. If I were him, I'd go to Mesonia to grab more soldiers and brainstorm something while the Ionians and the seamen prevented me from doubling back to the bridge."

Despite their grim situation, Danny chuckled. "Looking at those gigantic lances, a frontal attack would be suicidal. Viembo won't go for the gates."

Rayla nodded. "They're called broilers."

"The two cones?"

"Yes. You'll see when we get closer. They have holes in their interior faces called vents. Defenders funnel oil through the broilers and then set the oil on fire. Flames spew from the vents into the corridor, and the scorching heat burns anything between the broilers to a crisp."

Danny bit back a gasp. "Holy crap!" That would be a *horrible* way to die!

"But they consume a great deal of oil," Rayla pointed out in a matter-of-fact tone. "Viembo would probably realize that I wouldn't intend on using the broilers more than once."

Danny nodded. "Even so . . . He won't find volunteers for that first burst. And the bottleneck isn't any more appealing." Danny scratched his head, thinking about the problems Viembo would have to solve. Breaching the fortress seemed impossible, at least to him. "Nereida said you conquered the fortress—you were brilliant, she told me more than once. How did *you* manage to get inside?"

Rayla grinned. "I found a weakness to exploit. I used a device we invented a while back for military purposes: a spyglass. It lets you see details from far away. All of our scouts use them nowadays." She glanced at him. "I'm guessing you've never seen a spyglass? They're pretty remarkable."

Danny just shrugged. He had owned toy binoculars while growing up at the Rearing Center in Newisbel, but he wasn't about to tell Rayla that.

"Cael always carries a spyglass for me," Rayla continued. "I'll show it to you later. I'm sure you'll love it. But to answer your question, I used the spyglass to study the fortress and find my way." She pointed at the mountain to their right. "Can you see that road carved high on the side of the mountain? It accesses the tenth story of the fortress."

Danny squinted and managed to just make out a narrow road that stretched for about four hundred yards before it apparently turned into a tunnel that disappeared inside the mountain. "I see it. It's barely big enough for an oxcart."

"True, although it's a bit bigger now. That road was a supply route. To the right, the Normanians carved a tunnel. It exits on the other side of the mountain and gives them access to a coastal city named Sandless."

Danny frowned, puzzled. "So they built in a weakness?"

Rayla shook her head. "It wasn't a weakness against a traditional army—they wanted a secure supply route in case of a siege. The road and tunnel were both easy to defend because they were too narrow for an enemy to storm. We wouldn't have made it through the guards the Maraccians had posted." Rayla looked at Danny and smiled. "Care to guess how we did it?"

The answer came to Danny at once—he remembered how easily Kara's mother had climbed up the face of the mountain where the Normo rebels had ambushed Danny and his party. "Gatalans."

Rayla chuckled. "I led nine hundred Lathraias under the cover of night. We chose a sloping angle on the face of the mountain, and the gatalans climbed it like ants. We reached the road and sneaked inside the tenth story. The Maraccians didn't realize we were inside until we'd taken over the left side of the parapet.

"We fought our way in, creating a foothold that we expanded into a stronghold. But we didn't march into the fortress right away—instead, we widened the road, and gatalan riders poured in."

Danny's eyes widened as he pictured the scene. "Wow!" Nereida had been right—Rayla's tactic *was* brilliant.

"It was already over," Rayla continued. "I had over forty thousand gatalan riders at my disposal, but twenty thousand of them were more than enough to rout the Maraccians inside the fortress." She gave Danny a somber look. "Roaring gatalans are unstoppable in close quarters, Danny. They're incredibly ferocious, and the enemies either flee or freeze when they see a pack of charging gatalans." She resumed looking ahead. "I got all the credit, but now you know the truth: our gatalans took down the impregnable Narialy Fortress, not me. I barely gave them an opening, and they unleashed hell."

Moss and rust covered nearly every surface. The Narialy Fortress was a solitary monument of stone and iron carved out of the mountains. Nature now seemed eager to reclaim it, coating everything with a layer of neglect.

For the first week, logistics teams rushed about the fortress, rehabilitating bathrooms, lunchrooms, kitchens, and storage rooms. Danny was the only one impressed by the amount of work the teams accomplished so quickly—everyone else seemed to expect it. Danny took his hat off to them. Kasmanians were a well-oiled war machine, evident in how they managed logistics and operations.

Positions and roles were assigned early on, and Danny became one of six hundred people stationed on the tenth story. Almost everyone else had been assigned to levels one through four, where any heavy fighting would likely take place.

As promised, Rayla gave Danny her spyglass. He used it frequently while he was stuck on the tenth story without much to do other than wait. A whole week went by before he spotted any approaching enemies.

The Ionians arrived first, and their numbers were a surprise—they were only thirty thousand strong, not the fifty thousand they'd been when they amassed at the western side of the Singing Bridge. Danny wondered where the missing twenty thousand had gone or if Rayla, Nereida, and Aia had erred in their estimate of the Ionian forces at the Singing Bridge. But what were the chances that three experienced military leaders were wrong in estimating enemy forces? Danny shrugged. Perhaps it wasn't likely, but anything was possible.

The Ionians set up sky-blue tents one mile away from the gates. After that, they didn't make any moves—apparently waiting for the other two armies to arrive. Their flying banners were white and blue and blazoned with the letters ION.

"Why do they need so many of the same banners?" Danny muttered aloud. He counted over thirty of them.

"It's one banner per company," a soldier next to him said.

"Oh," Danny said, nodding. He remembered that a company in the Kasmanian army consisted of up to 931 soldiers, although according to Cael, companies rarely had all of their members available due to injuries, sickness, deaths, and leaves.

"You can't see it from here," the soldier said, "but each banner has a number following its acronym. That number corresponds to a specific company in the brigade. Banner positions and movements communicate orders to its company during battle."

"That's pretty cool!" Danny said with raised eyebrows. Then he frowned. "But only during battle? Is that why I didn't see Nereida's troops using banners?"

The solider nodded. "That's right. Although if two different armies traveled together, they'd use banners to indicate their respective campsites."

Danny nodded back. "Good to know." So then the numbers of enemy banners would likely quadruple in the following days.

Even though the arrival of the Ionians made for a more sober mood on the tenth story, Danny's routine didn't change, and no one was issued any special instructions. And so the waiting went on.

Anxiety made Danny restless; all he could do was watch impending doom swell below them. He felt like he was standing under a bucket filling with oil from an open faucet. He couldn't step away—he could only watch helplessly, knowing that no one was going to shut off the valve. The oil would eventually spill out of the bucket, drenching him, with his enemies waiting to light a fire.

But his growing anxiety wasn't even the worst part—the worst part was how much he missed Kara. Although he understood why she couldn't be with him, that didn't help. As soon as they'd arrived at the fortress, every rider had removed the saddle from their gatalan and sent them away to roam the nearby mountains and hills. Danny could barely contain his tears when he sent Kara away. It didn't matter that Aia promised Kara would know when to return.

"Be reasonable, Danny. We can't have gatalans confined inside the fortress," Aia had said.

"Prolonged accumulations of indoor poop create bacterial outbreaks," Corina added.

"Not to mention the stench," someone else pointed out.

"We can't afford to feed gatalans during a siege," Cael chimed in. "They'll be happier outdoors where they can spread out and hunt."

But Rayla's remarks had settled the matter for a reluctant Danny. "This is a war between Canyos, Danny. Gatalans won't participate in it. However, if they're confined inside the fortress, they *will* get in the way and they *will* get hurt. And about the saddle . . ." She paused and gave him a kind look. "I know what removing it feels like. But many of us will die during the next few weeks—that's inevitable. Lots of gatalans will become widowed. And widowed gatalans become depressed, Danny. They'll stay in the wild. The younger ones will reproduce, but most will die quickly after the passing of their masters. A widowed gatalan's life is hard and short. Still, it's even *more* difficult for them if they have to hunt with a saddle on their back."

Danny lowered his head and removed Kara's saddle in silence. So if he died, Kara would soon follow. *How horrible.* Was it out of sadness? Loyalty? Had she known that when she decided to bond with him but did it anyway?

The saddle fell to the ground, and Kara stayed beside Danny awhile as if saying goodbye. Then she licked his face and sauntered away. Danny watched her leave him for the first time since they'd been together. Would this be the last time he'd see her? His heart sank to his feet. Then he set his jaw, promising to survive for her. *I'll see you again, Kara*, he vowed to himself. Then they'd trot to Torinth together and he'd introduce her to his dad.

Another week went by, and still nothing had changed—the Ionian army remained in its encampment, not making any other moves. With ample free time on his hands—and a need to *do* something, anything—Danny found a way to quickly reach the first level of the fortress if needed. The fortress featured stone slides next to each staircase, coated with paint for a smooth ride. At Danny's insistence, Cael rehabilitated the slides, allowing anyone to quickly slip down one level at a time. That route let Danny reach the first floor within just two minutes, but he only tested the full route out once. Climbing back up the steep steps wasn't nearly as much fun.

On the fourteenth day, Aia came by for a visit. "Why did you stop practicing with Cayacoa's bow?" she asked him, referring to the guacanari that Captain Quecia had procured for Danny in Narian.

He frowned. Danny had only stopped practicing two days ago, but apparently people were keeping tabs on him. "It's not Cayacoa's bow," he replied. "I'm sorry to say it, but it's just a poor replica"— assuming that Cayacoa and his golden guacanari actually *did* exist . . . but he kept that thought to himself.

Although he had easily adapted to the guacanari's extraordinary length of seven feet, its weight of fifteen pounds made it feel impractical and even grotesque. The amount of force required to pull the bowstring to a full draw was ridiculous. The payoff was an arrow that traveled up to four hundred yards, sure, but accurately hitting targets beyond eighty yards with this particular guacanari was impossible— the bow had the fatal flaw of pulling left. By the fourth day, Danny had stopped trying to hit targets three hundred yards out.

"Did you try piercing armor with it?" Aia asked.

Danny nodded. "Yes. I could do it with the right arrowheads, but only within sixty yards."

Aia's shoulders slumped, but she kept her tone even. "What are you saying, Danny? You're a Cayali! You just need more practice."

He shook his head, hating to disappoint her. "Believe me, Aia, even if I practiced for a lifetime, I'd never hit targets consistently with that particular bow. I don't think anyone could."

A brassy horn sounded atop the fifteenth story, interrupting their conversation. Danny's hair stood on end as the vibration reverberated down the length of the fortress. Danny and Aia waited, but a second blast didn't come. "Only one horn," Danny said in disappointment.

Aia nodded. "More enemy troops." She hurried to the parapet, and Danny followed her. The tenth story's parapet had a parabolic shape, the same as levels five through fifteen, while the first four stories had larger, squared-off parapets. Aia and Danny reached the outermost edge of their soaring parapet and looked down at the valley below.

Danny pulled out his spyglass and looked beyond the Ionian

camp. He stifled a gasp—a sea of soldiers marched at them from the south, an army three times bigger than the Ionian forces. Danny had never before seen that many people massed together, not even at concerts or sporting events in Newisbel. His hands turned clammy as he looked at what had to be a hundred new banners waving in the air. They were dark blue, like the soldiers' uniforms.

He turned to Aia. "That's General Fabris's army!"

"Let me see," Aia said, putting a hand out for the spyglass. Danny passed it over to her. "Yeah, those are seamen," Aia said after a moment of studying the sprawling valley. "Over ninety thousand of them. That's quite interesting! Their numbers grew somewhat."

Aia's calm demeanor surprised Danny; he could feel his own shoulders tightening. She gave him a soft smile. "No worries, Danny. Not even twice that number can breach this fortress, not with my eken defending it."

Danny forced a smile. "Good to hear . . . So General Fabris's army is bigger than expected, but the Ionian forces are much smaller. What's all that about?"

Aia laughed. "It's because of you."

Danny paled. "What . . . ?"

She lifted a hand. "Let me explain. Over fifty thousand Ionians waited for us at the Singing Bridge, but only thirty thousand arrived here. Rayla, Gadai, Nereida, and I had a long discussion about it, and we all agreed on why. It's the same reason that caused Captain Quecia to step aside: the Ionians saw you in action and heard our riders call you Cayali. A Caya is a clear sign of Kas's approval. Many Kasmanians will refuse to fight you."

Danny shuffled his feet, feeling heat rise in his cheeks. "That's . . . quite something. What about the seamen, then?"

She frowned for a moment, thinking. "It's possible that General Fabris is controlling the flow of information or that he's trained them differently. Seamen don't attend battle school like gatalan riders and army soldiers do. Or maybe they just don't know what's going on. I guess we'll know more once Viembo's army arrives. If we're wrong,

Viembo's army will be much bigger than the sixty thousand he was bringing to the Singing Bridge."

That didn't ease the strain in Danny's shoulders. "He should arrive any day now."

The cool and collected Aia smiled. "And we'll be ready for him."

* * *

The brassy horn blew once more two days later, setting the fortress abuzz. Danny rushed to the parapet and looked through the spyglass. His suspicion was confirmed: General Viembo had arrived on the battlefield with about forty thousand soldiers from Mesonia.

The diminished turnout should've made Danny feel better, but the cold sensation in his chest didn't allow him to feel anything but rocks tumbling in his stomach. The view from the tenth story had gotten even more ominous: the valley brimmed with glittering swords, armor so polished that it was nearly blinding, and thickets of banners snapping in the breeze. Danny tried to swallow and couldn't. One hundred and seventy thousand enemy soldiers loomed large out there, all eager to kill a pseudo-Cayali to gain glory on the battlefield.

Danny clutched his stomach. How the hell had things turned out this way? He didn't regret sticking around to help—it was the right thing to do. But this Cayali business had gotten out of hand. *He* wasn't the reason for this war. Hell, he wasn't even from Kasmana! And yet this idolized version of him had become a rallying cry despite Rayla's efforts to protect him. Danny could only imagine their enemies' reactions. Even though those rebels didn't know a thing about him, they likely hated his guts.

Danny recalled Aia's words and did his best to calm his nerves: Viembo needed twice that many troops to breach the fortress. Still, Danny's heart relentlessly pounded his chest.

A Lathraias came to the parapet, followed by twenty soldiers in orange uniforms. Danny straightened his spine and tried to focus on his next action. He raised a hand in greeting, and the Lathraias waved back. The soldiers behind him carried a dozen red baskets full of arrows for Danny and three devices called flamers. They consisted of two small trays connected by a gutter-shaped bridge filled with water. One of the trays was a shallow bowl that held tar; on the other tray, a miniature sun stick jutted up.

"Where do you want them, Cayali?" the Lathraias asked.

Danny pointed at three spots along the left side of the parapet. The man nodded and issued instructions to the soldiers. They quickly deposited the flamers in the indicated areas and placed four red baskets next to each flamer.

Danny strode over to a red basket and checked to see that it held fifty arrows. He picked up one to inspect it. Yes, it was a flaming arrow. Danny had never seen flaming arrows until he'd practiced shooting with them the previous week. Their shafts were longer, and their arrowhead had a rag affixed to it with wires. If he decided to use them, Danny could dip the arrowheads in tar to coat the rags, light them using the sun stick, and then shoot.

"Can you please put two extra bows next to each flamer?" Danny asked the Lathraias. Better to allow for errors—during practice sessions, he had dipped the arrows too deeply into the tar, and the thick black liquid had smeared the bow's grip and caused the bow itself to catch on fire a few shots later.

The Lathraias nodded. "Will do. Do you want the green baskets next to the flamers too?"

"About half of them, please. I want the rest spread throughout the parapet," he answered. Those would be filled with regular arrows. He was planning on strapping his double quiver onto his back as soon as the fighting started, but still, having more arrows waiting throughout the parapet would be ideal for quick refills.

He expected to mostly use regular arrows if he had to fight at all. That was a big *if*. It was an open secret that Rayla had assigned him to the tenth story in an effort to keep him safe, away from the heavy fighting that would ensue on the lower levels.

"Will do," the Lathraias said again. "We have everything we need. With Kas's blessing, we'll all do our part."

Danny nodded. The six hundred people on this level were responsible for defending the entrance Rayla had used to conquer the fortress five years earlier even though it was unlikely that Viembo's troops would find a way to access the narrow road. They didn't have gatalans, for one thing—all fifty thousand war felines in the Kasmanian army served under General Nereida, the master of Gatalans. The only exceptions were the Lathraias and the midnight gatalans under General Gadai. Still, Aia had said she'd have reinforcements at the ready in case of a breach on the tenth story. But six hundred soldiers should be enough to fend off any feeble attacks that came from the narrow road, especially with the Cayali amid the defenders.

Danny had agreed with Aia's assessment. The parapet curved outward around the fortress, its left side offering positions for him to shoot at any troops trickling along the road. He wouldn't have to defend much, really—the road only stretched for about four hundred feet before turning sharply and becoming a tunnel.

The Lathraias and his soldiers left the parapet. Danny moved to the front of it again and gazed at the valley. Not much had changed—a mile away, the sea of enemy soldiers still buzzed about, getting ready to attack. Nothing earth-shattering happened for the next two hours . . . but then a horn blew four times behind enemy lines.

Danny pulled out his spyglass again. Giant catapults pulled by oxen were crawling forward from the rear, twenty in total; soldiers at the front made way for them. Dozens of drums beat a two-stroke pattern, their percussive sound rumbling through the valley.

"That's weird," a female voice said next to Danny. He lowered the spyglass and glanced at the young woman. Semery had sneaked up next to him. She was a lieutenant in Nereida's army who'd been put in charge of defending the tenth story. Semery came off as a younger and friendlier version of Aia, with an easy smile and lively eyes, and she towered a good six inches above him. She pulled out her own spyglass to look at the enemy's movements.

"Do you mean the drumbeats?" Danny asked.

Semery kept looking through her spyglass. "Not at all. That's standard gamesmanship, you know—riling up your troops, intimidating the opposition, getting into their heads, that kinda thing. I mean the catapults. That's not a bluff! They're preparing to use them."

Danny scratched his head, glad to be confused rather than anxious for a change. "Why is that weird? Attacking us is the whole point, no?"

Semery lowered her spyglass and smiled at him. Danny's confusion deepened; she was smiling for real. Wasn't she concerned at *all*? "It's rushed," Semery said. "Their commanding general just got here."

"Right . . . but the bulk of their troops have been here for two weeks. It makes sense that they've been ready for a while."

Semery shook her head. "Not really. Those catapults just arrived with Viembo, and a siege has a slow rhythm to it—you wear out your opponent psychologically *and* physically. Attacking right away is not a good move, not at all. They should've milked Viembo's arrival for a few days, shown off a gadget or two, let us sit here sweating. But those catapults seem like the main event."

Danny wasn't convinced. "An all-out assault is a valid strategy, Semery."

She shook her head again. "Not against the Narialy Fortress and not against Cacique Rayla. No, Cayali, that's a desperate move."

Danny wanted to believe her, but one hundred seventy thousand soldiers were amassed in front of him. Why would they be desperate? "Could they know something that we don't? Maybe they found a weakness they wish to exploit before we can find it and fix it. There could be an advantage in attacking right away."

Semery shrugged. "Everything is possible, sure, but I think it's the other way around. Waiting to attack is a disadvantage for them."

Danny raised his eyebrows, remembering what Rayla had said: time was on her side. Kameiros operated in the shadows of deception; the light that came with morning was his mortal enemy, not Rayla. Danny wondered if something was unfolding out there and Viembo knew about it. If so, Rayla just had to survive long enough.

"Umm . . . Interesting," Semery said, still looking through the spyglass.

Danny squinted through his again. "What?"

"The catapults. Check them out."

Danny examined them. "They're all brand-new. Seems like they just built them."

"True. But there's something else. At first glance, they appear identical, but they aren't. Look at the six on the left."

Danny did. "You're right! Those aren't for hurling boulders. Check out the carts behind them—they're filled with ropes, not rocks."

Semery grinned at him. "Exactly. I'm sure my eken has already noticed that." Semery was referring to Nereida, of course.

A faint chant made its way into their ears amid the beating drums. Two drum strokes one second apart . . . and then a single word . . . then two drum strokes . . . then a single word. As more and more enemy soldiers joined the chorus, the chant became increasingly clear. Drum, drum, "Fake!" Drum, drum, "Fake!" Drum, drum, "Fake!"

Danny opened his eyes wide and burst out laughing. He couldn't believe how ridiculous the whole situation had gotten! Semery followed suit. "They're talking about me!" Danny said amid their laughter. The outburst made him feel better—if they only knew that *Danny* didn't think he was a Cayali either. "Unbelievable!"

Semery snorted. "You believe me now, right? They're desperate!" Danny just shook his head.

As the chanting grew louder, a group of soldiers advanced in a horizontal line, carrying large drums and playing the two-stroke pattern. Danny counted thirty drummers.

"At least they're in sync," Semery said, still chuckling.

The drummers opened a nine-hundred-yard gap between them and the rest of their forces. Dark blue banners billowed out behind them, changing positions and describing patterns in the air.

Semery peered through her spyglass again. "The seamen are moving first."

She was right. About ten thousand of them marched ahead, keeping pace with the drummers and maintaining the nine-hundred-yard gap. They came closer and closer to the fortress, beating their drums and chanting their war cry of "Fake!"

Rayla's troops on the fourth story shot a small bevy of arrows at the drummers. The arrows landed far short of their target, and the drummers kept advancing.

"Are they trying to establish our range?" Danny asked.

Semery gave him an approving nod. "Right. Our guys try to trick them by not putting their backs into the shots. So add another twenty yards to what you see."

"I'm guessing both sides know that . . ."

"Yep, gamesmanship. Gotta love it!"

Danny shook his head at Semery's flippancy . . . but when he looked past her at the others, he saw that all six hundred soldiers on the tenth story wore interested and calm expressions too. Their cohort included the three platoon leaders under Semery's command. The one named Lion, in particular, looked nonchalant.

Danny stared at them for a few seconds. He knew Rayla had assigned battle-hardened warriors to protect him, but this was beyond typical confidence born out of experience. These Canyos had been bred for war—they were clearly having fun. Or maybe Rayla had purposely chosen a light-hearted lieutenant to watch over him? She never seemed to forget that he was a teenager.

"They're getting closer," Semery said. Danny looked back at the valley. Rayla's troops shot a fresh bevy of arrows; those landed about thirty yards in front of the drummers. The line of drummers advanced another ten yards and then stopped. The seamen behind them stopped in tandem, nine hundred yards behind the drummers.

Danny gauged various distances as the enemy chant continued. The drummers had formed their final line fifty yards past the tips of the broilers. That meant they stood one hundred fifty yards from the gates. The new enemy line behind the drummers sat over one thousand yards away from the fortress.

"Oh, that's weird," Semery said again.

Danny sucked in a breath. "What? Tell me, please! I don't know what's supposed to happen . . ."

"Well, the drummers figured out the range, but they aren't retreating. They're supposed to move back behind the new frontline. They're just standing there, drumming." She tightened her jaw. "Those cheeky bastards."

"Are they taunting us?" Danny asked.

"Darn right."

A massive volley of arrows from the fourth story suddenly flew at the drummers. The men stubbornly held their ground, still beating their drums, and watched the arrows fall short by about fifteen yards. The chant behind them grew louder. Drum, drum, "Fake!" Drum, drum, "Fake!"

"What's going on?" Danny asked, baffled by the display.

Semery sighed. "It's ridiculous. They're full of themselves and thinking that they scored the first point. Assholes. They're lucky *you're* not down there. You'd put an arrow through their stupid drums in a heartbeat."

Danny considered it. She was right. Rayla's archers were falling short by fifteen yards, but if he were on the fourth level, his arrows would have hit their targets. He'd worked hard to build up his core and shoulders, and they were the backbone of his accuracy—he could pull bowstrings to their full draws and extract the maximum rage out of any bow.

A curious thought came to him. Why not turn the tables on those taunting bullies? Sure, he was farther away from the drummers than

Rayla's troops on the fourth level were, but he was also much higher up. A higher release point meant his shots would travel a greater distance. His accuracy would suffer, but at least he'd make them hesitate. He'd settle for that result. A confident enemy was never a good thing.

"Could you lend me your bow?" Danny asked a soldier leaning against the parapet. "I want to test something."

"Sure thing," the soldier said, handing it over.

Danny grabbed the bow with thanks. He reached for an arrow from the quiver at his back and shot it at an upward angle toward the drummers. The arrow flew high, flattened, and then dove down, speeding in a parabolic curve. The shot accelerated for a while and then hit the ground. The arrowhead disappeared, buried deep in the soil.

Danny smiled. The arrow had struck past the drummers' line.

"Please step back and give me some space," Danny said to the soldiers standing along the parapet. They all moved back, hushed and curious. "A little bit more, please," he requested, and they complied. "Thank you."

Danny walked to the left edge of the parapet and gazed down at his targets. These would be the longest shots he'd ever dared. He closed his eyes and took a deep breath, feeling his muscles relax and fall into sync. A calm state filled him, one devoid of thoughts but brimming with certainty. He kept his eyes closed until he knew in his core that he was at his best.

Danny opened his eyes, reached for arrows, and fired two shots. He moved two steps right and fired two more, repeating the cycle as he kept moving to his right.

A first wave of "Oh!" reached his ears. He kept firing. A cheering murmur grew inside the fortress's lower levels and the drumming stopped. Danny came out of his zone when he shot for the fifteenth time. His last four arrows were still arcing downward, and the remaining drummers were fleeing their positions, some tossing their drums away to run faster.

He quickly assessed the scene as the cheering from Rayla's troops grew louder. His last four sets had missed because the drummers had fled so abruptly, but the rest of his arrows had struck and killed ten of his first eleven targets. Danny grinned at Semery, whose eyebrows had stayed high.

Danny said it first: "Fake, fake, fake," he chanted, smiling. The soldiers near him in the parapet laughed and imitated him. "Fake, fake, fake," they repeated, their chant growing louder as all six hundred of them joined in.

"Fake, fake, fake," cascaded down the Narialy Fortress, echoes bouncing along iron and stone. Soon, thirty-two thousand soldiers on the lower levels joined in: "Fake, fake, fake," they shouted mockingly at the soldiers massed below. "Fake, fake, fake!"

Chapter Forty-One

10. Kendar

K endar arrived at Fodora View Estate at sunset. It was one of the four residences that Bosi Darios called home. The manor sat atop a lush hill on the southern coast of Belphi, near Prince Port, and it overlooked the Sapari Ocean; a white-sand beach stretched for miles before it. The majestic view from atop the hill captivated Kendar. Foamy, deep blue waves curled softly onto the shore, filling him with peace.

Given his Highlander ancestry, Kendar was surprised by how much he enjoyed just looking at the ocean. In Casmare, where waves constantly rammed the towering bluffs, Kendar couldn't get enough of that relentless display of power, violence, and beauty. Here at Fodora View, the waves kissed the shoreline, resembling the hands of a mother endlessly caressing her child's back. Kendar fell in love with that view, too, and took a moment to soak it in before entering the manor. The hill sloped gently down to the white sand beach peppered with palm trees whose long fronds danced with the ocean breeze, waving goodbye to the last morsel of sunlight.

The sound of squawking seagulls reminded Kendar of Stargazer Hill even though Darios's home was six times bigger and built in an entirely different style, with bars and glass forming a large section of the front wall. Kendar nodded approvingly as he imagined how daybreak would look from inside the house.

He scanned the hill. Dozens of sun sticks lined a zigzagging path toward the beach that was paved with flat cobbles and guarded by palm trees. On the beach itself, remnants of a bonfire on the white sand painted a picture in Kendar's mind. He could almost see it: a group of friends gathered under a starry sky, enjoying each other's company and the sound of the waves; a full moon hanging over the ocean, twinkling on the heaving water; food, drinks, laughter, and perhaps music. Those burned logs whispered to Kendar. *Don't miss it next time*, they said. *We'll return like these waves, wasting happiness with every sliver of burning wood.* The invitation excited him and made him wish he could be part of that scene. But could such a thing be real?

A pair of house workers dressed in brown overalls walked by Kendar. "Good evening, Fuzu," they said. Kendar nodded at them, recognizing the phrase he'd learned that morning. In Belphi, "Fuzu" was said as a sign of respect, used for anyone who had the authority to issue them orders. The workers went down the hill carrying a lighting pole and used it to ignite the sun sticks.

Kendar's thoughts returned to the burned logs. They had sparked a new concept in his mind: would he draw more pleasure out of life if he had friends? Probably, now that he was thinking about it. After all, he'd felt the happiest during his time with Gemina in Isiagi, and he'd felt downright elated with Lunai in Stargazer Hill before truth had crushed that mirage.

He gave the idea a moment to simmer in his head. Relationships were meant to end just like a good meal or a memorable night of lovemaking. But he could enjoy relationships while they lasted. They were not a waste of time, he decided. Relationships required a steady investment of time and attention, certainly, but the payoff was equal to the effort—they were worthy. Good relationships had enhanced hundreds of moments for him, making experiences deeper, more meaningful, and sometimes even more memorable. He nodded to himself. Perhaps he had found a new source of pleasure.

Then a frown flitted over Kendar's face. Friends and lovers also had the power to anchor him to a place. If Gemina had lived longer, Kendar would've stayed much longer in Isiagi. He would've stayed in Stargazer Hill if Lunai had loved him for real. Relationships came with a hidden fee, one paid for with freedom. Given that reality, were they still worthwhile?

"Lovely view," said a soft voice behind him. Kendar turned. A man with blond hair and blue eyes stood there, aided by a cane. He was as tall as Kendar and wore a blue ankle-length tunic embroidered with gold. The man seemed to be in his mid-forties, but he was underweight to the point of looking unhealthy, with sunken eyes and cheeks. When he smiled at Kendar, the gesture only exacerbated his sickly appearance. The man moved closer to him, braving each painful step.

Behind him, the house had come to life. Lamps in the shapes of trees had been lit, with dozens of wicks playing the part of flaming leaves, and two rows of people stood before the house in a chevron formation. The people to the left wore various uniforms, suggesting that they were housekeeping staff. There were over twenty of them.

The row of people on the right was only half as long. The first six seemed to be cultured folks, and . . . oh my. Kendar's eyes opened wide. The last four were women, tall and slender, with glossy skin. Three were in their mid-twenties, with blond hair and blue eyes; the fourth had red hair and green eyes and was a few years older than Kendar.

He blinked. These women were Highlanders, no doubt. And they were simply *stunning*. Kendar had been thirteen the last time he'd seen Highlander women in the villages surrounding his hideout near Ypsilos. Kendar the child hadn't paid much attention to them back then. Now, though, these Highlander women seemed to be the most attractive girls in the world. Not counting Lunai, of course.

"Lovely view indeed," Kendar said.

The man chuckled. He extended a hand and closed the final gap between them. "My name is Darios. Welcome to my home."

Kendar shook the man's hand, noticing Darios's efforts to weather his physical pain. Perhaps greeting Kendar outside was a polite custom for a host in Belphi, but this sickly man should have been sitting and resting, not standing and greeting.

"Thanks for the invitation," Kendar said. "It's a pleasure to be here. Would you like to go inside the house? I could use a nice comfortable chair right now."

"Oh, no!" Darios laughed. "Thanks for that, Kendar. I'll be okay for a little while. Watching you stand here reminded me of the first time I stood on this spot. Oh, that sweet memory soothes the pain in my bones . . . This view is hypnotic to Highlanders, right?" He laughed again. "I bet you didn't realize you've been standing here for over twenty minutes."

Kendar jerked his head back. He opened his mouth to disagree, but then realized it was true—the sun had been setting when he arrived, and now it was dark. He lowered his eyes. "My apologies. That was quite rude of me."

Darios laughed a third time, and his laughter felt sincere. "You have nothing to worry about. The same happened to me years ago. It's healthy to enjoy beauty—it'll help you live longer. I'll tell you what, Kendar, seeing as it's not a cold night, we shall have our first meeting right here."

Darios gestured to the rows of people. Three of the house staff and the redhead sprang into motion. Kendar couldn't take his eyes off the woman as she walked into the house. Then he dragged his eyes away from her and looked at Darios. His appearance might have been sickly, but Darios's eyes hinted at great intelligence.

"You probably know I spent my first night here in jail," Kendar told him.

Darios nodded. "Yes, I know."

"My jail mates said I could pass for you."

Darios chuckled. "That could've been true two years ago, I

216

suppose. I haven't been seen in public in over eighteen months; few outside my household know of my condition. As you can see, I've been quite ill. Before that, yes, you and I could've gotten away with saying we were brothers. A content heart makes a Highlander age well . . . and I was very content."

The three house staff came back, two carrying lounge chairs and the third bringing a table. As soon as Kendar and Darios sat down, the redhead appeared with a bottle of spirits and two glasses. She was even more stunning up close.

"This is Aziri," Darios said as she poured their drinks. "I've tasked her with making your stay at Fodora View memorable. She's been with me the longest. Aziri is a fantastic hostess; I'm very proud of her. Bring any concerns or requests to her, and you'll see what I mean."

Aziri curtsied. "Pleasure to meet you, Fuzu. At your service."

"Thanks to both of you," Kendar said. He looked at her green eyes, beautifully set off by the red hair framing her oval face. "Please, call me Kendar." She nodded. "Aziri sounds like a Belphian name," Kendar continued. "I assumed you were a Highlander."

Aziri smiled. She had perfect teeth. "I am, but I decided to change my name after moving here to mark my new beginning. I love Belphi and its people, and I'm grateful to this land. It's been most welcoming."

Kendar smiled back at her and then looked at the beach. "It *is* beautiful here! I almost left Prince Port with the wrong idea. My first impression of Belphi was the Furaha Ghetto."

"Lots of hardworking people in the ghetto," Aziri said. "I'll take my leave." She nodded at Darios, then Kendar. "I'm sure my masters have lots to discuss. And we've prepared a special dinner in your honor, Kendar. There's a bath drawn for you in your room and some clean clothing in case you'd like to freshen up before dinner."

"Thanks, Aziri." Kendar forced himself to shift his gaze back to Darios as she returned to the house. Encountering so many Highlanders in one place was a pleasant surprise. Aziri was gorgeous, and the other three women were equally stunning. If they were a fair representation of Highlander women, he'd consider making a trip back to his homeland as soon as possible.

Darios chuckled, and Kendar realized he hadn't hidden his reaction to Aziri's beauty well enough. "This morning, as a joke, I asked the four of them to fool around with you tonight. They giggled in response this morning, and then they giggled again when they saw you arrive."

Kendar stiffened. "What's your relationship with them?"

"They are my . . . no, they *were* my lurias. That's a Belphian word meaning concubine." Darios leaned forward and looked Kendar in the eyes. "There's a lot I need to tell you, and it's all related. I'll start with the girls and move on to more serious matters. And I'll be quite forward with you, Kendar. I hope you don't mind. I've been told you appreciate honesty."

Kendar nodded. Darios had probably spoken with Lunai. "Please."

Darios smiled and sat back in his chair. He took a slow sip of his drink. "You know I'm the ruler of the Mongad province. I've been the bosi here for twenty years. My domain includes the cities of Mongad, Prince Port, and Avianer. Mine is the largest province by territory and population, and it's second in importance behind the Narabi province, which hosts the nation's capital. My territory also includes the kingdom's seaport and the largest military garrisons in Belphi."

Kendar's eyebrows rose. "That's impressive. Especially considering that you're a Highlander."

Darios smiled. "That's an advantage here, believe it or not. Standing out helped me win my first election and crush my next three challengers over the years. The challenger's fee goes higher every time I win a vote, so there isn't much appetite to come after my position. Especially given my relationship with King Bakia."

Kendar raised his glass. "To good relationships!"

"To good relationships!" Darios said cheerfully. Both men drank.

Kendar set down his glass. "I'm still surprised that a foreigner can become an elected official here though."

Darios nodded. "Such a thing is only possible in a kingdom like Belphi. That's thanks to their religious beliefs."

"How so?"

"Akoni is the one god for all Normos around the world," Darios explained. "He's a deity who's fond of law and order. Belphians believe all humans are equal before Akoni, even if they come from other nations."

"I remember that," Kendar said, nodding. "Normos from different nations agree on a single god, but each Normo nation believes in a different prophet."

"That's right. Lady Makena is the divine prophetess in Belphi. She demands goodwill and obedience to all fair rulers. According to her, that's Akoni's will. Except for the position of king, anyone—even a foreigner—can be a ruler if they're lawfully elected. People are satisfied with a fair ruler. If they elect one, it's a sign that the people have Makena's blessing."

Darios paused for a long while, swirling his glass. "My parents died when I was a child, and I moved to Belphi with my aunt. By the time I became a teenager, I'd discovered something important, namely that most races in this world have a positive bias toward Highlanders. Don't ask me why—that's just the way it is. They tend to embrace us."

Kendar gave that a thought as he brought his glass to his lips. Neros and the Wetlanders had been hostile toward him, but that was understandable, seeing as Kendar had traveled to Vepos to kill Neros. Other than Vepos, though, everywhere Kendar had gone, people had welcomed him.

"But there is *one* exception," Darios continued. "Kasmanians consider themselves to be superior to other races. They look down on everyone else, including Highlanders."

Kendar hesitated before responding. "I haven't met any Kasmanians yet . . . but the few things I've heard about them are consistent with your view, yes."

Darios blew through pursed lips. "Nah. We're likely biased, I'll admit it. Most of our dislike is just fear. Can you believe the Kasmanian army has over one *million* fucking soldiers? Compare that to the Belphian army. The last report I read said we have two hundred thousand soldiers, and frankly, I believe those numbers are inflated."

Damn! That halted Kendar's breath. "What about the Sebesian army? Do you have an idea about their numbers?"

Darios waved a hand in the air. "They claim to have four hundred thousand soldiers. I don't have a way to confirm it."

Kendar sighed. A war against Kasmana would not be a fair fight. And Darios hadn't even mentioned the Kasmanians' gatalans. Someone had told Kendar that each of those beasts counted as eight elite soldiers. Canyos would steamroll through Belphi and Novusland once they were ready to attack.

When Darios spoke again, his tone was much lighter. "Hey, let's not talk about depressing subjects just yet. We'll deal with doomsday later. Look!" He pointed at the house. "Isn't my staff wonderful?"

Kendar turned. Two of the blond Highlander women walked toward them, carrying trays heaped with food. Kendar smiled. They had anticipated what he and Darios needed without being told. That spoke well of them *and* his host.

The women placed the steaming dishes on the table. "This is Mayla," Darios said, tilting his head toward one of them as the smell of onion and chilis filled the night air.

Kendar nodded at her. Like Aziri, Mayla wore a tunic similar to Darios's, but the two women had sashes wrapped around the waists that accentuated their slender figures. In contrast, the girl next to Mayla wore tight pants and a blouse, looking much like the girls in Sebes. The style of clothing showed off her small waist, curvy hips, and ample bosom. Her blue eyes kept darting toward Kendar. She gave him a coy smile as she set down a bottle of wine close to him.

"The flirty one is Phoebe," Darios said, and the girl's face turned red. "She's the youngest. The poor thing has been with me more in sickness than in health. That breaks my heart; it isn't fair to her—all that youth being wasted. Phoebe would be happy to be the first one in your chambers later tonight."

"Master Darios!" Mayla said with a hard face. "You're embarrassing the poor child."

Darios shrugged. "Oh! Do you mean Kendar?"

Mayla shook her head. "We'll take our leave now," she said, and Darios laughed. Phoebe darted a final furtive look at Kendar before following Mayla back inside the house.

"I haven't had this much fun in a while," Darios said, reaching for a piece of fried fish.

Kendar poured himself a glass of wine. "If you keep joking, I'll believe you're serious."

"Oh, but I'm not joking."

Kendar frowned. "If I had concubines, I'd never share them with another man."

"Me neither . . . until a year ago." Darios fell silent for a spell, his drawn features burdened with a sudden sadness. "Lunai said you're good with secrets, so I'll tell you something that only King Bakia and my four lurias know. Can I count on your discretion?"

Kendar looked at him intently. Darios looked sincere, but Lunai had crushed Kendar's confidence in being able to tell whether someone was being honest. Kendar looked down, clenching his teeth. He was second-guessing himself, something he'd never done before. He cursed in silence. He couldn't allow Lunai to scar him for the rest of his life! He wanted to trust himself again and pay more attention to red flags moving forward. On the plus side, being objective with Darios—or anyone else—should be much easier than being objective with Lunai.

Kendar looked up. "Yes, you can trust me."

Darios gave him a sad smile. "Thanks. I appreciate it." He took a deep breath and reached for his drink again. "Eighteen months ago, I fell ill with this cursed disease. Doctors don't even know what to call it, but they tell me it's worsening. And it's true. The pain is unbearable, Kendar. I feel like my bones are shrinking inside my body and then stretching sideways. The screaming has damaged my voice . . ." He paused and sipped, grimacing. "The doctors came up with a concoction for the pain, and I'm grateful. They call it *mowezi*. It manages my pain, all right. But mowezi leaves me unable to perform as a man. For eighteen months now, the needs of my lurias have gone unmet."

Something flashed through Kendar. Somehow, he understood Darios's physical and mental pain deeply, even feeling it as his own. Kendar lowered his gaze, gritting his teeth. What the *hell* was going on? This newfound empathy was probably a side effect of the damage Lunai had caused. Curse that girl!

Kendar's eyes returned to his host. "I'm sorry to hear that."

Darios gave him a sad nod. "There isn't much left of a man's pride after that. That's why I'd be grateful if you could entertain the girls while you're here. I'd be in your debt."

When Kendar didn't answer, Darios sighed. "Six months ago, I lost hope of ever recovering and gave permission to all four of them to find new lovers. They agreed, but none have done so yet."

Kendar smiled. "That means they're loyal to you. They probably love you."

"Well, yes and no . . ." Darios sighed again. "First, the girls had difficulty finding anyone they liked. Speaking from experience, I think Highlanders just aren't attracted to Normos. It's a bit different with Naldos, though, especially Sebesians."

Kendar frowned, puzzled. Even though Belphi was the smallest of the three kingdoms, it still had about five million people. There had to be plenty of men whom these girls would find attractive. Kendar wondered if they went out much.

"Second," Darios continued, "I'm sure you've noticed that all four lurias share the same status." Kendar hadn't, but he just nodded, and Darios went on. "That's because I haven't fathered a child yet and probably won't." He waved a hand at the estate. "According to Belphian law, a man of my status can wed up to six lurias. The first concubine to carry a baby to term becomes the official wife, and her child is the official heir."

"I see," Kendar said, reaching for a helping of pasta. It was a waste of time judging the customs of other nations.

Darios gazed at him intently. "It would be obvious the child isn't mine if one of my concubines gave birth to a baby fathered by a Normo, but I told my lurias this morning that if any of them get pregnant while you're here, I'll recognize the child as my own. You're a Highlander, so no one would notice. I need an heir. I would consider the situation akin to an adoption."

Kendar stiffened. Was this man seriously asking him to impregnate *a* woman, let alone *four?* Darios had obviously spoken with Lunai, so Kendar could assume that Darios knew about his powers. Was Darios hoping that a child he fathered would be born with supernatural abilities? Was this his plan all along?

Kendar set down his plate with a sharp clink. "It's amusing that you invited me here to have sex. Does Lunai know?"

Darios's eyes turned hard. "Lunai knows nothing about my suggestion. Providing for my lurias' needs is a family matter; I would hope you'd keep this conversation private. And you are wrong, Kendar—no, I didn't invite you here to have intercourse. We have serious matters to discuss, grave matters. Fooling around with my concubines is a side business, a personal favor to me. I'm sure that at least Phoebe will take a shot at you later tonight, and I'm telling you that it's okay to fuck her. All four of them, if they want. But whether you do or not is up to you. And them."

Kendar sucked in a breath. "I understand. I apologize if I offended you. I'll stay the night . . . Let's see how things evolve."

Darios's gaze softened. "Yes. The rain falls where it pleases. I'm hoping you'll stay here much longer than one night, but that's up to you as well."

Kendar nodded. "Understood. Let's hear about this serious matter you wish to discuss."

"Very well." Darios gulped down the last of his drink and poured himself another. He looked at Kendar, the skin bunching around his pained eyes. "King Bakia sent me his best physician two months ago. That man came here, did all sorts of silly stuff, and then gave me the grave news: I'm to die before the end of winter, and I'll become incoherent a month or two before that."

The air thickened as Kendar stared at Darios. The man wasn't lying—he truly only had a few months to live.

Darios reached for a peach and bit into it. Juice dripped down his chin. "I have made my peace with the end of my manhood, but I'm still struggling with the idea of death."

Kendar's throat bobbed. "I'm sincerely sorry. Let me know if I can help somehow."

Darios gave him a brief smile. "You can help a great deal. Entertaining my lurias is a totally unrelated affair. I hope that offer didn't derail our potential partnership."

Kendar shook his head. "It won't affect anything else. I promise."

Darios settled back in his chair, looking slightly mollified. "That's a relief." He toyed with his glass, his face still etched with pain. "King Bakia came to see me after my terminal diagnosis. He stayed for a whole week. Can you believe that?"

Kendar smiled. "You must be good friends."

"That we are, that we are . . . We discussed many things and eventually found ourselves discussing state matters. The king had just concluded a series of meetings with his Sebesian counterpart and military brass from both kingdoms. Kendar of Ypsilos came up during those meetings."

Kendar's eyebrows went up. "Seriously?"

"Yes," Darios said softly. "Very seriously."

Kendar stared at him awhile, his face reddening. That meant lots of people knew about him . . . which also meant his life would never be the same. He should've realized what was happening—he should have paid more attention and been more aware—but Lunai's betrayal had made him stupid.

Kendar reached for the bottle of wine and took a swig directly from it, thinking. Lunai had mentioned a General Lazaro during her conversation with Tares. And she was a spy sent to manipulate him. Of *course* the Sebesian military knew about him. Damn it all! For how long? And now Belphi knew as well . . .

"You seem upset," Darios said.

Kendar took another gulp. "This changes everything!"

"Perhaps for you, but not for us."

Kendar tilted his head. "What do you mean?"

"There is no new information that would change our thinking. Sebes and Belphi still share the same purpose: we want you as an ally."

"And this is important to you?"

Darios snorted. "Of course it is! Think about it. Kasmana is an existential threat to both of our kingdoms. Saying that your help is vital would be an understatement." He waved at the coastline. "That's especially true for me. When the Kasmanian navy launches their assault, they'll invade Belphi through the largest city on the east coast. That's none other than Mongad. This is my home, Kendar. It pains me to know what the future holds."

Kendar stood up, bottle in hand, and looked at the beach. The sky was cloudy, obscuring the moon, but some waves nonetheless twinkled with starlight. He gulped down more wine. Could he still enjoy his life now that his secret was out?

He turned back to Darios. "I have to assume that you know everything about my powers."

"I believe so, yes. We don't understand them, but we know your powers are real."

Kendar scratched his chin. "You seem surprisingly calm about this. My abilities don't baffle you?"

Darios chuckled. "Kendar, have you seen Hellsmouth?"

"No, I haven't. But I've heard it's impressive."

"'Impressive' doesn't begin to cover it. Hellsmouth? Now *that* is baffling. Miles and miles of divine fury have been lashing out for centuries. We don't understand it, but Hellsmouth is right there, and no one can deny it or ignore it." Darios lifted a finger. "Something else that baffles me is the bond between Canyos and gatalans. It defies all logic, but it's real. It's like the gods were having fun at our expense. But you, Kendar of Ypsilos, *you* are the great equalizer. Your existence doesn't baffle me. If anything, I expected someone like you to appear, something divine to balance the fucking unfairness. You're the answer to a million prayers."

Kendar suddenly laughed, his mood shifting to amusement. Being Akoni's hammer was appealing! But something still bothered him. "Let me make this clear. I'm standing right here, and you know what I can do, and you're not afraid of me?"

"Why would I be?"

Kendar frowned. He sat down and looked Darios in the eyes. "I could kill you right now as easily as I can blink."

Darios shrugged. "I could say the same thing. Well, perhaps I couldn't kill *you*, but . . . Take my household staff, for instance. I could kill any of them without consequences if I just took a little precaution. I'm a bosi. I have such power, I'd get away with it. But why would I do that? Only a deranged person would wantonly kill. Sebesian intelligence followed you for a while and concluded that you're not deranged. And now I know they're right."

Kendar stayed silent as Darios reached for a bowl filled with dried figs. "You know I've killed people before," he finally said.

"Yes."

"And that doesn't concern you?"

"From what I've been told, you killed to protect or expand your interests. Is that a fair description?"

Kendar thought about it. "Protecting and expanding" seemed about right. He nodded.

"Then you've behaved just as any government does. So, no, I'm not concerned."

"But you don't know me," Kendar said, frowning.

"I don't know details about you, but I know the important facts. You act in your self-interest. That's normal. You like comfort and pleasure. That's normal. You are generous and popular but prefer that your powers be kept a secret. That's eccentric, but it could be arranged. And another thing I know: Kasmana will invade Belphi and Novusland, destroying everything we hold dear. So why *not* offer you anything you could ever want in exchange for helping us protect this country, Casmare, Isiagi, and the Highlands? We embrace you for what you are: a blessing from the gods."

A long silence ensued. Darios reached for the bottle of spirits and refilled his glass and Kendar's. "Did you know that Belphians believe Lady Makena intervened on their behalf centuries ago? She asked Akoni to shield Belphi from the Kasmanian armies, and Akoni cast Hellsmouth in response. That wall has protected Belphi for five centuries. It represents a great victory for the only Normo nation that follows Akoni's true prophetess. And now *you're* here at a time of great need. You're like Hellsmouth—a godsend. If any fool tries to cross it, Hellsmouth kills him. No Belphian would ever question the wall's divinity because a fool has died."

Darios let that sink in as Kendar sipped his drink. Anyone who had crossed Kendar had died. Except for Lunai. "So . . . you want to make me an offer," Kendar said.

Darios smiled. "I spoke with King Bakia. The terms I'm about to offer have been approved by him. If you want to make substantial changes, I must discuss them with the king."

"Does Lunai know about all this?"

"She doesn't know the details, but the Sebesian government agreed to let us take a shot at you. But just so you know, Kendar, Lunai sent a letter of resignation to General Lazaro the day after you left Casmare. She came to Belphi on her own looking for you, and I managed to contact her. I figured it was an effective way to get your attention."

"Did you give her money to pay my prison bill?"

"No," Darios said in a neutral tone. "She paid with her own money. It was a considerable amount."

"Oh . . ."

"There's more. General Lazaro rejected Lunai's resignation. They call her Gaelie, by the way. The general ordered her return to Sebes, but Gaelie hasn't complied. She told me she won't go back until she's made sure that you're okay and have moved on. She is risking being arrested and thrown into prison for desertion."

Kendar briefly closed his eyes, unable to decipher what came over him when his mind's eye saw an image of Lunai being thrown into prison. Was it sadness or rage? Did he want to crush anyone who dared lay a finger on her? Why did he care?

Darios smiled at him again. "I daresay the Madonalee grew fond of you, Kendar. I can see why. I like you myself already."

Kendar chuckled, his mood lightening. "You want something from me, Bosi Darios. Forgive me for considering your fondness to be transactional."

Darios laughed. "Good for you, young man! You'll make a great bosi."

Kendar wrinkled his forehead. "Bosi?"

"That's right. Here's what the king and I propose. I'll be dead in a few months, and I have no heir. I'll pass all my possessions to you before my death, including this home. All I ask is that you take care of my lurias. They are my treasures. You don't have to wed them, but keep them in your employment and look after them. They have no future in the Highlands; please don't make them go back there. I must have your word on this. My estate is considerable, Kendar—you'll be one of the wealthiest persons in any kingdom. How does that sound so far?"

Kendar shrugged. He never had any problem getting everything he wanted. "This house is very nice. I like it."

Darios grinned. "Ha! Sebesian intelligence was right. They said possessions would not entice you. That's why they didn't try that angle."

Kendar almost laughed. These people considered themselves clever, but all they had to do was ask. Especially Lunai—Kendar would've been happy to protect her and Casmare from any invading Canyos. And he would've done it without any recompense if he could have only found a way to remain anonymous.

His thoughts returned to the conversation at hand. "Are you implying there's more to your offer?"

"Yes, of course! King Bakia will issue a decree naming you my successor. You'll be bosi of the great Mongad province, the second-most-powerful man in the kingdom. The decree will prohibit anyone from challenging your title for ten years. That should give you time to develop your political base. If you have no interest in political matters, the king will send you three of his best advisers. They'd run the province on your behalf, and you would decide your level of involvement in the administration of Mongad. In any case, you'd get to enjoy the power of the position. Let me assure you, it's like nothing you've ever experienced! If I'm right about you, it'll be exhilarating. You'll be intoxicated by this type of power."

Kendar drummed his fingers on the arm of his chair, considering. "That does sound a bit interesting . . ."

"What are your initial thoughts?"

"I'm not entirely sure," Kendar said with a smile. "Can I think about it?"

Darios swept an arm through the air, indicating the ocean, the house, the grounds. "Of course! My home is open to you. I invite you to stay at Fodora View for a few nights. Mull over my offer and enjoy my hospitality."

Kendar stood up and looked at the beach. He wouldn't mind owning this place and playing at being lord of the realm for a few years. "If I agree to do this, one of my conditions would be that Lunai is granted her freedom and reimbursed for the money she spent on my prison bill."

Darios nodded immediately. "That could be arranged."

Suddenly, the voices in his head spoke to Kendar. *Get them all! Get them all!*

Kendar smiled, remembering. A child similar to Neros lived on the other side of Hellsmouth. Kendar would find and defeat that child, absorbing all of their powers to become even more formidable. But the child in Kasmana could wait. At the moment, he was consumed with debating whether or not to seriously entertain Darios's offer. Kendar liked the appeal of becoming a bosi, no doubt. What kind of experiences came with that title? What kinds of pleasures became available with that position? It was an opportunity almost too good to pass up.

The front door of the house opened, prompting Kendar to turn around. He saw Aziri walking toward them with another bottle of spirits in her hands, her slender figure casting shadows from a dozen sun sticks and her red hair dancing with the ocean breeze. When her green eyes landed on Kendar, the slight smile in them set his manhood ablaze. He imagined her naked legs wrapped around his waist, her warm breath in his ears, the shape of her breasts, the sounds of her moaning . . .

Kendar looked at Darios and smiled. "I'll stay a few nights and enjoy your hospitality."

Chapter Forty-Two

11. Danny

Rayla's troops were enjoying themselves inside the fortress, but their mocking, "Fake, fake, fake!" chant met an abrupt end when a horn blew four times behind enemy lines, its brassy bellow imposing silence. A new set of drums beat in a four-stroke pattern, and the massive patch of humanity moved forward. The sun glittered on the enemy's armor, nearly blinding Danny; the sea of approaching foes suddenly seemed insurmountable.

Danny's eyes widened, his heart racing. There weren't enough arrows in the entire world to kill that many enemies! If they managed to breach the wall . . .

A male voice called out, jeering, "Morons, come crash against my cliff!" Scattered laughter filled the parapet as Danny searched for the source of the shout.

A platoon leader next to Semery snickered. "He's grabbing his balls again."

The lieutenant sighed and shook her head. "That raging idiot . . ." Danny finally spotted the man—he was holding his privates with one hand while brandishing his bow with the other. His eyes met

Semery's, and she shrugged. "He can grab his equipment punishment-free today."

The soldiers around them laughed. Danny shook his head and forced a chuckle. In Newisbel, that soldier would've been labeled a dick. "You guys are unbelievable," Danny said.

"You're one to talk, Cayali. *You* are unbelievable," Semery replied. "Taking out those drummers all the way from here . . . those shots were mind-blowing!"

Danny rolled his eyes and looked straight ahead. How could these people be so carefree in the face of death? Equally weirdly, Semery had taken what he'd said as a compliment. He refocused on the scene unfolding below them.

As the enemy advanced, their twenty catapults split into five groups. Two sets of four each veered to the left, two catapults were pushed straight toward the front gate, another set of four moved slightly to the right, and a final set of six were trundled toward the far right.

Danny peeked at the activity happening in the lower levels of the fortress and saw soldiers on the fifth story pulling wooden machines toward their parapet. "I didn't know *we* had catapults too," he said to Semery. But theirs were much smaller than the enemy's, and he only counted five of them. The crews on the fifth story aligned their catapults to counter the positions of the enemy's catapults.

Danny pressed his lips together. They had the higher ground, sure, but five catapults against twenty didn't look promising. He glanced at Semery again. Lieutenants like her attended daily briefings with Rayla and the generals. "We can't out-duel their catapults, can we?" he asked, hoping to get information from Semery on the defensive strategy.

She shrugged again. "No. Despite our position, our catapults will be greatly out-ranged by theirs."

"By how much?"

"Depends on the size of the boulders they use," Semery answered nonchalantly. "I'm guessing they can launch heavy boulders from three to four hundred yards and extra-heavy ones from about a hundred yards. They'll try to find a hollow spot on the outer wall and then pound it over and over."

Danny's throat bobbed. If the enemy broke through the walls and that army poured into the fortress, it would be all over. And fairly quickly.

Semery jostled him slightly. "Chin up, Cayali! It's not going to be easy for them. General Viembo is going against Cacique Rayla and General Nereida. He's outclassed, believe me. There are ways to counter his catapults."

"How?" Danny asked eagerly.

Semery chuckled. "You'll see. That's why the enemy has twenty catapults—they know they'll lose some. I'm sure my eken is talking to Cacique Rayla right now. And I bet she's recommending using a tactic the Normanians used against us a while back during a siege in Antilla."

Danny vaguely remembered Cael telling him about that particular battle. "The Normanians were the ones defending a fortress, right?"

"Yup. But that fortress was nowhere near as formidable as this one. And they had smaller catapults, too. Still, they gave us hell—the Normanians hurled oil barrels instead of stones at our catapults. The barrels are much lighter than wall-bursting boulders, so they have a greater range. Once our catapults were drenched in oil, they shot flaming debris at us. We lost catapults left and right. We had to move the rest back out of their range."

Danny flinched as he imagined the fires burning on the battle-field. "What happened then?"

"The increased distance meant we could only launch lighter stones at their walls, causing less damage. If we can manage to do the same now and push Viembo's catapults out of the striking range he needs for his heavy boulders, this fortress could handle a rain of pebbles for months."

Danny felt a wave of relief ripple through him. "You're pretty familiar with all of this."

Semery smiled. "I'm older than I look."

"I better not comment on that."

"Smart Cayali," someone else said.

With Semery's words in mind, Danny examined the enemy's movements again. It would take them a while longer to bring their catapults into range. Meanwhile, a large portion of the army had reached their new frontline, which was nine hundred yards behind the line drawn by their drummers. Danny couldn't imagine the fortress catapults being able to reach that far.

Then, sky-blue banners rose in the enemy camp, fluttering and snapping in the brisk breeze. About four thousand Ionian soldiers advanced in a tortoise formation, marching to the rhythm of the drum's three-stroke pattern, with the soldiers grunting and realigning every third step. Danny had never seen anything like it. Thirty-six soldiers composed each square formation in six-by-six lines, with those on the right and left flanks standing sideways, facing outward. Each soldier positioned their shield to create an overlapping cover that protected the formation's front, flanks, and overhead, making their formations resemble square turtle shells. Four thousand soldiers advanced in five waves, each wave consisting of at least twenty-two tortoise formations. They all headed toward the iron broilers that narrowed the path to the gates.

Danny took a deep breath. The real fight had started. If the enemy managed to breach the walls, he would die. He'd never find his father, and Kara would die soon after him. Danny looked at Semery and the other soldiers with wide eyes. They were impressive —their silent confidence had not wavered. Danny flattened his lips and thrust his chest out, trying to draw their demeanor into himself.

The afternoon sun had perched itself high in the sky; the air hung heavy with sweat. The first and largest enemy wave consisting of about twenty-five tortoise formations entered the range of Rayla's archers. Danny's gaze was glued on them. Why weren't the archers shooting?

Semery noticed his wrinkled brow. "It'd be a waste of arrows," she said, like she could read his mind. Danny nodded, imagining the overlapping shields probably would be quite effective . . . "Look at the parapet on the fifth level instead," she added.

He did. A crew had aligned their small catapult with the gate, and now they were bustling about, gathering barrels of oil and preparing to attack. "Oh . . . Fire instead of arrows."

Semery nodded. "They're likely to wait until the *fourth* wave is within rage, and then they'll launch oil barrels at that one first. If we're lucky, it'll trap the first three waves and block their escape route."

Danny looked at Semery, impressed by the strategy. "That sounds like a brutally effective plan," he said. "So why not shoot at the fifth wave?"

"Two reasons. First, the crew on the fifth level doesn't want to disclose the full range of our catapult yet. And second . . ." she paused and grinned ". . . for dramatic effect. Watching the fifth wave running back in defeat will demoralize the others."

Danny raised his eyebrows. "War gamesmanship . . . Brutal."

The crew on the fifth level lobbed the first barrel of oil. It splashed just past the second wave of oncoming soldiers. They didn't launch another barrel for forty-five seconds; meanwhile, the tortoise formations kept crawling forward, inching closer to the broilers.

The crew manning the catapult hurled another barrel of oil, and this one splashed right in front of the fourth wave. They stepped up their attack and shot out eight more barrels, launching each one within ten seconds. Six barrels exploded onto the ground around the fourth wave, spattering the enemy soldiers with oil. The other two barrels directly struck the formations and crushed them, the soldiers tossed aside by shattering wooden barrels and gouts of oil.

Then, flaming arrows rained on them, setting an entire formation on fire. The flames spread with vicious speed, and the screams of dying men reached Danny's ears. His hair stood on end when the smell of smoke and burning flesh entered his nose, but he kept looking. Fourteen formations in the fourth wave were ablaze, and three other groups around them had broken their formation, the soldiers flailing about in confusion. A fresh volley of flaming arrows swooped down upon them, wiping them out. Still, despite the death and destruction, the rest of the fourth wave kept advancing. And the fifth wave behind them did the same, maneuvering around the smoldering remains of their fallen comrades. Danny could only gawk at the scene.

Barrels of oil flew out from the fifth story again, splashing onto the fifth and third waves. But the soldiers kept moving forward even as flaming arrows torched entire formations. Screams and smoke, fire and charred skin; nevertheless, the dwindling formations crawled ahead. Something invisible pinched Danny's heart. The soldiers being killed were brave Canyos too. Why did they have to die? Was there a way to stop this war before the casualties mounted even higher?

One of the remaining formations reached the tip of a broiler. A soldier in the group broke formation, carrying a hatchet, and smashed a thin rod above the iron cone, causing all the vents in the broiler to open. The soldier reached behind her shield and drew a small sun stick, lit it, and shoved it inside one of the vents. The broiler roared into flames at once, killing the soldier before she could scream. The rest of her unit maintained their tortoise formation and approached another broiler. But it caught on fire on its own, blowing the vents away; scorching flames jetted out, engulfing the narrow corridor leading to the gate. The entire group was caught on fire and perished, tumbling away in flames.

Danny gaped, not believing his eyes. Was he witnessing courage or madness? Had they known it was a suicide mission? He wondered if he would ever have the courage to do something like that.

"Oh no," Semery murmured as the surviving formations slowly retreated. Danny glanced at her and saw a tinge of worry in her eyes. "Their mission was to set the broilers on fire. That move cost us a tremendous amount of oil."

More barrels splashed down around the fleeing formations, followed by flaming arrows and screams of burning soldiers. At least three thousand of them had died by the time the crew on the fifth level stopped lobbing barrels of oil.

Everyone on the tenth story stood with clenched jaws and hard eyes. Despite their horrific losses, the enemy had just scored the first meaningful victory in the war.

* * *

The surviving tortoise formations retreated to their lines, where their comrades welcomed them with mild cheers. The broilers kept burning, their black smoke darkening the sky.

A horn blew two times in the enemy camp five minutes later, and the twenty catapults halted their advance. A large white flag was hoisted in the enemy camp. Danny squinted at it, confused. The flag depicted a syringe in its center.

An absolute silence engulfed the enemy camp as the flag waved; soon, the same stillness took over the fortress. Danny looked around him. Everyone had turned to stone, their hands hanging loosely at their sides. He felt a cold fist pressing on his chest. He didn't know what was happening, but he could tell that something meaningful was taking place.

A moment later, an identical flag rose above the parapet on the first story and the horn atop the fortress blew twice, matching the tone the enemy horn had used moments earlier. Viembo's frontline parted, and thousands of soldiers poured out, carrying stretchers. They were unarmed, and they hurried toward their fallen comrades. No one else moved or spoke as the soldiers arrived and loaded the dead and injured onto the stretchers. The solemn silence lasted until the last enemy soldier had rushed back into their camp and the frontline closed its gap. Then the enemy horn blew once. The horn atop the fortress responded in kind.

The lull went on. Danny glanced at Semery as the quiet

continued for another minute. "It's called the mercy flag," she said, looking straight ahead. "As far as I know, it's the first time an enemy army has requested a mercy break. It's also the first time a Canyo army has granted it."

Danny lowered his head. He could only imagine what they were feeling. Such a flag was a Canyo gesture, and it reminded them of whom they were fighting and killing: their brothers and sisters.

The enemy horn blew four times, and the twenty catapults resumed crawling ahead. "Well, so much for that," Semery said as both sides began to shift about again. She turned to Danny. "Keep an eye on the six catapults moving to our far left—I think they're gonna be our problem."

Danny nodded, thinking the same thing. That catapult crew was heading for the area he had to defend: the narrow road carved high on the mountain that granted access to the tenth story.

The eight catapults moving toward the other side of the fortress had stopped advancing, remaining four hundred yards in front of the wall. Their crews aligned the catapults in a parallel formation and then jumped into hectic activity. Their efficiency impressed Danny—in less than two minutes, they loaded their launchers with massive boulders and fired them all at once.

The heavy stones flew high into the air . . . but then thudded into the ground short of the wall, tumbling forward harmlessly. The crews got into motion again, cracking whips to spur the oxen to move the catapults another hundred yards closer to the fortress. Semery poked Danny in the ribs and then pointed at the lower levels.

Danny looked, rubbing his side. On the fifth story, two small catapults were already firing barrels of oil at Viembo's catapults as enemy crews rushed to load their artillery. One barrel flew over the enemy; another hit the ground near them and exploded.

In response, Viembo's soldiers launched eight boulders at once. Their heavy stones traveled three hundred yards in the air. One shattered the top of the parapet on the first level and tumbled into the fortress just as two others cleared the parapet and crashed into the courtyard, cracking apart the cobblestoned ground. Five boulders hit the outer wall. One barely reached it, and three thudded weakly into the wall and fell to the ground, leaving only shallow marks behind. But one of the heavy boulders smashed into the wall closer to the gate, triggering the formation of large cracks. Fragments of stone sprayed out as fissures spread like spiderwebs. Viembo's men gave a loud cheer and hastily began adjusting their launching angles to take advantage of the damage.

Danny peeled his eyes open. Was the wall about to crumble? Two defensive catapult crews went into a frenzy, launching barrels of oil every seven seconds. One kept missing its marks, but the other struck with pinpoint accuracy, hitting three catapults.

Viembo's men released a third volley of boulders just as Rayla's soldiers launched flaming debris at the catapults. The two salvos crossed each other's paths. Two boulders landed short of the wall; six others hit it squarely in rapid succession, but only one caused any real damage. The heavy stone smashed into the already formed cracks, unleashing a thunderous explosion, and a layer of the wall crumbled like sand. The cracks tripled in size.

Flaming debris rained down on Viembo's men, setting four catapults on fire and engulfing the crew of a fifth one in flames. Oxen and men yowled in pain as Rayla's men rushed to launch new barrels of oil. Three surviving enemy catapult crews turned back; a fourth catapult was abandoned. Danny breathed a sigh of relief—the wall had survived, at least for now.

Rayla's forces hurled more barrels and managed to hit one of the three fleeing catapult crews. Still, by the time the flaming debris came, all three had escaped, while the fourth one left behind caught on fire and burned to the ground.

The catapult crews inside the fortress didn't let the rest of the enemy artillery get close enough to launch heavy boulders—they lobbed barrels of oil as the enemy moved in, with barrels landing five hundred yards from the wall. One barrel hit an enemy catapult aiming for the front gates. The enemy soldiers quickly pulled back that set of catapults, saving the one drenched in oil.

The six final catapults that aimed at Danny's side of the fortress kept moving forward; they had advanced the least, and Rayla's defensive catapults couldn't reach them. They stopped six hundred yards away from the fortress. Their crews leaped into motion.

Danny pulled out his spyglass and looked at them closely. Semery had been right—these catapults were different. Their launching gear was designed to shoot pairs of harpoons instead of rocks. The harpoons were linked in the middle by a rod, making them look like oversized H's, and each harpoon had thick ropes tied to one end.

A bald man who wasn't wearing any armor rushed about, giving instructions to the crews. "That's a fabricator," Semery said. Danny figured that was some kind of engineer. "He's about to run a test," she added with mild curiosity.

Semery was right again. The crews loaded one harpoon without ropes into a catapult and then shot the harpoon at the mountainside. It flew at a tremendous speed and buried itself deep into the face of the mountain. The rod joining the two harpoons prevented it from plunging all the way into the rock.

"Holy crap!" Danny gasped. That was a bull's-eye shot.

The fabricator issued more instructions. This time, the crews loaded harpoons with ropes attached to them. All six catapults fired, and the ropes stretched out as the harpoons barreled toward the mountain, revealing what they were hauling: rope ladders.

Danny was almost disappointed. "Oh wow . . . They plan to climb up." He scratched his head. This wasn't a surprise climb in the dead of night, like the strategy Rayla had deployed when she'd used gatalans. Viembo's plan was flawed.

Semery watched them with her head tilted to the side. "That's almost clever! I'm wondering if they got the idea from the seamen. Kasmanian ships use rope ladders all over the place."

Danny gave her a skeptical look. "I don't know how practical that plan is. Even if they make it, the soldiers will be exhausted by the time they reach the top."

Semery shrugged. "They gotta try something." She looked at him with narrowed eyes. "Can you cut through the ropes with arrows?"

Danny thought about it. Those were thick cords—arrows would just bury themselves in them. He'd need to fire dozens of glancing shots to cut the ropes with arrows. Then he looked at the flamers arranged on the parapet. "I have an idea," he said. "It should work, but prepare your defenses in case it doesn't."

"Already planning on that," Semery said. She gave him a quick nod and left, taking all of her soldiers with her.

Now the six catapults had shot two new sets of rope ladders at the mountain. Eighteen ladders dangled all the way down to the ground. A soldier standing beside the fabricator waved a large flag; seconds later, a similar one flew inside the enemy camp. Then two dozen dark blue flags weaved back and forth . . . and over twenty thousand seamen charged ahead.

Danny's heart raced again. A new fight had started.

Two small catapults on the fifth story began launching barrels of oil at once. The first barrels exploded short of the enemy catapults, splashing the ground with oil. The crews lobbed more oil, targeting areas closer to the fortress wall and the mountain. They managed to drench the ground before the seamen could get there. Meanwhile, the parapets on levels one through four were suddenly brimming with seamen. Danny felt the weight of his own quivers pressing reassuringly against his back.

The seamen kept flinging themselves forward, shaking the ground as they ran past the catapults. They lifted their shields and kept heading for the rope ladders even as more barrels of oil bombarded them. Flaming arrows rained down upon them, setting off a sea of fire that trapped thousands within it.

Unlike the Ionians, the few hundred seamen cut off by the fire halted their advance and took cover behind the catapults while the ones who were already past the fire pushed ahead. Rayla's archers shot waves and waves of arrows at them, decimating their ranks. Still, a few thousand got past the archers' range and reached the rope ladders. They quickly strapped their shields onto their backs and began to climb.

A horn blew again in the enemy camp. This time, thirty thousand seamen ran forward, aiming for the rope ladders. Danny shook his head, tightly gripping his bow. What were they *doing*? Sending in more troops to be burned alive seemed desperate. Soon enough, the small catapults resumed launching barrels of oil. Much of it splashed into existing flames and caught on fire at once. Rayla's crews halted their efforts and waited for the reinforcements to enter the killing zone.

The seamen ran as fast as they could, jumping over dead bodies and staggering through smoke and fire. A surprising number of them —Danny guessed it was as many as eight thousand—made it to the ladders. The bulk of them massed at the base and waited for their turn to climb. They used their shields to fend off scattered arrows from the handful of archers who were still able to target them.

Danny took a deep breath. It was up to him now. He looked around and chose the best position in his parapet for launching his counterattack, then moved one of the three flamers to his chosen spot along with a basket of flaming arrows. He nodded to himself; one basket should be more than enough. Then he waited. The best moment to strike would come soon enough. From here, only three rope ladders were out of his range, the three closest to the tunnel.

He spotted Semery in the background issuing orders, posting archers on the parapet where they could protect the last thirty yards of the narrow road and barricade the entrance. That was reassuring, although he wasn't planning to let the seamen get that far.

His gaze dropped to the first level, where crews had installed abatis obstacles behind the wall that had been damaged earlier by the enemy catapults. The abatis were sets of interlaced trees with sharpened branches that jutted upward and created a thicket of spears. Danny nodded, admiring the imposing structures. The abatis would cause havoc if Viembo's troops managed to breach the wall and then tried to pour in. Although the abatises couldn't offer as much protection as the wall, they were formidable and likely to slow down the enemy. Danny remembered Rayla telling Captain Quecia that she could defend the Narialy Fortress for months with just a third of her current numbers. It appeared that Rayla hadn't been bluffing.

Danny looked back at the rope ladders. Streams of seamen dangled from them, but none had yet reached the halfway point, while a large pool of soldiers at the bottom waited for their turn. He decided to hold off a bit longer.

Moments later, Danny nodded to himself and reached for an arrow. He dipped it in tar, set it on fire, and shot it. The arrow barreled toward the top of the middle ladder. Its tip buried itself in the rope near the ring that attached it to one of the two harpoons, and smoke and flames flared from the first arrow as Danny shot a second one. The new flaming arrow hit the same ladder, striking the rope attached to the second harpoon.

The first rope frayed apart, and the ladder swayed, swinging screaming seamen wildly back and forth. Then the second rope burst and the ladder plummeted like a rock, pulled down by soldiers plunging to their death.

Rayla's troops began cheering as Danny shot more flaming arrows, taking down four more ladders. He paused and looked down as the cheering inside the fortress intensified. The remaining seamen had begun to climb back down.

Danny ceased firing, watching the enemy soldiers reach the ground and retreat to their camp. Rayla's troops didn't shoot at the seamen as they escaped. Danny smiled at her gesture. Even though he was proud of their collective defense, Danny didn't want to see more Canyos die. He had to protect himself and his friends, but a heaviness had begun to seize his heart. So much death was a senseless and unnecessary tragedy. Yet Danny had been swept away by the strong current of war and was trapped, unable to escape the riptide of suffering.

Down below, the fortress celebrated; the second round belonged to Rayla.

Chapter Forty-Three

11. Anaya

Cookies and cheesecake were great, but learning how to fly was the best thing ever! Asa almost ruined the whole thing though. He went on and on in the morning, explaining boring details about flying to Anaya instead of just showing her. In the end, though, she had to admit that the explanations had helped a little.

Flying and moving objects from a distance had turned out to be the same skill. Asa referred to it as a "zero-gravity field." Anaya imagined that Dian gave her invisible steel threads, which she could use in a dozen ways. She envisioned spinning the steel threads like gossamer from invisible spinnerets all over her body. Not only were they unbreakable, but she could also make them as flexible or rigid as she wanted. Once they were spun, Anaya hung them on trees or even clouds. She used them to grab fruits or prey and pull them toward herself. She transformed the threads into nets or thick ropes as needed, using them to lift objects, including herself. Eventually, she managed to turn them into slabs for climbing like stairs. However, Asa described the skill in an entirely different way.

It was weird at the beginning, but Asa's explanations gave Anaya a new way to use Dian's powers. To fly, nanobots surrounded Anaya's body or the object she wanted to move, creating a zero-gravity field. Inside the field, Anaya or the object was always either falling or not, as Asa explained. She laughed the first time he said it, but he was right—Anaya could fall upward, downward, or sideways at will inside the zero-gravity field. It was as if someone was rolling the world around her. The same force that pulled objects down now lifted Anaya up, left, or right as she wished. To an observer, however, she appeared to be flying upright and in straight lines. She seemed to stand atop an invisible elevator when moving up or down, or on an invisible plane when moving horizontally—always flying upright and in straight lines. She controlled the rate of her fall and could reach breathtaking speeds or turn sharply left, right, up, or down with ease. But to her, it all felt the same—she was either falling or she wasn't. *That* was flying.

Anaya had never laughed so hard before, especially when she flew in stealth mode. Her battle suit sprang into existence on its own to protect her body whenever she wanted to fly; whenever she flew too fast or too high, a helmet encased her head.

She would forever remember the day she learned to fly. It would have been the best day of her life, but something strange ruined everything later that evening.

Marko was all smiles as Asa helped him prepare a celebratory dinner. They said they were proud of Anaya and kept patting her on the head and making her giggle. She was really looking forward to dinner, and not just because it was going to include cheesecake.

But midway through dinner, without any warning, Anaya turned pale and threw up. She felt dizzy, confused, and weak; she couldn't prevent herself from sliding out of her chair and falling to the floor. She felt cold and shivery. As Anaya lay there unable to even speak, she heard plates breaking and a chair screeching. Marko called out her name, but she couldn't respond.

"Take her to my room!" Asa nearly shouted. *You don't have a room,* she wanted to say, but her voice wasn't there. She developed a high fever within minutes, and a heavy fog clouded her mind.

Strong hands grabbed her and carried her to a comfortable bed. "What's happening to her?" Marko asked, fear in his voice.

"Bring me the synapse meter," was all Asa said. Anaya recognized that name. The talking doll wanted her purple sphere, but he'd forgotten to ask for her permission first. She would scold him later.

Asa and Marko kept talking, but Anaya couldn't make out the words. She slipped in and out of consciousness, unable to tell what was reality and what was dreams.

Hours later, she heard a voice next to her. "The IV looks good. Not bad for your first time."

"It's not my first time, Asa, and you know it."

The doll sighed. "I wish it were. Sorry, Marko. I guess I just want to forget."

"I'm sorry too, Asage. I know this is rough on you."

Asa sighed again. "At least we found her."

"Yes, my friend. We found her."

The voices faded away again. That first night, Anaya dreamed of being underwater but still being able to breathe thanks to her suit and helmet. She was playing at the bottom of the Naldo Lake, and her big brother Casar was there. They were playing a game of tag. Her big brother didn't need a suit to breathe underwater, plus he was faster than her, as always. Then Albi joined them. The gatalan took Anaya's side, and she rode him to outrun Casar. They played for hours beneath the water until the dream faded into something she forgot.

The voices came back. "Did you figure out how many?"

"Yes. Her bionanobots increased by a staggering eleven percent," Asa said.

"That's incredible! How did she get that many?"

"Anything within a hundred miles flocked to her when she began flying that fast."

"She was amazing up there!"

"Yes, she was. I never expected her to master flying so quickly. She has the potential to surpass Isbel's speed."

"Can't say I know what that means, exactly," Marko said. A smile crept into his voice. "But Anaya had a blast flying in stealth mode! She'll want to do it again as soon as she recovers."

"I know. But we need to limit her flying time to one hour per day. Although it's unlikely, this same thing could happen again."

Marko chuckled. "Good luck with that, Asa."

"I'm going to need your help telling her, Marko. She's closer to you."

"Like I said, good luck . . . By the way, what about the other threat?"

Asa sighed. "Same. He's still around, looking for her."

"You're sure he isn't a Satiu-X?"

"Positive. He's human, but the virus he's carrying is the same one that weakened Isbel and left her vulnerable all those centuries ago. The virus he carries is dormant, set to activate upon touching Anaya."

Marko sounded incredulous. "But that would infect *him* too."

"Yes. Which means he's clueless."

Marko sighed. "I see . . . Our old enemies are pulling strings."

"No doubt. But I've had five hundred years to prepare. No virus will survive Anaya's cleansing field! The virus will be eradicated long before he touches Anaya. Our little girl will be just fine."

Anaya's symptoms didn't worsen, but her recovery was slow. She spent two more nights in a foggy state, having a recurring dream: she was a warrior princess, gorgeous at age sixteen, powerful at age twenty-five, experienced and beloved at age sixty. Time went on, but she never died—instead, she kept hopping into a new and identical sixteen-year-old body. She lived a new life with all of her memories intact. She repeated the process over and over, living for thousands of years. She traveled to many places and fought in hundreds of battles; she slew monsters by the thousands and protected humans. She was Dian's favorite, able to do so much! But then one day, a needle pricked her. Anaya fell unconscious and never woke up.

"Good morning, Anaya," Marko said in a soothing voice on the third morning.

Anaya struggled to open her eyes. She was lying on Marko's bed in familiar surroundings. She felt rested, but something was bothering her left arm. "Why does it hurt?" she asked, touching her forearm.

"You were in and out of consciousness for three days," Asa answered. He was standing next to Marko, and although his face was expressionless as usual, Anaya sensed concern in his voice. "We fed you nutrients and fluids through a tiny tube plugged into a vein in your arm. The tube is called an IV. We removed it last night when your fever broke. It will stop hurting soon."

Anaya frowned. An IV . . . She knew what that meant. Where had she heard that word before?

"I prepared porridge for you," Marko said. His eyes had dark circles underneath them. "Can you smell it? Do you want to eat some now?"

Anaya's eyebrows remained furrowed. The scent of porridge was making her mouth water, but an image was stuck in her mind.

"Are you alright, Anaya? Is there something bothering you?" Marko asked.

She took a moment to respond. "I had dreams . . . Many dreams. They felt so real . . ."

Asa came closer. "Do you want to tell us about it?"

Anaya hesitated, wondering if she wanted to re-experience all that. She eventually nodded, sat up on the bed, drew her knees into her chest, and wrapped her arms around them. She laid her head on her knees and spoke without blinking as she stared at the wall. "I fought and fought, over and over, battle after battle. It went on and on. I wished for arrowheads, and Dian made lots of them appear in front of me. There were so many! And they were so sharp!"

She rubbed her fingertips together, remembering. Marko and Asa just waited for her to continue. "I shot them all! The arrowheads flew tightly together like an avalanche, chasing after mean monsters. They couldn't escape; I wiped them all out. Sometimes the monsters didn't run—they fought me instead. They were scary! Silver and black, and there were thousands and thousands of them. They changed forms whenever they moved—they stood like hyenas, rolled like balls, and ran like spiders, but they had scissor blades instead of legs. There were so many monsters."

She had to take a breath; Marko and Asa stayed silent. "I wished for even more arrowheads. Dian formed them in front of me and behind the monsters, and the arrowheads came together like clasping hands. I wished for more still. Dian made arrowheads appear above the monsters' heads and dropped them like heavy rain while I shot more at their sides." A hint of pride crept into her voice. "I never missed! I killed them all."

Asa and Marko glanced at each other, staying silent for a few tense moments. "Isbel had many weapons," Asa told Marko. "She called this one Swarming Legions, where she used fasma-piercing rounds in astonishing numbers. It was her second deadliest weapon."

Episode Twelve

Chapter Forty-Four

12. Danny

Danny gave the plan a thumbs-up when he heard it. Rayla had ordered the removal of wooden and textile items—along with any other flammable materials—from the lower levels. She wanted to prepare the fortress for the only attack she had determined Viembo could carry out effectively: lobbing barrels of oil followed by flaming debris. But Viembo never tried that tactic.

"He doesn't have oil," Semery suggested.

"He doesn't have brains," someone else said.

After the ill-conceived attack with the rope ladders, Danny had to agree. He could only imagine the amount of work that had been poured into building and transporting those catapults. They had likely built the launchers in Mesonia and pushed them all the way here. Danny could almost see the presence of the brand-new catapults arousing Viembo's troops and boosting their confidence as they marched toward Narialy. And then they had rushed into an aggressive attack within hours of their arrival, expecting a swift victory.

Danny shook his head. All of those efforts seemed so dumb now, not to mention futile and morale crushing. General Viembo had lost a staggering number of soldiers during the first day of battle—at least a quarter of his forces. He had little to show for it but a scarred wall and burned oil. What an idiot! He would've been fired in Newisbel for such a pathetic failure.

In contrast, Danny's confidence in Rayla as a general had skyrocketed, in part thanks to the competence and swagger of her troops. After the first day, his heart no longer raced whenever the enemy camp blew its horn or launched an attack—instead, he managed to relax, knowing that they were likely to survive the siege. A confident smile came to his lips. He would see Kara again. Who knew? Perhaps he would also see Castellana Loen's lovely face in Newisbel again, and sooner than expected. He would have so much to tell her!

With nothing to do, the best bowman in the world watched the second day of fighting unfold from his parapet. The enemy camp flew its mercy flag again in the morning. After retrieving their dead, other crews moved the harpoon-hurling catapults behind their front-line. In the afternoon, Viembo's men attacked the damaged wall, using nine conventional catapults this time. They drenched their artillery with water often as they advanced. But Rayla's oil burned anyway, and Viembo's men retreated after losing one catapult.

The third day brought what Danny considered to be a better attack: the enemy used their catapults to hurl double harpoons at the damaged wall without any rope ladders, and they did so from a distance that was far beyond the range of Rayla's defensive catapults. But the enemy appeared to have run out of the specially made harpoons—after they had launched thirteen of them, piercing three holes in the wall, they stopped. Rayla's troops retrieved the harpoons later that night and used them to reinforce the defenses behind the damaged wall.

The rest of the week trickled by with little action.

"They're trying to kill us with boredom," someone complained to Danny. "They sent for more harpoons!" became a popular rumor inside the fortress, followed by, "Viembo is sick with danguela," and, "Kameiros was killed by a gavian on his way here."

Viembo's men tried to probe Rayla's defenses with tortoise formations, sending thousands of soldiers to advance in sync with the rhythm of beating drums. And then they would retreat quietly before entering the range of the defensive catapults.

"They're trying to provoke us into wasting oil," Semery said to Danny, laughing. But that wasn't about to happen. Rayla had instructed the catapult crews *not* to launch any barrels until the enemy was close enough to trap tens of thousands of them in the fire. Danny scratched his cheek when he heard that. Rayla was a caring friend and leader, but as an adversary, she was ruthless.

Danny entered into a quiet routine soon enough. There was an open area on the tenth story near the spot where Cael had raised Danny's tent. He practiced archery there for an hour in the morning and another hour in the afternoon. For the rest of the day, he watched the battlefield from his parapet, often chitchatting with Semery and other soldiers between food breaks. He grew fond of her.

On the seventh day of fighting, Danny retired to his tent earlier than usual, driven there in part by boredom and in part by the memories swirling through his thoughts. He would've loved to have his electronic tablet! Then he could have written down a few of the most amazing moments he'd experienced since crossing the Atmospheric Disturbance. Bonding with Kara was at the top of his list, followed by the feelings he had experienced while on the Singing Bridge.

The image of the Singing Bridge stayed with him. As he relished that memory, Danny realized a growing certainty within him. As soon as he returned to Newisbel, he decided, he'd resume his studies and spend a few years specializing in structural engineering. He'd program trillions of virgin nanobots to coalesce into breathtaking bridges and buildings that would define cityscapes for centuries. He'd work hard, and his creations would inspire people long after he was gone, like the Singing Bridge had done for him; he'd make things better for future generations. He'd also spend time finishing the arrow he had made out of nanobots back in prep school. *And* he'd come up with new devices for everyday use inspired by the experiences he'd had in Kasmana.

"Cayali!" came an urgent male voice outside Danny's tent, startling him.

"Come in, please," Danny called back.

"No need, Cayali. Please come to the parapet! Lieutenant Semery requests your presence."

Danny grabbed his double quiver and rushed out of his tent. It was already dark. His heart raced a bit; Semery wouldn't have bothered him at this time if it weren't important. He followed the soldier to the parapet, where Semery and her three platoon leaders waited for him.

"Why are all the sun sticks extinguished?" Danny asked. The moonlight was bright enough to let him see everyone's faces up close, but turning off all sun sticks felt ominous.

"There," Semery said, pointing at the far end of the narrow road that gave access to the tenth story. That entire area was submerged in darkness, the same as the parapet.

"You mean inside the tunnel?" Danny asked, squinting past her finger.

"Yup. There's something in there. It arrived a few minutes ago and it's still inside the tunnel. We extinguished the sun sticks to level the playing field."

Danny looked closely. Semery was right. Someone stood inside the tunnel, moving now and then.

"It could be more than one person," a platoon leader said. Semery nodded.

"Bring me the guacanari," Danny said with an authority that surprised even him. "Please," he added, a bit embarrassed.

"Do as he says," Semery told one of her platoon leaders.

The soldier fetched the guacanari and offered it to Danny. "Thanks," Danny said, grasping it. He then reached for an arrow, dipped it in tar, and set it on fire. He aimed at the tunnel, angling the bow slightly to compensate for how much it would pull left.

"You can hit something that far out?" someone asked. It was a fair question, given that the tunnel was over four hundred yards away. There was no way Danny could have shot a flaming arrow into the tunnel using a standard bow, but the guacanari would cover that range.

"I can't hit anything with this bow past eighty yards," Danny answered without taking his eyes off his target. "I just want to get close enough to the tunnel to glimpse what's inside before the flame goes out."

He let loose. The arrow sped to the right, then veered left until it hit the face of the mountain just above the tunnel. The arrow bounced off and fell onto the ground near the tunnel's entrance.

Semery gasped. "Did you see that? I saw riders atop gatalans! But just for a second."

"Midnight gatalans," Danny said with confidence.

"Are you sure?" Semery asked with surprise in her voice. "Of course you're sure," she answered herself a second later. "A bowman's eyes are blessed."

Danny shrugged. Weirdly, the compliment made him doubt himself, but he was going to stand by his assessment.

Semery turned to her platoon leaders. "Midnight gatalans mean the people in the tunnel are allies." She turned back to the tunnel in time to see one of the riders get off his gatalan and pick up the flaming arrow. He brought the fire close to his face and then waved.

Semery waved back. "Do any of you recognize him?"

"He won't see you waving back unless you light the sun sticks," one of the platoon leaders pointed out.

Semery laughed. "I swear to Kas, Lion, I don't know why *you* aren't the boss around here!"

"Not cute enough," another platoon leader answered.

Lion snorted. "Agreed." He gestured for someone to light several sun sticks.

Danny was still staring at the waving man. "I think that's Rolan!"

Semery looked surprised. "Rolan? As in Lieutenant Rolan? The Lathraias?"

Danny gave her a brief grin as their sun sticks flared into brightness. "That's the only Rolan I know!" He started waving himself. "Hey, Rolan! Is that you?" he yelled.

Rolan hesitated for a moment. "Yes, Cayali," he finally called back.

"Why didn't you call for us?" Danny shouted.

"I can answer that," Semery whispered, but Rolan beat her to it.

"Didn't want to alert the enemy of my presence!"

"Too late for that," Semery mumbled.

"Sorry . . ." Danny said, realizing he'd messed up. He wasn't sure what, but doubtless there was a strategic advantage in keeping Rolan's presence under wraps.

"Didn't want to be shot by you in the dark either," Rolan added.

"It's safe to come out now, Lieutenant," Semery called out in a clear voice. "I'll restrain Danny myself."

Rolan chuckled and then walked onto the narrow road, followed by his gatalan and another twelve midnight gatalan riders Danny didn't recognize.

"What's strapped onto the lieutenant's gatalan?" Lion asked.

"That's for me," Danny answered with a smile, recognizing the shape of the item Rolan had set out to procure for him.

* * *

Semery's soldiers removed the abatis obstacles blocking access to the gate, and Rolan hurried up to the tenth story with his companions. Their faces were covered in soot, making their features hard to see in the flickering light of the sun sticks.

"It's great to see you, Cayali!" Rolan said in a rush. He handed Danny the bow he was carrying. "It belonged to the Cayacoa," he added unnecessarily. One of Rolan's companions bowed to Danny and gave him a wooden box. "That's the armor," Rolan said. "We'll talk more later—I must see my eken right away. I bring important news for Rayla." He paused long enough to smile. "It's good news." Then he rushed off before Danny could respond.

"Thank you!" he yelled at Rolan's back. The Lathraias waved a hand at Danny without turning.

"I better go down with him," Semery told Danny. "Do you need help with any of that?" She nodded at the bow and box of armor.

"No, I'm good," he said. "Go do your thing. I'll check out these in my tent."

Semery smiled and left. Danny hurried to his tent, carrying the box and bow. He nearly tripped in his haste. He arrived moments later, entered his tent, and placed the box on the floor. As curious as he was about the armor, he was nearly on fire with curiosity about the bow.

He sat down on the bed and took his time reverently unwrapping Cayacoa's legendary possession. When he had finally freed the length of it, his mouth fell open. The naked bow was a thing of beauty. Its limbs resembled curving flamingo necks while each string nock bloomed into a tuft of feathers. The riser was larger than anything Danny had seen. It was adorned with finger grooves, but the grip was too big for a normal-sized hand.

The bow's colors were hard to pinpoint. Except for the golden stripe that coiled around its limbs, the bow oscillated between blue and green; the feathers at each end shifted their colors as light bounced off them at different angles. He wondered why some people had described it as being a golden bow. Perhaps they meant the armor? Or maybe the bow looked golden in the sunlight?

Danny pulled the guacanari close to his eyes and looked at it carefully, trying to ascertain what material had been used to craft such a magnificent bow. His eyes widened. "No way!" he said in disbelief, jumping to his feet. He examined the bow again, squinting so hard his eyes felt like they might glue themselves to the bow . . . Then he gently placed it on the bed. Danny paced for a few seconds inside the tent. "There is no way," he mumbled a few times, refusing to believe his eyes. He inspected every inch of the bow yet again. "But that's impossible!" he muttered aloud.

Finally, he blew out a breath. There was no denying it: the famed Cayacoa's bow was made out of nanobots. Danny was very familiar with the material created by virgin nanobots. It was called fasma, a type of metallic fabric. To create it, nanobots swirled amorphously until they bonded through identity programming and coalesced into a final form. Fasma could be rigid, flexible, or elastic. It was also soft to the touch, light, and nearly unbreakable . . . except by more advanced technology.

Fasma could take on any shape or form—it could be as thick as construction slabs or as thin as a needle. Once bonded, nanobots became hardware and software in one, collecting and processing data autonomously according to their identity and then running complex algorithms. Essentially, fasma turned buildings into intelligent computers. Most of Newisbel's infrastructure was built of fasma.

Danny stared again at the bow in his hand. Cayacoa's guacanari featured *very* advanced technology. No wonder Canyos couldn't copy it! But what was it doing in Kasmana? Had it come from Newisbel? Danny shook his head. That wouldn't make sense. According to legend, Cayacoa wielded this bow four hundred years ago. No one in Newisbel could've built such a weapon back then—except for the Invoker, of course. But this bow was a toy compared to the weapons the Invoker had. Danny couldn't imagine a person like him wasting time with a bow.

Then he shrugged. "You never know," he muttered. The Invoker could've used it as a hobby—maybe he had hunted with it. Or maybe there was much more to this weapon than met the eye.

Danny's foot bumped against the box still on the floor, prompting him to finally tear his gaze away from the bow. Cayacoa's armor . . . someone had said it was *matching* armor. He gasped. "Could it be?" He put down the bow and hurried to open the box.

He wasn't disappointed. "Yup! Fasma . . ." he breathed. But the design gave him pause. Why would the Invoker wear something that looked like an earlier version of Kasmanian armor? As a disguise, perhaps? To pass as a wealthy local?

He took his time examining the helmet and cuirass, setting each one aside. Then he inspected the gauntlets. His heart skipped a beat. "No way!" he gasped. They were a *perfect* fit for the grip in the bow's raiser. A thought came to him. Could the armor be part of the bow?

He reached for the bow and tried to bend it without the gauntlet. Like the guacanari he had used earlier that night, pulling the bow's string to its full draw required a ridiculous amount of force, taxing the strength of his core.

Then he reached for the left gauntlet and slid his hand inside. Danny gasped and giggled—the gauntlet felt like velvet! His curiosity spiked. This was high-quality fasma. He grabbed the bow and wrapped his gloved hand around the grip. He heard gear humming and then a click . . . and the bow suddenly felt weightless. His eyebrows shot up. The technology in this bow and armor was much more advanced than he'd imagined it would be. When he tried pulling the string again, this time, it smoothly drew back like a curtain. His excitement grew.

Danny grabbed an arrow from his quiver and rushed out of his tent toward the parapet, adrenaline surging through his veins. Once there, he paused for a moment, then dropped the arrow he'd brought and grabbed a flaming one instead. Now he'd be able to follow its trajectory in the dark.

He lit up the arrow and shot it straight at the tunnel. The bow twanged like a guitar, and the flaming arrow rocketed away, striking the rock right above the tunnel in less than three seconds. "Holy crap!" Danny gasped. The arrow kept burning, its tip buried in the stone, flames illuminating the entrance to the tunnel.

He glanced at the bow and chuckled. That shot had traveled over four hundred yards. And it flew with lightning speed! No one could've dodged that arrow. It would pierce through several people at short range. No wonder Cayacoa had killed Nephilim with this weapon. Danny raced his fingers through his flowing black hair. He could strike targets five or six hundred yards away with this bow. Maybe even a greater distance if he could see that far.

A new thought came to him. Wearing *one* gauntlet had made a tremendous difference. What would happen if he wore the full suit of armor?

"Danny Elsberra," said a male voice behind him. Danny froze, not recognizing the voice. A cold sensation spread through his body. No one outside Newisbel knew Danny's last name. Whoever it was, he was dealing with someone from home.

He turned. His eyes saw no one, but Danny was certain of it—he sensed a dominant presence on the parapet, right in front of him.

"The last Ciberus Slayer has made its way to you," the voice continued in a pleasant tone.

Danny didn't answer for a while, goggle-eyed. He only knew of one person who was capable of becoming invisible. His throat bobbed. "Invoker?" he asked softly.

"Quite right, Danny Elsberra."

Chapter Forty-Five

13. Danny

Danny's eyes saw nothing, but the rest of his body yelled it—the man responsible for his father's exile was standing before him. His neck stiffened, thoughts colliding like rocks inside his head. He looked straight at the seemingly empty space and felt an old pain stirring in his chest.

Danny lowered his gaze. This was a momentous occasion. Still, it was hard to wrestle himself under control and keep a cool head. But he had to find a way to stay calm. Whatever the Invoker had come to say, the consequences of it were sure to ripple outward in all directions just as they had with his father. A single decision from this man could affect the lives of many people for many years; Danny knew that hard truth all too well.

He clenched his teeth. He'd grown up both admiring and resenting the Invoker. Newisbel owed everything to this man, but the Invoker had left Danny fatherless, something he hadn't understood as a child. When he became a teenager, logic said that his resentment was misguided. Then his grandfather Randal had confirmed it: Marko Elsberra had broken a "consequential rule" by smuggling advanced technology into Kasmana. The Invoker could've executed his father, but instead, he had allowed Marko to live. Danny was grateful for that decision. Yet he'd always felt a tinge of resentment that would never go away.

"Shall we speak inside your tent?" the Invoker asked. "I can guarantee privacy there."

Danny gave him a slight nod. A second later, he somehow knew that the Invoker had left. Danny blew out a breath and started slowly walking toward his tent, head hanging.

What the *hell* was the Invoker doing here? He'd hear an explanation soon enough, but could he trust a single word from that man? Danny had to admit that he was biased against him. Even so, being skeptical was probably the right move. No one in Newisbel knew the Invoker's real name, let alone any personal details about him. The only thing people knew for sure was his desire to resurrect his daughter Isbel. Everything else was a darn mystery. On the other hand, the Invoker had founded Newisbel, a fantastic place to live—it was peaceful, beautiful, and free. That counted for something.

His tent came into view. In another fifteen seconds, Danny would be face-to-face with the most important man in the world. All of Danny's questions would be answered. Probably.

His heart raced. The Invoker's stature made the man intimidating. He was powerful in every way, beyond any kind of artificial authority based on a title. Danny had to tread carefully. Should he listen or ask questions first?

He reached the tent, stopped at the entrance, and frowned, thinking. The Invoker showed up right after he had tested the bow. So that was probably what the Invoker wanted to talk about.

He pursed his lips, considering it. Everyone he'd met since shooting down that gavian had been wrong. This weapon wasn't Cayacoa's bow at all! A Canyo named Satsani might well have used it four hundred years ago, but Danny doubted that Satsani had ever tapped into the bow's true power. What had the Invoker called it? "The last Ciberus Slayer," Danny muttered. The word "Ciberus" felt familiar. Why? Perhaps more importantly, what did it mean?

Danny opened the tent flaps and stepped inside. The feeling of thick static in the air made the hairs on his arms stand on end.

The Invoker noticed his reaction. "I set up a soundproof dome around the tent. No one will hear us." He shimmered into view, turning completely visible.

Danny took a good look at him. The Invoker was about five feet, ten inches tall and was wearing a fasma battle suit. The suit shifted colors as the Invoker moved, mirroring the hues of whatever objects were nearest to him. Even though the Invoker was visible now, Danny still had to make an effort to differentiate his body from the background.

Danny kept staring. The Invoker's head was larger than a Canyo's and perfectly symmetric, with a heart-shaped jawline and a round chin. His features were so delicate that the Invoker could've passed for a woman—his rosy lips were a stark contrast to his pale white skin, and he had striking silver eyes and matching flowing hair. But Danny's eyes moved away from all that beauty, his attention drawn back to the suit.

The Invoker laughed. "You can touch it if you want."

The comment startled Danny. "Oh, no. Sorry. That's okay. My apologies," he said, embarrassed. He had been gawking. But who could blame him? That suit was *not* your everyday fasma.

Danny suddenly remembered the Invoker once describing his suit. His comments had gone viral. He'd called it a bio-suit and said that its trillions of interactive nanobots were an extension of his body. The nanobots responded to the Invoker's thoughts, and various parts of the suit could act at a distance, taking on different shapes, like projectiles. That explained the Invoker's ability to shoot bullets that appeared only a second before they struck their target. It was a devastating skill, especially considering that the fasma bullets returned to him after piercing his enemies, ready to be fired again or turned into something new. The Invoker would never run out of ammunition.

That reminded Danny of another skill. "Is your bio-suit the source of your remote surveillance?"

The Invoker smiled. "In a way, Danny Elsberra. As we speak, clusters of my nanobots are swirling around this fortress. I have the potential to know everything that's going on outside."

Danny frowned. "The *potential?*"

"Quite right. The feed is like background music. Unless something draws my attention, my focus will remain on you."

"That's just remarkable."

The Invoker gave him another smile. Danny frowned. These smiles were beginning to look fake. Then again, that suit was truly amazing. "I know you don't have much time," he said. "But I just want to tell you, it blew me away when you talked about the suit's stealth ability. You used a three-letter acronym to describe it, right?"

The Invoker nodded. "DRT. It stands for *detached reflection technology.*"

Danny's eyes sparkled. "Right! That was it!" Photons appeared to go through the suit and reflect the light off the objects behind it, making the suit invisible to the human eye. "Out of everything you can do, lots of my friends envy that skill the most."

The Invoker shrugged. "It's useful on this planet, yes. On others, creatures with pentachromatic color vision can see me. But none of those are here on Palaios."

Danny nodded, remembering the Invoker had said so before.

The smile returned. "Danny Elsberra, a curious mind like yours will have five hundred questions. It would take twenty-six months of chatting to satiate your curiosity. Unfortunately, we don't have that kind of time. I want to gain your gratitude, though, so I'll grant you one more question, and I'll answer it to its fullest. But then you will listen."

Danny lowered his head. He would take that deal, although he wasn't sure which one of his many questions was the most important. Should he ask about his father? Should he find out about the little girl he was supposed to find in Kasmana? He'd always been curious about the Atmospheric Disturbances. Had the Invoker created them? And what was the Invoker's real name? Where did he come from and why

—and how—had he lived for centuries? Was he even a man? How did he plan to bring his daughter back to life? And what about the bow?

More and more questions kept piling into his mind, over-whelming him. Danny was sure that this visit had nothing to do with the war going on outside his tent—the Invoker would never get involved in a dispute between the locals. No, something much bigger was going on.

Danny looked into the Invoker's silver eyes and fired his question at the man like an arrow. "Why are you here?"

The Invoker blinked. "Excellent question." He took a second to answer. "If you were a local, I'd say I'm here because of a prophecy."

Danny frowned at the awkward answer. "But I'm not a local."

"No, you are not." The Invoker dropped his shoulders, sighed, and sat down on the bed.

Danny sensed that this was going to be a long conversation. He pulled the wooden box over to him and sat down on it.

"Are you familiar with predictive algorithms?" the Invoker asked.

Danny half shook his head. "Only the basics." He quickly riffled through what he'd been taught in school. In advanced civilizations throughout the galaxy, everyday citizens, governments, and private enterprises shared information freely and willingly. The available real-time digital data had reached staggering proportions in such civi-lizations, and their societies prospered for centuries. The free flow of information became a way of life for advanced peoples; it was a new form of religion, an intrinsic code of conduct. But over time, inevitably, powerful and deadly algorithms emerged in those soci-eties. They were known as IIs, a variation of their original name of infinity intelligence processors.

Like organic viruses, no one knew where IIs came from. The algorithms predicted what was about to happen based on the massive flow of information. They were a free service, available to everyone. IIs assigned a degree of probability to their predictions, but anything calculated to have more than a sixty-five percent chance of happening almost always came to pass. At first, they seemed innocuous, and people embraced IIs, claiming a decisive advantage over those who didn't use them. But inexorably, within a few short years, the appearance of predictive algorithms resulted in the collapse of those societies.

"Do you know what was wrong with the algorithms?" asked the Invoker.

"They . . . they altered the natural way humans behave . . . ?" Danny more asked than answered.

The Invoker nodded. "That's correct. The source of human power lies in our ability to form large societies. We behave across the centuries like a single, evolving organism—always advancing, learning, adapting. No other species in the galaxy creates mammoth societal structures like we do or enjoys its resulting exponential power. However, IIs struck at the heart of that ability, exacerbating individuality and self-preservation. They set afire the invisible threads that bond human societies together. It was like bees forgetting they were part of a colony, each one deciding to keep the pollen for themselves. They enjoyed a temporary benefit, but in the end, everyone died."

Danny frowned. "But I thought IIs were defeated . . ."

"The largest societies bounced back, yes. But dozens of remote, smaller ones didn't make it. Now, Danny Elsberra, I expect you'll keep what I'm about to tell you confidential. Can I count on your discretion? This is very important. I won't continue with this answer unless I have your assurance."

Danny hesitated, but he was too curious not to hear more. "I promise, yes. I won't breathe a word. I swear it."

The Invoker sighed. "An II emerged in Newisbel seventeen years ago."

Danny subdued the urge to jump to his feet. "Is everyone in danger? Did you come here to ask for my help?"

The Invoker waved at him. "Calm down, Danny Elsberra. Everything is fine. I managed to contain the II back then—I trapped it inside a virtual replica of Newisbel, a place it can't escape from. It lives in a closed digital world; nothing can come in or out. But I'm able to see its predictions."

Danny's eyes got even bigger. "Oh wow! So you know everything that's going to happen?" That seemed almost unfair.

Surprisingly, the Invoker chuckled. "Not at all. After a week, the virtual world diverged from the real Newisbel. The two are now nothing alike, and the calculations are worthless. But the II's predictions during that first week *were* based on accurate data."

"So one of those predictions—"

The Invoker lifted a hand, interrupting Danny. "If you don't mind my eccentricity . . . Since the process can't be duplicated, I've been calling those rare predictions prophecies. It helps fight my perpetual boredom."

Danny scratched his head. Someone had once told him that brilliant people were weird. "Okaaaay, sure. So one of those prophesies was about me, right?"

"Not quite. It was about the bow. The II predicted that someone from Newisbel would find the last Ciberus Slayer and use it to change both worlds, meaning Newisbel *and* the locals."

Danny's head spun. There was that term again, *Ciberus Slayer*. He'd heard those words before, but he couldn't remember where. Suddenly, something else clicked into place. "My father . . ." he muttered.

The Invoker's head jerked back. "That was quick! You truly are worthy, Danny Elsberra. I'm almost proud of you." He gave Danny one of his odd smiles. "You deserve to know the truth. When your father smuggled technology out of Newisbel, yes, I thought the prophecy referred to him."

At least one piece finally fell into place in Danny's mind. "So you let him live . . ."

"Yes. The appropriate punishment for his actions was death by execution; I never doubted that, but the bow's importance outweighed any potential damage your father might have caused through his actions. You could say that the II's prediction saved your father's life. Except it turns out that the prophecy was about *you*."

Danny's shoulders slumped, and he lowered his head. He felt like a faceless pawn. How many forces out there were constantly influencing people's lives without them ever knowing it? He'd thought that his *own* decisions and desires had led him here, yet a machine had predicted this outcome seventeen years ago. How was that even possible?

The Invoker remained quiet as Danny thought about the major decisions he'd made on his way to this moment: choosing to become a ranger, crossing into Kasmana, setting out to find his father, joining Rayla . . . He would make each one of those choices all over again. Was all of that predictable?

He finally straightened his spine and looked the Invoker in the eyes. "People make choices within their circumstances. You've been setting up my circumstances, haven't you?"

The Invoker's eyes softened. "This encounter is shattering your delusion of control. Good for you, Danny Elsberra! But you're wrong. Until a week ago, I was still convinced that the prophecy referred to your father."

Danny hesitated. That part made sense. "But how could a machine predict that *I* would be here?"

"You'll have to get out of your head to see it. Humans are complicated to other humans, but not to an infinity intelligence computer working with enough data. The algorithm predicted that *someone* from Newisbel would acquire the bow. *Someone* would eventually appear who fit its profile."

Danny frowned. "That still tells me we're not in control of our own lives."

The Invoker shook his head. "You're looking at this the wrong way, Danny Elsberra. Your comment reminds me that you're a young man. Here's a piece of advice that has served me well for centuries: when things get complicated, return to simplicity."

"What do you mean?"

The Invoker smiled and lifted a finger. "I mentioned bees earlier. Think about them now. Do bees feel like they're being controlled when they're collecting pollen, or do they feel bliss?"

Danny pinched his lips together. "I don't understand."

The Invoker ignored his angry tone. "All you can do, Danny Elsberra, is follow your heart and pursue your happiness. There are limits to being a human just like there are limits to being a bee. You'll feel miserable if you start acting outside of what you know and desire. Yes, you're a piece in other puzzles, but those puzzles are above your head. They represent someone else's life, and you won't see *that* picture. But you have your own picture and your own goals and desires. Pursue those! Live your life to its fullest, Danny Elsberra, within what you know. Go after what you want. That's all you can do. Resenting what you don't understand will only frustrate you."

Danny crossed his arms and remained silent for a long while. He disagreed—if his mind could question something, then he had the potential to understand it. The Invoker just waited, staring at Danny. "What is it you came here to ask me?" Danny eventually said.

"I didn't come to ask you anything. I came here to fix the Ciberus Slayer."

Danny frowned and reached for the bow. What in the world was this weapon supposed to be? He gave the bow a once-over. "It doesn't look broken to me."

"It's broken *and* incomplete," the Invoker said. He stood up and tapped something invisible in the air. A rectangular glass box appeared, encasing a flat quiver that matched Cayacoa's armor.

The box drifted over to Danny and then settled down at his feet. The flat quiver inside contained twelve fasma arrows; their fletching matched the tufts of feathers on the bow's string nocks. When Danny reached for the glass box, it opened, allowing him to withdraw one of the arrows. He examined the shaft and arrowhead and saw that they shone with the same amazing colors as the bow's limbs.

"They're made with interactive nanobots," the Invoker said. "After being shot, the arrows disintegrate as soon as they stop moving, coalescing inside the quiver a moment later and reforming themselves back into their original forms. You'll never run out of arrows to shoot, Danny Elsberra."

Danny scratched his head. "How am I going to explain that to the locals?"

The Invoker shrugged. "Say it's a divine bow or something. They'll be in awe but won't question you further."

Danny jerked his head back, surprised the Invoker could lie so easily. He would remember that. No doubt the Invoker would lie to *him* that easily too.

"Why the long face?" the Invoker asked, squinting at him.

"You're asking me to spread superstition."

"Do you want to explain the truth instead? Interactive nanobots? Fasma arrows?"

Danny just gave him a blank stare.

"There is nothing wrong with mental crutches, Danny Elsberra. Superstition is an effort to explain an effect when the mind can't grasp the cause. Don't label superstition as something evil, young man. That doesn't suit you. Superstition is a stage in the evolution of knowledge. The human mind doesn't produce an error message the way a computer does when it doesn't have sufficient information. Instead, we make something up to fill the void. Call it a defense mechanism to avoid paralyzing confusion."

Danny sighed. This was turning into a lecture. "You seem to know a lot about the bow," he said in an effort to change the subject. "That bit about the fasma arrows is amazing."

The Invoker's eyes hardened. "I know everything there is to know about the Ciberus Slayer. That weapon took down my spaceship five hundred years ago and killed my daughter in the crash."

Danny flinched. The Invoker certainly wouldn't lie about his daughter's death. He glanced at the bow and blinked rapidly, wondering how something so small could've taken down a *spaceship*.

"You haven't seen its full power, Danny Elsberra," the Invoker said, seemingly reading Danny's mind. "One Ciberus Slayer would've been enough, but they ambushed us with eight of them. This weapon was specifically designed to sneak past my ship's defenses and kill my daughter." His tone hardened. "That same tactic wouldn't work now. But back then, the bow's novelty made it deadly."

An avalanche of questions rumbled inside Danny's mind. Whoever had created this weapon was clearly the Invoker's enemy. Was there a war going on involving the Invoker? And what had happened to the other seven bows? "I'm sorry to hear that," Danny said, genuinely meaning his words. "But who killed your daughter? And why would they target Isbel?"

A slight smile came to the Invoker's face, easing his expression. "Because she was amazing! No one has ever been like my little girl. Isbel grew into the greatest weapon to ever fight Satiu-X." Pride shone in his voice. "She nearly wiped them out. The group that attacked us here in Palaios was the last of them." The Invoker gazed steadily at Danny. "It was them, Danny Elsberra. Satiu-X killed my daughter. They designed the Ciberus Slayer and ambushed us here."

Danny ran a hand through his hair. He felt like his head was overheating. "I'm sorry, Invoker—I have no clue what you're talking about. I've never heard of Satiu-X, and I don't know what a Ciberus is, either."

The Invoker twisted his lips. "I'm . . . I'm sorry, Danny Elsberra. I don't have time for this." He started pacing. "This meeting has gone on much longer than I anticipated," he muttered. "What was I thinking?"

He stopped pacing and looked Danny in the eyes. "This is what we're going to do. Pay attention. First of all, the helmet is broken. I'll take all of the armor with me and fix it. It will be ready for you by the time you wake up tomorrow morning.

"Second, I understand that it isn't great to feel so confused. I'll upgrade the Slayer and connect it to your tablet in Newisbel, then upload a book titled *Designing Gods*. You can read it and learn all about *Homo ciberus* and Satiu-X in there."

He paused and tapped his left thigh. A small compartment opened on the side of his suit, releasing a jet-black bracelet. He grabbed the floating bracelet and offered it to Danny. "Third, hold this with your right hand until it glows."

Danny did so. The bracelet felt soft; it was obviously also made of fasma. It scanned Danny's right hand and eventually glowed to indicate that it had completed the process. The Invoker gestured, asking for it, and Danny handed it back.

"I'll give it back to you tomorrow morning," the Invoker said. "Once you have it in your possession, place the bracelet on your left wrist and touch it with your right hand with all five fingers until the bracelet glows. That will activate voice commands. Say, 'Slayer, activate.' The armor will coalesce around your body. With the helmet on, say, 'User guide.' That will give you access to all the information you'll need to operate it, including how to summon the bow."

The Invoker stopped talking and stroked his chin for a moment. He nodded. "I think that covers everything. We're finally done here."

Danny felt a shudder of excitement and confusion. "I've never heard of you using voice commands."

The Invoker smiled at Danny, making him frown. There was that fake smile again. "That's because your armor isn't a bio-suit," the Invoker said. "My suit responds to my thoughts just like my limbs do, but *Homo sapiens* can't operate bio-suits. You don't have the physiology for it."

Danny's eyes narrowed. "So you aren't human after all . . ."

"Of course I'm human!"

Danny leaned toward him. "You just implied you're not a *Homo sapiens*."

"No, I'm not. *Homo sapiens* are my ancestors *and* my descendants."

That didn't clarify anything. "I . . . So what are you then?"

"I'm *Homo ciberus*. Read the book I'll send you. You'll understand everything."

Danny gritted his teeth. "I will, I will, I promise. But can you just take the edge off my ignorance? Please? I won't sleep tonight if you don't."

The Invoker sighed. "I'm *not* looking forward to meeting you again, Danny Elsberra. So many questions! But I understand. Very well. Here are one hundred thousand years of human history in forty-five seconds:

"First there were the original *Homo sapiens* from Earth. They upgraded themselves into *Homo deus*. *Homo deus* created *Homo ciberus*. That's my species. You'll read all about us in the book. The short story, we conquered the galaxy. *Homo deus* coexisted with us for a long while. Those were good times; *Homo deus* was highly creative.

"Then, about fifty thousand years ago, *Homo deus* created *Satiu sapiens*. That was a catastrophic mistake." The Invoker paused, his eyes briefly shadowed. "*Satiu sapiens* spawned Satiu-X and another species that isn't relevant right now. Just know that Satiu-X was a scourge. They first eradicated their creators, and then they eradicated *Homo deus*. They tried to do the same to us. We fought back and won."

The Invoker began pacing. "The fighting lasted thousands of years across vast regions of the galaxy. But we didn't eradicate Satiu-X back then—scattered pockets remained for a while. We believe that Satiu-X were the beings who created predictive algorithms. That was the type of harm they inflicted for a period of time . . . until my Isbel almost wiped them out. Once Satiu-X was sufficiently degraded, we succeeded at bringing *Homo sapiens* back to life."

His inward gaze returned to focus on Danny. "That's why you're here. We seeded *Homo sapiens* on hundreds of planets across the Milky Way, including Palaios. We consider you to be our children, people who will eventually upgrade themselves into *Homo deus*, our ancestors."

His voice took on a tone of finality. "And there you have it, Danny Elsberra: the history of humans. I still recommend that you read the book, although it doesn't cover Isbel's story."

"Wow!" Danny said, wide-eyed. It was going to take him a week to digest just half of all that. "I won't sleep tonight after all."

That made the Invoker laugh. When he gestured in the air again, a large glass box appeared inside the tent. He gathered all of the armor and the bow and placed them inside the box as Danny moved to sit on the bed.

A helmet appeared around the Invoker's head, as sleek as the rest of his suit. Then he and the glass box became invisible. Still, Danny could feel his presence when he walked closer to him and spoke into Danny's ear.

"You need a good night's sleep, Danny Elsberra. It doesn't take a predictive algorithm to tell that something significant will take place tomorrow. Sleep."

Danny noticed a sweet smell in the air, like strawberry cake. Before he could say, "Thanks for everything," his eyelids turned heavy and he fell back onto the bed, sound asleep.

Chapter Forty-Six

11. Kendar

Kendar stayed at the stunning Fodora View Estate for six days, a time filled with feasting, drinking, and lovemaking.

He discovered it the first night with Aziri and spent the rest of his stay confirming it with the other three: these were gorgeous and passionate women, but sleeping with them was not the same as making love to Lunai. Kendar couldn't have explained it, but having sex with anyone else felt like eating soup with a fork or gazing at a colorless rainbow—without Lunai, an entire dimension was missing. He couldn't figure out what the hell was wrong. He spent his last day at Fodora View walking on the beach with hands behind his back, cursing. Lunai had ruined lovemaking for him forever.

"I'm planning to accept your offer," he told Bosi Darios on the final evening. Kendar had decided to inherit Darios's title and wealth and become the bosi of Mongad. He'd play that game for a while since the experience promised to be unique. Kendar would join the upcoming war as part of the deal and crush the greedy Kasmanians. It had to be done anyway—Canyos were a threat to his way of life whether he lived in Belphi, Casmare, or Isiagi. He had yet to figure out the specifics, but he'd find a way to unleash his power on the battlefield while maintaining his anonymity.

"But I must do something first," Kendar continued. "It's the reason why I came to Neojoppa. I'll be back as soon as I'm done—probably in less than a month."

The bosi shook Kendar's hand, sealing the deal. "I can only hope Kasmana hasn't invaded us by then." Darios thanked him for everything, wished him good fortune, and gave him two dozen gold coins for his trip.

Kendar said his goodbyes to the rest of the staff and left Fodora View within the hour, using his invisible limbs to fly northwest through the night.

He arrived at the city of Avianer before daybreak and continued his journey by horse until the evening, taking only short breaks. Once darkness fell, he returned to the skies. He got his first glimpse of Hellsmouth four hours later. He slowed down and then came to a complete stop, hovering in midair, as the enormity of what lay just ten miles away overwhelmed his senses.

Ahead of him, the greenery carpeting the land abruptly ended, giving way to a sandless desert that stretched for miles before the wall. It was dotted with barren hills; Kendar couldn't spot a single bird or animal in the starlit landscape. Bright flashes of lightning had replaced the sun, their unrelenting fury stinging his eyes as he moved closer. From a distance, the wall seemed like a curtain of rage hanging from the sky, sprawling east and west as far as Kendar could see. Continuous flashes of lightning branched down and out like jerky veins of light, forking and connecting, forming a moving mesh of white fire.

Kendar inched closer. A protective layer of feathers and scales sprang up around his body, thicker than it had ever been. A low rumble of thunder reached his ears. The acoustic shock waves increased in potency as Kendar neared the wall, growing into explosions that shook the air and the senses. The rolling thunder grew so loud that it threatened to damage his ears, prompting

Kendar to spawn an invisible sphere around his body that muffled the sound.

He kept advancing. Gradually, the wall gained definition. Mammoth twisters came into view, swirling with dust and rocks, moving and bending like drunken men. Smaller tornadoes whirled and touched down from dark clouds, merging into giant twisters, spawning and dissipating, yet never dwindling in number. Something strange kept them contained within a stationary patch of severe weather, creating the wall.

Kendar stopped, the muscles in his legs tightening. His hands became clammy as he contemplated the monstrosity before him. He was strong, but was he strong enough to make it through *that*? Should he reconsider? He had planned to cross into Kasmana through Hellsmouth to save a considerable amount of time. The other option was to travel west, all the way to the Vipes Ocean, requiring him to fly one or two days straight over open waters, circumventing Hellsmouth, then landing in freezing-cold western Naldora. After that, it would take him an additional two days to reach Kasmana's border.

Crossing through Hellsmouth had made sense when Kendar had looked at Neojoppa's map, but now he wasn't so sure. When the sound of howling winds reached his ears again, Kendar spawned a second invisible sphere around himself, then a third for good measure. The interior space became soundproof, giving him some confidence.

Kendar cracked his knuckles, deciding to move forward. He could always pull out if anything went wrong. He'd fly close to the ground, using dozens of invisible arms and feet to anchor himself and move ahead. He should be alright.

He spawned yet another protective sphere as he neared the wall. The relentless flashes of lightning became so blinding that he had to close his eyes and shield them with his forearm. He entered the wall. The pressure and resistance were incredible, but Kendar's invisible limbs proved powerful. He struggled ahead, grunting and breathing hard, making ground. He perceived the blinding flashes of lightning through his closed eyes. Pebbles and rocks hurled around in the powerful winds crashed against his protective sphere. Now and then, larger stones rocked the sphere—and Kendar with it. He spawned yet another layer in response.

Then, a flying boulder struck his right side. The sphere tumbled and bounced, and Kendar lost control of his invisible limbs. A twister picked up the sphere with Kendar still inside and tossed them high into the air. Lightning struck the sphere, and the electric current shook everything inside it. Kendar's teeth rattled, the chattering sound echoing through his skull.

Powerful gales hurled Kendar's sphere about. He tried to open his eyes, but furious flashes of lightning forced him to shut them tightly again. He shot invisible arms out in all directions, vainly trying to grab hold of something, *anything*. Stones kept hitting him, making the sphere ricochet unpredictably in all directions.

Then the sphere hit something solid. It felt like an actual wall. Disaster struck—the sphere exploded outward, shattering like glass and leaving Kendar unprotected. Deafening thunder rattled his brain; large stones struck his body, the blows hurting despite his protective layer of scales and feathers. Then a bolt of lightning hit him squarely in the chest. Kendar screamed as he felt his bones breaking and his muscles tearing apart.

One of his invisible arms finally grabbed onto something. Kendar pulled as hard as he could, blind and desperate.

He flew out of Hellsmouth, but a second lightning bolt struck him as he shot away, exploding his eardrums. He twirled in the air, unconscious and helpless, and then crashed onto a barren hill outside Hellsmouth.

* * *

Gradually, light seeped past Kendar's eyelids. He opened his eyes and blinked in the late-afternoon sun. He was resting on a makeshift table, feeling groggy. Grass covered the ground beneath him, and tall trees surrounded him. The sounds of chirping birds and running water reached his ears. In the distance, he could make out Hellsmouth's lightning still raging across the skies.

Kendar glanced down at his body. His right arm and both legs were splinted, yet he felt no pain. The stupor enveloping his head told him he had been drugged. He tried to sit up but couldn't. An almost-stifled grunt left his lips.

"Ah! You're finally awake," a male voice said.

Kendar looked to his right. A figure walked closer. He was wrapped in a ragged gray cloth, but underneath it, the man wore a strange metallic fabric that tightly covered every inch of his skin except for his head. It reminded Kendar of his protective layer of feathers and scales, except the man's garment was clearly made of a different material. A black mask shaped like butterfly wings covered his face. It hid his forehead, mouth, and chin; not even the color of his eyes could be glimpsed. But when he spoke, the man's voice came out clearly, as though nothing was covering his lips.

"Don't try to move," he said when he reached the table.

Kendar's thoughts were scrambled. He wanted to ask who the man was, what had happened, and how long he'd been unconscious. Instead, his hand reached out to the man's face and touched the black mask. The man said nothing—he simply touched Kendar's face in return, as if responding to an unfamiliar greeting.

Kendar frowned. Was that a sign of caring? Sympathy? Moments later, the man nudged Kendar's hand down, and Kendar noticed his injured forearm. His skin was cracked and burned, with crevices exposing raw muscle tissue. Kendar scowled. That would hurt like hell as soon as the drugs in his system wore off.

The man reached behind his back and then brought his hand back a moment later, revealing a small metallic box. He placed it on the table next to Kendar, opened it, and pulled out a piece of broken armor. It was made of the same material as the man's clothing.

"I found you four days ago," the man said, his voice soft and soothing. "You were unconscious and dehydrated. The injuries themselves weren't going to kill you, but you were healing too slowly. You would've reached terminal dehydration before regaining consciousness."

Kendar frowned. What the hell did all of that mean? He would've died of thirst? And what did the man mean by "healing too slowly"?

The man gently but firmly grabbed Kendar's forearm. "Please don't move," he said. He held the piece of broken armor close to Kendar's injury. Nothing happened. "C'mon, c'mon!" the man muttered, apparently talking to the broken piece. Kendar could only watch in confusion.

"That's it," he said a moment later. "That's it."

The tip of the piece disintegrated, turning into a layer of thin dust that floated above it. The rest of the piece followed suit, and then the particles swirled and flocked toward Kendar's injured forearm. His skin absorbed them like they were water dripping onto dry sand. Kendar's eyes opened wide. It felt soothing, reinvigorating. The wound healed as the last particles entered his forearm; not even a scratch remained.

"What . . . what is that?" Kendar managed to ask, dazed.

"Oh . . . I don't know how to explain it to you . . . Call it 'divine dust.'" The man gave a single, sharp nod. "Yes, that should work just fine."

"Divine dust," Kendar mumbled, remembering. The same substance had come off Neros's body when Kendar had touched him. The particles left Neros and swarmed toward Kendar, increasing his powers. Neros's body had withered away, his cheeks caving in and his eyes sinking inward when the last of the particles left him. It hadn't been a pretty sight.

"I'll use all I have left to heal your more severe injuries. The rest will heal on its own," the man said.

Kendar reached for the man's mask again. "Who are you?"

He intercepted Kendar's hand with a firm grip. "By now, you understand the need for anonymity, don't you?"

Kendar hesitated. "Are you like me?"

"Not quite," the man said. "Now, you need to rest. I have little time and much work to do." He waved his right hand over Kendar's face. A sweet smell entered his nose, and Kendar's eyelids turned heavy.

"By the way, before you fall asleep, please don't try to cross Hellsmouth again, okay? The wall was designed to keep things out, especially people like you and me. Go around it next time."

Kendar's eyes closed. "Oh!" the man said as Kendar lost consciousness, his words fading away. "When you find Anaya, don't underestimate her—only a sneak attack will work. Go for the head and . . ."

* * *

Kendar woke midmorning atop the makeshift table. There was no sign of the masked man or anyone else. Kendar clearly remembered being injured while trying to cross Hellsmouth, but that was all he felt sure about. Could the masked man have just been a sickly dream?

Kendar looked at his body again. The splints were gone, and all of his injuries had healed. His mind was clear now, although his muscles felt stiff. That was probably from having slept for too long on a hard table. How long had he been here? He had no way of finding that out.

He sat up and noticed a black mask in the shape of butterfly wings lying next to him. He picked it up and looked at it carefully. "It wasn't a dream . . ." he mumbled. The masked man *had* been real, and he'd helped Kendar—he had healed him with divine dust.

Kendar knew it then: divine dust gave him his powers. Without it, he would die just like Neros had. He remembered all of the children who had perished in his village many years ago. Divine dust had entered their bodies, too, but they hadn't been able to assimilate it.

Kendar scratched his cheek. *He* could obviously absorb divine dust. That made him unique. Did this ability also make him a divine being? Bosi Darios had said Kendar was the answer to a million prayers. Perhaps he *was* Akoni's hammer after all, destined to protect the world from the bloodthirsty Kas and his hordes of Canyos.

Kendar tried the mask on. Not only did it fit perfectly, but his vision was unimpeded—it was as though he wasn't wearing anything on his face. He smiled. The mask was the answer to his desire! Wearing it would allow him to conceal his identity while fighting in the upcoming war. Perhaps gods *were* real. And perhaps Akoni favored him, providing Kendar with whatever he needed and wanted.

Kendar looked to his left. Hellsmouth rose up in the distance, towering and monstrous. Unending flashes of lightning told him how stupid he'd been for trying to weather that beast. He had been lucky to survive and just as lucky that someone had come to help him.

A new thought bothered him. The masked man had implied that someone had built Hellsmouth to keep people like Kendar outside. Outside of what? It certainly wasn't outside of Kasmana—more than forty million Canyos lived there.

He sighed. "People like you and me," the masked man had said. Kendar already knew there were others like him, but now he'd begun to suspect that some of them were more powerful than he was. Yet there was so much he *didn't* know, placing him at a tremendous disadvantage when dealing with those other beings. The masked man had even known that Kendar was after a little girl—Anaya he'd called her. Kendar wanted to know more about divine dust, the wall, and the masked man, but it would be a waste of time to wrestle with those mysteries right now. His priority was clear—he had to focus on becoming more powerful.

He glanced at Hellsmouth one final time. The builder of such a thing was indeed mighty. Something inside that wall had destroyed a large amount of Kendar's divine dust on contact, shattering his protective spheres. That wall could kill him. He'd listen to the masked man's advice and forever stay away from

Hellsmouth. Traveling around it was infinitely preferable to being slaughtered by it.

Still wearing the mask, he stood up and jumped into the air, knowing the gods favored him. He resumed his journey toward Kasmana a bit wiser than he'd been before. His path was clear: he'd become a bosi and fight against the Canyos and their gatalans. He'd learn more about emotional pleasure, the elusive type of joy he'd only enjoyed with Gemina and Lunai. But first he would travel to Kasmana, where he could steal more divine dust. There, he'd find a little girl named Anaya, defeat her, and take her powers.

* * *

Kendar traveled at night and rested during the day. He wore his mask whenever he flew and tucked it safely away whenever he wasn't wearing it.

He flew north of Narabi, the kingdom's capital, and touched the cities of Ababis and Mjikoni on his way to the west coast. He flew past the Belphian shoreline and landed on the island of Asmar. Then he flew over the Vipes Ocean for two days and arrived at the Naldorian island of Vigani, going around the stretch of Hellsmouth that jutted out past the continental landmass. From Vigani, Kendar hopped into Naldora and then traveled east to the Kasmanian city of Palaumone. A three-week journey had ended; a new search had begun.

"Find the girl," Kendar commanded the voices in his head at the Kasmanian border.

As you wish, they responded.

The girl piqued Kendar's curiosity. The masked man had said her name was Anaya and advised him not to underestimate her. She was probably stronger than Neros, but Kendar just needed to touch her. Then Anaya would die, her divine dust would flock to Kendar, and he'd acquire new powers. He stroked his chin. Would he be strong enough to take on Hellsmouth after? Perhaps that wasn't too smart, but would he ever get the chance to see what was hiding behind the wall?

The voices in his head guided Kendar northeast, all the way to the city of Torinth, where it rose up next to Naldo Lake. Anaya managed to evade him for an entire week, but he finally found her one midafternoon in a forest of sequoia trees. The little girl stood alone amid the giant redwoods with a rag doll underneath her arm. She was looking with delight at a purple ball in her hands that flashed wiggly characters, unaware of Kendar's presence.

Kendar's mouth fell open. The seven-year-old was protected by the same metallic fabric the man who had helped him had worn! But Anaya wasn't wearing anything over it, making it easy to see that the fabric was some kind of armor. And it seemed to be more powerful than Kendar's protective layer.

His shoulders tightened, and a cold sensation spread through Kendar's guts. His head twitched back. Was that fear in his belly? He felt like a rabbit standing in front of a gatalan. Was it possible that this little girl was more powerful than him? Perhaps he should retreat. The masked man had said not to underestimate her and that only a sneak attack would work. Maybe Kendar was in over his head.

The girl's glossy black hair shifted, and her eyes finally left the purple ball. She placed her rag doll and ball carefully on the ground, still not looking at Kendar.

Kendar caressed his chin, wondering. Perhaps he was over-thinking things. He could kill her in an instant. If he moved around her, he could swoop down on her from behind. She'd never see him coming. A blow to the back of the head would mean a quick victory. He nodded to himself. Yes, that would work.

He hovered a foot off the ground and glided surreptitiously around Anaya. She kept looking straight ahead, probably daydreaming like the little girl she was. Kendar approached her back. He formed an invisible fist and shaped it into a sledgehammer, readying to jump forward and strike Anaya's skull. Her head was the only part of her not covered by her armor. One blow, and it would be over.

Kendar inched closer . . . and the air changed around him. Anaya hadn't moved, but he felt warm all of a sudden, as if he'd entered an invisible bubble that she had cast. Kendar had no doubt about it—he had stepped into a hidden field.

Flee! the voices in his head told him. *Flee!*

But before Kendar could run, Anaya turned and looked at him. He froze. Her eyes were silver colored, just like Lunai's, and her caramel skin made Anaya even more adorable.

Flee! the voices in his head repeated. Kendar's mind went blank. His protective layer of feathers and scale sprang into existence just in time.

Anaya flicked a hand, and a mighty wallop struck Kendar in the back, driving him to the ground. His face bounced off the soil. He jumped to his feet, bleeding from his nose. He took on a defensive stance and rushed to erect a protective sphere around himself. But before he could complete it, an invisible cannonball clobbered his chest, pushing him back. Kendar bent forward, trying to counteract the force, and fell onto his knees. Something else struck him hard in the face and shoved him even farther back.

He slammed into a sequoia tree and fell to the ground again. Only half believing what was happening, he got to his feet, grunting and pressing a hand against his throbbing ribs. This time, he managed to put up a protective sphere.

He looked, but Anaya had disappeared. His mind raced. Kendar turned left and right, trying to spot her. The corner of his eye caught movement to his right. He looked. No one was there, but the leaves on the ground shifted as if the wind had disturbed them. Kendar frowned. There was no wind . . .

Then a punch drove into his ribs, powering through his sphere. Anaya appeared beside him as Kendar's protective layer cracked at the point of impact. He fell to the side, winded. When he looked up, the girl was gone again.

Kendar pushed himself upright, his heart racing as fast as his mind. What the *hell* was going on? He formed six protective spheres around himself as he scanned his surroundings. Anaya was nowhere in sight.

Something disturbed the leaves on the ground to his left. Kendar swung invisible fists wildly at the area, aiming at something he couldn't see, striking over and over again but hitting nothing. How could Anaya turn invisible? He couldn't understand it. Worse still, her strikes were devastating—each one shook him to the core. He was in real trouble.

A tactic flashed into his mind. Kendar created a large sphere dozens of meters in diameter in an effort to trap Anaya inside. He sensed that he had succeeded, although he couldn't be sure. Then he shrank it and released three dozen invisible arms, covering every inch of the area. He felt her small form run right into one of them. Quickly, Kendar grabbed her, wrapping the invisible arm around her like a rope.

Anaya struggled for a brief moment, but then she stopped resisting and became visible. Her expression was surprisingly neutral—her eyes held no trace of fear. Kendar breathed a sigh of relief. No matter how strong she was, Anaya couldn't escape. For a second there, he'd thought he was a goner.

He walked toward her, still trying to catch his breath. He felt blood trickling from his nose; his ribs burned with each step. But it was over now. He would touch her, and Anaya would die, giving him her powers. Then he'd return to Fodora View stronger than ever, and he'd become a bosi.

Kendar got closer. Anaya looked into his eyes and smirked. His heart dropped to the ground as a visceral fear gripped every inch of his guts.

Flee! the voices echoed inside his head. But it was too late.

Anaya's armor suddenly gave off a dim glow, and the arm Kendar had wrapped around her shattered like glass. Kendar stepped back, gawking. His invisible arm had burst just like his protective sphere had shattered when it touched something inside Hellsmouth! His eyes opened wider still. This girl had the same ability—she could destroy divine dust.

Kendar readied himself to turn and flee, but a sudden onslaught of devastating blows demolished all six of his protective spheres and knocked him down. He jumped into the air a second later . . . and then something that felt like a rope caught his foot, pulled him down, and slammed him into the ground.

She let go of him. Kendar threw invisible punches at her. She dodged them all with ease, as if she could see them coming. He threw a few more as a distraction and jumped into the air again. This time, no invisible rope grabbed him. He took off flying as fast as he could, relief flooding through his veins.

Anaya appeared right in front of him, standing in the air, cutting him off.

He stopped, the sudden halt knocking the air out of his lungs. Anaya could *fly* too! And much faster than him. Sweat moistened his face. He was screwed! But there was one last attack he could try: Neros's fireball.

He opened his hands and brought his wrists together before his solar plexus, drawing on every ounce of his strength. A dense ball of fire formed in the palms of his hands. Anaya just watched him with amusement, not taking a defensive position, her hands hanging loosely at her sides.

Kendar clenched his teeth. This was his chance. Anaya was underestimating this attack, just like Kendar had done with Neros. He regretted that, and Anaya would too. Even though he doubted the blow was likely to kill her, he could use the opportunity to escape.

He drew his hands back and shot the fiery ball. It hurled toward Anaya. The little girl still just watched it and made no effort to evade the attack. The ball hit her and exploded in her face. Flames splashed around her body like waves crashing against a cliff.

Kendar waited with bated breath, hoping for the best. But when the flames and smoke cleared, Anaya stood there in midair, unscathed. A slight smile crossed her lips.

He gasped and stared at her incredulously from behind his mask.

Then a flaming wall sprang to life behind Anaya, tall and wide. Over a hundred spears of fire emerged from it. They hovered around the little girl, twisting and turning to aim themselves at Kendar.

His eyes bulged and he drifted backward. He couldn't possibly hope to evade all of that!

The sound of crackling fire behind him reached his ears. Kendar turned, dreading what he would see. He went limp. A second flaming wall floated there; another hundred spears were pointing at him.

He closed his eyes and curled up, spawning a dozen protective spheres around himself as he did so. Anaya released her spears. The first wave shattered the first layers of his protective spheres. He dropped to the ground in an effort to avoid the worst of it.

Other waves of spears collided and exploded above him, and fire rained down upon him. He hit the ground just as the forest caught on fire. Smoke filled the air, and soon it was difficult to breathe or see. Kendar hastily took cover behind a sequoia tree. He saw Anaya back on the ground, looking for him amid the flames.

Kendar was breathless. He was out of options too. He couldn't beat Anaya or outrun her, and he couldn't stay hidden for very long among the growing fire and smoke. He decided to make a final gamble. He didn't *have* to beat Anaya through force, he reminded himself. If he simply touched her, Anaya's divine dust would flock to him. Sneaking behind her and touching her was his final chance.

Kendar levitated and glided around her, hoping to catch her off guard. Anaya had an elbow around her mouth and nose to protect herself from the smoke, a posture that was undoubtedly reducing her peripheral vision a bit. He approached her stealthily, the crackling fire and smoke serving as his allies.

She stood within reach with her back toward him. The masked man had said to strike her head. Kendar's legs were longer than his arms, so he went for a kick—he lifted his right leg and swung it at her.

Anaya turned in time and grabbed Kendar's ankle. They stood frozen for a moment, looking at each other.

Kendar smirked. He hadn't managed to kick her, but now they were touching. He'd done it! Soon, her divine dust would be his.

Suddenly, an excruciating pain flared inside his leg; it felt like his nerves were on fire. Kendar screamed, anguish contorting his face. The pain rapidly shot outward—it was as if a wild creature was clawing at his leg and carving away live tissue.

Kendar watched, horrified, as dust particles started coming off his legs and flocking toward Anaya. His eyes opened wide. The particles flowed toward the strongest one! The pain and shock were unbearable. He screamed again, his voice that of a wounded animal, feeling on the verge of passing out.

Surprise flooded Anaya's face. She looked at Kendar's mask, and through eyes slit almost shut with pain, he glimpsed a hint of empathy in her eyes. She let go of his leg and struck him in the guts instead. He tumbled backward.

The divine dust stopped leaving him. He rolled on the ground, the flames in the forest growing more and more wild. The pain in his leg was unrelenting. Kendar tore away his pant and looked at the leg. He screamed again, this time more in despair than pain. The divine dust wasn't leaving him anymore, but his leg had withered like a broken branch—it was black and sunken into itself.

The forest fire around him intensified even more, the thickening smoke threatening to asphyxiate him. Kendar tried to stand up and kept falling back down. His withered leg wouldn't work; his mind had deserted him. Hope fled. Kendar knew it then: he was about to die.

Then, something invisible grabbed his back, lifted him, and tossed him high up into the air. The mighty throw hurled him miles away, saving him from the smoke and fire. He twirled helplessly as he hurtled through the air, trying to use his invisible limbs to steady himself, but his powers were out of whack. Moments later, he fell, speeding downward uncontrollably, his arms flailing. He splashed into the middle of the Naldo Lake.

The impact slapped through his entire body. Kendar sank to the bottom of the lake without offering any resistance—bloodied, battered, and defeated, he just let go. But still, his invisible arms and feet turned into a bubble around him, and a tube shot upward, elongating itself toward the surface, providing him access to air.

Everything hurt, yet a heavy numbness blocked all feelings and thoughts. Kendar sank deeper into the water, encased in his invisible sphere. A ringing in his ears took over and eased him into unconsciousness as the last of the sunlight faded away.

His limp body reached the bottom of the lake. His mind slid into his mother's womb; he felt warm, safe, and quiet, not caring about anything anymore.

Chapter Forty-Seven

14. Danny

The sun was shining brightly by the time Danny woke.

He sat up on his bed, surprised at how rested he felt. It had been a while since he'd had such a good night's sleep. Then he glanced at the sky and frowned. It was already midmorning.

"Damn that Invoker," Danny muttered, remembering the sweet smell that had knocked him out the previous night. He probably should have felt guilty for oversleeping or angry at the Invoker, but instead, he felt amused. He wouldn't mind finding out what the Invoker had sprayed on him—whatever it was made for a great night of sleep. He'd like to get his hands on some of that . . .

He yawned and stretched, then noticed a tray of food sitting near his bed. His eyebrows rose. Someone had entered his tent, yet he hadn't noticed at all. He'd been *really* out of it! Kudos again to the Invoker.

Danny reached for the tray, wondering who to thank for the thoughtful kindness. The aromas of porridge, honey bread, and fresh orange juice made his mouth water. He felt famished all of a sudden and ate like he'd been in prison for a week.

He felt bubbly. The day was off to a superb start. Not only did he feel incredibly refreshed, but he was enjoying room service in Kasmana for the first time. He entertained himself by guessing how the food tray had made its way here. Surely everyone in the lunchroom had noticed that the Cayali was late for breakfast.

He had fun imagining a mild uproar over his absence and let his creativity fly . . . "How would you explain to Rayla that the Cayali has gone missing?" someone had teased Semery. "He finally ran away with the petite archer from the second level," another offered. "Rayla will be proud of her," Semery said, and the laughter that followed settled the matter. Halfway through breakfast time, someone felt intrigued enough to come and check on him, only to find him sound asleep. Danny chuckled, imagining what Lion might have said about that. "Was the petite archer still in his tent?" "No. She left no evidence but the exhausted cub." Then Semery made a witty remark and told everybody to let Danny sleep. Maybe she had asked someone to set aside some breakfast for him. She might have even brought in the tray herself.

Danny laughed as he finished the made-up story in his head with the last bite of porridge. Probably the only thing true about his imagined sequence of events was that someone had brought him breakfast. That was nice. He was surrounded by good people and terrible circumstances, that was for sure. He'd never forget any of it.

When he set down the empty porridge bowl, the jet-black bracelet adorning his left wrist caught his eye. His eyebrows went up. The Invoker must have returned with it and put it on his wrist—and Danny hadn't noticed any of that either.

His heart started to race. The Slayer was ready! Its original power had been restored. Danny sprang to his feet, eager to command trillions of interactive nanobots for the first time in his life. He touched the bracelet with all of the fingers in his right hand, keeping them there until the bracelet glowed. "Slayer, activate," he whispered.

The bracelet pulsated. A wisp of tiny particles as white as salt emerged around his left wrist and swirled around Danny. The wisp swooshed and multiplied. They thickened into strips, enveloping Danny's body as they twirled and rustled. More particles emerged, glittering silver and gold, swelling into a cloud.

The strips settled into place and sucked in the cloud. The fasma suit coalesced, dressing Danny in the legendary Cayacoa's armor. "Raise your left foot," a digital female voice said in his ear. Danny complied, and a sabaton shoed his foot. It felt weightless. When Danny put down his foot, the thick sole and heel lifted him up a full two inches. "Raise your right foot," the voice said. Danny complied, and the armor was complete.

He smiled as he eagerly removed a gauntlet and touched the golden armor with naked fingers. It felt as soft as velvet. He stretched his arms, squatted, and jumped; he twirled and broke out a dance move. He couldn't help giggling. The armor felt as light and flexible as sportswear. He couldn't believe his luck . . . the quality of this fasma was beyond anything Danny had ever seen. And it was over five hundred years old! The Invoker had said that he'd upgrade the suit, but Danny assumed that just meant adding a feature or two, like allowing him to upload books to read.

Danny touched the bracelet again. "User guide," he said. The front of his helmet turned into a one-way glass, the interior functioning as a screen that no one would see from the outside. A list of available voice commands appeared. The last one read "Danny's Tablet." He'd look at that later.

A wild idea came to him. Danny reached for the quiver at his back and withdrew a fasma arrow. The bow appeared at once in his left hand, glittering green and blue, the feathers at the ends of both limbs shifting colors as Danny turned the bow.

His face turned into a giant grin, and he laughed, adrenaline rushing through his body. As soon as he nocked the arrow, the screen before his eyes changed into a telescopic sight. The reticle pinpointed where the arrow would strike, and data around the screen's edges told him the distance the arrow would travel along with its trajectory, time of flight, and anticipated force of impact.

He pointed the arrow upward and pulled the bowstring to its full draw. The fasma arrow would travel nine hundred yards straight up into the air if he released it, according to the display.

"But that's not high enough to strike a spaceship," he muttered out loud. Then he noticed a line of text at the scope's upper right corner. It read, "Compound Thrust Setting = 0." His eyes opened wide. The weapon's power was turned off!

He slid the arrow back into the quiver and touched his left wrist. "User guide," he said, followed by "Quick start." The screen started to play a video, showing Danny the depth of the bow's power.

* * *

Danny finished viewing the basic instructions for the Slayer. The Invoker had been right—it was an *incredibly* advanced weapon. Yet the Invoker had implied he'd found a way to counter it. That said everything about the man and explained why he hadn't confiscated the Slayer. Plus, of course, there was that so-called "prophecy" the Invoker seemed to care about.

After viewing the series of short instructional videos, Danny made two decisions. First, he'd call the weapon guacanari for the sake of the locals; the name Ciberus Slayer confused even him. Second, he'd never fire the guacanari while astride Kara since the kickback would hurt her legs. If he had to shoot while galloping, he'd use a regular bow. Satsani had gotten away with shooting the guacanari while astride because the bow had been broken back then—he'd never used fasma arrows.

The armor may have functioned to disguise the Satiu-X that had used it to bring down the Invoker's ship. But the armor's true purpose was to serve as a mount for the bow—it projected an invisible platform to handle the recoil when the weapon's compound thrust was set between 1 and the maximum of 7.

Right then, the horn atop the Narialy Fortress blasted.

"Oh no!" Danny gasped. A single bellow meant that new enemy troops had arrived in the valley. How many more thousands of reinforcements had arrived this time? Was there no end to this? Would he have to use the incredible power of the guacanari to end the war?

He took a step forward, ready to grab the bow and head for the parapet. But then the horn sounded for a second time. Danny froze where he stood and waited with bated breath. A third blast made him grin. "Allies!" he said, pumping his fist.

He grabbed the guacanari and rushed out of his tent for the first time that day. "No way!" he exclaimed when he noticed the sun's position. It was noon already. He'd watched instructions and played with the bow for two full hours.

Someone yelped as he rushed to the parapet, and Danny glanced at her. "Praise Kas!" she added as Danny kept going. That seemed weird, but perhaps she was also excited that reinforcements had arrived.

He nearly ran to see for himself what was going on in the valley, thinking that the Invoker had been right again—something significant had occurred on the battlefield. The Invoker had probably used his remote surveillance and spotted Rayla's allies closing in on the fortress. Danny spent a moment wondering who the ally was, but then he shrugged. Probably the name wouldn't mean much to him anyway.

He neared the parapet and slowed down. It buzzed with people looking down at the valley, pointing at various locations, and chatting excitedly. Danny smelled a victorious mood in the air. He smiled, remembering Rolan's words the previous night when he'd said he had brought good news for Rayla.

"Oh, mighty Kas!" someone yelled. Dozens of soldiers turned to Danny and gawked. The entire parapet froze a second later; a complete silence took over as everybody looked at him. Six soldiers right in front of him fell to their knees, muttering praises to their god.

"What the hell?" Danny whispered.

"Cayali, is that you?" Semery asked in a booming voice.

Suddenly, Danny remembered that he was still wearing the helmet. The darn thing was so comfortable that he'd forgotten about it. Danny removed it and gave Semery a nervous smile. "Yes, it's me. Sorry about that."

He expected people would laugh and return to normal, but they didn't—instead, a few more fell to their knees. He chuckled. "Guys, guys, guys, it's just me! Can you please stop doing that? It's embarrassing."

No one stood up. "Please?" he added. More fell to their knees. He turned to Semery and begged with his eyes.

She laughed. "Can you blame them, Cayali? I feel that way myself. None of us has ever seen that armor before. Seeing you right now is a blessing from Kas. We'll talk about this for the rest of our lives. Can you let us be in awe for a few seconds longer?"

Danny scratched his head and dropped his shoulders. "C'mon, guys, it's still me . . ." he said weakly.

"Okay, okay," Semery said, shaking her head and still chuckling. She strode to the center of the parapet. "He's the Cayali, but he's also a teenager. We talked about this, remember? Everybody, come here. Get closer to him. That's it, that's it . . . You, too, guys. Good. A bit closer . . . Now, on the count of three, we're going to yell 'Cayali' as loud as we can. The loudest we've ever yelled, okay? We'll scream it five times in a row, all right? Let it all out. Feel free to stomp your feet too. Ready? One, two, three—"

"Cayali!" their voices erupted. The parapet rumbled as six hundred people yelled and stomped. "Cayali! Cayali! Cayali! Cayali!" Then the screaming broke into group laughter, and all of the tension dissipated. Hundreds of soldiers resumed chatting enthusiastically, many making their way to Danny and touching his armor. Some gave him hugs, Semery included.

"You make me proud, young man," she said with moist eyes. Danny could only nod in response.

Eventually, they drifted away, and he was moved to the front of the parapet, glad the furor had died down. He'd forgotten to bring his spyglass, but he didn't need it to spot a new party in the valley—the new group was about twenty thousand strong, and many of them were riding gatalans. They occupied a spot on the far left, distancing themselves from Viembo's men. Danny didn't recognize the golden flag they flew, although he instantly loved it, seeing as it featured a prancing gatalan. He thought about putting his helmet back on and using its telescopic sight to take a better look, but he decided that might make him seem too mysterious. He didn't need to draw more attention to himself.

"Can anyone please tell me what's going on out there?" he asked no one in particular.

Platoon Leader Lion came closer and offered Danny his spyglass. "That's General Helikex, my friend."

"He came to save his girlfriend," Semery said behind them, and dozens of soldiers laughed. Danny knew she meant General Nereida, because Rayla had implied that Nereida had broken Helikex's heart.

Danny grinned. "Wow!" Helikex's presence was indeed significant news. A while back, Cael had said that Helikex had been Rayla's predecessor, the former cacique of armed forces. Danny didn't know much about Kasmanian politics, but that seemed like a major endorsement for Rayla.

Semery walked over to stand next to him. "Can you tell which one he is?" she asked. She didn't wait for a response. "Helikex is right at the front of his troops, atop his gatalan and staring into Viembo's camp." She laughed. "That traitor is likely squirming like a worm inside his tent! I bet he's pissing his pants right now."

She squinted into her spyglass again and tapped Danny's shoulder. "There! See that woman just behind Helikex? That's Lieutenant Laramie, Rayla's best friend. She had the smarts to find General Helikex in central Kasmana before the Ionians blocked the bridge."

Danny strained his eyes at where Semery was pointing. "Yes, I see her."

She lowered her spyglass to grin at him. "Laramie had time to do her thing! Whew. Helikex is a big, *big* deal. There's no telling how many more troops will show up to support Rayla because of him."

Danny grinned back. Rayla had always said that time was on her side. "Perhaps that's why Viembo's attacks seemed desperate—maybe he knew about Helikex?"

Semery gave a curt nod. "That's right. He tried to take Rayla down before the general could show up with his forces. The fool!"

"How many more troops do you think will show up?" Danny asked. "Enough to end this?"

Semery's grin disappeared. "Cayali, keep in mind that the Kasmanian army has over 1.3 million soldiers and riders."

Danny raised his eyebrows. He hadn't known that . . . Suddenly, the support Viembo had boasted at the beginning of the war didn't seem so impressive.

Semery went on. "A lot more will come. The question is, how many of them will support Rayla, and how many will support Cacique Kameiros? Even Viembo is a small fry in all this—he's nothing but Kameiros's pawn. With General Helikex here, though, the answer is becoming clear. Kas's truth is beginning to shine through, my dear Cayali! This is almost over."

Just then, a cluster of Viembo's men moved south, away from their camp. Murmurs swept through the Narialy Fortress, growing louder with each passing second.

"They're leaving Viembo's camp!" someone yelled from a higher story. "They won't fight against Helikex! There are about fifteen thousand of them."

The soldiers in the tenth story cheered as the ones in the lower levels looked up, wondering at the commotion.

The horn inside Viembo's camp blew four times, and the remaining soldiers rushed to take offensive positions—over one hundred thousand of them.

"They're about to attack General Helikex!" Semery nearly shouted.

Danny looked. Helikex's camp had broken into hectic activity, readying themselves for battle.

Semery leaned on the parapet, gripping its edges tightly. Her voice came out laden with fear. "Most of the Ionians left . . . Viembo's troops are mostly seamen, but still, he outnumbers Helikex five to one."

Her words were nearly drowned out when a horn above the fortress blew—one, two, three times—announcing the arrival of more allied troops.

Semery eagerly resumed looking through her spyglass, her demeanor shifting back to a more confident one. "Colonel Clamer and Lieutenant Nibel are coming! They're about three miles away. Looks like they have about twenty thousand troops with them."

"They're here to support Rayla?" Danny asked.

"Yes! They're loyal to Helikex for sure." She let out a hissing breath. "But they won't make it in time. Helikex is in trouble!"

A trumpet sounded on the lower level, and the gates opened with a low rumble. Rayla burst onto the battlefield, carrying a two-handed sword, piercing Viembo's men with her gaze. Aia ran beside her, screaming battle cries. Thousands of Lathraias and Nereida's soldiers poured out of the gates behind the two women.

"Wow . . ." Danny whispered, his eyes wide. Rayla was the first one on the field, spearheading the troops and risking her life. Her chances of survival and victory would have soared if she had stayed inside the fortress and waited for Colonel Clamer and Lieutenant Nibel to arrive, but instead, she had rushed to protect Helikex and Laramie.

Danny's eyes remained peeled open. Rayla ran to the left, aiming to join General Helikex before Viembo's men could overwhelm him. Thirty thousand troops followed Rayla, all running as hard as they could.

Flags flapped madly in Viembo's camp. Semery watched them through her spyglass, studying their patterns. "Oh no!" she gasped.

Her tone poured a bucket of ice into Danny's heart. "What's happening?"

"Viembo is splitting up his troops! Only twenty thousand are heading toward Helikex—the rest are veering left to intercept Rayla. They'll use a crescent moon formation to encircle her. She'll be outnumbered nearly three to one . . ."

With his teeth clenched, Danny watched Viembo's army divide itself exactly the way Semery had predicted. An invisible hand squeezed his chest. Rayla's life was in imminent danger—Viembo's men were about to swallow her up and attack her from every direction. Danny had to *do* something!

He activated his helmet and rushed away from the parapet. Every second counted. He ran toward the slide on the tenth story and used it to reach the ninth level, then the eighth. He repeated the process until he landed in the first story two minutes later. He ran into the courtyard. One quick glance told him that the ground level had completely emptied.

The front gates were wide open. Without a second thought, he ran through them and into the corridor where dark plumes of smoke from the broilers were still smoldering. Grimly, he covered his nose and pressed forward.

Ahead of him, thousands of Canyos were fighting in a confusing melee. Armor clashed against armor; swords clattered; soldiers screamed and grunted. Cut limbs flew through the air even as bodies thudded into the ground and blood splattered onto the powdery dirt.

He stopped, trying to make sense of the sea of combatants. He saw it then: Viembo's men had already engulfed Rayla's troops. The bulk of Viembo's soldiers were pushing in from the right, overwhelming Danny's friends.

He reached for his quiver and shot fasma arrow after fasma arrow, striking one, two, three of Viembo's men at the same time. The arrows flew, struck, and then reappeared inside Danny's quiver. But even that wasn't enough . . .

"This isn't gonna cut it!" Danny yelled in frustration. A dozen shots hadn't changed anything on the battlefield. He glanced at the data on the one-way glass in his helmet. The Compound Thrust Setting read 0.

He touched his bracelet until it glowed. "CT Setting 1," he commanded.

The armor hummed, and an invisible platform lifted him three inches off the ground, expanding into a circle and casting a long tail that resembled the neck of a guitar. Danny drew a fresh arrow and nocked it, feeling the tension force mount and pass through his armor and into the platform. He pulled the bowstring to its full draw and let loose.

The arrow blasted away like a rocket, and the bow released a boomy, heavy sound like a gigantic bass. The arrow barreled toward the bulk of Viembo's troops, exploding on contact and plowing through them, blowing aside the mangled soldiers. A gap opened up that looked like a furrow running through a plowed field.

Soldiers on both sides of the furrow stopped and gawked at the devastation. Then they looked over at Danny and froze at the sight of his golden armor glittering in the sun's rays. But the clanging sounds of ongoing fierce battle and the density of the fighting prevented the other soldiers from realizing what had happened—Viembo's forces kept hurling themselves at Rayla's troops.

Danny touched his bracelet. "Microphone, activate. Maximum volume; tactile control." The armor hummed, and a microphone icon appeared on his left wrist.

Danny drew a new arrow and shot it. Amplified by the armor's sound system, the accompanying boom thundered through the valley. The deafening noise reverberated back from the mountains as the arrow struck Viembo's troops and blew them away, carving a new furrow of death on the battlefield.

Everyone froze. Then most fighters turned hesitantly, looking around in confusion. One by one, they spotted Danny standing between them and the fortress, wearing the golden armor.

Two dozen of Viembo's men started toward Danny with tentative steps. All eyes were on him, but not everyone understood what had just happened. Danny clenched his teeth. The time had come to put an end to this!

He drew a new arrow, aimed it at the soldiers coming at him, and shot for a third time. The sonic boom rocked the valley; every soldier in the arrow's path was killed. A third row of desolation opened up on the battlefield.

No one moved. Silence reigned—the soldiers could only gawk and glance at each other as if asking whether they had seen it too.

When Danny spoke, his voice was amplified by the armor. "Canyos, stop killing each other! End this madness right now! You've been deceived by Kameiros's lies and led astray by Viembo's greed."

"Nooo!" a lone voice yelled at the other end of the battlefield. "*Noooo!*" he repeated, running toward Danny, his sword held high.

Danny recognized the man: it was Viembo. Everyone stood motionless as he rushed toward Danny. The general wore a fierce look on his face, willing to either kill or die.

Danny tapped the microphone icon, muting it. "CT Setting o," he said. He didn't want to shoot at Viembo and kill everyone behind him. But even shooting at Viembo with no compound thrust could cause additional casualties . . . He drew a fresh arrow and nocked it, planning to only pull the bowstring halfway.

"He's mine!" yelled a potent female voice. Everyone turned and watched. Rayla charged ahead to intercept Viembo. Her face was stony and her eyes spat fire.

Viembo saw her, and his face transformed. That fierce expression turned into a terrified one. He faltered as he ran, then tumbled and fell. Clumsily, he staggered back to his feet and assumed a defensive position.

Rayla never stopped running. She jumped at Viembo, slashing her two-handed sword downward. Viembo parried the blow, but her mighty strike knocked the sword out of his hands. She swung again, upward this time, and caught Viembo's jaw. The tip of her sword bit into him deeply, splitting his face in half.

His body went limp. A thin line of blood started running from his forehead to the middle of his nose. A second later, he fell backward and thudded into the ground. He moved no more.

Rayla spat on him. "Your miserable death is not enough!"

A gatalan wailed twice in the background, probably Viembo's. No one moved; no one said a word.

Danny shifted his gaze from Rayla to everybody else. All eyes had returned to him. The silence grew thick and heavy, covering the battlefield like a tent, spreading as far as Danny could see.

He reactivated the microphone. "Long live Rayla!" he shouted. "Long live Rayla!" He lifted his bow in her direction.

No one echoed his call. Over one hundred and fifty thousand pairs of eyes continued to stare at Danny. His legs grew weak. Heat and cold blasted through his body alternately; his head felt as though it were swelling, like someone inflating a balloon.

Rayla sheathed her sword and walked to him in the silence. "Take off your helmet, Danny," she said. Danny complied. Rayla's commanding voice didn't need a microphone.

A murmur swept through the battlefield. "He's just a child!" someone gasped.

Rayla stood next to Danny and faced the crowd. Everyone quieted down.

"Canyos! Brothers and sisters! What you heard is true—lies and deception have divided us and caused untold deaths. What has come to pass in our beloved Kasmana is despicable. Mark my words: come tomorrow, we'll march toward the holy palace. We'll bring Kas's justice to the man who murdered my eken, King-Priest Altanarian. We will have justice and vengeance and the restoration of our holy nation, I swear it to you!" She paused. "But that is tomorrow."

"We suffered many losses today," Rayla went on with pain in her voice. "And many more Canyos died earlier this week in this senseless war. Tonight, we'll bury our dead and lick our wounds. We'll raise our glasses to them. We'll pray to Kas, asking for the eternal rest of their souls, and we'll thank the Almighty for the honor of sharing our lives with them." Rayla paused again, and authority returned to her voice. "But that is tonight."

She paced away from Danny. "Right now, I feel the same way you do: words choking my throat, eyes unable to blink, a racing heart, and warmth in my chest. We witnessed Kas's light shine before our eyes like never before, and our minds can't grasp it."

She turned and pointed at Danny. "He's fifteen years old. He saved my life near the Triple Peaks, shooting arrows while astride a galloping gatalan. Then, with a few shots, he prevented a bloody battle between my army and fifty thousand Ionians, saving thousands of lives. In Narian, the sound of his name stopped another battle from happening between my forces and Captain Quecia's troops. And now he stands before you wearing Cayacoa's golden armor. Praise Kas Almighty! You saw it yourselves: with just three arrows, he stopped this war."

Rayla approached Danny, and his eyes widened. He couldn't feel his legs anymore. Was the armor the only thing keeping him upright?

"It is my honor to introduce him to you," Rayla said, sweeping an arm from him to the surrounding soldiers. "He is not a Cayali. He is not a Cayacoa. Brothers and sisters, witness the first Caya-*king* in Kasmana's history."

Rayla turned back to face Danny, who struggled to assimilate what she'd said. He couldn't believe his ears.

"Caya-king!" she hailed, falling to one knee. He almost stepped forward to ask her to stand up, but he didn't get the chance . . .

"*Caya-king!*" hundreds of Lathraias shouted behind Rayla, kneeling before Danny. He froze where he stood.

"*Caya-king!*" thousands and thousands repeated. The cry spread until the entire valley was brimming with prostrated soldiers.

Danny couldn't so much as blink. What was going on? What was he supposed to do?

"Caya-king!" all of them mumbled in prayer, facing the ground.

"Caya-king!" they said as one, lifting their faces to gaze at Danny.

"Caya-king!" one hundred and fifty thousand people chanted, rising to their feet.

"*Caya-king!*" they yelled in one voice, grins on their faces and tears in their eyes.

They roared the word one final time, making it echo in the valley, announcing it to the world: "*Caya-king!*"

Afterword

Thank you for reading *Fragments of the Gods, Book Two, The Great Caya*. I hope you've found it entertaining and rewarding.

If you enjoyed it, please consider leaving a review on Amazon. Reviews help other readers discover this story and support my work. Even just a line or two would be greatly appreciated and mean a lot to me.

Best wishes,

JCR Paulino
https://jcrpaulino.com

About the Author

JCR Paulino is an emerging author in the fantasy and science fiction genres best known for his debut novel, *The Swords of Blood and Gold*. This book has garnered several accolades, including:

· The Literary Titan Golden Book Award.

· The Artisan Book Review Book Excellence Award (in Mystery, Thriller, Urban Fantasy).

· The 2022 Readers' Favorite International Book Award Silver Medal in Fiction – New Adult.

· A B.R.A.G. Medallion listing from indieBRAG, LLC.

In January 2023, Paulino introduced readers to *The Crystal Canvas*. His high-fantasy series, *Fragments of the Gods*, was released in January 2024.

Balancing a full-time career as a Human Resources executive with his passion for writing, JCR resides in Southern California. He enjoys life's adventures with his wife and two children.

Also by JCR Paulino

Anaya Awakens

The Swords of Blood and Gold

The Crystal Canvas